In a primitive time, on the shores of a strange and beautiful island, one woman forged a new life and a dream that would last forever. . . .

DAUGHTER OF THE REEF

"The author's masterful grasp of the history of the South Pacific—the ancient rituals and customs—suffuses this exciting romantic novel of Tahiti . . . The cruelty of the time comes through, but so does the magic. Readers will come away with an appreciation of the rich and complex society that existed before the first Europeans arrived in 1767."

—SHIRLEY STRESHINSKY, bestselling author of *Hers the Kingdom* and *The Shores of Paradise*

This book includes a special excerpt from the next enthralling novel by Clare Coleman . . .

SISTER OF THE SUN

. . . continuing the breathtaking story of *Daughter of the Reef*

D0683988

DAUGHTER OF THE REEF

CLARE COLEMAN

JOVE BOOKS, NEW YORK

DAUGHTER OF THE REEF

A Jove Book / published by arrangement with
the author

PRINTING HISTORY
Jove edition / December 1992

ISBN: 0-515-11012-4

Jove Books are published by The Berkley Publishing Group,
200 Madison Avenue, New York, New York 10016.
The name "JOVE" and the "J" logo
are trademarks belonging to Jove Publications, Inc.

PRINTED IN THE UNITED STATES OF AMERICA

10 9 8 7 6 5 4 3 2 1

Acknowledgments

For their help I would like to thank:

At Berkley Books: Beth Fleisher, who originated the project, and Hillary Cige, whose efforts and enthusiasm brought it through.

Richard Curtis, my literary agent, who got things rolling.

The Bernice P. Bishop Museum of Honolulu, for its dedication to preserving knowledge about the ancient culture of Polynesia.

The San Jose City Library system for its inter-library loan program and helpful staff.

The Clark Library at San Jose State University, whose staff put up with many queries and endless renewals.

The Museum of Tahiti and the Islands, Papeete, Tahiti, whose staff took time to answer questions.

The Tahitian Tourist Advisory Board office in Papeete for advice and direction.

Dorothy Wall, for editorial input.

The members of the Wordshop Writing Group: Kevin J. Anderson, Michael Berch, Dan'l Danehy-Oakes, Avis Minger, Gary Schockley and Lori Ann White, for helpful comments and critiques.

Dorothy Bradley, for proofreading.

The computers and printer, for not breaking down.

All the researchers and scholars who have devoted themselves to the peoples and ways of life in the South Pacific.

Historical Note

The Pacific island of Tahiti lies below the equator, about 2500 miles south of Hawaii. What is known of ancient Tahitian society comes from the journals of early visitors, from records made by Tahitians after they adopted a system of writing, from archaeological studies, and from the work of anthropologists in collecting and recording the remnants of a once-rich oral tradition.

The first documented contact between Tahiti and the outside world did not come until 1767 with the arrival of H.M.S. *Dolphin* at Matavai Bay. The early explorers—French, English and Spanish—discovered a rich and complex society that had flourished in isolation for more than a thousand years.

Anyone attempting to delve into Tahiti's fascinating past soon discovers that the references are often sparse, contradictory and subject to varied interpretations. This can be a frustrating roadblock or a delightful springboard for the imagination.

In re-creating the world of Pre-European Tahiti, I have attempted to remain true to those sources that I feel were authentic and open-minded. Any omissions, misinterpretations or mistakes are solely mine.

Pronunciation

The vowels of the language of Tahiti are pronounced as follows:

> a - as the "a" in "father"
> e - as the "a" in "say"
> i - as the "e" in "me"
> o - as the "o" in "so"
> u - as the "u" in "rule"

When two vowels are adjacent in a word, each is pronounced as a separate sound. The accent on a word usually falls on the next to last syllable. The presence of an apostrophe in a word indicates a break or glottal stop.

NOTE: A glossary of unfamiliar terms appears in the back matter of this book.

1

WIND gusted against plaited sails, speeding a two-hulled voyaging canoe on a course between coral atolls. The young men and women aboard wore headdresses decked with seabird feathers. Their skirts were finely woven from dried leaves of pandanus palm. Painted bark-cloth capes fluttered brightly as the passengers chatted of the wedding festivities to come.

The wind strengthened as it raced across the sea. Spray flew in sheets from the twin bows, and the deck that stretched over the twin hulls tilted steeply. Several young women shrieked, more from excitement than from fear, while everyone scrambled to counterbalance the boat. But one did not join them, for tradition demanded that she remain in her seat.

Tepua-mua, the eldest daughter of a chief, sat rigidly on her seat of honor in the middle of the deck. Her four-legged stool was lashed to a raised bamboo platform, making her the center of attention. Those who glanced at her saw a tall, slender girl at the verge of womanhood, a face slightly too narrow to be called beautiful, and glistening black hair that flew back in the wind.

That morning Tepua had been proud and happy to be sitting so high while the canoe glided across her home lagoon and out into the placid sea. Now she wanted to be down on the deck, instead of up here on the platform, where height intensified every buck and heave of the boat. The wind tore at the feathered crown in her hair and whipped the long robe of bark-cloth about her legs.

She stared down at the knotted backs and arms of the men working the sails, and then beyond, to the water, whose color had gone from a peaceful blue to an ugly gray green.

Over her head the boom of the rear sail arched upward like
a bow.

How the weather had changed since this morning. When
Tepua had mounted to her place on the canoe, the lagoon
had been warm and calm, the white beaches dazzling. Along
the shore, gifts from two families—her mother's and her
father's—had been laid out for all to see.

These presents for the bridegroom's kin included pearl-
shell fishhooks, wreaths of rare feathers, and rolls of
bark-cloth from distant Tahiti. For the wedding feast the
families had collected plump fowls, heaps of clams, and
boatloads of coconuts. Best of all, they had obtained a dozen
pigs from traders. *Pork!* Tepua's mouth watered at the
thought of that costly delicacy, so rarely offered to women.

Now, atop her seat on the sloping deck, she worried
whether she would even reach the feast. She watched a
priest standing at one bow waving a bundle of sacred red
feathers at the sky. She could not hear him, but knew that he
was intoning a prayer to soothe the spirits of wind and
water.

The crew struggled on with the steering oar and sails.
Tepua felt useless as she watched them. She was as tall and
strong as some men, for she was descended from Tapahi-
roro-ariki, a chiefess of strength and renown. From childhood Tepua had drawn the bow and thrust the spear for
sport, in the manner of noble families. Why remain here,
idle, when she could help? She slid forward on her seat to
step down.

A hand stopped her, an ancient hand. Tepua glanced into
the rheumy eyes of Bone-needle, the woman who had
attended her for many years. "No," Bone-needle said.
"Stay where you are."

Tepua thrust out her arm, making a fist to show Bone-
needle that her limbs had strength. "I can hold a sail as well
as I can a bow," she said.

"You have skill for the bow. You have none for the
sail," the ancient noblewoman answered. "You must stay
in your place of honor and show your faith in the canoe
master. He will take it as a deadly insult if you do not."

Tepua gritted her teeth and tried not to slide off the smooth wooden seat as the swaying threw her from side to side. Under her breath she said a small prayer to the spirit of her ancestress.

The cords that tied the platform to the deck creaked loudly as each wave struck the boat. Tepua shaded her eyes against glare from the heaving seas and searched the horizon for other canoes in the wedding party. There they were, behind her, diving through wave tops, in winds that threatened to tear sails from masts.

She shivered from cold, for her bark-cloth robe was thin and already softening from repeated drenchings of seawater. First fear and then anger intensified her trembling. She hated being forced to sit here. She could help if the crew let her, even if the task was only bailing. But she was obliged to stay in her seat, though it meant she had to cling like a coconut crab.

Even if the wind breaks this seat from its lashings and tosses me overboard. She bent down toward Bone-needle, speaking directly into the aged woman's ear. "Why is the storm still chasing us? Does this mean the gods disapprove of my marriage?"

"At home, all the omens were good." Bone-needle had to raise her voice against the wail of the wind. "Perhaps the wind rises to speed you on your way. Your husband has waited long enough for you. His manhood stiffens in eagerness and you are not there to please him."

Tepua refused to accept that answer. What, after all, did she know of the man she was about to marry? The go-betweens spoke of his many virtues, but poetry was designed to flatter, not speak truth. Given the choice, she would have found a husband who lived closer to her home.

Now regret tormented her. How could she look forward to giving up her own family and friends, and taking up a life with strangers? She did not know how the customs of her husband's atoll would differ from those of her own. At home she had enjoyed freedoms that her new life might not allow. Would her husband let her swim in the lagoon whenever she pleased, or roam the shore in search of shellfish? And what if she failed to quickly give him an heir?

These worries fled as the boat lurched again, and heavy rain began pelting the deck. Surely the canoe master would seek shelter now, as soon as land came into view. Tepua looked out and saw only white-tipped waves. Heavy clouds covered half the sky.

She felt the two-hulled canoe swing around as the helmsman leaned hard on his steering oar. The crew worked both sails, pulling on lines that swung the upcurved booms about their masts. Sailing close-hauled, the canoe picked up speed, its hulls planing over the surf.

Tepua felt her trembling ease. The canoe master must have decided to seek refuge. She squinted to the northeast, trying to spot any small hump of land breaking the horizon, but saw none. Perhaps the master's eyes were better than hers. If he was guiding the craft by the direction of the sea swell, she hoped his art would prove true.

The canoe continued to beat upwind, the sails close-lashed and straining. Everyone who was not struggling with the ropes or bailing the hulls lay together under mats for shelter. The passengers had fallen quiet as they watched the grim effort to gain land. Tepua realized that the fleet was far downwind of the outermost islands her people knew. The weather and current seemed determined to drive the canoes even farther into unknown seas.

Again Tepua moved to descend from her seat, but the old noblewoman's stare pinned her. You must show your trust, Bone-needle's gaze said. It is the burden of your position.

Tepua's eyes teared against the cutting wind. She felt her headdress fly off, and she snatched at it too late. Her cry of dismay sent crewmen and passengers scrambling after the circlet of feathers and precious shells as the wind spun it across the deck.

The headdress eluded its pursuers, catching for an instant on the edge of the deck before a gust dragged it overboard. Tepua felt a clench of fright in her stomach. Had she felt divine fingers snatch the feather crown away? What had she done to anger the spirits?

Her eyes sought the canoe master, a small wiry man whose corded arms and ever-squinting eyes told of his many struggles with the sea. Would he think it such an insult to his skill, Tepua wondered, if she came down on the deck and took shelter with the others? Her wet bark-cloth robe was now plastered against her arms and breasts, making her misery worse.

The old woman's eyes still said no, but inwardly Tepua rebelled. She had had enough of being battered by the gale.

Suddenly the wind changed direction, making the great curved booms swing across the deck. As each slammed into the limits of its line, the boat lurched while men rushed to regain control. Tepua froze, one foot already touching the matting on the deck. The gods themselves must be displeased with her lack of faith in the canoe's master. She withdrew her foot, hoping that the wind might steady.

Instead the storm grew fitful, blowing harshly from one quarter then quickly shifting to another. The boat slowed as it lost direction and headway; men went to sit in the hulls, feverishly stroking with long paddles.

Beyond the forward sail she saw the boat's master and the priest conferring once again. They spoke rapidly, with worried grimaces and a glance in her direction. A crewman hurried forward, carrying an armload of young coconuts. He skidded on the wet matting, dropped one. It rolled into the waves.

Tepua saw the priest shake his head. Not a good omen. The sea was hungry and unwilling to wait.

The youth managed to deliver the rest of his burden to the master and the priest. The priest went to the bow of the right hull. Tepua saw him kneel, his robe and feathered headdress fluttering in the wind. One by one he lifted the young coconuts in offering to the storm, pierced each with a sharpened bamboo cane, and poured the milk into the sea.

Again the wind turned, now wilder than ever. It struck the sails like a fist, bending the masts, driving the left hull so deep that it threatened to fill. A crewman rushed aft toward Tepua, carrying a length of sennit, coconut fiber cord. She could scarcely see him through the curtain of heavy rain

shrouding the canoe. "Bind yourself!" he shouted through
the sound of the storm. He thrust the cord at her. Numb with
cold and fright, she took it.

She glanced down, saw people huddling under their mats
and wraps about the base of her platform. Eyes looked up to
her in appeal or reproach. Except for Bone-needle, these
people were from her new husband's family. She had
known them only for the few days they had stayed on her
father's island.

Now she saw that she could not leave her place. Apart
from the lack of faith it would show, the space around her
was completely covered by bodies.

She reached down, threaded the cord around several
pieces of bamboo in the platform beneath her, then about
her body, drawing it tight so that it crumpled her bark-cloth
robe and bound her to the seat. After she had knotted the
sennit, she let one end, about twice the length of her arm,
hang free. She had another use for this piece. It might help
her find guidance that no human wisdom could supply.

Quickly she coiled the cord in her hands, preparing
herself for the difficult art of *fai,* making string figures. *Fai*
was well-known throughout her islands, but to most people
it served only for amusement. Tepua had become unusually
adept at it, able to make patterns on her fingers without
conscious effort, until a final figure emerged.

The results often surprised her. At times she was certain
that the spirits guided her, allowing her to see in the strings
the answer to a baffling question. Now, the sea gods were
angry. She needed to know what they wanted of her.

"No!" rasped Bone-needle, who had long known of
Tepua's rare gift. "It is the priest's duty, not yours, to deal
with the spirits that trouble us. Put that aside."

Tepua hesitated as she peered ahead, listening to the sails
creak and bang. She could see almost nothing through the
heavy rain. What had happened to the priest and the master?
The rain curtained them from her, silenced their voices.
Despite his offerings and his sacred red feathers, the priest
clearly had failed. Her fingers tightened about the coil of
fiber cord in her hand.

Another sailor hurried by, appearing out of the rain like a ghost. Scowling at Tepua, he defied wind and spray to climb the ladder along the mast. She caught her breath when she saw him starting to pull down the sail. When he was done, they would have only the paddlers' strength to drive the canoe.

Again she prayed to Tapahi-roro-ariki, begging her ancestress to intercede. Then, as she began to tie the cord into a loop, she heard a crash that made the boat shudder. Mixed with screams, cries, and the beat of rain came a terrible splintering. She saw the outline of the forward mast as it broke and toppled, the falling boom sweeping across the deck, dragging mats and men into the sea.

Beneath her, voices mixed in a babble of frenzied prayers. The canoe bucked and dived, caught in the roiling storm. She saw the deck timbers shift as strain twisted one hull out of line with the other. The tension broke a lashing that held her platform to the deck. She glanced down and saw another fraying. Sweating with fear under her barkcloth robe, Tepua fumbled to untie herself.

The people around her groaned, and tried to hold her seat fast as another binding broke. The stool began to shift with every lurch of the canoe. Above her head she heard a stream of angry words while the man aloft wrestled with a sail that would not come down.

Tepua was thrown violently from side to side. The platform beneath her began to break apart as people screamed with anguish and reached up to keep her from falling. Then the boat pitched so sharply that she was torn from their hands, tossed sideways, tumbled into a swirling madness of rain and spray and sea.

For a few instants Tepua felt stunned, but the shock of hitting the water brought her back to awareness. A good swimmer, she kicked herself to the surface. Now she was free of the bridal seat, though she felt trailing bits of cord and bamboo. She spat brine and managed to suck in a short breath before another wave spilled over her.

Again she came up, rising with a swell, and searched for

the canoe. When she finally spotted it, she groaned in despair. Surf poured over what remained of the deck while paddlers stroked frantically. Every wave pushed the hapless craft farther from her.

The sea pulled her down again. When she surfaced this time and glanced out, the mast looked like a tiny stick and the canoe itself a battered leaf that was rapidly growing smaller. It would not be coming back for her. The people still on board would be lucky to save themselves.

What of the other boats in her party? They had been sailing close behind and might have been blown this way. Each time the sea lifted her, she searched the horizon but found nothing.

Alone in the water, she wondered how long she could survive. Tepua had seen death often, had mourned for the loss of kin both young and old, but never had her own death seemed so near. Now as she felt its approaching embrace she cried in outrage and anger. She wept and prayed, hoping that the gods who had doomed her might relent.

But the waves kept washing over her, filling her nose and mouth with brine. Each time she kicked her way back up, she lost more strength. She knew a way of staying in the water—at least in calm seas—without tiring. As a young child, Tepua had found that she could let herself hang below the surface, her legs and arms loose, her head down except when she needed a breath. Now, though her temples throbbed and her lips trembled with chill, she tried to enter that slow rhythm: kick, lift the head, breathe, relax, and sink under. Kick, lift, breathe, relax. No. To relax was impossible now.

Rain pattered down, a rain colder than the sea. She thought about the fate of the doomed. As a noblewoman it was her right to enter the paradise of Paparangi and dwell with the other favored souls. But what if the gods had found her impious? They might send her to the place of darkness and suffering instead. No, that was not possible, she told herself. She, who had served as ceremonial maiden-to-the-gods, would surely be accepted in Paparangi. Thinking so, she lost her will to keep struggling.

When the sea lifted her, she rarely bothered to open her eyes. The coming paradise seemed to surround her. Yet once in a while, as she rose to the surface, she noticed the water growing calmer. She saw clouds starting to disperse, the sky brightening. And something unexpected—long and dark—was bobbing on the swells. *A canoe?*

Hastily she spoke a prayer to her guardian spirit, and then she began to swim. She lost sight of her target, halted in panic, turned to scan the waves. "Tapahi-roro-ariki," she called again. Still she saw nothing but churning water.

Then suddenly, a short way off, she spotted what appeared to be a drifting wreck. She threw herself after it. Her hand reached out and she felt something solid.

She clawed at the wood, dug in with her nails as this new hope revived her. She pulled the wet hair from her eyes and tipped her head back to get a better view of what she had found. The single-hull craft was empty. Capsized. She flung one arm over the upturned bottom, tried to heave herself atop it. The craft only rocked, dumping her back in the sea. Frantically she grabbed on again and clung with both hands, determined not to let the wreck get away.

When she had caught her breath, she inspected the boat, moving hand over hand along its side. She found no obvious damage to the single hull, which was made of small planks sewn tightly together. The long outrigger float, attached by flexible poles, also appeared sound. If she could right the craft and bail it, Tepua thought, she might survive. If a paddle remained lashed inside, she would have some hope of reaching land.

But how to turn the boat over? Watching from shore, she had seen vessels capsized by sudden winds. What the boatmen often did was stand on the outrigger of an overturned canoe, shoving it down and under. Then, once the craft righted, they would rock it violently, slopping enough water out so that they could climb in and bail.

Tepua had never done this, but saw how it might work. Balancing on the outrigger, she curled up with her knees beneath her chest. Taking a deep breath, she straightened her legs. The outrigger went down, but it came right back up

again, pitching her off. The second time, her feet slipped off
too soon. The outrigger surged up, smacking her on the
rump. She rubbed the bruise and kept trying.

The rain had stopped. An edge of sun peeked from behind
the clouds. But the canoe remained upside down. She began
to think that the canoe was just too big for her to right by
herself, the outrigger too buoyant to go under. She thought
about breaking or cutting the outrigger loose, but she had no
knife, and she doubted that the water-filled hull would float
without its outrigger.

With anger fueling her effort, she made one more try,
kicking down as hard as she could to sink the outrigger. She
went down with it, gave it one more shove with the soles of
her feet, then surfaced, gasping. She was sure she had lost
once again when she saw the water frothing and the hull still
spinning. Then the outrigger shot up on the side away from
her. The canoe wallowed in the swells, its bare, wet mast
pointed at the sky!

Crying and laughing at the same time, Tepua laid her
arms over the sunken splashboard. She looked within the
flooded hull to see if any supplies remained. A sack of netting
lashed to a thwart held large gourds—water bottles—though
by now salt water had probably seeped into them. Beneath
the gourds lay a pile of coconuts. All the paddles were gone.

Tepua's grief welled up again as she realized that this
craft had belonged to her wedding party. How many people
had been lost to the storm? She could only hope that some
larger canoes had rescued the passengers from this one.

For now she had to put aside her worries about kin and
friends. Her throat burned with salt and thirst. She glanced
again at the large gourds, and prayed that one still held fresh
water.

With trepidation she began to rock the canoe, fearing she
would accidentally overturn it once again. But now that the
canoe floated upright, the outrigger made it steady. In fact
the whole craft was so stable that she found it difficult to
rock. After spending a short time fighting with the swamped
boat, Tepua finally pulled herself in over the side and sat in
the water that remained.

Under her weight, the canoe tipped away from the outrigger, its splashboard almost level with the sea. She tried bailing with cupped hands, but for every handful of brine she tossed out, the waves slopped another in.

Frustrated and weary, she stopped. A scrape on her arm stung, leaking blood into the water. She looked at it, alarmed. Blood in the sea would soon bring sharks. To remain long like this could only bring death.

But how was she to get the boat bailed? Again she eyed the gourds. If the water inside wasn't drinkable, then she could break one open and use it as a scoop. With stiff fingers she undid the netting and selected a gourd that felt half-empty when she shook it. She pulled out the sticky plug and tipped the gourd, letting a few drops onto her tongue.

She tasted salt, but perhaps that was just from her skin. She let a bit more dribble into her mouth, and then drank the rest greedily. Slightly brackish, perhaps, but it would sustain her.

Then she smashed the end of the empty container against a hard edge of the splashboard until she opened a hole in the gourd. With a few more blows she was able to fashion it into a crude bailing scoop.

The sun brightened, giving a blue tinge to the water. The sea, calmed now, lapped gently at the sides of the boat. Only an occasional wave splashed in. Working with the gourd, Tepua began to feel that she might actually be throwing more water out than was coming in. Wiping her brow, she kept going, even though her arm ached and weariness made her dizzy.

Gradually the canoe began to rise as Tepua gained more freeboard. Finally the flood within dwindled to a few annoying puddles. With a huge sigh, she fell back in the canoe.

Only then, when she felt something sharp against her back, did she remember the tangle of cord about her waist. She reached back to find a few sticks of broken bamboo, the remnants of the bridal platform, still tied to her. Tossing these aside, she lay down with her head pillowed on the

remaining gourds, her torn bark-cloth robe spread over her.
She told herself she would rest for only a few moments.

Tepua woke, half-immersed in brine, her arms and legs
stinging. The boat shuddered as something bumped it. She
sat up with a start and a cry. She had no idea how long she
had slept. Her shadow stretched out of the canoe, far across
the water.

Angrily she groped for her makeshift bailer and began
once again. Boats such as these, with so many seams, leaked
constantly. She knew that; why had she let herself fall
asleep?

"Fool!" she said aloud. "Stupid child!" She flung bilge
water in an arc over the side. Another bump shook the boat,
jarring Tepua from her rage.

This time she saw a shape passing the hull, a high dorsal
fin. She froze in her bailing, then started once more in a
frenzy. The shark was as long as a man was tall. She knew
why it had come.

Blood from her cuts, mingling with the seawater, had
seeped through the hull. Even a trace could draw sharks
over great distances. She was fortunate that only one had
found her.

Scooping water out as fast as she could, she kept a close
watch on her enemy. This was not a great blue or a roaming
tiger shark. It swam with stiff, rapid tail beats, speeding
back and forth just beneath the surface, the blue and silver
of its sides flashing with each turn.

The tail was a full crescent, like a waning moon. Its shape
mimicked the tail of an albacore or bonito, the fastest fish in
the sea. Only one shark had such a tail, or the speed and
power to prey on those fish. All Tepua's people knew the
mako.

She summoned what reserves of strength she still had. If
she released her guard, she thought that the shark would ram
the hull with enough force to pitch her into the water. Now
it seemed just to be testing her defenses. It flicked into a
turn, slicing by the canoe and giving Tepua a glance from its

large round eyes. No white or color showed in those eyes. They were entirely dead black.

Tepua sat upright in the half-bailed boat. She reached for her coconut-fiber cord, now lying waterlogged under her feet. She took a length between her hands, forming a loop.

A warning in her head spoke with the voice of Bone-needle. *If you meddle in the realm of priests, you will be punished for it.*

"But there are no priests with me now," Tepua cried aloud. She set her teeth. She had hesitated when the storm struck her bridal canoe. When she might have found a way to soothe the gods, she had let Bone-needle dissuade her. For that advice, perhaps the old woman herself now lay within a shark's belly.

Quickly Tepua looped the string about her hands. She wrapped the cord so that one strand lay across each of her palms. With the middle finger of the right hand, she picked up the strand crossing her palm and then drew her hands apart, forming the beginning of the figure. Quickly she worked, not even watching as the image took shape, for her fingers knew the art far better than her eyes.

And then the first figure was complete. By the looping and crossing and knotting of string, she had created between her hands the form of the mako. She held it up between trembling fingers and thrust it at her enemy. She rolled her eyes to the sky and chanted:

"Father of Sharks, I have made you between my hands. Give me strength to fight the hunger of your son. Send him to the bonito. Send him to the albacore."

The mako shot forward, ramming the canoe and biting at the planks. Clawlike teeth curled from its lower jaw in rows, their tips slanting back into the mouth. Some were needle thin and long as a man's finger.

Tepua braced herself against the thwarts and sides of the craft. Anger and fear ripped her voice as she cried, "Mother of Sharks, I hold you between my hands. Make me your daughter. Give me your teeth, your belly, your anger, or else I die, Mother of Sharks!"

And as she held the figure aloft she felt a hot rush of

strength come through her. Yes, it was magic, it was a gift, it transformed her insides from those of a woman to those of a shark, and she no longer felt weak with fear. With an abrupt motion of her hands, she brought her palms together, crushing the figure in the way she wished to crush her enemy. The mako jerked in the water as if it had felt the blow. The shark backed off, but remained close by, swimming in tight circles.

Tepua was not finished. The gods had not yet shown her how to destroy her foe. She pulled her hands apart again, intending to try another figure, but then something unexpected happened. A few strings became tangled. As she tried to pull the cord tight the shape distorted. Within the strings she suddenly caught a vision of a real shark, its nose arched back against its tail.

Then the mako charged the canoe again and the image disappeared. She cast off the string, snatched up a broken length of bamboo that had been tied to her. As the mako struck she thrust her makeshift dagger hard and deep into the shark's nostril, twisting fiercely.

The mako snapped its jaws, the rows of curled teeth just missing her hand. It writhed, jumped, then seized the splashboard of the canoe. Tepua threw herself back toward the outrigger. For an instant she thought the shark's weight would overturn the boat. Then, with a splintering sound, the splashboard split lengthwise and the mako toppled back into the water.

Tepua crouched, breathing rapidly, astonished that the canoe remained afloat. The shark dived out of sight, giving her a moment to recover. She turned to see what damage it had done. The splashboard must have been cracked previously, for now it had split along its entire length, shedding a long spearlike piece that trailed in the water. Tepua seized the splintered section with shaking hands and twisted it, tearing it off.

The canoe had less freeboard now, but she had gained a weapon against the mako. And the shark itself had given it to her! She laughed aloud, then steadied herself, letting her racing heart slow. Carefully she tore a strip of bark-cloth from her robe and wrapped it around the middle of her makeshift spear for a better handhold.

Chanting an appeal to Tapahi-roro-ariki, she watched the mako as it surfaced, zigzagged away, then came back. One nostril was torn, leaking blood. She knew she probably could not kill the shark with only a bamboo dagger and a short spear. She had seen fishermen club and stab at sharks repeatedly. Even after one seemed long dead, it could suddenly thrash or bite. All she wanted was to keep the shark from taking her.

And then she remembered what the string figure had shown her, how the shark's nose had been tied to its tail.

With one hand still hefting the spear, she gathered up her fiber cord. It was slender but strong. Strong enough? She would soon know. She took the loop of string and wedged one end between two jagged splinters at the tip of her makeshift spear.

She hesitated, wondering if she could really do what she had planned. As if the mako sensed her hesitation, it made another run at the boat. Tepua dropped her spear, grabbed a heavy coconut from the sack, and flung it at the shark's snout. The mako seemed briefly stunned as the coconut splashed harmlessly into the water beside it. She pitched another, hitting the shark at the same sensitive spot.

In fury, the shark snapped, and tried to swallow the offending coconut in one gulp. The hard shell caught in the back of its jaws, wedging the mouth open. The fish began to writhe and shake its head to dislodge the object. Tepua had only a few moments. . . .

She aimed low, at the wounded nostril. With all her weight, she thrust the spear, driving it into the shark's nose to break out through the skin at the other side of its head. The spear point carried the cord with it, threading it through the hole. The pinned mako thrashed and snapped, wrenching the splinter spear around in her hands. Sweating and panting, she braced herself against a thwart.

The shark rested briefly, turning one eye toward her. She knew from its cold gaze that it would not give up. Biting her lip, Tepua leaned out of the boat. One end of her cord loop trailed from the nostril, while the other came out through the wound on the side of the mako's head. She grabbed the first end and then the other, finally yanking her spear free.

The mako went crazy, writhing and twisting until it bent back on itself, its crescent tail close to its snout. Tepua saw her chance to do what the vision had showed her. Deftly she slipped both loops of the fiber cord over the high tail fin. The loops caught, strained, and held. The mako's body formed a ring, tethered nose to tail. The shark struggled helplessly, unable to bite through the cord or thrash free.

Hastily she used her spear to poke the ring of angry mako as far as possible from the boat. At any moment the cord might break or other sharks might arrive, drawn by blood scent or the splashing.

Another glance at the mako surprised her. The shark was sinking! Now she remembered fishermen saying that a shark needed to swim to stay afloat. And this one could do nothing now but chew its own tail. Triumphantly she praised the spirit of her ancestress, then turned to bailing out the canoe.

Making a paddle was her next task, for without one Tepua would only drift helplessly. Now that her cord was gone, she needed a new source of lashings. Surveying her few possessions, she turned to the netting that held the gourds. The cords appeared strong enough, but she had no hope of unknotting them. She would have to cut away the unwanted parts, wasting more than she saved. And without the protective net, she would risk losing her drinking water and food if the boat capsized again.

Finding no other choice, she took her bamboo dagger, washed off the shark's blood, and set to cutting apart the net. Then she laid her short spear and her bailing gourd together. The bailer was squat and bowl-shaped. With a little cutting and trimming, it could serve as a paddle blade.

Using her edge of sharp, hard bamboo, she worked the softer material of the gourd. She cut away the rim to make the bowl shallower, then filed two notches each at the top and bottom. Across the width of her short spear she also scored two grooves, being careful not to weaken the shaft.

Finally she bound the gourd paddle blade to the shaft by fitting cord into the notches of both parts. She examined her work with misgivings. The shaft was too long and the blade too bowl-shaped, but it would serve. And she could also still use it as a bailer.

A chill in the wind made her glance toward the horizon. The sun was only a half disk, the rest melting into the sea. Soon the light would be gone. She wrapped the remains of her bark-cloth robe about her, knelt at the stern, and tried the blade. The paddle was awkward but workable. Slowly she began to dip and stroke, turning the prow to the setting sun.

West. Other islands lay in that direction. Other islands with strange names and unfamiliar people. She felt a surge of fright and homesickness, telling her to turn the canoe and paddle eastward toward her own island.

No. She knew that she could not fight the current that was bearing her westward. She would only waste her strength in the attempt. Her best chance was to paddle with the current, and then pull away from it when she came within sight of land.

Tepua settled into a rhythm of paddling, switching her strokes from one side to the other to keep the boat on course. As daylight diminished she squinted up, trying to sight any stars that might be following the sun down across the violet arc of sky.

She knew that navigators steered by knowing where certain stars fell below the horizon. Though she had rarely sailed at night, those few times remained vivid in her memory. She recalled the gnarled fingers of a canoe master pointing at the night sky, his voice speaking of stars that followed each other down certain paths. When one dropped into its pit below the sky, the steersman would watch the next. In that way he would always have a guiding star over the bow.

Looking toward the final glow of sunset, Tepua chose her first star, then paused to ease her thirst. She punctured a young coconut, lifted it to her mouth, but hesitated to drink.

The gods had been good to her, sending her the canoe, then the strength and wit to fend off the mako. She had so little to offer in return.

Leaning over the side, she carefully poured part of the coconut milk into the sea. She chanted: "*Tapena, tapena, tapena. Kai!* An offering to the gods, come and partake. . . ." Had they heard? A gust of wind stirred her hair and she felt that the spirits had touched her.

It was a long weary night. Tepua's arms and shoulders ached from paddling. Her eyes hurt from squinting at fickle stars that vanished among their twinkling companions each time she blinked or let her head drop. Finally she chose a star that lay apart from its fellows, so that she could follow it more easily. But soon it grew blurry as tears and exhaustion dimmed her vision. When it sank beneath the horizon, she couldn't keep her gaze fixed on any following star. Overwhelmed by sleep, she toppled forward and lay in the bottom of the canoe, clutching the paddle to her breast.

She woke to glaring daylight and a hissing wind. She bailed out the hull again, for more water had leaked in during the night. Her skin was raw and chapped from brine, her eyelashes and mouth crusted with salt. To sit up and move around was difficult; she felt leaden and dizzy. She also felt queasy and could scarcely make herself swallow the soft meat of a coconut. She drank from the water gourd and used a tiny amount to wash the stinging salt from her eyes and mouth.

She knew she had to reach land soon or die of exposure. Her head throbbing, she pushed back her tangled hair and squinted at the horizon. Nothing except waves and sky and more waves and sky. She sighed, put her stern to the rising sun, and paddled.

Two more days and nights went by. She ate the last coconut, drank all but the last of her water. Though she made a sunshade by tying the remains of her bark-cloth robe to the canoe's mast, the sun constantly beat down on her. Heat and sea glare made her disoriented and brought frightening visions.

Once she thought that the mako had broken its bindings and returned to haunt her. She raved—shouting, cursing, striking the water, trying to beat off the shark's image. Again it attacked and again she stabbed it with the pointed end of her paddle shaft. Only when her spear pierced nothing but water and she nearly tumbled overboard did she realize that there was no shark. She fell back, sobbing and panting into the bottom of the boat.

And then, when she had lost track of days and nights, or where the canoe was pointed, she turned her bleary gaze and saw in the distance a long shelf of cloud like none she had seen before. She blinked, unable to make sense of the dark and towering form that lay beneath it. *Another illusion?* She had heard of high islands, said to be huge heaps of stone, but had never glimpsed one. She knew only low, flat, coral islands.

Shaking with weakness, she seized her paddle again, changing course, then stroking in a frenzy toward the impossible sight. She could not keep it up for long. Soon she slowed, falling into a pattern that allowed her a rest between strokes. Her mind went into a daze, her vision tunneled so that she could see only the jagged mass of grays and greens that lay ahead. She tried to remember the names of the high islands that lay in this direction—Eimeo, Urietea, Tahiti.

Dip, stroke, dip, stroke, change sides, dip, stroke. The canoe creaking, the wind hissing, the expanse of water as endless as ever, lips dry, skin cracking. Dip, stroke, dip, stroke, arms screaming, knees aching, everything whirling in a vortex of sea and sky, except at the center, the white mass of cloud and the craggy shapes beneath it.

Then she was far above herself, watching a little figure that sat in the canoe, paddling forever toward an island that never got any closer. Sun glistened on the waves, and on the tiny paddle that kept dipping and rising. Red-tailed seabirds passed overhead, making shrill cries. And far behind her appeared another canoe, terrible and shining, slowly drawing closer.

It was *Mahina*, she knew at once, the canoe of the dead. It had come to take her soul! Its huge sails billowed and its

twin hulls plowed deep furrows in the sea as it approached.
Its fierce master glowered from the deck, pointing his long
finger in her direction. He opened his mouth to call her, his
voice deep and harsh. . . .

Suddenly a prolonged and violent scraping jolted Tepua
out of her trance. She felt a wave lift the canoe, then drag it
sideways. Surf pounded all around her, foam spurting above
her head.

Wiping her arm across her eyes, she saw in the distance
a vast panorama of green-clad peaks that seemed to ascend
to the sky. At the shore lay a sliver of beach lined with
innumerable coconut palms. Ahead, beyond the breakers,
calm water gleamed with delicate shades of aquamarine.
Yet all about her lay frothing sea. . . . She shook her head,
trying to clear her mind. She realized that she had struck a
barrier reef.

An incoming roller lifted the canoe again, spinning it and
smashing it down on an outcrop of coral. A plank on the hull
broke with a harsh crack. The hull started to sink, leaving
only the outrigger afloat.

Grabbing her paddle, she jumped from the waterlogged
boat, crying aloud as her bare feet were cut by the harsh
coral. Quickly she flung herself out of the way as surf rolled
the damaged boat toward her, then heaved it aloft and
slammed it down again on the reef. The canoe shuddered,
cracked open.

Scrambling wildly to escape the beating surf, Tepua
staggered across the submerged reef, catching herself with
her paddle when she could, but sometimes falling heavily.
Ignoring the scrapes and gashes from the rock, she flailed
forward, knowing her strength was almost gone. When her
next step plunged her into deep water, she felt a strange
sense of relief as she went down. Now it was over. The pain
and weariness would end. *Mahina* would take her after all.

For a moment she let herself go limp, resting in the
buoyant water as she would in her mother's arms. Behind
her, the surf still pounded. But the waves were gentle in the
lagoon.

She thought she heard her mother whisper to her,

reminding her how well she could swim. "I want to sleep," Tepua murmured, but the voice urged her on. *Just show me you can reach the shore. Then I will know you are a chief's daughter.*

"No, Mother." But despite herself, she felt her arms sweeping, her legs kicking. *Someone else must be swimming,* she thought, *for I am already asleep.* She began to dream—of other lagoons and calm, blue, welcoming waters.

2

On the mountainous island of Tahiti, in a deep valley cutting inland from the sea, two boar hunters emerged from the shade of hibiscus trees. The men, dusty and perspiring, carried long hardwood thrusting spears across their well-muscled shoulders. Overhead, clouds covered the sun, but the air in the valley remained warm, humid and still.

In the lead walked Matopahu, brother of the district's high chief. He was a tall young man with black, wavy hair that spilled from beneath his turban of bark-cloth. For this hunt he had left behind his feathered headdresses and capes; he wore only the simple loincloth of a laborer. But anyone could see by the elegant tattoos on his back and thighs, by his stature and the grace of his movements, that he was a man of the highest rank.

"The tusker has slipped by us once again," said the second hunter, Eye-to-heaven, as he wiped his brow. Eye-to-heaven was an important priest in the tribal *marae*— the sacred walled courtyard of the high chief. Yet today the priest also wore only a loincloth. He was shorter and stockier than his friend, and a few years older, with a pleasant oval face and crisply curled hair.

"The beast will soon have to make a stand," replied Matopahu, glancing at the ribbon of water that cascaded down a steep cliff at the valley's head. From behind the hunters came the crackling and rustling of underbrush as beaters drove the wild pig toward sheer walls that towered on three sides.

The men had been chasing this animal since dawn, losing it in another valley, but finally trapping it here. Standing in the open now, Matopahu paused, wishing for a breath of wind to cool his face. In this narrow river gorge no breeze stirred.

"I say the pig will go on," replied Eye-to-heaven. "And try to find a hiding place."

"Is that your own judgment, my amiable priest?" asked Matopahu with a wry smile. "Or has some spirit whispered in your ear?"

Eye-to-heaven, who was his *taio,* his sworn friend, with whom he shared everything, laughed. "When I decide to make a divination, you will know," the priest answered. "I was just offering my own opinion."

"Then I will take it, my *taio*." They walked on, passing more stands of hibiscus, whose yellow, trumpet-shaped flowers smelled so rich that the odor became cloying. Daylight would not last much longer, and Matopahu did not want the boar to get away from him. It had done too much damage, frightened too many people, destroyed too many garden plots. He had been hearing reports for a month, but only today had he been fortunate enough to catch up with it.

"This pig is leading us a chase worthy of the legendary Pua'a-mahui," he said to Eye-to-heaven. "If night were not coming so soon, I would ask you to consult the spirits right now." He turned toward the shallow river that ran down the center of the valley, studied the tangled foliage along its bank, but saw no sign of his quarry. Matopahu wondered if—as some people said—this boar indeed had been possessed by the Man-slaying God. If so, then it was unlikely that either spear or priestly incantation could stop the destruction.

Pushing aside his misgivings, Matopahu continued up the narrowing valley, passing dark *rata* trees whose trunks were surrounded by wide, curving buttresses. His footing grew difficult as he crossed a slippery tangle of roots. Behind him, on both sides, the beaters kept to their work, lashing the brush with bamboo flails.

The forest thinned and the club mosses beneath the *rata* grew more luxuriantly. Huge fronds of bird's-nest fern sprouted from decaying stumps, creating a maze of greenery in which the prey could hide.

Far ahead, Matopahu caught a rare glimpse of the pig—a dark, woolly tail vanishing beneath a giant fern. This was about as much as he had ever seen of the elusive beast. But now he began to think that his *taio* had been right after all. The animal was still running. It might seek a hiding place under the cliff.

Matopahu remembered the fear-whitened faces he had seen that morning as he questioned householders at the other end of the valley. "Oh yes, noble sir," one man had told him. "The beast was huge and terrible. See how it rooted up my taro patch and knocked down the wall of my house. It is surely Pua'a-mahui, driven by the Man-slaying God."

"Eeeyah, but it was monstrous!" said another. "Just as the legends say. One jaw pointed to the sky, and the other to the earth. The mouth could have swallowed a man."

Matopahu's palms became moist with sweat as he remembered. Frightened people often exaggerated, but he had seen for himself the damage that the creature had done. Even if it was not the legendary beast, it was surely powerful enough to kill a man.

Perhaps that is why I am here, he thought sourly as he continued up a rise. Matopahu knew that some people considered him a troublemaker. What better way to get rid of such a man than to have him die a hero's death?

The high priest, Ihetoa, had maneuvered him into leading this dangerous hunt. At an audience with the high chief and his retinue, Ihetoa had loudly bemoaned the dangerous pig until Matopahu had felt obliged to offer his help. In these peaceful times, what better way for the chief's brother to prove his valor?

"What do you say, my *taio*," Matopahu asked, turning to his friend behind him. "Do you think Ihetoa is hoping that we never return?"

Eye-to-heaven smiled. "Perhaps so. But he will not get rid of us so easily."

There had long been ill-feeling between the high priest and Matopahu. Ihetoa considered himself the only one who understood the gods' wishes. Yet sometimes a man who was not a priest fell into a trance and uttered words of prophecy. Such oracles might have divine favor, but Ihetoa viewed them only as his rivals.

Matopahu was one of those inspired men. He had no wish to compete with the priests, but when his god spoke through his lips, he lost all awareness of what he was doing or saying. Eye-to-heaven had taken on the task of remembering and interpreting his friend's pronouncements, and so he, too, had come into disfavor with his superior, Ihetoa.

"I will be depending on your spear, my *taio,* to make certain that the high priest is disappointed," replied Matopahu. Recently his god voice had spoken again, warning of famine. The annual season of plenty was at its peak, yet the usual season of scarcity would follow.

Matopahu's voice had declared that the difficult season would be uncommonly long and severe this time. Until he could confirm Matopahu's pronouncement, Ihetoa refused to urge the unpopular practice of storing away extra reserves of food. To Matopahu's annoyance, the high priest still delayed his decision.

Now Matopahu halted, sniffing the breeze. The distinctive swine odor had grown stronger. He looked about warily, eyeing the nearest ferns. Behind him, the beaters advanced.

Then a shrill cry went up as a huge gray-brown form shot from cover. Before the pig vanished into another stand of ferns, Matopahu got a better glimpse of his quarry—the curved yellow tusks, long snout, and huge humped shoulders. Yes, this one was big, the largest boar he had ever seen. Sweat trickled down his chest and back as he gazed at the place where it had vanished.

More cover lay ahead, but the valley was narrowing. Eventually there would be only the river flowing between dark walls of stone. If the boar could find no refuge under the moss-covered rock, it would have to turn and attack the men.

Matopahu waved the beaters back. With spears leveled, he and Eye-to-heaven moved in. He could not judge how close he was to the animal. His mouth grew dry; his heartbeat quickened.

The stretch of rocky ground along the bank narrowed, forcing one man ahead of the other. Then they reached an impasse, a water-slick wall that edged the river. Matopahu turned back, and saw that Eye-to-heaven was already fording the shallow stream. Reaching the other side, he climbed the bank.

On the far side, with no warning, a clump of ferns near the priest exploded, releasing a gray-brown woolly streak. The huge boar, jabbing with lightning thrusts of its head, was on Eye-to-heaven before either man could react. The priest lunged wildly, ramming his spear point between the beast's ribs. Then he dodged from the assault, blood welling from his right thigh. Squealing its death challenge, the boar drove after him as he stumbled backward.

Pua'a-mahui! Matopahu's breath caught in his throat as he splashed across the stream. The pig's rage stink billowed up around him as he hefted his long weapon, but he was still too far away to use it. He saw Eye-to-heaven go down, crimson streaming from rents above his knee. Mouth open, tusks gleaming, coarse brown hair flecked with spittle, the boar charged the priest again.

Matopahu shouted his own challenge, hoping to draw the boar's wrath, but the beast plunged on toward the priest. Eye-to-heaven retrieved his fallen weapon, but could not get it into position. Awkwardly, he clubbed the pig across the snout, deflecting its charge. With a snort of anger, the boar turned toward the oncoming Matopahu.

He choked up on the spear, locked the shaft against his body with his arms, and lunged to meet the attack. The impact pushed him back over slippery ground as the point rammed into the boar's massive chest. Matopahu drove his heels into the rocky dirt and shoved, feeling the spear cut through the beast's muscle and plunge deeper. Now Matopahu's nose lay within a hand's breadth of the disk-shaped snout and slashing tusks. Red-rimmed amber eyes glared at him like coals surrounded by fire. Foam sprayed from the pig's jaws onto Matopahu's face.

He wrestled against the boar's thrashing. Surely that thrust had gone deep enough to pierce the heart! A river of blood poured down the shaft, but still the beast would not die. Far behind him, Matopahu heard the beaters coming.

From the corner of his eye, he saw Eye-to-heaven limping forward, his own weapon dragging on the ground. "Keep back!" Matopahu warned his friend. But the priest tried another thrust, into the belly. This made the creature fight harder, for a moment. Then it paused, flanks heaving, spittle flying.

The foam from its jaws turned from pink to red. For an instant Matopahu thought that the animal had succumbed, but then he felt a sudden crunch of jaws against the bloodied spear shaft. In a new frenzy, the boar gnashed at the pole, sending Matopahu scrambling back hand over hand to keep clear of its jaws. He thought that the pig would chew the spear to splinters. Beside him he heard Eye-to-heaven's voice in an impassioned prayer as the priest tried to jab once more. The sweat of panic washed Matopahu's body.

With a crack, the shaft broke and the boar came hurtling at Matopahu. He stepped back, aimed the splintered end at the animal's gullet, and leaned all his weight into it. The pig gagged, staggered, skidded in the soil as it fought for breath. Spasms shook the body, each one weaker than the last, until finally the boar lay still. Then Matopahu threw back his head and gave a howl of exultation.

"You have finished him," cried Eye-to-heaven, hobbling up and embracing his friend. "What a fight!"

"We did it together, my *taio,*" said Matopahu. "We both share the victory. Now you must tell me; was it merely a beast we just faced, or the spirit of the Man-slaying God? I have never seen such a fight."

The priest did not answer at once. Matopahu saw crimson stains on Eye-to-heaven's leg. Quickly he examined the two ugly gashes. One lay on the inner side of the thigh, close to the groin. He shivered as he realized what the boar might have done to his friend. "You have not lost your manhood, my *taio,* but it was close."

"Yes, very close. Here is my answer. If the evil god had

been inside that beast, we would both be lying there in the mud.''

At last the beaters and the rest of the company arrived. They danced with joy at the sight of the dead boar, but Matopahu had a more urgent task for one of them. ''Bind my friend's wounds,'' he ordered the healer he had brought with him. Then, holding his pearl-shell knife, Matopahu bent over the carcass, intending to gut it on the spot.

''Wait,'' said Eye-to-heaven, hobbling over to him, the new cloth about his thigh already stained with red. ''Let me.''

''But you are wounded and in pain,'' Matopahu protested.

''The pain is a small thing. This animal was a powerful opponent. Surely he carries a message of the future within his belly. I would be failing in my duty if I lost this chance for a divination. And the message will be for you, my friend, for the gods gave you the honor of the killing blow.''

Matopahu put his knife away, watching while the priest prayed over the dead boar, rolled it onto its back, and slit its underside with his own blade. The pig's belly fell open, revealing the entrails nestled in the gut cavity. Eye-to-heaven studied them, frowning and murmuring to himself.

Matopahu left the priest to his exercise. The sight of pig innards did not bother him, but the method used to extract meaning from lobes of liver or loops of intestine was a mystery reserved for priests. Only rarely did a diviner hint at his techniques.

While Eye-to-heaven poked and pondered, and the beaters watched in awe, Matopahu stood up to let a freshening breeze dry the sweat on his face. He stretched and shook out the stiffness in his muscles. He had decided what to do with the pig's carcass. It had been a valiant animal, even if it had not proved to be the beast of legend. Such a pig would make a worthy gift for the high chief's dinner.

Relations between Matopahu and his brother had grown cool of late. Perhaps this gift would help prove Matopahu's good intentions.

"My *taio,* come and see what lies ahead for you," Eye-to-heaven called suddenly.

When Matopahu knelt down beside the priest, Eye-to-heaven swept his palm above the entrails. "See how knotted and tangled they are? This can only mean that complications will enter your life."

"That will be nothing new," Matopahu answered.

"And the pattern of vessels in the gut membrane tells me there will be problems involving a woman."

Matopahu laughed. His only problems with women were how to get rid of them. "But what of my disagreement with Ihetoa?" he asked the priest impatiently. "That is a real problem. The high priest continues to reject my prophecy. The longer he delays, the more everyone will suffer."

Eye-to-heaven peered and squinted at the entrails. The meaty smell was beginning to attract flies. "I, too, wish to know how that will end," he said. "But here I see no answer."

The priest finished his divination with a short prayer of praise to the gods. Reverently he buried the viscera, for it could not be cooked and eaten if it had first been used for prophesy. Then Matopahu ordered his men to finish cleaning the carcass and tie it to a pole.

When the party was ready to leave, the beaters crowded forward, all begging for the honor of carrying the prize. Matopahu had intended to share the load between himself and Eye-to-heaven, for he enjoyed the thought of marching home in triumph with the prize on his shoulders, watching the amazed faces of the people in the settlements.

But Eye-to-heaven was too badly wounded to help now. And to ask someone else to share the victory with himself, Matopahu felt, would be an insult to his *taio.* So he chose the two strongest men among the beaters to carry the pig while he and Eye-to-heaven walked modestly behind them. With his arm about the limping priest, he followed the jubilant procession along the riverbank path that would finally emerge at the coast.

My brother will be pleased with this outcome, Matopahu thought. *He is easily flattered. But the high priest will not celebrate our return.*

3

As evening approached, a Tahitian fisherman sailed home in his small outrigger canoe. Ahead he saw a line of foaming surf, waves breaking over the barrier reef. He steered toward a narrow stretch of smoother water, a pass into the calm, blue lagoon that lay between the outer reef and the shore.

The fisherman was called Rimapoa—"the one who fearlessly handles the unpleasant." His darkly tanned skin and wiry build marked him as a man who worked hard and received little for his efforts. Today not a single albacore lay in the bottom of his boat.

Rimapoa glanced for a moment at Front-tooth, the boy who assisted him. "I know why the gods did not send fish today," said the youngster. "It is because you argued with your sister this morning." Angrily Front-tooth hit the splashboard with his fist.

The fisherman gave the boy a weary look. "I am always quarreling with my sister," he answered with a growl. "By now the spirits have lost interest in our arguments." It was useless, he knew, to tell Front-tooth to keep his thoughts to himself. He had little control over the boy, who was bound to him only through a friendship between families. If Front-tooth didn't like the arrangement, he would quit and join up with some other fisherman. Then Rimapoa would have no help at all.

"Then tell me why no fish took the bait," said the boy. "It was good mullet and I hooked it on well." Front-tooth leaned over the splashboard and stared moodily across the lagoon.

Rimapoa did not reply, and he wondered whether Front-tooth was right after all. Rimapoa was a solitary deep-line fisherman. The parties of men who trolled for albacore from large double canoes constantly warned him to keep away from their fishing grounds. Today he had gone as close as he dared, but not close enough to lure the elusive albacore. Yet on other days, the fish had found his hooks. . . .

The fisherman sighed, and turned his attention to the churning water that lay just ahead. Shooting the pass was always risky. He leaned on the long steering oar, turning his bow to the channel's entrance. Water boiled in whitecaps to either side of the canoe as waves struck the submerged coral.

Slackening the line to the boom of his curved claw sail, he let the fore part luff in the wind, waiting for the right moment. As his gaze crossed the frothing boundary between sea and lagoon, he saw a wreck—a battered half hull, its sternpost canting up. The reef had taken its toll once again.

Rimapoa was in no hurry. He had no fish lying in the bottom to spoil. Ignoring Front-tooth's impatient grimaces, he let several rollers sweep by before choosing the strongest. He felt the surge as the wave gathered behind him and he pulled hard on the sail, catching the wind. The outrigger lifted on the wave's crest and rode through.

Leaving the breakers crashing behind him, Rimapoa tacked into quiet waters. The sail bellied and the outrigger surfed, making his spirit lift. He knew that even if there were no fish and he had to make his living ashore, he would still sail his canoe. There was nothing like the feeling of a well-built craft leaping like a flying fish across the sea.

The love of it was in his bones, for one of his ancestors had been a canoe master on an island far to the west. This heritage showed in the fisherman's long legs, his wiry frame, and the tight curl of his hair. It showed also in his daring, in his willingness to face the sea in all its moods.

The canoe was gliding toward the narrow, sandy beach when Front-tooth shouted, "Look over there!" The boy flung out his arm toward shore.

Rimapoa scowled and squinted. With the sun so low, every rock and piece of driftwood on the beach cast a shadow. Yet he saw something at the water's edge that did not roll like driftwood when the waves lifted it. It moved loosely, like a half-filled sack . . . or a human body.

"Who is it? Who is it?" asked Front-tooth excitedly. Then, without warning, he leaped over the splashboard and swam toward the beach.

Rimapoa shouted after him, but to no avail. He wanted Front-tooth's help when he reached shore, and now he would have to manage alone. Angrily, he lowered the sail and brought the canoe in, struggling to pull the dugout hull to dry ground. Front-tooth was calling him, but he ignored the boy while he secured the boat.

He found Front-tooth crouched beside a lifeless young woman who lay sprawled in the sand. The boy had dragged her up from the waterline and was now poking her ribs and peering into her face.

"She is dead!" announced Front-tooth. "Drowned!"

Her black hair spilled down in salt-and-sand-encrusted tangles. Her closed eyes were sunken. Her jaw was so slack, her skin so ashen and colorless, and her limbs so still that Rimapoa thought she had been dead for some time. "Careful," he warned, pushing the boy aside. "Do you want to anger her spirit?" Her soul might still be nearby, able to wreak harm.

But Rimapoa suddenly noticed a faint flush under the skin of the woman's cheek. He dropped to his knees and touched two fingers to her throat just beneath the angle of her jaw. At first he found nothing, and then he was not sure of the small flutter beneath his fingers. He brought his cheek to her open mouth, hoping to feel the gentle pressure of her breath.

"Why do you bother?" asked the boy scornfully. "She looks like she's been dead for days. She smells like it, too."

Rimapoa glared back at him. "Go get help, you useless son of an eel! Fetch Hoihoi!"

"Your sister won't listen to me," Front-tooth said with a whine. His feet did a nervous dance on the wet sand.

The fisherman grunted his agreement. Hoihoi was not easily roused into action. He focused again on the unfortunate woman, tipping her head back, using two fingers beneath her chin and his palm against her forehead. By custom, one did not touch another person's head, but he knew no other way to help her.

For a moment he studied her face. The sculpted cheek-bones and the strong chin that drew to a point were unlike those of Tahitian women. Not long ago, he imagined, she had been beautiful.

He ran his fingertips down her arm and shuddered at how cold she felt. He pinched her nose shut, took a deep breath, placed his mouth on hers, and breathed out from deep in his chest, the way a healer had taught him long ago.

The first breath would not go in.

"You have to empty the water from her chest," said Front-tooth with a superior air.

Rimapoa did not answer the boy. He rolled the woman on her side, swept the inside of her mouth with a finger, and hooked out a plug of mucus and seaweed blocking her throat. He breathed into her again, holding her tongue with his thumb so it could not slip back and choke her. This time, when he blew, he saw her chest rise. He gave her several strong breaths and then felt her throat again. The pulse was there, weak but persistent.

Front-tooth repeated his suggestion with an air of arrogance that irritated Rimapoa. "Boy, you know nothing," the fisherman answered. "What you say comes from old tales. I have pulled people from the sea and I have never had to empty them like pouring out a bucket. There is only a little water in her throat." He stopped his tirade to blow more breaths into the woman.

He continued breathing for her until he met some resistance as he blew in. He turned his head to one side and felt the tickle of breath on his cheek. He felt hope flood over him. She was starting to breathe on her own at last.

"The sun is dropping fast," said the boy, edging closer. "And she is dead, anyway."

"Be quiet," ordered the fisherman, wiping the sweat of tension from his forehead. He hadn't realized until now how much he wanted this woman to live.

Rimapoa began massaging her feet and hands, trying to

bring some warmth back into them. He paid no attention to the boy and was surprised to hear Front-tooth calling him again.

"Look, Rimapoa. Part of a canoe washed up here."

"Maybe it was hers," he answered, recalling the wreck he had seen on the reef. He frowned, wondering if there were men who had come with her. Surely she could not have been sailing in the open ocean by herself.

Front-tooth dragged a piece of the wreck closer to show him. "See. Patchwork pieces, all sewn together."

Rimapoa glanced quickly at the dripping lengths of board. He knew at once that the boat had been made by *motu* people, who lacked trees large enough for building dugout hulls. "Then maybe she is an atoll woman," he answered testily. "What does it matter?"

"Atoll woman?" The boy's eyes widened. "Then she is a *savage*!" He backed away. "Why save her? If she lives, she will probably *eat* you!"

Rimapoa wanted to laugh aloud at Front-tooth's ignorance. Instead he focused his attention on the young woman. Though she shivered, her breathing was stronger, enough to sustain her awhile. Now she needed a warm, dry place.

He slipped his callused hands beneath her shoulders and rump. She was heavier than she looked, telling him that much of her weight was muscle. He began the lift with care, hoping she had no injuries that might be made worse. Grunting with effort, he got to his feet, rolling her up against his chest.

"Go on home," he told the boy. "Your father will be looking for you." Carrying the woman in his arms, he strode past Front-tooth, crossing the beach into a stand of coconut. The fronds were rattling in the brisk wind as the slender palms bowed high above his head.

The fisherman walked quickly, scowling to himself at Front-tooth's foolishness. It was said that atoll dwellers killed and ate their enemies, but how could he fear this poor woman? Perhaps, he thought, feeling a twinge of sympathy, she had fled her homeland to escape just such a fate.

His concern for her grew, and he quickened his pace,

eager to reach home. At last, just as darkness fell, he saw a glimmer of light at the doorway of his small, thatched hut. "Hoihoi, we have a visitor," he called as he carried his burden, still dripping, inside.

His plump sister stood waiting for him, her meaty fists on her hips. Looking at her now, he could scarcely see how she had once been known as a beauty of the district. Nor could he recall that she had ever been sweet-tempered or even agreeable. As he approached, her eyes widened with surprise and then her expression darkened.

"Is this what your fishhooks dragged up?" Hoihoi asked scornfully, shaking her double chins. "What sort of bait have you been using?"

Rimapoa did not reply in kind. "Have you forgotten what our ancestors taught us? *Begrudge nothing to the stranger who passes your door.*" He knelt to let the woman down on a sleeping mat. He tried to arrange her limbs to make her comfortable.

"Ha. This one has not passed anyone's door. Not on her own feet."

"Even so, sister, I have made her my guest." He gave Hoihoi a challenging stare. "And now it is your duty to help me."

He glanced back at his charge, studying her pale, haggard face. He doubted that his sister could see the promise of beauty that lay within. He gently brushed one strand of brine-soaked hair from the woman's face. Suddenly he felt clumsy and awkward.

He looked up again, studying Hoihoi's plump figure and stout, muscular arms. She had tied her hair back tonight, in a way that did nothing to flatter her face or her body. Yet her expression seemed to be softening now as she saw the firmness of his resolve. "Help her and I will bring you the next albacore I catch," he promised quietly. "Even if it means I am late with my gift to the headman."

"Make it a white-belly," she muttered, marking the length of fish she wanted on her extended arm. "Nothing smaller." Then she sighed and took a few steps closer. "Well, brother. What are you doing sitting there when we have a guest who needs attention? Go to the stream and get me some fresh water!''

When Tepua opened her eyes, she saw a strange woman crouching beside her. A bluish, flickering light covered everything, and for a moment Tepua thought that she had entered the realm of undersea spirits. Painfully she turned her head and saw an unfamiliar kind of torch, a stick strung with oily kernels that sputtered as they burned. Above her, far higher than she was used to, hung a thatched roof, while beneath lay a coarsely woven sleeping mat on a grass-strewn dirt floor. Her lips felt swollen and stiff, her tongue clumsy. ''I—I am alive.''

The woman beside her merely grunted in response, her fleshy face showing no sign of friendliness. She wore a wrapper of thin and frayed bark-cloth, unlike the well-made material that Tepua's father obtained from traders. Tepua tried raising her head, then shut her eyes against a wave of dizziness. Surf seemed still to be roaring in her ears; her hands and feet throbbed from coral cuts. She saw again the anguished faces of the people from her wedding party.

''Where—where is this?'' Tepua asked weakly. The night air felt heavy and moist. Strange, intoxicating scents drifted in through the open-weave walls.

The woman muttered something, then picked up an open coconut and held it out to Tepua. The young woman struggled to sit up. She found her hands bandaged with moist leaves tied on with sennit cord. Now she remembered every scrape and bruise, the damage that wind and sun had done to her skin, the blisters on her palms. She cried out with pain as she took the coconut between her bandaged hands and began to drink. The milk was sweet and rich. She gulped it eagerly.

''Slow,'' said the woman, taking it away from her.

Tepua had never tasted anything so delicious. She reached out and pulled the coconut back to her lips.

''Stubborn,'' said the woman. ''You must be. Otherwise, you would be in some fish's belly by now.'' She spoke with a lilt that left out parts of words and made other parts run together. Tepua had to strain to understand her.

The large woman let her finish the half coconut, but afterward would give her only water to quench her thirst. Tepua had to struggle against the weakness and vertigo that made her head swim, but she stayed propped up on her elbows. "What—what island is this?" She had to repeat herself before the woman understood.

"Tahiti, of course," she answered with pride. "Not one of your heaps of coral. This is a *real* island."

Tepua narrowed her eyes. She did not like the scornful tone in the woman's voice, a tone she was unaccustomed to hearing. But at least now she had some hope of speaking and being understood. She had listened often to her father's visitors—men from high islands, from Tahiti and its neighbors. These high islanders spoke a language similar to hers, but did not voice the hard "k" and "g" sounds of atoll speech, making only a breathy sound deep within their throats. She had to listen carefully to understand them.

She took another sip of water as she recalled what her father's guests had said of their journeys. Hope formed her words. "Tahiti? Then . . . I am only three days' sail from home! You can take me back!"

The other woman threw back her head, big body shaking as she laughed. "Girl, you don't have enough strength to sit up on a mat, let alone a canoe. Lie back and rest."

Tepua's body wanted to do that. Stubbornly she willed her tired head to lift, her eyes to stay open. "I can do it. Prepare a canoe."

"Prepare a canoe!" The Tahitian woman turned to a man in the far corner. "Did you hear that, brother? She is ordering us around as if she were the headman's firstborn daughter."

"She has had too much sun, Hoihoi," he answered from across the room. Then he came closer and crouched beside Tepua. Her vision was blurred, forcing her to squint at him. He had weathered skin, small wrinkles about the eyes and mouth, and he smelled of fish.

"You will take me home," Tepua said, addressing him as she would a servant.

The man glanced at the heavyset woman in puzzlement.

"Take you?" Hoihoi squealed in outrage. "He has no time for that. If you want to go home, you can swim!"

Tepua ignored her, concentrating her attention on the man.

"You must rest—" he began in a patient voice.

"What is your name?" she interrupted.

"Rimapoa."

"Rimapoa, I need to go home." She said the words slowly, trying to soften her "k" and "g" sounds. Surely it must be a matter of understanding. If these common people knew what she needed, they would do it. That was the way things had always been.

She didn't like the way his expression hardened, although a little kindness remained in his eyes. Perhaps she had better try a different approach. "My father will reward you," she offered, not allowing herself to doubt that Kohekapu, who had sailed with the wedding party, was still alive. "He will give pearl-shell fishing hooks, as many as you want. I know how much you value them."

The fisherman leaned closer, his interest evidently roused. "And who is this father of yours?"

Taking a deep breath, she recited Kohekapu's full name with all his titles, including even those now bestowed on her eldest brother.

Hoihoi began to laugh. "So many titles! One for each little pile of coral!"

"You would not laugh if he were standing here. Look. Here is the proof of my birth." She turned her hand to show the back, where she carried her special tattoo, a unique rosette that was reserved for her family.

Hoihoi wiped tears of mirth from her face. "That mark means nothing to me," she said. "And now I think I have heard enough from you. My brother has made you our guest. Otherwise, I would throw you out to sleep with the pigs."

You should be beaten, Tepua almost shouted in reply. Yet

a sudden fear stopped her tongue. Clearly, her father's authority meant nothing here. The Tahitians could do with her as they pleased.

If she wanted them to help her, she would have to use charm and tact, not threats. Even if she must humble herself . . . She glanced down at her body, naked but for a small cloth about the hips. Somehow Hoihoi had washed her and rubbed coconut oil onto her skin to help relieve the sunburn. She had wrapped leaves about Tepua's hands, with a poultice to ease the pain of coral cuts.

She swallowed hard and realized that she would have to show her appreciation. It was not something she was used to doing, especially to those she considered beneath her.

"It was . . . kind of you," she said, feeling awkward and a little angry. "I know you . . . did not have . . . to help me."

"Then let us hear no more talk about atoll chiefs," replied Hoihoi.

Too exhausted to say more, Tepua sank back onto the mat. Rimapoa stayed beside her. He looked down and gave her a sad little smile. "You need to rest," he said again, smoothing back her hair. She wanted to flinch from his touch, but found herself too tired to care. His hand was warm and dry, his fingers gentle.

"I would rest better at home," she tried again. "Is there no way to take me?"

"I have a small outrigger canoe that I use for fishing," he admitted.

"Then you could . . ." She tried to sit up again, but his hand on her shoulder pushed her back down.

"You are in no shape for an ocean voyage. The trip would be long and full of dangers."

"But I managed to get here—by myself—in a little canoe."

"With the gods' help, yes. But do not forget that winds and currents helped carry you to us. To go back in the direction of dawn is far more difficult. Let us not speak of it until you are stronger. Instead, lie still and let Hoihoi nurse you."

Tepua allowed herself to slump back. She felt as though the world were spinning away from her. Everything was so different here—the speech, the customs, the houses.

She shut it all out. Nothing here mattered. She would soon go home, to rejoin those of her family who still lived and to mourn those who did not. Clasping that thought for what comfort it gave her, she drifted into sleep.

4

TEPUA slept poorly that night, waking often and imagining that she was still in the canoe. In her panic she flailed about in the darkness, seeking the bailer or the makeshift spear, until she heard Hoihoi's soft snoring and remembered where she was. Then she would feel for the solid earth of the floor and convince herself that she no longer rode the waves.

What of the others—her mother, her father, her brothers and cousins? she would ask herself. *How many drowned?* She could think of nothing but returning home to learn their fate.

She dozed again, to be awakened first by crowing cocks and then by the whispering voices of Hoihoi and the fisherman.

"What if her story is true?" Rimapoa said. "With a bundle of pearl-shell hooks, I would not have to go out fishing anymore. I could sleep all day under the trees while other men brought me their catches."

"Ah, you fool. You are a fisherman, not a trader. Do you even know what stars to steer by to reach her island?"

"I know men who can teach me."

"So. And what if you do manage to find the place? How do you expect those *motu* people to treat you? They will have a feast to celebrate the girl's return, and serve *you*—baked in hibiscus leaves—as the main dish."

Tepua balled her fist and wanted to cry out against Hoihoi's lie, but she bit her lip and waited for the fisherman's answer.

"I do not believe her father would reward me so poorly."

"Ha. But do you remember, when you brought her in, how she started babbling about a wedding party? If canoes tipped over, then maybe she lost some of her kin in the waves.''

''But how does that—''

''Think a moment, brother, before you sail to your death. If she truly is a chief's daughter, she may now be his only surviving heir. If you bring her home, what if she finds a stranger ruling there now, a stranger who has taken a title that is rightfully hers? He may wish to be rid of both of you!''

Tepua pushed her knuckles into her mouth to keep from screaming. *It is possible,* a voice within her wailed. She did not know who remained alive to rule her people. Tears trickled down her cheeks as she forced herself to keep silent.

''Shhh! I hear our foreigner stirring,'' said Hoihoi suddenly. ''Say no more now, but weigh the risks carefully.''

Tepua could hold back no longer. She shuddered with grief, her single cry piercing the air before she fell back, exhausted, onto the mat. She did not wish to consider what awaited her at home. It was her duty to return, no matter what had happened there in the meanwhile. If this fisherman refused to take her, she would find another.

Cocks crowed once more. She heard Rimapoa stirring. He muttered a few words and rushed out into the dim early light.

When Tepua woke again, she found herself alone. Daylight streamed through the latticework walls of the fisherman's hut. How high the roof seemed, compared with the houses of her home island. The single room appeared tidy though spare. It held a few mats, several heavy wooden bowls, and smaller utensils made of polished coconut shells. Against the rear wall she saw a small wooden shrine, a pedestal holding the carved image of the god that the fisherman worshiped.

A post made from a smoothed length of a branching tree ran up through the center of the house. From its shortened limbs hung stoppered gourds and parcels of food—to keep them away from rats. Tepua glanced up at the rafters and saw a few small rolls of bark-cloth, perhaps the only valuables the fisherman possessed. If only Rimapoa would ignore his sister's poisonous words, he might change his lot. . . .

Tepua frowned, recalling Hoihoi's arguments. There might be risk after all for the person who took her home.

"So, my noble castaway," came Hoihoi's voice from behind her. "Perhaps you are ready to take your morning meal."

Tepua turned and saw the woman coming through the doorway carrying a polished coconut bowl. She raised her head, acknowledging the greeting.

"This is something you will like," said Hoihoi, who wore a wrap of bark-cloth printed with fern-leaf designs. She carried a white flower in her short, swept-back hair, and seemed more cheerful than she had been last night. Perhaps she believed that Rimapoa meant to ignore Tepua's offer.

The younger woman leaned forward eagerly, for a fierce hunger had appeared during the night. The dish, she saw, held a thick, pasty concoction.

"*Poi*. We make it many ways. This one uses cooked breadfruit with coconut cream."

"Breadfruit?" Tepua didn't know what the word meant.

Hoihoi clucked. "I forgot that you are an atoll girl. Come outside and let me show you the tree." She turned, taking the bowl with her.

Hunger drove Tepua to follow Hoihoi. She stripped the wrappings from her hands and found the skin sore but starting to heal. Wincing as she put weight on her foot, she tried to avoid pressing on the side, where coral had gashed it. Then she picked up the length of bark-cloth that had covered her during the night and wound it about her waist, tucking it in under the armpit. When she was finally ready, she limped out into the leaf-strewn shaded yard.

"Up there," said Hoihoi, gesturing at a handsome tree where broad, dark green leaves were deeply scalloped. The round, rough-skinned fruits were of varying sizes, the biggest as large as a man's head. "That is the food I like most."

On the ground, Hoihoi had set out on a broad leaf a

coconut-shell cup full of water for washing, and another for drinking. Now she put the *poi* beside the cups. When Hoihoi sat cross-legged at her own place, in front of a second bowl of *poi,* Tepua noticed the chain of tattooed sprig marks around her heavy ankles and wrists, and the delicate swirl marks on the backs of her hands. "Do you know how to eat this?" Hoihoi asked.

Tepua eyed the bowl hungrily. Vegetable food such as this was scarce among Tepua's people, who sustained themselves on reef fish and clams. When her island's version of *poi* was available, children usually ate most of it.

She cautiously plunged a forefinger into the yellowish mass. Gummy strings trailed from her finger as she raised it to her lips. The sweet creamy taste filled her mouth. *Wonderful!* Hurriedly, before she could even swallow, she plunged her hand back into the bowl.

"It is getting on your chin!" Hoihoi chided, holding up her own finger, which she had licked completely clean.

Tepua was too busy scooping *poi* into her mouth to worry about such niceties.

"You will have to learn our customs and *tapus,*" said Hoihoi. "I don't want my neighbors thinking I have a savage living here."

The young woman thought only about filling her empty stomach. She was using two fingers now, not caring how sticky her face felt.

"Did you hear how I said that word?" Hoihoi persisted. "*Tapu,* not *tabu,* as some foreigners say it. You must learn to speak properly."

What does it matter? I'll be leaving in a day or two, Tepua wanted to explain, but her mouth was too full of food.

Hoihoi waited until she had finished most of the bowl before continuing her lecture. "The women of a fisherman's household have a special duty that you must understand," she began solemnly. "And this applies to guests as well. While Rimapoa is away in his canoe, we never sport with men. A look and a wink, maybe, but no *hanihani.* Remember that spirits are always watching. If we do not obey, they will keep the fish from his hooks.''

Tepua felt her eyebrows rise, pulling the burned tight skin of her forehead. It took her a moment to understand and then she didn't know whether to laugh or lose her temper. Of all the things to warn her about, Hoihoi had picked the most ridiculous. Tepua smiled as she licked the last bits of *poi* from her fingers. ''You need not worry about me.''

''Yes, I forgot,'' said Hoihoi gruffly, waving away a persistent fly. ''A chief's daughter, and not yet wed. I know how they treated you at home. While the other girls went out to have a tumble beneath the bushes your father kept you under guard. But he is not here now.''

''What does that matter? I have my duty to my family, just as you have yours to Rimapoa.''

''But my brother is usually home by afternoon!'' said Hoihoi with a broad grin. ''Then I can go off and do as I please.''

Tepua tossed her head scornfully. The open lechery of this woman repelled her. She replied, ''After I am married and have borne my first son, I, too, will be free to do as I please.''

''Ah, but that is a long way off, my atoll flower.'' Hoihoi's voice softened, and she quietly finished her meal. She dipped her fingers in a half shell of fresh water. Tepua used her own bowl to rinse the stickiness of *poi* from her fingers.

''I have been thinking,'' said Tepua, when she was done, ''that I should not keep asking your brother to make this journey that he fears is so difficult. Instead I should go see your chief. Surely he knows men with larger canoes. He will grant me the customary hospitality.''

''If he is certain that your people are no enemy of his, he may help you,'' Hoihoi answered. ''But our high chief lives up the coast, far from here. We have an underchief, a headman, who looks after our affairs.''

''Then I must go to him and explain my predicament.''

''Yes,'' she said thoughtfully. ''That is just what you should do. After all, Rimapoa's boat is old and small. The

headman can find you one far better." With sudden
eagerness, she rose to her feet and straightened her wrap.
"Come now. I would like to settle this quickly, before my
brother comes home. Maybe we can get in to see the
headman this morning."

Spurred on by Hoihoi's encouraging tone, Tepua forced
herself to stand. After days of kneeling in the canoe, her
knees felt stiff as an old crone's. She still felt weak, and the
cuts on her feet stabbed her at every step, but she followed
the fisherman's sister out of the yard. They took a path that
led toward the water.

Every sight here was startling and new to Tepua. Wherever she turned she saw tall thatched houses like the
fisherman's, usually standing in clusters, shaded by breadfruit trees and surrounded by low bamboo fences. In open
sheds beside the houses she saw fire pits and implements for
cooking. The residences were spaced comfortably apart, yet
seemed endless in number. She could not imagine how so
many people could live in one area and get along with each
other.

Creatures that were rare in the atolls seemed common
here. In almost every shaded yard, she glimpsed dogs with
upright ears and coats of white or brown. Tame fowl—hens
and gaudy cocks—fluttered or pecked at the ground.

Plants of exotic shape and unfamiliar color grew wherever she looked. Trumpets with five-pointed crimson stars
in their centers bloomed among vines that snaked about
trees and over the trail. Flowers she could not name stuck
tongue-shaped petals out at her. Sprays of blossoms, colored
cream or pink, erupted like sea foam from the bushes.

When she let her gaze travel up the hillside toward the
distant green-mantled peaks, she grew dizzy and had to look
away. She longed for the familiar flat terrain of her
homeland and the simple plants she knew.

And here lay another surprise—a broad stream of water
in its own channel, flowing brightly toward the lagoon. At
home the only time that fresh water ran on the ground was
during a heavy downpour. Tepua's eyes widened. While
Hoihoi splashed indifferently across, the newcomer had to

muster her courage, fearing she might lose her footing and tumble onto the rocks.

At last, close to the seashore, the two women came to the bamboo fence that surrounded the headman's compound. Here a guard turned them away at once. "The headman is out, gone for two more nights," said the guard as he shifted his polished wooden spear idly from one hand to the other. Its slender tip looked hard and extremely sharp.

"What is your problem, Hoihoi?" a new voice interrupted. Tepua turned to face a pair of men squatting in shade outside the compound. Between them lay a pile of small stone disks, evidently part of a game. The speaker grinned up at Hoihoi. "You usually don't need the headman's authority. I have seen you settle many a quarrel without anyone's help."

His partner, a stocky younger man with a lopsided face, studied the stones and looked annoyed at the interruption. Tepua did not recognize the game they were playing. She noticed that both men were darkly tanned and had the callused hands and salt-roughened skin of fishermen. Their sides were tattooed above their hips with a series of dotted arches that vanished, front and back, into their loincloths.

"The problem is not mine," answered Hoihoi, gesturing toward Tepua. "This is Tepua-mua, my brother's guest. She is looking for a boatman to take her east, to her pearl-shell island."

"Ay," muttered the older fisherman, seemingly indifferent to Tepua's plight.

"What does she offer?" asked the younger fisherman— the one with odd features—as he suddenly showed an interest in the conversation.

"Pearl shells, of course. What else do those *motu* people have?" Hoihoi laughed as if she had made a great joke, her plump breasts heaving beneath her wrap.

"Then the journey is for me," said the second man with new enthusiasm. He stood up and addressed Tepua while his gaze took in her face and then made a slow excursion downward. Suddenly her cheeks felt hot. At home no man of his class would have dared stare at her so. She forced herself to endure his inspection silently.

He was young, not much older than Tepua, far stockier than Rimapoa. As for his face, she thought that his jaw had been broken and had not healed properly. She felt a stir of pity, thinking that he might have been handsome before the injury.

"People call me Tangled-net," he said, "because my net got snagged on the reef and I lost it. But if I had some pearl-shell hooks, I would not be wasting my time here. I would be out in my boat." He kicked with his bare toes at the pile of gaming stones.

"I want to leave at once," said Tepua, trying to ignore the weariness that still clung to her. She knew she needed rest and food before undertaking another sea voyage, but was too impatient to wait.

"At once?" asked Tangled-net with a laugh. "I must prepare a few things. Make an offering to the gods, of course, and see to my boat. After that, if you help me gather supplies, we can leave tomorrow at first light."

Something about his manner troubled her, but she quickly agreed to his plan. She could not stand waiting two more nights to see the headman.

"Then I will come looking for you later," he said. "In the afternoon—at Rimapoa's house. Meanwhile, try to fill your belly. We will have little to eat on the way."

When the women returned home, Tepua helped Hoihoi collect breadfruits from a tree near the house. The globular fruits grew in small clusters, two or three to a bunch, hanging amid the splendor of broad, glossy leaves. Hoihoi used a long forked stick to loosen one at a time, and Tepua's job was to catch it before it hit the ground. As she worked, her hands grew sticky with sap that oozed from the yellow-green rinds.

The two carried their harvest to an open-walled shed behind the house of a neighbor, where a fire was burning in a shallow pit oven—a round hole dug in the ground and filled loosely with rocks. The other Tahitian women stared at Tepua while Hoihoi gave a brief explanation. "Rimapoa found her on the beach, nearly drowned. And now she is ready to sail home again!''

The women were short and plump, though none matched Hoihoi's bulk. When they spoke, they used their eyes and hands as much as their voices. They stared at Tepua as if she were an exotic deep-sea creature. "What do you think of our island?" they kept asking.

When the fires burned out, the women wrapped sliced breadfruit in leaves and placed the packets between the heated rocks within the pit. They covered the food with more leaves and with earth, then sat talking while the food baked. Tepua could not keep her eyes open. She sprawled in the shade and fell asleep.

She woke to a tantalizing aroma. Hoihoi had brought her a steaming packet of food. "Do as Tangled-net told you," she said. "Fill your belly while you can."

Breadfruit! With curiosity, Tepua took a small bite. It had a faint sweetness, a mild flavor, and was slightly firm to the tooth. After seasoning it with a rich coconut sauce, she ate as much as she could, then dozed again along with the other women. She was startled from sleep by a deep voice.

"So this is where you hid yourself. I was looking in the wrong place."

She saw Tangled-net standing over her, grinning. The sight of his misshapen face gave her a start, until she remembered who he was. Then, flushing again in the presence of his frank stare, she sat up slowly and brushed sand from her wrap.

Nearby, Hoihoi was rubbing her eyes sleepily. The shadows had lengthened and Tepua saw that the day was almost gone. "Let me warn you, my friend Tangled-net," Hoihoi said to the fisherman. "Do not try any tricks with this girl. Tepua is my brother's guest. You will take her home as you agreed, or answer to both of us."

A brief look of worry came over the young man's features. "Your brother does not frighten me," he said, with a nervous laugh. "But nobody wants to be Hoihoi's enemy. You can trust me to take her off your hands."

Tepua stiffened. Evidently Tangled-net saw what Hoihoi

wanted—to get rid of the stranger before she caused trouble for Rimapoa. Even so, Hoihoi had helped her, and Tepua could offer nothing in return. "I will send gifts back to you," the young woman promised, feeling awkward as she spoke. "And to your brother." Hoihoi only grunted and folded her arms.

Tangled-net walked away, beckoning Tepua after him. For an instant she wanted to stay with Hoihoi. *And hide behind her as you did behind Bone-needle. You will never get home that way.* With a sense of loss she finally left Hoihoi.

Excitement quickened Tepua's pulse as she hurried after Tangled-net. She became acutely aware of the gritty beach sand beneath her feet and how the rhythm of the sea beat in her ears like a booming temple drum. As she caught up with the fisherman a startling thought made the hair of her nape stand on end. *She had never, in her memory, been alone with a man.*

It was true. Chaperons and guardians had always watched over her. Bone-needle had been with her constantly since early childhood. On long, lazy afternoons how Tepua had envied the other girls their freedom to go off with young men. She had remained on the beach, close enough to hear the soft laughter and cries from behind the bushes.

Now she watched the fisherman striding ahead of her, his brown back supple and the muscles in his buttocks bunching to either side of his loincloth. His face might be marred, but otherwise he was attractive.

Tepua had been sheltered far too long. What would it be like to touch him, she wondered, or to feel him touch her? She was obliged to preserve her maidenhood, of course, but what harm would come from sitting alone with him, breathing his scent, listening to his voice?

Tangled-net stopped, glanced back, appraising her in turn, though he had already inspected her thoroughly. Was he now trying to guess her thoughts? The way his hips thrust slightly forward against the low-slung band of his *maro* made her suspect that he knew exactly what she was thinking. She bit her lip, trying to keep the unwanted emotions at bay.

He led her seaward into a palm grove that was screened by surrounding foliage from sight of any dwelling. Odd little shivers ran up and down Tepua's back. Everything was quiet here except for the sound of Tangled-net's feet on fallen coconut fronds.

She had never imagined that a coconut grove could be so large or lush. The undergrowth surged up and into the trees like a restless sea. Vines wound everywhere and were full of blooms whose strong perfume made her dizzy. Tall, slender boles of the trees arched upward, crowns swaying with the breeze of late afternoon.

It was all so intensely green, the air moist and heavy. Sweat trickled down her face, her neck, her back, between her breasts. She looked for Tangled-net and found him waiting for her a short distance deeper into the grove.

"Whose trees are these?" Tepua asked as she caught up with him. At home, coconut trees were so precious that each was closely guarded by its owner. Even on bountiful Tahiti she imagined that someone had a claim on these.

"What does it matter?" he answered brusquely. "The nuts belong to those who need them." He carried a brownish-green drinking nut to a stake that stood in the ground beside a pile of broken husks. With a few quick blows he stripped away most of the husk, leaving a narrow fibrous strip attached to the shell of the nut within. "You can help me," he said, pointing to another stake.

Tepua had never bent her back in such labor. This was a job for servants, but now she had to do it. She slammed a husk down onto the stake and managed only to get the wooden point jammed inside. With an effort, she wrenched the coconut free of the stick. Wiping away the sweat that stung her eyes, she tried again.

"Do it like this," Tangled-net said. Before she could object, he came up behind her and began guiding her hands. She felt the heat of his body, his skin sticky with perspiration.

His chest muscles moved against her back as he showed

her how to aim the point of the stake. The knotted rough
cloth of his *maro* pressed into her through the light *tapa*
wrap. She found it difficult to focus on the work and was
relieved when he stepped away from her.

Taking up another coconut, Tepua tried to follow the
lesson. Tangled-net had made the task look so easy! Finally,
after a dozen blows, she managed to free the pale, veined
shell within. She was out of breath, but pleased with herself.

She continued working until Tangled-net told her she
could stop. Then he showed her how to twist the strips of
husk remaining on the coconuts, tying them into pairs. He
helped her sling the pairs over a stout pole.

Tepua had never before been a thief. Now, as she carried
her end of the pole, she felt an unexpected tingle. She had
almost forgotten her exhaustion, her coral cuts, her doubts
about the young man's ability or willingness to bring her
home. The excitement of the moment blotted out all else.

What an escapade for someone who had always been
protected by chaperons! Tangled-net glanced back, and his
eyes held a joyful look of mischief. His expression warmed
her. She realized that his face was not really ugly, just
unusual.

At last they approached the narrow, black sand beach.
Across the lagoon, she saw the sun sinking toward the
distant breakers on the reef. "Here is my boat," he said,
pointing to a weathered and patched sailing outrigger canoe,
smaller than the one she had paddled. "It will get us there."

Tepua had watched such canoes set out on long voyages,
so she did not question its seaworthiness. But she remembered the conversation she had overheard between Hoihoi
and Rimapoa. "How will you choose our course?" she
asked. "I cannot tell you which stars to follow."

"Would I offer to take you if I could not find the way?"
The fisherman sounded exasperated. "We will go east, so
we must put the setting stars at our stern," he explained, as
if she were a child. "Tonight, I will show you which ones
to choose. We can watch them from a shelter on the hill."
He pointed behind him. "But first, we need to load the
canoe. Now, before dark sets in."

They gathered another load of coconuts, and by then the daylight was growing dim. "This is not a good night for staying out," said Tangled-net. "It is a time when our spirits walk. Maybe on your island they come out on a different night."

Tepua felt a shiver. Her atoll had its share of ghosts, and she knew well what harm an evil one could do. She tried to remember the last moon she had seen. . . .

Tangled-net's voice interrupted her thoughts. "This is also a favorite night of thieves," he said with glee. "But I think you will be happier under a roof." He startled Tepua by grabbing her hand, and this time he had no excuse.

He had a powerful grip and calluses on his palms. She felt something shoot through her that was not exactly fright or desire, but a mixture of the two. It made her pull back, yet his hand remained, clutching hers.

"What is the matter?" he asked.

Tepua's pulse was racing and her breathing fast. She had hoped that she could avoid telling him, but now she dared not delay. "There is something that Hoihoi did not explain," she said, trying to speak firmly. "It is important that you understand this. I am a chief's daughter, and unwed. You must not touch me—not even my hand."

"Oh?" She heard the disappointment in his voice, felt the sudden jerk as he released her. She couldn't see his face, but she sensed that glow of friendliness in his eyes fading. She thought she had made another blunder, flaunting her high status before a lowly fisherman. Yet what else could she have done to prevent misunderstanding?

For an instant she wanted to turn around and run back to Rimapoa's hut. She bit her lip. If she did that, she would remain stranded here for days. Even if she waited, she could not be sure that the headman would help her. No, she must press on and try later to soothe Tangled-net's hurt feelings.

He said nothing more until an outline of a sagging thatched roof showed against the darkening sky. "Here," he said, vanishing into the shadows within. The tiny shelter had no walls, only a tattered mat that hung on one side and

swayed in the wind. Already feeling the coolness of the
night breeze, Tepua sat on the grass-strewn floor.

The shelter stood by itself, far from any other dwelling,
for nearby only a few faint lights glimmered. Glancing
higher, she saw the first bright stars.

Tangled-net crouched beside her, so close that she could
feel the warmth of his body. One part of her wanted to press
against him for protection from the chill. Another part
wanted to run. "Do you see?" he asked, pointing his arm
above the horizon. "That one is a western star. It will follow
the sun to his bed."

"That may be the one I watched," she answered,
recalling her exhausting nights on the sea. She was trembling now, possibly because of the memories . . . or the
wind that made the whole shelter sway overhead, its
lashings and poles creaking.

"Here is my plan. We will reach the swarm of atolls in
daylight. There are so many that I can surely hit one of
them. Then you will recognize where you are and guide me
to the one that is your home."

"Yes. I think I can do that. But now it is late, and I would
like to go to a warmer place to spend the night." She stood
up, waiting for him to lead her to the house where his family
lived.

His hand reached up to grip her forearm. The pressure
was harsh, unyielding, almost painful. "I told you that
ghosts walk tonight. We are safe here. They will not come
in under a roof."

"The spirits do not worry me," she answered, trying to
pull free. "As we go I will recite a charm that the high priest
taught me. Even ghosts respect a chief's daughter."

Tangled-net's grip became fiercer. She felt herself losing
her balance and cried out in protest. Now she could not keep
from falling. . . .

He pulled her down against him, and she tried to fight
him off with her free hand. She beat her fist against his firm
flesh, striking high and low, but he did not ease his grip. She
felt his other hand on her as well, moving her, turning her.

Then she was sprawled on her back, with her head against the hard ground and the pressure of his weight on top of her.

"Don't you understand?" she cried. "I am *ta . . . pu*. Sacred to the gods . . ."

"Your gods are far from here," he growled as his hands roughly pushed her wrap up to bare her thighs. "And so are your priests." She heard the cloth rip—a sound that set her teeth on edge—and felt him shift his weight. He had her knees pinned painfully to the ground, and his arm lay heavily across her neck.

For a moment she refused to believe what was happening. She had lived too long under her father's protection. She had learned to trust men, without thinking that they held themselves back out of fear—not only of the chief's wrath but of the gods' revenge.

She heard Bone-needle's voice shrieking at her, but the warning had come too late. "This is my death," Tepua said, gasping for air. "And yours as well."

"Quit your babbling, atoll woman. Now you must learn *our* customs. In Tahiti, we do not go hungry when there is food before us."

Outrage drove her into a frenzy of kicking and wild swings, but her blows missed their target. He laughed harshly as he caught first one wrist and then the other, imprisoning both in a single rough-skinned hand. As she strained against his force she stared up into the shadow of his face. Where were the gods with their revenge? How soon before they crippled him with pain?

She lay on her back, her eyes burning, her chest heaving, trying to find an answer. Was it true, as some said, that the gods could not protect her so far from home? She felt Tangled-net's free hand slide down her belly and over the hair that covered her womanhood. His fist forced her legs apart and his finger probed. . . .

No! She writhed as she had seen eels struggle on a fisherman's spear. She spat and screamed and threatened him with all the punishments she had heard from the priests.

"You are unbroken," his voice said softly in her ear. His finger had withdrawn, but something else much larger pushed between her legs. His hand and then his knee forced her thighs apart.

"Your manhood will die," she hissed. "It will shrivel and wither when it touches me. Stop now and you will be spared."

"I have already touched you, chief's daughter, and my manhood only grows stiffer." His nose and lips brushed her cheek. She thrust her head aside. "In the dark, you cannot see my face," he said. "If I am ugly, what does it matter?"

She felt his fingers opening her for that strong, hard spear. He was pressing, stretching her painfully. She felt helpless, numb. Then fury took the place of fear.

She had fought the sea; why could she not fight this man? As he made a harder thrust she felt his grip on her wrists weaken. With a sudden jerk she loosed one of her hands. Finding his sweaty face by touch, she jabbed with two fingers at his eyes.

His howl was followed by a fierce blow at her arms. She reached up for another attack on his face, but he would not stay still. Then, with a cry of victory, he rammed himself into her. Her voice could not find breath. All she knew was the agony of torn flesh between her legs. She tried to scream, but her fury was so great that the sound gagged in her throat.

A moment later a spasm rocked his body. He pulled himself free and rolled off her, but did not relax his grip on her arm. "It will be better for you the second time," he said quietly. "Better for me also." In answer, she kicked him in the belly. It was over. Pain meant nothing to her now. All she could think about was revenge.

While he struggled to catch his breath she crawled away from him, colliding with one of the flimsy poles that held up the roof. Overhead, thatch crackled as the whole structure threatened to topple. "Where are you going, *motu* woman," he gasped. "Did you forget . . . what I said about spirits?"

Tepua stood up and shook the pole, trying its strength. "The ghosts will not come in here," she said, her voice so deep and cold that it made her tremble. "Not while the shelter stands over you.'' She leaned against the rough pole, and this time felt it bend. If she applied all her weight . . . Suddenly, with a snap, the support gave way and she scrambled out to safety. Behind her she heard the creak of stretching cord and rattle of dried leaves as the heavy roof came down. ''Now the ghosts can do what they want with you!'' She listened with satisfaction to his howls of anguish as she raced into darkness.

Her feet seemed to choose the direction on their own. Outlines of trees and bushes rose up in front of her, but somehow moved aside so she could pass. Roots tried to trip her, but she was too nimble. ''You can do nothing to me now,'' she shouted defiantly to the spirits of the night. ''Nothing worse than what Tangled-net has done.''

She was heading downhill, toward the beach, she realized. And then she knew what else she was going to do.

The sand gleamed faintly under starlight, and waves lapped the shore with iridescent foam. Tangled-net's canoe was still here, loaded with supplies and ready to be launched. And he had told her that this was the night of thieves!

Hastily she made her way along the shore until she found the canoe, a long black shadow in the gloom. She reached inside, felt the rough shells of the heaped coconuts. Good. She would take them as well.

She checked by touch for the other things she would need. Paddles lashed to the thwarts. Mast and plaited sail. Ropes. Bailer. Then, for a moment, she paused to wonder if she truly meant to sail home by herself.

Rimapoa had warned her against the contrary winds and currents. Even if she could find her direction, she would have to sleep sometimes. And while she slept all her progress would be undone.

No. She shook off the doubts. All that mattered now was getting away from this place. She lifted a short log that fishermen used for launching heavier craft and dropped it beneath the boat's bow. Tangled-net could probably drag his canoe into the waves without such help, but Tepua knew that her strength was not equal to his. To lighten the load, she tossed out some coconuts. She placed two more logs ahead of her path, went behind the boat, dug her feet in the sand, and pushed.

The strain worsened the pain inside her. She felt warm fluid oozing from between her legs, but refused to stop. She gave another fierce push, her shoulder against the stern of the canoe. The bottom made a hissing sound as it shifted against the sand. Then the boat was up on two rollers and skidding into the lapping surf. One more shove and the canoe was in the water. Shivering with rage and triumph, Tepua climbed in.

Putting the outrigger to the leeward side, she sat up and began paddling. She would raise the sail later, she thought, perhaps at dawn when she could see better. She would probably have to wait for daylight to find a safe passage through the reef. But she must get as far as possible from shore. . . .

The feeling of cool water puddling about her ankles gave her a moment of dismay. But bailing was nothing new to her. Tepua put her paddle aside, scooped out most of the water, then took up her stroke once again. She went only a short distance, bucking some mild chop, before she realized that the canoe was refilling. Angrily she took up the bailer, but water seeped in almost as fast as she scooped it out.

Tangled-net was going to have the last laugh after all, she realized. She had stolen a leaky, worthless canoe!

She yelled oaths to the night sky. What a fool she was! Trusting Tangled-net. Stealing a boat that would sink before she got it out of the lagoon. Now she would have to paddle back and find something better.

And what if he came after her? No, dawn was far off, she told herself. Tangled-net would not come out into this haunted night. She peered toward shore, surprised at how far she still had left to paddle. If only the water would stop pouring in . . .

5

WHEN Rimapoa returned home at dusk and found that Hoihoi had sent Tepua with another fisherman, he flew into a rage. "You let her go off with Tangled-net?" he shouted.

Hoihoi met his gaze, unperturbed. "He was willing to take her to her island. What is wrong with that?"

"I do not trust the fellow. If he owned a coconut tree, he would steal nuts from himself just to keep in practice."

Hoihoi gave a patient sigh and Rimapoa knew that it was not for Tepua but for him. "Tangled-net has a boat and he is greedy for pearl-shell fishhooks. Nothing will keep him from making that journey. And if he never comes back from the atolls, who will weep for him?"

Rimapoa lowered his voice. His sister did not have to remind him of the problems that Tangled-net and his family had caused. A quarrel with them had cost Rimapoa his place on the communal fishing canoe. "I would not mind being rid of that rascal," the fisherman admitted.

"Then do not interfere. The two will sail tomorrow at dawn, and we will be free of them."

Rimapoa did not know how to answer her. Moodily, he turned, pushing aside the mat that covered the doorway, and gazed out at the darkness closing in. He had only been with Tepua a short time, yet he could still feel the touch of her skin beneath his fingers and see her face with the wet hair streaming back. The thought that she might be with another man, possibly even enjoying his company, made the fisherman feel hot and cold by turns. "Tepua should have stayed with us tonight," he muttered,.

"So that you could discourage her from leaving? Brother, I know what is in your thoughts."

He balled his fist. "She is . . . like no woman of Tahiti."

"She is not for you. Do you think you could make her forget those vows she believes in? And what would you want with an inexperienced girl? Worse still, she is so skinny that you can almost see her bones!"

His breath hissed through his teeth and he could not reply.

"Tomorrow, brother, come with me to the stream when I go to wash. You will find plenty of riper beauties there. Eager ones. They'll make you forget her."

Rimapoa was still staring out, though the twilight had faded. "She was my guest," he said. "When she came, the gods placed her where I could find her. Now I am obliged to see that she leaves Tahiti unharmed."

"What of your own safety?" Hoihoi asked in a rising voice as he suddenly stepped out through the doorway. "Brother, guard yourself against the spirits of the night!" But Rimapoa was already hurrying along the path that led to Tangled-net's house.

The younger fisherman lived with his uncles and aunts in a group of houses far from the beach. When Rimapoa put his head in the doorway of the largest dwelling, he saw people sitting in a circle and talking quietly. The room was lit by candlenut tapers, made of oil-rich nuts strung on ribs of palm leaf. Puzzled faces turned to stare at him in the flickering light.

"Where is Tangled-net?" Rimapoa asked.

"We think he's out somewhere with a woman," several people answered, making sly winks.

"*Woman!*" Half-delirious from rage and jealousy, Rimapoa turned around. He heard footsteps. A moment later, Tangled-net pushed past him and into the house. Rimapoa caught a glimpse of his face. The skin about Tangled-net's right eye was badly swollen and his expression was full of fright.

"What have you done with Tepua-mua?" Rimapoa demanded, following the younger male inside.

Tangled-net refused to face him. "That woman speaks lies," the younger man whispered hoarsely. "She is no chief's daughter. Any fool can see that. Why should I risk my head and my boat to take her home?''

"If you value your head, you will tell me where she is.''

"How do I know? She ran off when I told her I saw through her story.''

Rimapoa grabbed Tangled-net fiercely by the shoulders, thinking he might shake the truth from him, but the family members closed in to protect their kinsman. "You will hear from me later,'' Rimapoa growled. In fury he turned, pushing his way through the crowd. He snatched a lit taper from someone's hand and hurried outside.

Let them call me a thief for that, he thought defiantly as he knelt, lowering the taper so he could study the deep footprints that Tangled-net had just made. He needed no more help from this clan of thieves and liars. With the light he could backtrack along Tangled-net's trail.

It took him a short time to reach the collapsed shelter, and there he found a second set of tracks. As he studied them he remembered how small and delicate Tepua's feet were.

Now he noticed that the moon had risen over the heights and was almost full. Tossing aside the taper, he began to sprint down the wooded slope. Ahead he heard the distant crashing of surf against the reef.

He lost the trail and paused outside a thatched hut. "Have you seen a woman running?'' he called. Light flickered through the doorway, but he heard no answer. "I think she came this way.''

A face appeared. A heavyset man. "You crazy fish stealer! Why are you bothering us?''

"Just tell me if you heard anything.''

"There was a pig snuffling around.''

"Oh, tell him so he'll go away,'' said a female voice.

The man at the doorway turned and made an angry gesture at his wife inside. Then he pointed over his shoulder. "We heard footsteps going that way. Might have been a woman or a girl. Someone as foolish as you. Who else would be out on this night?''

Rimapoa did not wait to hear what else the man might say. He charged down the slope and toward the beach. Here moonlight shone brightly, gleaming on the wet shore. Catching no sight of Tepua along the beach, he stopped to search again for footprints.

In a few moments he found a fresh set of her tracks. He followed them, trying to read what he could from their appearance. In one place she had stumbled and fallen. Then she had gone inland a short way. . . .

Suddenly he saw the twin furrows, one broader and deeper than the other, crossing the sand and leading into the water. *The marks of an outrigger canoe!* "Tepua!" he bellowed. Unwilling to believe that she was gone, he searched to see if her trail continued past him, but found nothing.

"Tepua!" With growing dismay, he scanned the phosphorescent surf. Then, as he gazed far down the beach, he noticed a lone swimmer struggling to reach shore. Could it be her so far out? He began to sprint across the sand.

As Rimapoa drew closer he saw a waterlogged canoe adrift, and then he caught a glimpse of Tepua's anguished face. What was she doing in the water? The fisherman splashed into the surf and dived under, stroking hard to reach her. When he paused to catch a breath and fling wet hair from his eyes, he realized that she was not out there alone.

When he saw the fins of the first shark, he felt a stab of fear. When he caught sight of the second, he froze, his heart striking the inside of his chest like an adze hollowing out a canoe.

Suddenly he began to roar in grief. Why had his guardian spirit permitted this calamity? Now the fisherman knew he must swim for shore. In a moment Tepua would be gone. And once the sharks scented her blood, they would go into a frenzy, attacking anyone in the water.

But something held him there, breasting the swells, watching. He had seen how sharks took prey. They arrowed straight for their victim, bumping the quarry with their snouts before striking. These behaved differently. The pair came alongside Tepua, nudged her, but did not bite.

Rimapoa heard a faint murmur and saw Tepua's hand move, as if she were welcoming them. He began to stroke again, his heart making the decision for him. Recklessly he swam toward her, splashing and shouting, hoping somehow to drive the creatures off. To his surprise, they retreated as he approached.

He got a good look at one and the image remained fixed in his mind. The long, slim, pointed snout. The dorsal fin set far back from the head. These were not ordinary sharks, but great blues, beloved of the gods. Usually they stayed at sea. Now they were here in the lagoon. What could that mean?

He seized Tepua's wrist, pulled her to him. She seemed dazed, and he thought she had almost given up her struggle to stay alive. He wrapped his arm around her neck and stroked for shore as hard as he could.

When he gained enough of a foothold on the gritty bottom to stand and lift the woman, he dared a glance back. Before he could stagger ashore with her, the two sharks suddenly sped toward him. Yet they did not touch him as they brushed past. They merely lingered a moment before turning and swimming away.

Trembling violently, he carried her up onto the beach. Great blue sharks, he knew, were sometimes inhabited by the gods. Indeed, at royal investment ceremonies, high chiefs waded into the water and encouraged the huge fish to approach them. If the sharks came peacefully, everyone knew that the gods had approved the candidate.

Now Rimapoa recalled how his sister had sneered at Tepua's ancestry. Did this not prove her high birth? Why else would the sharks have swum so close—acting as if they had come to protect rather than devour her?

Unable to answer, he placed Tepua gently on the beach. As he brushed aside her streaming locks of hair, relief and tenderness rushed to the fore. But anger came also—anger with himself. What was this woman, this skinny, pretentious atoll *vahine* doing to him?

"Tepua," he said, his voice hoarse. "Are you hurt? Tell me what happened?" He put his ear to her lips, listening for thickness or gurgling in her breathing, and heard none.

She was wearing only a soggy cloth about her waist. Running his fingers quickly over her body, Rimapoa found no cuts or bruises. "Tepua! You must answer!" he insisted. When she replied with only a moan, he softened his voice, but still to no avail. She stirred, but said nothing.

Seeing the drops of salt water still clinging to her cheek, he could not resist touching the dampness with his lips. He found the taste far richer than that of seawater alone. A strange notion seized him. He imagined himself licking the salt, first from her chin, then her neck, then . . .

He snorted at the idea, though it made his manhood begin to stir. Instead, he slipped his wiry arms beneath Tepua, grunted, and lifted her. Just ahead lay a path that would lead him to his hut.

Suddenly he heard a whisper. "Tangled-net," she said softly.

"What did he do to you?"

"His canoe—"

"Tangled-net's?"

"Maybe someone's—old hulk. We filled it—with coconuts. Bottom—split open."

"And that is why you sank! But why did you try to go off on your own?"

Tepua did not answer, and the fisherman was almost out of breath from carrying her. In the glimmer of moonlight that came through the branches, he saw her eyes fall shut again and her face go slack. She was exhausted, he realized. He would have to let her rest before he could learn the full story. For a moment he set her down.

This was not a good night for roaming, he recalled suddenly as he grew aware of the shadows around him. Hoihoi had warned him earlier, but he had refused to listen. Thinking of ghosts now, he lifted Tepua again, took his bearings through the trees, and began to stride at his fastest pace.

A distant cry made him start. Perhaps it was only a bird, or a night-walking priest. Rimapoa hurried onward, bypassing a thicket, splashing through a shallow stream and then another. He thought of stopping to rinse the salt and sand from Tepua's skin, but dared not linger now.

Ahead lay his thatched hut, light filtering out between the

gaps in the wall. Hoihoi stood at the doorway with arms crossed and a frown of disapproval on her fleshy face.

"So you found her."

"Say nothing more, sister. Just get something dry to wrap her in." He placed Tepua gently on the sleeping mat she had used earlier.

"Ah yes, brother. I see you are beyond help now." With a toss of her head she reached for the smallest of the few bundles of cloth that hung from his rafters. "I thought we were rid of her, and now you carry her back. What calamities you bring on yourself."

"And why is that, my farseeing sister?"

"I know what will happen if she stays here long. She will break some *tapu* because she knows no better. Then you will be blamed. Is it not enough that you catch fish like a thief? You are already in danger, brother, and this woman will only make it worse."

"I know what you are thinking," said Rimapoa. "But I am safe from the priests. I have my arrangements."

"Arrangements! Will a gift of a few fish change anyone's mind? When the time comes for a man to be sacrificed, we both know what will happen. They always look for a troublemaker. Neither headman nor priest will hesitate to choose you for the offering."

"Then my head is at risk, not yours, my sister. Do not fret about me." Rimapoa was trying to peel off the last of Tepua's wrap. When the final bit of cloth came free, he gazed for a moment at the nest of curly hair between her legs. It looked so soft that he wanted to touch and stroke her there. But his pleasure was spoiled at once by the sight of fresh blood trickling onto the mat.

Hoihoi also saw this, for she pushed him aside and bent to inspect the injury. "Well, brother," she said with an air of satisfaction. "At least we will hear no more from her about highborn ways. Tangled-net has taken from her what she should have lost long ago."

Rimapoa slapped his own face hard enough to make tears come. He did not know whether to weep or laugh. He fell down and pressed his forehead against Tepua's cool thigh.

So this was the truth behind Tangled-net's story. Rimapoa imaged the younger fisherman's leering face as he forced himself on the woman. Rimapoa's breath hissed angrily between his teeth. "I will kill him," he whispered, knotting his fist. "But not with a knife. It must be done slowly, over many months, so that Tepua can enjoy his suffering."

"He has done you a favor," said Hoihoi coldly. "Now she will open her legs to you—or to anyone else who asks."

"To me only!" Rimapoa cried. He caught himself. Never in his life had he come so close to striking a blow at his sister. "And no more taunts from you," he threatened, "or I send you outside. Then you can match words with the long-toothed ghosts and see how you fare."

Hoihoi shook her head. She muttered under her breath, but then bent to caring for Tepua. Rimapoa immediately turned to a task of his own. The god he worshiped had been good to him this night. Tepua had been saved, from Tangled-net and from the sea. And now he had hopes of persuading her not to go home after all.

Rimapoa knelt before the small wooden image that stood on a pedestal in a corner of the room. He placed a breadfruit and a green plantain before the idol and whispered a prayer. "Forgive my angry words tonight," he pleaded. "Accept my offering for saving this woman's life."

When Tepua woke, she found herself alone with Hoihoi. She looked up once at the familiar disapproving frown, then closed her eyes. The past night's events seemed now no more than terrifying dreams—the sharks in the lagoon, Rimapoa bringing her back here. But Tangled-net's attack had surely been no dream. She stirred, feeling soreness inside.

"Come with me and wash yourself," said Hoihoi gruffly.

"What does it matter?"

"You are young," said the fisherman's sister. "In a day or two you will stop hurting."

"Between my legs, perhaps," Tepua answered bitterly. "But what of my heart? Tangled-net crushed every hope."

"You have yet to learn about the heart, girl," Hoihoi snorted. "When I was your age, I had three lovers, sometimes all on the same night."

"Lovers!" Tepua spat. "That is all you think about in Tahiti. Do you understand that my virginity served a purpose? At important ceremonies, I was maiden of the gods!" She could not go home now. That knowledge hurt more than the pain from Tangled-net's thrusting. Once the priests discovered her defilement, they would send for a warrior with a heavy club. For her offense there was but one punishment—death.

"Do you know what I was to become?" Tepua continued in a tone of despair. "The wife of a high chief. And my son was to be his heir. Now it is lost to me. Everything."

"You have lost very little, I think," answered Hoihoi. "What does it mean to rule a pile of coral? Who wants to live without breadfruit and yams and bananas?" Hoihoi tapped her fingers against her throat, as Tepua had seen Tahitians do when speaking of food. "You will learn that good eating gives you more pleasure than reciting your ancestry. And I am going to start fattening you now, while the season of plenty is still with us. Otherwise, the women here will give you no peace. They will call you a stick woman behind your back. And Rimapoa, a collector of sticks."

Tepua shook her head. "I do not know why he came after me last night."

"Nor do I. But you are here, a guest in his house again, and now I think you will stay awhile. Are you coming with me to the stream?"

"So your friends can gawk at me?"

Hoihoi tossed her head. "They have seen you once. You are no longer a novelty. And they will not dare say anything unkind while I am there. Have you ever seen me wrestle? No woman in the district can beat me." She flexed her stout arms.

"I could have used your strength last night." Tepua sighed. As gloomy as she felt now, she could not deny the appeal of a bath in fresh water. With an effort, she roused herself from the mat.

Outside, the morning sun cast sharp shadows over the

leaf-strewn ground. Sweet scents drifted beneath the trees. From the clearing ahead sounded shouts and laughter.

"Hoihoi is coming," the fisherman's sister announced loudly as she walked. "All of you, move aside." She flung off her wrap and plunged into the pool, spreading waves. Tepua, glad that all eyes turned to Hoihoi, hoped her own arrival might go unnoticed. She waded in, unwrapping the cloth barely in time to keep it from getting wet. She plunged ahead until cool water covered her to the waist.

"Who is that new, slender beauty?" asked a male voice, hidden in a thicket just upstream. The laughter that followed made Tepua's face burn. Small green *nono* fruits splashed into the water, tossed by men at women they wished to attract. She was grateful that nobody tossed one at her.

The rushing water helped calm her. She crouched, ducking her head, letting the current rinse her long, dark hair. She scrubbed at her skin, trying to wash off every trace of Tangled-net's touch. But one part remained tender and she left it alone.

The women chattered, boasted, and teased each other as they bathed. Hoihoi's voice was the loudest of all and her jokes were more ribald than any Tepua had heard spoken by men. A few days ago she might have enjoyed the fun, but now it only reminded her of her recent ordeal. Quietly she finished bathing, waded ashore, and stood in the sunlight to dry.

Tepua glanced at Hoihoi, now queen of the pool. Surely Hoihoi would not mind if she slipped quietly back to the house. She felt a pervasive weariness in her limbs and a need to think things out. Arranging her bark-cloth wrap about her, she made her way back down the path.

Inside, she lay down once again. A tear seeped out of one eye, rolled down the side of her nose. She thought of Hoihoi and the other women with their boisterous talk. Their first time with a man had surely not been like hers.

Often, at home, she had wished she could take a lover. The experience, she thought, would be gentle and pleasurable, and raise the kind of tingling she felt when she caressed herself. But after the ramming and tearing she had suffered last night, she thought she would never want to see a man again.

Recalling what Tangled-net had done made her face flush with rage. Until last night, her misfortunes had seemed bearable, like a strange dream that could be endured because she knew it would end. Now she realized that it would not end. Her home had become the dream and this foreign place, Tahiti, her life. She moaned, burying her face between her hands, but she could not deny the truth.

Her thoughts slipped back to a time when her family had gathered under one roof, entertaining each other with singing while a storm howled outside. The favorite song was *te ara matangi,* which told of the great canoes and how they were sailed. *Ko te piu.* She could still hear the words. *E ko ne a, hirika.* She remembered the feeling of warmth as everyone pressed together in the narrow house, so that even as a child she did not fear the storm. *Here I go, cleaving the waves, here I go. . . .*

At last, Hoihoi returned to the hut and plumped herself onto a mat opposite Tepua. "Still mourning for your coral island, are you, girl? Well, you will find life here more comfortable. How can you live in a place where nothing grows?"

"We have pandanus trees, and coconuts. . . ." Tepua protested, but her voice trailed off. There was no way to explain what had been taken from her.

Hoihoi merely smiled, opened her large hand, and held out a mound of damp moss. "This is what you need now. Put it between your legs to ease the ache."

Tepua's face burned as she accepted the moss. Perhaps Hoihoi was not as uncaring as she seemed. Tepua offered a word of gratitude, but Hoihoi just snorted. "Now rest yourself, girl. And then we will see what kind of Tahitian we can make of you."

Tahitian? Can it be done? Tepua wondered. The songs kept echoing in her mind, telling of spray and flying fish and the joy of sighting land on the horizon. Now she would not be sailing anywhere.

6

FOR a day, Tepua remained inside and let herself heal, coming outside only to eat. Hoihoi brought her *poi*, and a paste called *mahi*, made by fermenting the breadfruit. "You will learn to like it," said Hoihoi, when Tepua grimaced at the taste. "*Mahi* keeps well underground in pits. Long after the trees are bare, we still have good food."

"Why not eat fish?" asked Tepua.

Hoihoi snorted. "We are not *all* noblewomen here. Go walk through the valleys and count the houses where *teuteu* and *manahune* live. Tell me how anyone could catch enough fish to feed all those people. No, girl. We thank the gods for our breadfruit, and you must do so as well. Without it, we would starve."

Tepua frowned and reached into her bowl again. Though the mash was sour and its taste vaguely unpleasant, it did fill her belly. She hoped that Rimapoa might bring home something from his catches, but until then breadfruit would have to do.

Another day passed. Tepua struggled against feelings of despair. She did not belong here. When the canoe had sunk under her, it should have meant her death, the punishment for her defilement. She should be dwelling now, not in a bright and fragrant paradise, but in that other place—the land of eternal night.

So much had happened that she could not explain. The gods had let her fall into the sea, but had helped her to reach Tahiti. They had not stopped Tangled-net's attack, yet had kept her from harm in the lagoon. The sharks had spared her. The gods had told her to live.

Whenever she was alone, she whispered prayers, begging to know why, but no answer came. Finally, in a dream, she heard the resonant voice of her ancestress, Tapahi-roro-ariki. She was so startled by this rare visitation that she woke up, and lay in the darkness with her pulse pounding. She could only recall fragments of what her guardian spirit had spoken. *I have not forgotten you. . . . You are still my daughter. . . . Go out and see what this new world offers. . . .*

Heeding these words, Tepua began to accompany Hoihoi on her morning rounds. There was a ritual she followed that started with a bath in the stream. Later, the fisherman's sister would look over her soggy taro patch and her yam garden, then harvest a few vegetables for the afternoon meal. These, along with shellfish she gathered from nearby shoals, she placed for cooking in the earth oven that she shared with the neighboring women.

Later in the morning Hoihoi sometimes sat with her friends at a long board, making *tapa* cloth by pounding the inner bark of young trees. Tepua listened to the rhythmic clatter of their wooden mallets and the chants that the women sang as they worked. She could not help thinking of her own island, where women gathered in similar groups, pounding dried cones of the *fara* fruit to break out the edible kernels. When she asked herself, would she ever hear that familiar sound again? Yet, as she blinked away her tears, she found her fingers keeping time to the beat of *tapa* mallets.

In the afternoons, while she and Hoihoi rested and chatted beneath the trees, Tepua learned a bit more about the man who had rescued her. The fish that Rimapoa caught went mostly to others. Here, as on her own island, albacore was a food reserved for noblemen and chiefs. Rimapoa made gifts to the men of importance and delivered the rest, when he had any, to families who paid him with coconuts or *ava* roots or—for a season's work—with rolls of bark-cloth. Cloth was the principal medium of exchange here, and could be traded for almost anything one needed.

It did not surprise Tepua that the fisherman was absent at mealtimes; custom and *tapu* required that men and women eat apart. When Tepua asked where Rimapoa ate, Hoihoi tossed her head and said, "Sometimes with the people who take his albacore. Or with other fishermen, when they tolerate him."

"Why should they not tolerate him?" Tepua asked. To her, Rimapoa seemed inoffensive; she felt sorry that he led what seemed an odd existence.

"It is the way he fishes," said Hoihoi stiffly. "Some say he hurts the catch for others. Some even accuse him of fish stealing."

Tepua frowned. *Rimapoa, a thief?* But Hoihoi would say nothing else about her brother. Well, that was one more thing Tepua did not understand.

There was another mystery the next morning. Tepua woke on her mat with a start, feeling someone's shadow pass between her and the sunlight that streamed into the hut. But when she rolled over and looked up, she found no one there.

As she leaned on one elbow, blinking, she smelled a delicious aroma. Roasted fish, something she hadn't had in days. She saw a moist, leaf-wrapped packet next to her mat.

She glanced toward Hoihoi, who twitched and mumbled in her sleep as if she, too, had smelled the fish. Quickly Tepua drew her wrap about her hips and scurried outside with the packet between her hands. Feeling slightly guilty, she found a place behind a tree.

She should share this with Hoihoi, she thought. But the older woman would probably eat most of it, or worse yet, tell her that eating it was *tapu* for women, then take the packet for herself. Tepua's mouth watered. She was tired of breadfruit, even when served as *mahi*. Carefully she opened the packet.

Albacore. She knew it by the aroma, by the pale tan color and the firm flesh. Eagerly she popped a piece into her mouth. Mmm! A delicious morsel, seasoned with salt water. She had finished most of the fish before she admitted to herself who had brought it. Of course, Rimapoa.

Suddenly she stiffened. How many *tapus* had she just violated? In Tahitian eyes she was a commoner now. Such women were forbidden albacore. Nor was any woman supposed to eat what a man had cooked. Yet women sometimes ignored these restrictions.

She glanced about nervously, hoping that no one had seen her. More troubling thoughts surfaced. Rimapoa had brought her a gift. Was this his way of courting her? If so, then how could she avoid disappointing him?

The next morning, when Tepua was returning with Hoihoi after gathering mussels, she saw Rimapoa waving to her from farther down the beach. "You talk to him," said Hoihoi brusquely. "I have work to do, and the sun is getting hotter." She snatched Tepua's basket of shellfish and continued on her way, leaving the younger woman to greet the fisherman.

Tepua watched Rimapoa as he drew nearer. She did not like recalling how she had first thought of him—as little more than a kindly servant. But what servant would brave sharks to rescue his master?

Now she had begun to see him simply as a man. By Tahitian standards, she knew, he could not be called attractive. He was tall, but not broad. His arms and chest were wiry instead of fleshy, his skin tanned and roughened by the sea. He had the long legs of a runner, and she could easily imagine him speeding down the beach, his loincloth flapping about his narrow hips.

His eyes, dark gray brown like the outer husk of the coconut, were wrinkled at the corners from squinting against sea glare and wind. Today the lines around his eyes and across his brow gave his face a touch of worry.

As he walked up to her the fisherman smiled, erasing the lines for a moment. His grin had a rough charm that warmed her as she looked at him. "I left early and fished well today," he said. "Now I would like to do something for you. I would like to show you a special place."

At these words, she grew uneasy. Up to now she had enjoyed a pleasant friendship with Rimapoa, but she knew that he wanted more than that. "Hoihoi has gone off without me," she answered.

"Good. Then you are free now. Let me take you up to the

hills. It is a pleasant walk.'' The lines on his face deepened again, as if he feared she might refuse him.

Her first impulse was to do just that. But he had always been kind and gentle to her. Would it do any harm to go with him, even if she had to fend off a few caresses?

She glanced inland toward the towering green heights, a sight that still startled her. Her life had been spent on a low island, close to the sea. She could not imagine what it would be like to climb toward the sky.

''I will go,'' she said, and added, ''but not for long. I think Hoihoi will be looking for me soon.''

''We will be back before she needs you.'' The fisherman smiled. His teeth were even and white and his lips, especially the lower, curved on the inner margin, giving a unique roguishness to his grin. Once again she felt the warmth of his charm.

They took a path that wound toward the hills. Now and again they passed men carrying bundles of firewood suspended from poles across their shoulders. The wood carriers stared at Tepua with open curiosity, recognizing, she thought, that she was not a native, not Maohi.

She felt a chill as they passed her, as if they had penetrated some inner secret. How much could they tell about her just from a glance? She knew that she was not only slimmer but also taller than the women she had seen here. And perhaps her manner of walking also marked her as different. A sharp-eyed observer might realize that she carried herself like a chief's daughter.

A chief's daughter! What did that matter now?

She tried to focus her attention on the trail as it wound along wooded slopes. For a time she could see little more than the trees and brush that surrounded the path. ''Look over here,'' said Rimapoa when she had been climbing long enough to need a rest. She followed him as he skirted a bamboo thicket. Then she gasped as she emerged on an open hillside far above the coastal plain.

Now she knew how a bird saw the world. The height made her dizzy, but she fought the sensation long enough to glance at the view. Along the distant shore she saw the tops of coconut palms, looking like feathers mounted on sticks. Beyond them stretched the milky blue waters of the lagoon.

"From here," Rimapoa said, "you have a good view of our neighboring island, Eimeo."

But Tepua felt a rush of panic. She was not accustomed to such heights. The hillside seemed to be tilting, pushing her over. She stepped backward, then fell and clutched the ground.

"Tepua!" She felt Rimapoa sit down beside her and put his arm about her shoulders. His touch was comforting, sheltering. "I am sorry," he said. "I did not know this would frighten you."

"Never been . . . so high before," she answered. "Climbed palm trees, but . . . never anything like this."

"Close your eyes. I will carry you back to the trail."

"No." Tepua felt the stubborn part of herself take hold. She had never handled a canoe alone before her accident, yet she had salvaged one from the sea and sailed it here. She refused to let a hillside overwhelm her.

She tried looking out again. The vertigo wasn't so bad when she was lying down. Cautiously she rolled onto her stomach and lifted her head. That was better.

Beneath her, forested slopes swept sharply down to meet the lowlands. The broad plain was thickly planted, mostly with breadfruit trees, and between these she glimpsed many thatched roofs.

On a point of land that jutted out into the water rose a stepped tower of stone—the *ahu* of a sacred courtyard, where prayers were offered to the gods. And behind that the lagoon shimmered with transparent shades of azure and sea green, the color deepening farther out. Shading her eyes against the glare, she saw the churning of distant breakers, and beyond—far beyond—the jagged green peaks of Eimeo.

She blinked and tried standing up, feeling Rimapoa close beside her. "The waterfall is only a few steps away," he said. "Are you ready?"

When she nodded, Rimapoa slipped his hand in hers. His touch was so reassuring that she did not pull away. He turned and led her up the path. Tepua was glad when the screen of forest surrounded her once again.

Shortly, they came to an opening in the trees at the base of a high, dark cliff. A glistening cascade shot over the clifftop, sparkling as it fell in an unbroken sheet into a basin surrounded by stones. Children were bathing in the pool, splashing each other, racing in and out of the spray.

Tepua gazed in astonishment. She had finally grown used to the streams and rivers of Tahiti, but this scene was startling and new to her—the coolness of the mist . . . the huge, glossy leaves of the plants along the bank . . . the rich scents from blossoms high in trees. The atolls held nothing like this.

Rimapoa found a dry place above the bank and invited her to sit. She enjoyed being beside him, feeling the firmness of his hand as it pressed against hers. The surroundings were so lush that she felt she could lose herself here.

A warning sounded in her mind. Rimapoa's company was pleasant, and the surroundings exhilarating, but she was content merely to sit and drink everything in. Rimapoa would not be so easily satisfied.

"Why are you so quiet?" he asked when she continued to sit stiffly beside him. Slowly he withdrew his hand.

She felt relieved at this gesture, yet saddened at the same time. He was so considerate, so kind. What more could she want from a man? She did not wish to hurt him, yet she feared she had already done so.

How confusing and awkward this all was! If only she could tell Rimapoa that she found him attractive, but felt more comfortable with him in the role of a friend.

"How beautiful this place is," he said, letting his arm rest gently against hers.

"The waterfall is pretty," she replied. She did not wish to withdraw from the comfort of his touch. If only he could be content to remain this way, wanting nothing more.

"Tepua, I sense something still troubling you. Not the heights—"

"No."

"Is it Hoihoi? She will not need you for a while."

He had given her an opening, a way to steer his thoughts in another direction. "I was just remembering something that your sister told me."

He sighed and Tepua realized, with a twinge of regret, that she had succeeded in breaking the mood. At least he did not move away from her this time. "What lie is my sister spreading?" he asked in a pained voice.

"I hope it is a lie," she answered. "But Hoihoi says that the other fishermen speak unkindly of you. They use a word I do not understand."

Rimapoa glanced away. "What is that word?" he asked. *"Mafera."*

He flinched, squeezing his eyes shut for a moment. Tepua wondered how that word could hurt him so, and regretted that she had said it. He gave her a long, appraising look. "Let me ask you this, pearl woman. Do you know how albacore are caught?"

Tepua confessed that she did not. At home, the fishermen would bring the gleaming albacore and bonito in baskets as tribute to the family of the chief. She had never asked how they made their catches.

"Then let me tell you, for there are two ways. The first uses a twin-hulled canoe and many people. Some men paddle while others throw out baited lines to trail in the water. At the end of the trip, they share whatever they have caught. But if no fish rise to their hooks, they accuse someone in the crew of breaking a *tapu* and angering the spirits. Too many times I was blamed unfairly, so I no longer fish with the large boat."

"Then—"

"The other way is my way. I go out alone to deep 'holes' in the sea where the albacore gather. I drop my hook far down and wait. Sometimes the fish strikes so hard that I am nearly pulled from my canoe. I have fallen in. I have lost fish that the other men who work together could have landed."

She felt a rush of sympathy. "That must be hard."

"It is. But when the fish hits and the battle begins, I

cannot stop—until he is thrashing in the canoe or breaks from my line.'' Rimapoa paused, his eyes bright and the muscles knotted in his arms as if he were straining against a wildly fighting albacore.

To Tepua, something hidden in his spirit seemed to emerge. He was, for a moment, no longer Rimapoa the outcast and rogue, but the fisherman-hero of myth, who could draw up great islands on his hook. She sensed that Rimapoa at sea became a very different man than when he was ashore.

"Some men say that fishing my way spoils it for others,'' he continued. "They say that if albacore are caught on deep lines, they will not come to the surface. So they use ugly names for what I do, and they shun me.'' He lowered his voice. "Sometimes I fish at night so I will not be noticed. That is the worst offense of all, in some eyes. That is what they call *mafera*.''

She saw the pain in his eyes and wished she could soothe him. Gently she replied, "I see no harm in it. One man alone cannot take many fish. If the others do not like it, what can they do to you?''

Rimapoa's grin returned, though some bitterness remained. "They will do me no harm. Hoihoi knows a bit of sorcery and they fear she would take revenge on them if they tried. But the next time the priest calls for an offering, my name will be mentioned.''

Hair rose on Tepua's nape as his meaning became clear. *"Offering!''*

"You do not sacrifice men to your gods?'' The worry lines about his eyes were deeper now than she had ever seen them.

Tepua shuddered. "We have so few people—''

"Here, on Tahiti, it is different. When the gods demand an offering, the chiefs pick someone they can easily spare—someone like me.''

Again she stared at him, not knowing what to say. How could the Tahitians do such a thing to a man who seemed so gentle? "Then why do you stay here?'' she managed to ask.

"Where else can I go? Here I have my arrangements. The

headman takes my fish and lets me live on his land. Though I have enemies, they keep their distance. In another place, as a stranger, I might suffer an even harsher fate.''

"Perhaps your friend the headman will warn you if your name is chosen. Then you can hide somewhere and let them take another man.''

"Friend?'' Rimapoa snorted. "Pigs-run-out is not my friend. He tolerates me only because of the tribute I pay him. But I have a spirit who protects me and will give me warning. When the time comes, I will get away.'' He smiled, though she knew he did not feel as confident as he sounded. "But we have spent too much time in gloomy talk,'' he said.

"I think we should start walking back,'' she suggested, before his amorous mood could show itself again. "Let me teach you a game I know. We can play it on the way. You hold your hand like this and cover your thumb. . . .''

She tried not to see his look of disappointment.

The next morning Tepua and Hoihoi went out early to gather seafood. The air was quiet, the beach still shaded by coconut palms. Low tide had drawn the lagoon down, exposing shellfish beds. Tepua saw Hoihoi's eyes brighten when she spied a cluster of oblong blue-black shells in among the whelks and limpets.

"Mussels,'' Hoihoi said, licking her lips. "Just the right delicacy for this day.''

"What is so different about today?'' Tepua asked, yawning. She still didn't know why Hoihoi had gotten her up so early.

"Today we will have feasting and dancing and special visitors. The Arioi will perform for us. We must feed them well.''

"Arioi?''

"You will see.''

When the baskets had been filled to overflowing, Hoihoi marched ahead, leading the way to the assembly ground, a large clearing above the beach. In the wide pits that served as communal ovens, Tepua saw fires blazing, heating the stones within.

As was customary, men and women worked separately, each group preparing their own part of the feast. Hoihoi took her basket first to one of the men and emptied half its contents onto some coconut leaves. She waited until he acknowledged the gift. "Do you expect pork in return, woman?" he chided. "Take some of those bananas."

Hoihoi snorted her anger, then told Tepua to pick up the largest bunch. They delivered their load of food to the women's oven, staying on to help until everything had been wrapped in leaves and buried to cook. "Now," said Hoihoi, "we must go to the house and get ready."

Along the way, they gathered green coconut fronds, brightly striped leaves of the *ti* plant, *maire* ferns, and flowers. At the hut they wove these into colorful head-dresses. Then they joined the other women in the stream for a midday bath. The mood that day, Tepua thought, was unusually bright, each woman boasting about how much she would eat and how long she would dance at the celebration. There was also lusty talk about men, but Tepua did not listen to it.

She did follow the lead of the others, rubbing herself with scented oil and combing out her long hair. Suddenly she heard drumming from afar. "Arioi!" shouted the women, running off in several directions.

In a few moments Tepua was following Hoihoi, who was already bouncing to the drumbeat as she walked. Decked in fresh wraps and their new headdresses, the women hurried toward the beach. There Tepua drew in her breath as she gazed across the lagoon.

A flotilla of double canoes was coming in to shore. The tall prows, elegantly carved, and decorated with red and yellow streamers, were like none she had seen before. On the decks stood men and women in festive costumes, their faces painted black and red. They danced and paraded while musicians behind them played on tall drums and slender nose flutes.

"Who are these people?" Tepua asked as Hoihoi danced to the music, and the crowds grew thick along the shore.

"The followers of Oro," Hoihoi answered. "They entertain us, and teach us, and help us please the gods. Tonight you will see."

"And who is that—a great chief?" Tepua pointed to a tall, heavyset man who stood by the shore, apparently waiting to greet the arriving Arioi. He wore an elegantly painted cape and a feather headdress that spread out like a fan. She saw his feathers shimmering and gleaming in the sunlight, but could not get a glimpse of his face.

"He is but the headman here, the underchief, the one called Pigs-run-out."

The man who might have helped me. Tepua pushed that thought aside. She did not wish to remember that she had met Tangled-net outside his compound. The underchief turned briefly, assessing the crowd. Then Tepua saw his middle-aged face, dignified in expression, with a trace of petulance about the mouth and the lower lip.

A moment later the first of the Arioi came ashore, and the crowd made way for them. Tepua watched the underchief warmly greet the man who stood at the fore of the troop, embracing him and pressing his nose to each cheek. Then a woman leader stepped forward and was greeted as well. These head Arioi, unlike the others, had solid black tattooing covering them from ankle to thigh. They wore cloths painted scarlet and yellow, necklaces of pearl shell, and feather headdresses as tall as the chief's.

The remaining Arioi were decorated in a variety of styles, some with cowrie shells and feathers, others with necklaces and fringed gorgets. They strode forward, smiling and laughing, toward places that had been set for them on the ground, men and women in separate sections. Tepua smelled delicious steamy odors as servers hurried from the ovens to feed the guests.

Tepua and Hoihoi found places of their own, far from the honored guests, and they had to wait a long time to be served. When the food finally came, Tepua thought it the best she had ever eaten—roasted fowls, savory with sea salt, and yams, plantains, reef fish, steamed leaves of taro. At home there had been feasts, of course, but none with this variety.

While she ate, Tepua glanced occasionally across at the gathering of men. Rimapoa was seated at the edge of the crowd. When he saw her, he grinned and flourished a leg of fowl. Tepua returned his greeting, but she felt uneasy. Later, when the dancing started, she knew he would come looking for her. There would be no distracting him then. . . .

At last she realized that she had finished all the food before her. She saw other women around her moving into the shade beneath the palms to escape the fiercest heat of the day. Some had brought sleeping mats. Others, like Hoihoi, dug themselves hollows in the sandy soil. Tepua made herself a resting place and curled up on her side.

The entertainment was still to come. She was curious to see why these Arioi merited the great welcome that the headman's people had provided. But now, as she heard the snores and the buzzing of flies, her eyelids fell shut.

Tepua awoke to drumming. It grew louder and faster, picking up a two-toned beat. *Boom, ba-boomba, boom ba-boomba,* almost the same as the drumbeats of her homeland. When she stood up, her feet began moving to the rhythm. It got into her, making her skin tingle.

As she followed Hoihoi in the slanting sunlight of late afternoon, she saw the Arioi gathering about the level area in the center of the assembly ground. Underlings were laying down mats. "For the performance," Hoihoi explained. The musicians had already taken seats at the rear of this simple stage.

So many people in one place! Tepua feared she would be lost in the midst of the crowd around the mats, but she felt Hoihoi's hand close about her wrist and draw her through. Then the noise quieted and people knelt or sat on the ground.

The chief Arioi stood and raised his hands to still the drums and the crowd. "Let us remember," he said in a booming voice, "why it is that we feast and laugh and dance here today. Let us recall the god who inspires us. Let us do honor to Oro-of-the-laid-down-spear.''

For a moment the crowd fell into a respectful silence for the god. Then, at the chief Arioi's signal, the drums and flutes started once more, joined by a chorus of male singers. They began chanting a history of Oro, starting with the story of his search for a wife, finally telling how he inspired the start of the Arioi society.

To Tepua, much of this was new. Oro was known in her islands, but her people held no rites in his honor. He was a god of many aspects, feared as the patron of war, yet admired as the spirit of peace when enemies sat down together. From the words of the chant, she gathered that both aspects were important to the Arioi. They kept themselves ready for war, should it come. But they devoted themselves to promoting Oro's peaceful nature, when he presided over rich harvests.

The chanting continued as the sun dropped toward the horizon. Tepua felt gooseflesh as she listened. Oro was more powerful than any god her own people dared call on. It was far wiser, she had been taught, to beg favors of a lesser spirit; the great gods could not be bothered by human troubles. Yet these Arioi told of Oro coming to earth, allowing his power to touch men and women.

After the introduction, the mood of the audience turned from sober to gay as a small group of players took their places on the stage. These Arioi wore outlandish costumes— oversized or undersized wraps, necklaces made of discarded shells and coconut husks. Tepua saw people grinning, leaning forward in anticipation. ''And now our first entertainment,'' announced the Arioi chief. The players began to perform in mime, strutting about the stage while the chorus spoke for them.

Tepua looked on in puzzlement, wondering why people were laughing. One player after another stepped forward, each with a distinctly mannered gait, each earning an enthusiastic response from the crowd. She had seen something like this at home—performers mimicking well-known people.

Suddenly she stiffened as a man dressed like a plump woman, with bundles of straw stuffed under his wrap, sashayed onto the stage. As the actor raised a fist angrily the chorus chanted:

> ''What is this you serve to the women?
> This is no festive meal.
> Give me good food.
> Give me succulent pork!''

A man dressed in mock chief's attire came out to rebuke the ''woman.'' He stood with his legs wide apart and waved an absurdly decorated staff. The chorus chanted:

> ''This is our privilege.
> We men will eat the pig.
> No pork for you, woman.
> No pork for you, Poipoi.''

Poipoi? Tepua glanced at her companion's smile of embarrassment. Others around Hoihoi began to slap their thighs in appreciation. Tepua tried to hold back her own laughter as the two characters traded insults and boasts, but suddenly it was too much for her. Tears of mirth ran down her cheeks.

So even the Arioi knew Rimapoa's sister! For a moment, sitting so close to the center of attention, Tepua felt a part of this boisterous throng. She watched the victim herself begin to laugh. *Yes, these people are not so different from my own.* In a surge of feeling that surprised her, Tepua flung her arms around Hoihoi.

One entertainment followed another, until finally all the actors left the stage. Then the drums, which had been restrained, began booming again. The flutes joined them in a pulsating melody. Tepua sensed the mood change once again as people followed the beat with their heads and their hands.

A couple appeared on stage, both wearing wreaths and dancing skirts. They stood opposite each other, and slowly the woman began to roll her hips in the beginning motions of the dance.

The wreath about the woman's waist accented her hip motion. She stepped in time to the drumbeat while holding her arms above her head. Her hands fluttered in the air, fingers making graceful gestures as her hips picked up the tempo. She inclined her head, sending her partner sly looks.

Her partner crouched on his toes, his upper body straight, his knees bent. He clapped his knees together and apart, matching his partner's rhythm. He was well suited to his role, Tepua thought, for his muscles were huge and ropy, bulging along the top of his upper leg from knee to thigh.

More performing couples joined the two on stage as the drumbeat accelerated. The onlookers bobbed their heads and sang along with the music as the dance grew faster and more intense.

"May Oro be pleased! Everyone dance!" came the deep bellow of the head Arioi.

By now night had fallen and the area was lit by bonfires and torches. With excited cries the young men and women in the audience leaped to their feet while their elders drew to the side. Tepua felt her heart jumping. This dance was almost the same as one she knew. At home she had been the best, making up for her slender form with suppleness and speed.

But right now she did not want a partner. She glanced around, wondering if she dared step out into the crowd of dancers on her own. Then she saw other women, swaying in clusters, paying no heed to the men. "Go," said Hoihoi, giving her a push. "Show us how they do it on your coral island."

The drumming was too powerful to resist. She went to the darkest part of the clearing, raised her arms, and began to move with the beat. Men turned to stare at her, some with scowls. *Because I am a stranger?*

She redoubled the speed of her dance, the rotation and swaying of her hips, the sinuous movement of her arms. No longer shy, she stepped forward into the light. She saw men and women watching, their eyes widening at her skill.

"*Motu* woman!" A brawny male dancer sneered.

Undaunted, Tepua turned in another direction. Anger lent vigor to her dance as she realized how many others were watching her now. In the place of honor, where torches flared, she saw the headman seated with other people of rank. When she noticed how their eyes glistened as they studied her, she tossed her head and danced harder.

"She is in the god's frenzy," came shouts from the crowd. "In the grip of *nevaneva*. The Arioi should see this."

"But no man will dance with her!" others replied.

No partner? Tepua knew how to answer these scoffers. She had seen Rimapoa waiting eagerly for his chance. Now she moved toward him, inviting him to join her.

With a cry of delight, the fisherman leaped into place and took up the male part of the dance. Gales of laughter broke out in the crowd. "Here is a treat! The scrawny cock fowl joins the starved chicken!"

But the laughter soon died as Tepua's flowing hands and artful movements began to draw murmurs of appreciation. And Rimapoa, though lacking the grace and control of an Arioi, displayed his wiry strength and endurance. He balanced on his toes, clapping his knees together and apart so fast that they were just a blur in Tepua's eyes. He jerked his hips so lustily that his loincloth threatened to fly up.

"They do well together," someone said. "Oro should be pleased."

Now Tepua no longer watched her partner as the mounting frenzy of the dance enveloped her. Her body grew weightless and her arms seemed to move of their own accord. The lights and shadows flew past her, merging into haze.

Had the god brought her to this pitch of excitement? She only knew that now she could not stop. Her skin felt charged with heat. The music became part of her, echoing through her veins. . . .

And then, suddenly, she felt tired and dizzy. The music

tried to hold her, but she could not keep up with it. She felt herself falling, saw Rimapoa's worried face peering down at her. "You did well, *motu* flower," he kept saying as he helped Tepua up. "You are the best dancer I have ever seen."

Her legs felt numb. She leaned against the fisherman and managed to hobble a few steps, then a few more. "We will take you home now," he said gently, with just a hint of disappointment in his voice. Hoihoi had arrived to help as well. Tepua closed her eyes, refusing to look at the crowd. They had seen her in her glory. They had also seen her fail.

"Look how thin you are," chided Hoihoi. "You need to eat more if you want to dance all night."

Tepua tried to straighten up. She knew that the long voyage had weakened her. She had not fully recovered. How could she have expected to sustain her impossible pace? But as she walked slowly along the path, with the music still pounding in her ears, Tepua found herself wishing she could run back.

She was dancing again in her imagination, dancing with the Arioi, dancing for Oro-of-the-laid-down-spear.

7

THE next morning, Tepua thought she would never want to get up. Still feeling exhausted from her dance, she drifted in and out of sleep. Much earlier she had heard cocks crowing. Now, when she opened her eyes, she saw streaks of sunlight crossing the floor.

What had happened during the dancing? she asked herself. Had she truly been touched by the god? Suddenly she sat up, wanting to ask Hoihoi a host of questions, but the fisherman's sister was gone and the house empty.

Tepua put on her wrap and hurried to the stream, where she found Hoihoi sitting on the bank with her large feet dangling in the water. "Ah," said the fisherman's sister dreamily. "You should have stayed longer last night. After I took you home, I went back to try my own dancing. What a man I found!"

"Tell me about the Arioi," Tepua asked brusquely, unwilling to listen to her chatter.

Hoihoi laughed. "You heard their chants and watched them perform. When they return, you will see more."

"Who are they? I know nothing about them."

"They are sons and daughters from the highest families." Tepua frowned. "Only highborn people?"

Hoihoi splashed her feet playfully. "No. A commoner can become one of them, though it is not easy. If you are interested—"

"I did not say that," Tepua answered cautiously. She tossed aside her wrap and waded out into the pool made by a half circle of black rocks. The steady flow of water helped ease the stiffness in her legs and back.

Hoihoi watched from the bank. "Then let me tell you about this Papara man I found. . . ."

The talk was soon interrupted by deep voices and the rustling of footsteps in dry leaves beyond the stream. Tepua turned and saw two warriors, each carrying a long spear, staring at her. Hastily she covered herself as she came out of the water. The intruders gave her a disturbing chill. She had seen one of them before—standing guard at the headman's compound.

"What do you mean, bothering us at our baths?" Hoihoi demanded.

"Headman's business," came a curt response. "The visitor—the atoll woman—must come with us."

Tepua turned with a start. Enjoying the pleasant surroundings, she had allowed herself to relax. Now hair prickled at the nape of her neck as she drew her wrap about her and tucked it in firmly. What could the headman want?

Nervously she turned toward Hoihoi, hoping for an answer. "If Pigs-run-out calls you, you must go," Hoihoi said in an angry whisper. "But I will send my brother after you. If the headman asks what you are doing in his district, then Rimapoa will answer."

"And what can he say?" Tepua glanced again at the impatient guards and felt herself starting to perspire.

"That we honor the Maohi customs," said Hoihoi. "That we have taken you in as our guest."

Guest. It pleased Tepua to hear that word. She recalled, not long ago, how Hoihoi had scorned the fisherman for trying to help her. At least Tepua had two friends now, though she doubted they could influence the headman.

While Hoihoi hurried off to find Rimapoa, Tepua followed the guards. With only a few grunts for conversation, they took her on the same path she had followed days earlier, finally nearing a fenced compound close to the beach. Just as they reached the pebbled path she heard footsteps and a familiar voice behind her. The underchief's men turned, and when they saw Rimapoa, they waved their spears at him. "Go home to your bigmouthed sister," one guard called.

At the compound, they marched through the gate without a glance at the man on watch. Behind them Rimapoa began arguing loudly, but the guard refused to let him pass. Tepua stiffened as she heard his anguished voice.

"Let me speak to him," she said to the guards. As she turned to the fisherman she felt the point of a spear against her back. Her lips trembled, but she managed to get out a few words. "Rimapoa, go home. There is nothing . . . you can do for me here."

"If the headman takes from me what I value the most," he said harshly, "I will show my feelings." In his hand he carried something she had seen before, a shark's tooth lashed onto a short stick. This implement was similar to those from her own island, and the fact that he carried it made her trembling worse. To show grief, a person used it to strike himself. . . .

"You do not need that," Tepua hissed. "Nothing has happened to me. I have not even heard yet what the headman wants." Her throat tightened and tears burned at the corners of her eyes. She felt the guard's hand on her shoulder.

"I will wait for you, then," the fisherman said gruffly. "If you do not come back soon . . ."

Tepua turned away, trying to hold her head up and walk in the manner that had been drilled into her. She was a daughter of a chief, after all. She could trace her ancestry to the great creator god, Tangaroa. Why should she be frightened of a mere underchief?

Within the bamboo fence lay a neat cluster of thatched houses. Pigs, dogs, and children roamed freely under the breadfruit trees while servants scurried about keeping the grounds spotless. Tepua heard the clattering of *tapa* mallets and turned to see a row of women hammering out bark-cloth on a long beam. They stopped to glance at her, their gazes lingering. The men called for Tepua to hurry.

Then she entered the wide doorway and saw Pigs-run-out sitting on an elegant four-legged stool. The underchief was not garbed in the finery she had seen the previous night. Instead, he wore a simple turban of yellow bark-cloth and a white, printed cape.

"May you prosper, noble chief," Tepua said when she knelt before him.

He held a polished coconut shell in his pudgy hand and took a sip from it before speaking. Then, with an arrogant sniff, he acknowledged her greeting. "You are a foreigner," he said in a harsh tone. "A woman from the pearl-shell islands. Tell me your name and how you got here."

For a moment Tepua's tongue refused to budge. "I—I am called Tepua-mua. I was washed ashore."

The chief leaned forward. "Your canoe sank?"

It pained her to remember. "I fell overboard. Then I found a smaller boat. The currents carried me, and I paddled—"

"You came a long way," he said. "But now what is your intention? Do you ask permission to live in my district?"

She struggled with his question. Was this a trap? How did he want her to answer? His knit brows and piercing gaze gave her no hint. "I—would be pleased to stay."

The underchief narrowed his eyes. "You do not wish to go back to your family?"

How could she reply truthfully? "I would like to learn Maohi ways. And remain in Tahiti."

He smiled coldly. "Then that is all I need ask you for now. The rest I have seen for myself."

Tepua felt her face grow hot. Last night she had noticed him watching her, but his expression had remained distant. Even now she felt that he was examining her as he might study an unusual fish. He still had not said whether she could stay.

"Look," the headman continued. "This is my youngest daughter—Small-foot." From the corner, a figure crept out. It was a slender girl, who eyed her shyly, then scampered back to her hiding place. "She is very pretty, is she not?"

Tepua whispered her agreement.

"She will grow up to be as beautiful as her mother," declared the headman. "Yes. And she will be the best dancer on the island as well. That is why I am granting your request."

"Dancer?" Tepua felt bewilderment as well as relief.

"You will teach her. Do not be modest about your skills. Everyone watched you last night. And I am a generous man. I do not ask exactly where you came from, or what enemies might pursue you. I take you into my household and grant you my protection." He turned to one of his attendants. "Let Hard-mallet take charge of this new one," the headman said. "And be sure the dancing lessons start at once. I am expecting important company in a few days." He waved Tepua and the others away.

Tepua did not know what to make of this new situation. The headman had offered her protection, but what would he want in exchange? Surely more than just lessons for his daughter. And what of her own hopes? If a chance did come for her to join the Arioi, would she be free to take it?

With dismay, she realized that now she must leave Hoihoi and her brother. How she would miss Hoihoi's coarse humor! And what of Rimapoa? If she remained with him much longer, she might well do what had once seemed impossible.

She frowned, knowing that the fisherman would not take this separation well. Coming out into the shaded yard that surrounded the houses, she glanced around but did not see him. She darted toward the bamboo fence and peered between the gaps. There he stood, scowling, scuffling his feet on the ground. "Rimapoa!" she called.

His woeful expression did not ease as he came up to her. "What does that scoundrel want?" he whispered.

She explained hastily, and the fisherman's reaction was exactly what she had feared. With a groan of despair he swung the shark's-tooth flail at his forehead, striking until blood began to flow. "Is this how he rewards me," he cried, "for all those plump fish I brought him?"

"This is neither reward nor punishment!" she answered, thrusting her hand between the poles to stop his frenzy. "It means nothing to the headman that I have my own wishes, or that you care about me."

"Then I will make it mean something to him." He shook free of her and gashed himself again.

"No!" Tepua caught his hand between hers, cradling it.

His anguish seemed to ease for a moment. "Listen," she said quickly, for she heard footsteps coming. "I am not caged here." For proof she shook one of the bamboo staves of the fence, showing how loosely it was set into the ground. "He does not hold me prisoner."

"Then you will come to me?"

"When I can. Now go home and put the shark's tooth away."

Gradually his scowl began to soften. He thrust his other hand between the poles and pressed her fingers. "Yes," he said. "I know you will come. You will not forget Rimapoa." With a wary glance toward the approaching guards, he scurried off, looking back at her after almost every step.

Tepua sighed, admitting to herself that she was relieved to see him go. His display had embarrassed her, and she hoped it had not drawn much attention. Yes, she cared for him, in a way she had never cared about a man. Often, while working, she would recall something he had told her, or remember a certain roguish look in his eye.

Now she would be living among a different class of people. How could she expect the women of the underchief's household to understand the bond between herself and the fisherman?

Drawing in her breath, she lifted her head and turned to face the underchief's compound. This was to be her new home now. She must adapt to it, as she had to Rimapoa's hut. Perhaps she would even find a friend.

Returning to the yard, she saw a short and attractive young woman, with a broad face and small mouth, approaching her. "I am called Hard-mallet," said the other pleasantly. "They say I am to show you around. As a stranger among us you will have a few things to learn."

Tepua nodded, following Hard-mallet to where the other women sat hammering bark-cloth on a long wooden beam. "The chief gives many gifts of cloth," Hard-mallet explained. "That is why he keeps us so busy with this work. You will be expected to do your part."

Tepua protested. "He told me I am to be his daughter's teacher."

"That is but one small part of your duties."

"And what are the rest? Must I share his sleeping mat as well?"

Hard-mallet grimaced with distaste and looked away. "I do—sometimes," she said softly. "The best I can say for him is that he is quick about it."

Tepua stamped her foot in anger. Suddenly she remembered a servingwoman her father often called for his pleasure. The arrangement had seemed so natural that she had never asked herself how the woman felt about it. *So now I must see life from the other side. . . .*

"Do not fret, slender one," said Hard-mallet. "I know the headman's tastes. He likes women who eat well. You are pretty, but not . . ." She held her hands out to suggest a bulk that Tepua did not possess.

"Then I will stay the way I am."

A brief grin lit up Hard-mallet's broad face. "We have talked enough for now. Come. Join us. We chant to the hammer's sound as we work, and the time passes pleasantly."

In this way, Tepua was introduced to the first of her duties. She learned later that she was also expected to help prepare the women's meals, keep the houses and grounds tidy, and tend vegetable gardens that lay outside the fence.

Only in the evenings did she have time to spend with her young pupil. Then Tepua would take Small-foot into a corner of the women's house while a drummer sat just outside. They would practice the simplest hip movements until the girl yawned and begged for sleep.

During the first few days in the headman's household, Tepua saw Rimapoa several times, but always from a distance. He would gaze over the fence, call to her, and wave mournfully. Tepua always waved back with more enthusiasm than she felt.

She had promised to go to him, yet a reason always came to hold her back. It was true that she wanted to see both Hoihoi and the fisherman. But if she went to him when he was alone, he would surely think she had come for *hanihani.* As much as she liked him, she was not ready for that. Each day she found some excuse not to leave.

She consoled herself with Hard-mallet's growing friendship. Often they worked side by side. When their turn came to uncover the women's fire pit and take out the cooked food, Tepua taught her a chant of celebration from her own island.

> *Oho! Taku manu e pekepeke*
> *Taku manu e peke. . . .*

Hard-mallet gamely tried to repeat it, though she stumbled over the sounds that were strange to her. Tepua encouraged her to keep going, laughing and clapping as they chanted together. "I will make you into a coral islander," Tepua promised. "And then I will not feel so far from home."

Just as she was getting used to her new routine, a sudden flurry of activity within the compound drove all stray thoughts from her mind. A visitor was coming—a nobleman she had heard about—the brother of the high chief. Starting at dawn, everyone worked to get ready.

The women shook dust from the sleeping and sitting mats, brought in fresh *aretu* grass to cover the floors, and rehearsed dances for the entertainment. The menservants gathered foodstuffs and piled firewood beside their huge earth oven. The pigs and chickens were herded into bamboo enclosures so they would not be underfoot.

At last, when the guest arrived in early afternoon, the entire household turned out to greet him. "*Manava,* my friend Matopahu!" called Pigs-run-out in welcome as he went to escort the visitor inside the compound. Tepua, standing far back with the womenservants, wondered at his unusually genial tone. With most people, the underchief displayed a distant or even sulky manner, but this time he looked genuinely delighted.

"*Ia ora na,*" replied the arriving guest to the underchief's greeting. "May you live, may you prosper."

Over the heads of the other women, Tepua stared with curiosity at the high chief's brother.

The visitor was far younger than the headman, but the intent look in his eyes and the set of his mouth hinted at a dignity and wisdom beyond his years. He had a strong-featured face and a head covered by waves of black hair that gleamed beneath the band of his turban. Matopahu was a tall man, taller than the underchief, and he had with him a small band of warriors all nearly his own height.

Even among the group of handsome warriors, Matopahu stood out, drawing everyone's attention. Tepua found it difficult to let her gaze wander from the young nobleman. His limbs were smooth, but when he walked, Tepua could see the strength in his arms and chest. About his shoulders Matopahu wore a cloak of richly painted *tapa* cloth. His legs were elegantly tattooed, though she could not see the details of the design.

The visitor called a greeting to everyone, then went inside the main house with the headman. The women and servants were dismissed. "First the men will talk and eat," Hard-mallet explained. "The entertainment will come later." She smiled shyly. "Not only singing and dancing. This Matopahu has been here before. After the lamps are out, you can be sure he will keep someone up late."

"I think you would like to be that someone," answered Tepua. She had come to like Hard-mallet and wished her friend the pleasure this noble stranger might bring. Yet Tepua was more than curious about Matopahu. He had a striking face and an impressive manner. She found herself wondering what sort of spirit might lie behind that face.

Tepua could see the excitement in her friend's eyes as well. "What you say is true," said Hard-mallet. "He has chosen me before and I did not regret it."

"Then let me help you," Tepua said, putting her affection for Hard-mallet ahead of any possible interest she might have in the visitor. "Shall we make an offering to the gods and ask their favor?"

Hard-mallet laughed. "Yes. Quickly, then, before anyone sees us." They raced back to the women's house and gathered several pieces of ripe fruit. At the small wooden shrine behind the house, they set their offerings before the idols and chanted a quiet prayer.

8

THE welcoming celebration began at once, with feasting, then performances and dancing in front of the underchief's main house. Pigs-run-out and his guest sat on stools in the place of honor while important people of the district sat on mats to each side.

Tepua and the other servants had to stay out of sight, except when they were summoned to entertain. From afar she watched a group of young men strutting through a spear dance, but she took no interest in their performance. She could only sit and wonder when she would be called to show off her pupil. Impatiently she balled her fist and stared at the ground.

As the afternoon passed she began to think that Pigs-run-out had forgotten her. Perhaps he had stolen a glance at Small-foot's progress and decided that she wasn't ready to perform. Tepua felt a twinge of disappointment. It was true that the underchief's daughter still had much to learn, but the girl had worked hard to prepare herself.

As darkness fell the servants lit torches and the entertainment continued. Musicians played and men chanted, though they were no match for the Arioi performers she had seen. Hard-mallet explained that these were merely local people and not seasoned players. "But our guest is having a good time anyway," she whispered. Tepua could scarcely see Matopahu in the flickering firelight.

She forced herself to look away, uncomfortable with the intense and unexpected effect he had on her, even at a distance. Then she was startled to hear her name called. A servant beckoned. Tepua's pulse began racing as she and her student came to stand before the headman and Matopahu.

Small-foot stood in front, Tepua several steps behind. The drummers took up their beat.

Eager as ever, though far from graceful, the headman's daughter began to wiggle her small hips. Tepua tried not to laugh, though the girl's exaggerated motions were comical. The first lessons had helped, but Small-foot would need many more.

Tepua saw a frown growing on the headman's face. Had he expected his daughter to be performing like an Arioi? she wondered. She kept her own dancing subdued to avoid drawing attention from Small-foot. For a moment she watched her pupil's small tan back, the child's smooth skin catching the light from a dozen palm-rib torches. Then Tepua looked at the headman and Matopahu.

She saw how Pigs-run-out's scowl softened when he glanced at his guest. Once again she found herself curious what sort of person this visitor might be. She had heard only a few hints from Hard-mallet.

The pleased expression on Matopahu's face confirmed what her friend had told her—he was truly enjoying himself. Occasionally he spoke to his host, gesturing with long-fingered hands. She noticed his powerful shoulders, sinewy forearms, and guessed that he was skilled in the usual pursuits of the chiefly class—archery, throwing the javelin, sailing for sport. This was no indolent nobleman, she thought, devoted to eating and other sedentary pleasures.

She caught herself casting too many looks at Matopahu and lowered her head, hoping he hadn't noticed. He was not watching her, she saw, relieved. His attention was completely on Small-foot, for he nodded with appreciation each time the girl tried something new.

Despite her decision not to upstage her pupil, Tepua found herself starting one of her more exotic flourishes. Her hands and arms seemed to be moving of their own accord. . . .

From Hard-mallet, Tepua had learned a few things about Matopahu. He was older than his brother, who was high chief over several districts. If, as some said, Matopahu had been deprived unfairly of that office, no sign of disappoint-

ment showed on his features. His face was clear of the lines
that bitterness or pettiness could engrave. Yet a certain look
about his eyes said that he was no stranger to pain.

The drumbeat quickened and Tepua watched Small-foot
struggling to keep up. Tepua did not need to think about
what her hips and legs and fingers were doing. *Restrain
yourself,* came a warning voice in her head. *Here you are
nothing but a servant.*

Her body, moving in the fast rhythm of the dance, grew
more supple, her skin more sensitive, her senses more acute.
Her breasts, rubbing against the flowered wreath she wore,
began to tingle, and the side-to-side thrusting of her hips
began to waken the pleasant feeling that dancing often
produced.

*It is the dance that is arousing me, not the closeness of
that man,* she thought fiercely, but something beyond her
will seemed to take possession of her and she turned in
place before Matopahu, displaying herself.

For an instant Matopahu's gaze went to her and his brows
rose, but his attention was drawn away again by a remark by
Pigs-run-out. Feeling deflated, Tepua faced away and continued to dance, but some of the spirit had gone from her
performance.

At last the headman clapped his hands and the drumming
ceased. Small-foot, laughing and prancing, raced off to
rejoin her mother. Tepua received no praise for either her
dancing or her instruction. Pigs-run-out dismissed her with
a curt wave. She could only slip into the shadows and wait
for the entertainment to continue. When she looked toward
the two men, she saw them in animated conversation.

Her frustration with the headman flared into anger. She
was already weary of being his servant, set to tending crops
or pounding bark-cloth at his whim. And now he had
brought her out like a bizarrely colored bird, to display her
for his guest and then quickly put her aside.

What did you expect? she scolded herself. *That you would
be included in such noble company? You are but a brief
amusement for these men. They would be far more excited
by a cockfight.*

She watched with little interest as the headman called
Hard-mallet to him. But then, to her surprise, Hard-mallet
made her way back to Tepua and whispered that the
underchief wanted her. He had invited his daughter's
dancing teacher to come and sit beside his guest.

Tepua's heartbeat quickened again. Matopahu had noticed her after all. But she realized, with a growing sense of
shame, that she had betrayed her friendship with Hard-
mallet. She had let her own desires take control of her
during the dance.

What about the offering to the gods? she asked herself,
shaking her head and frowning at poor Hard-mallet. Had
they mistaken the purpose of her offering to the idol, turning
the guest's attention to the wrong woman? Whatever the
reason, she could not refuse the headman's invitation.

Slowly she got up and made her way around the edge of
the audience. Feeling her dancing skirt brush against her
legs as she walked, she took her place on the mat beside the
guest. Uncomfortably she faced forward, not wishing to
meet his gaze while the headman's attention still focused on
both of them. What did Pigs-run-out expect of her?

Or Matopahu himself? Though she was not looking at
him, she could not help being intensely aware of his
presence. Warmth seemed to radiate from his body, unless
that was the flushing of her own skin. Her breasts throbbed
beneath the flowered wreath, and the excitement woken by
the dance stirred again.

She glanced sideways at his legs, at the hard, well-
sculpted muscles of his calves and the elegant tattoo of an
eel that twined up around each one. A desire crept over her
to touch the glistening skin with her fingertips.

She could hear, almost feel, the resonance of his voice as
he spoke to Pigs-run-out. His tone was not deep, but still
powerful, and she knew he would not have to shout in order
to make himself heard. The air about her seemed charged
with his scent. The sweet oil he had rubbed on his limbs and
the smell of the bark-cloth cloak mixed pleasantly with his
own warm aroma.

She watched the next performance start and tried to let it

distract her from his presence. This was to be the *ponara,* a game she had seen played by Tahitian women, though they had never invited her to join them.

A group of women wearing wreaths, and waistcloths painted with birds and flowers, formed two lines and faced each other. They laid their arms about each other's shoulders so that they could dance in a line. One woman kicked a green, unripe breadfruit across the ground. It hurtled toward the opposing line, whose members tried to block it with their feet.

The breadfruit shot back and forth several times before it bounced past the legs of the first team. Laughing, they conceded the round to their opponents. For a penalty, the losers had to perform a song or a dance; then the breadfruit was put into play again.

Tepua stole a look at Pigs-run-out. The headman was absorbed in the *ponara,* cheering on the team that held the women of his family. She caught Matopahu also casting a quick glance at the headman.

The honored guest gave her a conspiratorial look from the corner of his eye. "Our host seems to be occupied," he said softly. He shifted, moving closer to her, leaning down from his seat. Again she inhaled his scent, a sweet, clean maleness fresh from bathing. She noticed his appraising glance, his nostrils flaring delicately as he took in her own aroma.

"I have seen women from the atolls dance as you do," he said, "but none with your ability. You are a foreigner, yet you have enough skill to teach our own dancers."

Tepua bathed in the warm glow engendered by his praise. It was not just polite flattery. For a moment she was so absurdly happy that she wanted to leap up and dance again, just for him.

Yet she sobered as she felt a sting of wariness. *How much does he know about me? I should be careful.* "I am new to Tahiti," she conceded. "I am trying to learn Maohi ways."

"Where did you come from and how did you get here?" The questions were friendly, but she sensed a sharp curiosity behind them.

She did not want Matopahu or anyone else to know her true background now, and she hoped that people would forget everything she had said earlier about her family. Traders from the low islands sometimes visited Tahiti. If she were recognized, and news of her presence here reached home, her kin might send someone to bring her back to them—in disgrace. She chose her words with care.

"You would not know my little island. There was an accident at sea. I was lucky to find a capsized canoe adrift, and somehow I brought myself here."

"Accident?" His eyes narrowed. "Then you came because the gods sent you, not of your own will. You must be homesick for your country."

Tepua stiffened. Of course she was homesick for her atoll.

"You do not answer," he said mildly. "Perhaps you find Tahiti to your liking." He waved his hand at the expansive compound with its spacious houses. "My friend Pigs-run-out surely lives better than any of your island chiefs. You could do worse than stay here."

Tepua felt her temper simmering. Perhaps it was not the slight against her homeland but the discovery that this man, charming though he might be, shared the arrogance that Tepua found in many Tahitians. This island might have its abundance, its green-clad heights and cascading streams, but she missed the stark beauty of her atoll, its landscape of sand and coral and water. Her people were not as rich or plump as the Maohi, but they were still her people.

"I am satisfied with my place," she said, trying to keep the edge from her voice. "For now."

The answer seemed to startle him. "And later?" he asked after a pause.

A motion on Matopahu's far side drew her attention. Pigs-run-out was heaving himself off the stool to go congratulate the winning *ponara* dancers.

Tepua decided that with the headman gone, she could be more candid. She lifted her chin. "Perhaps I will not pound bark-cloth forever."

"You could teach young girls to dance. I would not say

this to my host, but his daughter has little aptitude for the art. You have at least made her presentable.''

Tepua stared at him directly. Should she share her new dream with him? Something about this man drew her secrets from her. She did not know whether she resented this or welcomed it. She tried to put her wish into words that would not sound absurd.

"Sometimes . . . when I dance, I feel it is not just me doing the dancing. I become something more.'' She glanced up. "Do you understand?''

"I do.''

"Does such a thing ever happen to you?'' As soon as she finished, she wished she could take back her words. A little vertical line formed between his brows, as if her question had disturbed him.

"Not when I dance,'' he said. "But there are other times . . . yes.''

Tepua felt her eyes widen. He did understand! He did share something that was precious to her. She was seized by a hunger to know more, to share more, but she stanched her impulse to flood him with questions. If he wanted to tell her, he would.

"I have heard,'' she continued, "that Oro sometimes inspires a dancer. I think that happened when I danced for the Arioi.'' She took a breath, feeling her pulse beat at the base of her throat while something inside her screamed a warning in Bone-needle's voice. Yet she forged ahead, feeling her own voice start to tremble with intensity. "It may be, as you say, that the gods sent me here, to Tahiti. If so, then perhaps they wish me to honor Oro—by joining the performers of the Arioi society.''

Matopahu's brows rose. "One does not draw such a conclusion lightly. Tell me what you know of the Arioi.''

Tepua recalled what she had learned by questioning Hoihoi and Hard-mallet, but she knew how inadequate their explanations must be. Under his stare, she became tongue-tied. He smiled again, putting her at ease, and she felt another rush of happiness.

"You need not answer,'' he said. "The Arioi are important to us. They help keep peace in ways you may not understand yet. Young people of the best families are encouraged to join the society, so they will not breed trouble. They are kept busy trying to rise through the ranks.''

''Then that must please the chiefs—''

''Not as much as you might think. You see, the Arioi do not hesitate to make their views known—through their satires. If a chief is ridiculed by the Arioi, he soon mends his ways.''

Tepua paused, trying to take in all he had said. ''Then you have given me another reason to admire these Arioi. They have the courage to stand up to overbearing chiefs.''

''Yes. That is sometimes very useful.''

Suddenly a thought came to her, and she spoke in a rush. ''You say men of the high families are urged to join them. Does that mean you are a member?''

''For reasons of my own, I am not.''

She stared at him in silence, regretting her hasty words.

''But do not let that discourage you. The Arioi may be what you need. Certainly you seem out of place here, like a custard apple in a mango tree. You are the headman's servant, but you have the stature and grace of a noble-woman. Tell me your background.''

Tepua met his eyes again. They were deep, liquid, a color too rich to be called brown. She knew that if she tried to lie to this man, she would merely show herself for a fool. Yet how to explain?

''I was a member of the chief's court on my home island. I was sent away.''

''Intrigue?'' he asked. He reached toward her and gently cupped her chin, raising her eyes to meet his. His touch made gooseflesh rise on her nape. ''Jealousy among the ladies of the court?''

Inwardly Tepua smiled, though she kept her expression solemn. An arranged marriage was anything but an intrigue, but it had certainly led to her present troubles.

''Problems at court, yes. It will be better for me if no one learns where I have gone. They think I am dead, and I wish them to go on believing that.''

''I will not tell anyone,'' he answered. Then he leaned forward and pressed his nose against hers. The warmth of his touch did things to her that even the dancing had not done. The delicious sensation of one nose sliding against another intensified all her other feelings.

''Ha, I see you like my dancer!'' Pigs-run-out said lustily to Matopahu as he plumped himself down on the stool beside his guest. ''Of course, my good friend, I share everything I have with you. She is yours for the night.''

She is yours! Suddenly all of Tepua's warm feelings drained away. What an insult—to be offered to a guest in such a coarse way. However charming and desirable Matopahu might be, she would not be handed to him like a roll of *tapa* cloth. She was Kohekapu's daughter.

Her temper spoke for her as she turned to the headman. ''I am not yours to give!'' she answered angrily.

The headman's mouth fell open, and for a moment an ugly silence reigned. Pigs-run-out took a deep breath while the brown in his cheeks flushed to a dusky red. Tepua braced herself. Chiefs in her own islands did not bother scolding or punishing servants. They simply gave an order to have the offender killed.

Suddenly Matopahu began to laugh.

''What amuses you so, my noble friend?'' asked Pigs-run-out sullenly. ''That this woman does not respect her betters?''

''Not at all, my gracious host. You have mistaken my intentions and that is why I laugh. This dancer is not to my taste. Amusing to talk to, but no more. The woman I want is standing over there—Hard-mallet. See how she looks at me!''

All thanks to the gods. Tepua sighed. They had saved her by making Matopahu choose the right woman after all. Yet her joy for Hard-mallet was mixed with envy and anguish.

Tepua left her seat. She stood behind the men, uncertain of what to do next. Matopahu had rescued her from a bad situation, but his words hurt bitterly. She went hot and cold by turns as they sounded again in her memory. What a child she had been—trusting him, prattling about her dreams of becoming an Arioi.

The headman's expression suddenly changed to one of relief. "Hard-mallet is a good choice," he told Matopahu with a sly grin. "She will make your mallet hard, and more than once. I am happy to share her with you." He beckoned to the other woman, showing that she should sit where Tepua had been.

Tepua blinked back tears as she hurried away. If her father and brothers were here . . . No, she must not think of home. She did not even know who among her bridal party had survived the storm.

She left the yard and went to the servants' house, curled upon a mat, and covered her ears. She tried not to hear the raucous singing, tried not to weep, tried not to envy Hard-mallet.

She knew what the rest of the evening would bring. Entertainments always aroused the passions. Soon eager couples would go off together into the shadowy sleeping houses. Even in the servants' quarters she would hear the soft rustling of clothing, the sighs of pleasure. And she would spend the night alone, without Hard-mallet's comforting presence beside her.

If that ocean storm had not come, she would now be lying with her husband, a man who surely outshone Matopahu! She tossed angrily on her mat, blaming the nobleman for her unhappiness. He had charmed her, flattered her, made her desire him.

Tepua sat up, blinking back tears. She would not stay here, enduring the misery. Better to go to the comfort of her two friends, Rimapoa and Hoihoi, even if she risked the roaming night spirits. Pigs-run-out would not need her before morning. If he did call for her, too bad. She wiped her cheeks defiantly and stood up.

When she slipped back outside, she saw the audience watching a comical performance—a pair of clowns cavorting in painted costumes. *Call one clown Pigs-run-out and the other Matopahu,* she thought as she ran past the guards at the gate and out onto the moonlit path.

9

At dawn Tepua returned to her sleeping place, and found no sign that anyone had noticed her absence. The other women woke, groggily, to begin their morning tasks. They glanced at her but said nothing. Perhaps none of them had overheard Matopahu and the headman. Perhaps they did not know how she had been shamed.

But everyone knew that Hard-mallet had not slept in the women's quarters. When the women glanced at her empty place, they raised eyebrows and smiled at each other.

Tepua did her best to keep busy, and away from the men. When she heard a loud commotion—a chorus of sad cries as Matopahu departed—she was carrying water to the caged dogs at the side of the compound.

"Do not be angry with me," said Hard-mallet later as they went out to work in the yam garden.

"Why should I care?" asked Tepua. "He is not to my taste. The man I want is Pigs-run-out!"

Hard-mallet stared at her for a moment, and then she understood the joke. The two women laughed, and hugged each other. Tepua felt her pain easing.

In the days following Matopahu's visit, she was relieved to hear nothing more from the headman about the incident. He seemed preoccupied with his practical affairs, ordering the household to produce a vast quantity of bark-cloth. "He needs the *tapa* for gifts," Hard-mallet explained. "He is always generous with his friends. Especially if he wants something in return."

Tepua made no complaint when she was ordered to join in the task. The work would be tedious, she knew, but it would help pass the time until the Arioi returned to give another performance.

And then . . . She did not know what would happen.
Perhaps Oro would seize her once again, and this time the
players would realize that she belonged among them. It was
this hope that sustained her during the long, grueling days.

Until now Tepua had only worked on the final stages of
clothmaking. Now Hard-mallet showed her where the paper
mulberry trees grew in neat plantations, their lower branches
kept trimmed away so that the bark would strip off in
unbroken sections. Men felled the trees using stone adzes
bound by cords to stout wooden handles, then stacked the
slender saplings beside a stream.

Tepua learned how to slit the bark along the length of the
tree, then use a pointed stick to pry it loose. Then she
washed the sections she had stripped, laid them on a slanting
board against her knees, and scraped away the coarse outer
layer with a cockleshell. It was hard, repetitive labor, but it
kept her mind from things she did not wish to think about.

Despite herself, her thoughts drifted often toward Matopahu. His words of rejection still made her cheeks burn.
Perhaps he had saved her from punishment, but she thought
he could have done so more gracefully.

It was impossible to keep him long from her mind.
Sometimes another woman would speak his name, or
mention something she knew about him. Matopahu was a
skilled navigator, Tepua heard, a man who could steer by
waves and wind and stars. And though he was neither chief
nor high priest, the gods had marked him for distinction in
another way. At times he fell into a trance, and a god spoke
through his lips, warning the people of troubles to come.

These revelations did little to change Tepua's opinion of
the high chief's brother. For a time, she wished not to think
about men at all. She welcomed the routine of making *tapa,*
which occupied both her hands and her mind.

Once she had the inner bark scraped clean, she wrapped
it in plantain leaves, placed it in the stream, weighted it with
rocks, and left it to steep with similar packets. While the
fiber cured she stripped, cleaned, and scraped more, depos-
iting other packages to soak in the running water.

After two or three days, when she drew the bundle out,

she found the bark had become clammy and glutinous, ready for working. Now the enjoyable part of the task began. At their usual shady place in the compound, the women spread their bark strips atop a long mat of plantain leaves, overlapping the narrow pieces in several layers. When the bark sheet was dry enough to be handled, they spread one end over a narrow wooden beam, dampened the fibers, and began to pound them with their wooden beaters.

Hard-mallet had two *tapa* beaters that she prized highly and kept apart from the communal store by hanging them in her quarters with sennit cords. These beaters were long blocks of close-grained wood, four-faced on one end and rounded into a handle on the other. Each surface was scored by grooves, whose fineness varied on different sides.

The task progressed by striking first with the coarsest side, then slowly working toward the finest. Hard-mallet generously allowed Tepua to use one of her prized cloth beaters, and in many other ways tried to make her feel welcome. The hollow *tok tok tok* as the mallets struck the beam was a joyful sound and often the women's voices rose in chants or work songs.

These peaceful days did not last. One morning, as Tepua was kneeling at the beam, enjoying the fresh breeze and the clatter of mallets, the headman's guards admitted an unusual visitor. She paused in her work to peer at the newcomer. Between the dust and the bodies of the men who escorted him, she could see that he did not wear Maohi dress. In truth, there was a disconcertingly familiar look about the visitor, but he disappeared so quickly into the headman's house that she could not be sure what she had seen.

Uneasily, she turned back to her work. It was not long before a womanservant came from the house with news. The visitor was a trader, she said. He had come to pay respects, and ask permission to remain awhile in the underchief's district.

When the stranger stood in the shaded doorway, still speaking to Pigs-run-out, the words of their conversation drifted to Tepua. The trader spoke slowly, evidently unused to the Tahitian dialect. He used the hard "k" sound that Tahitians always omitted.

Her *tapa* beater froze in her grip. She knew the accent. And when he stepped out into daylight, she saw the finely plaited matting of his skirt and the patterns of tattoos— alternating squares of black—that swept down from each shoulder to border his chest. He must have come from an island in her own group!

She studied the stranger more closely. He walked with a quick determined step and swung his shoulders in an arrogant way. He had a rugged dark face and hard black eyes that returned the contemptuous stares of the Tahitians around him.

She found herself watching him with a mixture of longing and dread. Just to see a man of her own people made her heart hammer as hard as the beater she'd been using. Was he here only to trade, she wondered, or for some other purpose?

Suddenly the trader turned his head as if he knew he was being appraised. His sharp gaze crossed the courtyard and she felt it settle on her. His forehead wrinkled, then his brows rose. She tried to duck among the other women, who were still bending to their work, but he had already seen enough.

She heard him cross the courtyard with purposeful steps. Quickly she turned the back of her hand away from him. The tattoo of her family meant nothing to Tahitian eyes, but this man might recognize it.

Then he crouched before her, staring intensely into her eyes. He spoke rapidly in the atoll dialect, the "k" and "g" sounding wonderful to her ears. He asked her name and how she had come there. She longed to free her own tongue to answer, and to ask what he knew of her family, but she dared not reply. Instead she made gestures with her eye-brows and head to indicate that she did not understand. When he persisted, she answered only in the soft Maohi manner she had learned.

A hand on the visitor's arm brought his inquisition to a halt. The hand belonged to one of the headman's warriors, but Pigs-run-out, standing beside him, had given the order. The trader shrugged off the guard's grasp and turned away.

"I have given you permission to trade shell hooks for cloth, not to meddle with my women," the headman warned. "Be gone before I revoke your privilege."

The stranger looked as if he were about to argue. Then, with one last glance at Tepua, he turned and strode away.

With uncertain fingers she picked up her mallet again. The headman's guards had gone to escort the trader from the compound, but Pigs-run-out still stood over Tepua. When she glanced up, she saw his measuring stare.

"You have a knack for attracting attention, woman," he said in a caustic tone. "Perhaps I should learn something more about you."

Tepua averted her eyes and clenched the mallet.

"I have heard that *motu* women are different. Maybe you will show me." He laughed softly. "Yes, soon, when I feel the need for a change." Tepua stared at her work, saying nothing, until she felt his shadow slide off her and heard him amble away. Then she let out a long, low breath and hit the cloth so hard that she almost tore it.

"Gently, gently," said Hard-mallet, laying a cool hand on top of Tepua's. "He is all talk and little else. I have been with him many times, so I know." She gave Tepua a shy, yet roguish wink.

Tepua frowned. Compared with her new problem, the headman was a minor worry. This trader was not from her own island, but she realized that he might have seen her on a visit. Even if he did not know her, he had certainly heard by now of the sea disaster and the lost bride. Such news traveled quickly through the atolls.

He would be trading in the district, talking to all the men. What if he learned that she once had called herself a chief's daughter? She needed to find out what he was thinking, what he might do if he discovered her identity. She knew only one person who might be able to help her now.

Late in the day, after Hoihoi had gone off for a tryst with her Papara man, Rimapoa sat in his yard making a new albacore line from the inner bark of the *roa* bush. Raw fiber lay on a banana leaf before him and the growing cord he was making was tied to his big toe. Rolling fibers on his bare thigh, he formed two separate strands, then twisted the pair tightly into a two-ply cord.

When he glanced up and saw Tepua approaching his house, he yanked the cord from his toe and jumped up to greet her. "My flower, it has been so long," he chided, though he could not be angry with her for more than an instant. "And the headman's guards, I am sure, never gave you my messages." He put his hand on her shoulder and tenderly greeted her with a pressing of noses.

He felt his desire stirring, but sensed her reluctance. He sighed, knowing that he would continue pleasing her in every way he could. It did not matter to him how long he must wait. He looked at her face, and saw worry in her eyes.

"Rimapoa, I have been unkind to you," she said quietly.

"It is nothing. The headman keeps you busy. I understand why you cannot get away."

"Even so . . ." She looked down, her voice trailing off.

Then he noticed that the back of her hand was red and swollen, crossed by a network of newly tattooed lines that overlaid the old design. "What have you done?" he asked in alarm.

She winced when he tried to touch her hand. "Something I delayed too long. The *tatatau* who did this is a master of his art. He promised it will look like a flower when it heals."

Seeing that she was fighting her tears, he tried to soothe her, until she finally explained about the trader's arrival. "I do not know what this stranger wants," she concluded. "If he learns who I am, he may go back and tell my people. That is why I must hide the mark of my family."

Rimapoa laid one gentle finger on her lips. "Shh. We will talk more about it later. First, I have a gift for you."

He got down on his knees and reached for a loosely tied bundle he had stored under a bush. Over the past days he had often prepared similar ones, but Tepua had not come to claim them.

Hoping the shade had kept the bud fresh, he drew it out. Yes, it was still crisp, beaded with dew, and had opened into a star-shaped flower with petals whiter than the palest coral. He touched the moist waxy petals with his forefinger. With the flower cupped in his palms, he turned to Tepua. "I picked it early this morning in the hills. It is called *tiare-maohi*."

Tepua took the *tiare* by its stem, touched it, smelled it, all with such an open look of wonder that Rimapoa sorrowed for her. What kind of life had she led, so empty of such beauty?

"Did you have flowers on your atoll?" he asked softly.

"None like this."

"Let me put it in your hair," he said. With gentle fingers, he separated the strands of her hair and wove the flower's stem skillfully among them. When he stepped back to admire his handiwork, he felt a rush of tenderness. Standing there, her face tilted up to him, her body bronzed by the golden light of late afternoon, the *tiare* shining in her hair like a star, she seemed like a goddess from the old legends.

He was almost afraid to take her in his arms again, but when he did, he clasped her to him tightly, speaking old words that his grandfather had taught him, words that were the deepest expression of fondness for the beloved.

"*Ta'u tiare 'apetahi 'oe,*" he breathed into her hair. "The *tiare* itself wilts when compared with your beauty, woman of the atolls."

Though she clung to him for comfort, he sensed that she was still too troubled to think of pleasure. For her sake, he tried to turn his thoughts elsewhere. "Do you know that a flower like this once gave me a fright?" he asked as they sat down together beneath a breadfruit tree.

"A flower frighten you? Now you are teasing me."

"When I was a stripling and as arrogant as Front-tooth, I visited the island Urietea with my father. We stayed there for several days. One morning I rose long before sunrise and walked up a great mountain called Temahani. When the sun started to rise, from all about me came sounds like darts hitting a tree."

"Someone attacking you!"

"I thought so, and ducked fast. But then, just in front of me, I saw a bud pop open as the first rays of the sun struck it. The stem split and the petals flew out. And then another and another until the air was filled with the noise. Pop-pop-pop-pop, just like this."

"This same flower?" Tepua inhaled the fragrance of the *tiare*.

"No. Only on far Urietea do the buds make such a noise. Here in Tahiti we leave the task of frightening people to chiefs and high priests." He had meant only to be clever, but he saw that his words brought a shadow across Tepua's face. "I have been thinking about this atoll man who worries you so," he said, reluctantly coming back to her problem.

Tepua frowned. "I wish I could have talked with the trader. He might have heard what happened to my family. I do not know if I have anyone left!" Her voice shook and tears shimmered in her eyes. "But I cannot let him learn who I am. . . ."

Rimapoa stroked her hair and tried to comfort her. "Do you think the man actually recognized you?"

"I cannot be sure. He grew angry when I did not answer in his dialect. Perhaps he once came to a religious ceremony on my island and saw me—when I was still maiden-to-the-gods."

Rimapoa wished she would forget that part of her past. "Remember," he said gently. "Your life is changed now. You are under the headman's protection."

"Pigs-run-out," Tepua scorned. "He is but a big lump of *poi*. I know my people, Rimapoa. Tahitians may look down on us as savages, but we are like coconut crabs. We fight hard and we are tenacious. If this man wants to know who I am, he will find out. And then he will return with his friends and try to take me away."

"I will not let that happen. No one is going to take you from Tahiti. Tomorrow, I promise, I will find out what that scoundrel is thinking."

* * *

The next morning, Rimapoa rose early, hoping to get his fishing done before the day grew hot. He went out alone, because his assistant, Front-tooth, had gone to visit cousins in a nearby valley. Rimapoa did not follow his usual habits. Since the albacore had started biting well lately for everyone, he decided to risk sailing within sight of one of the double canoes used for trolling. The fishing would be better over the albacore hole where the *tira* worked.

He had a second reason for watching this other boat. When its fishing was done, he thought it might lead him to Tepua's trader. The *tira*'s crew always had a need for pearl-shell hooks.

He set a floating sea anchor and cast his lines, but his gaze kept straying to the *tira*. It was well made, better than any craft he could hope to own. So fine was the boat and so high its reputation that its owners had bestowed it with a name, something rarely done except with sacred craft that belonged to a chief. It was called *Reef-wrecker*, in honor of its hulls of tough *tamanu* wood, which had battled many a submerged shoal and broken off chunks of coral.

Rimapoa once had worked aboard that boat. He remembered the smell of sweating salt-sprayed men, the creak of the fish crane as it swung, and the splash of the albacore bursting from the water. He shook his head ruefully. If he had stayed with the group, he might have earned himself a share in the boat and its equipment. *Reef-wrecker* was communally owned—by women as well as men, for it was the fishermen's wives and daughters who netted the red mullet used as bait.

But too much quarreling had ended that possibility. He gazed at the great canoe with longing, recalling its solid feel beneath his feet. Now the men who had been his companions called him a fish stealer. He watched, trying not to feel envious as *Reef-wrecker* began to troll.

As soon as the crane swung down to drop the baited hooks into the water, a fish struck. When the men pulled it up, gleaming and thrashing, he saw that it was a big one, the albacore known as *aahi mapepe*. But soon his own lines grew active and he nearly forgot the other boat. He was busy for a time fighting to bring in several smaller, but no less tenacious fish. When he finally glanced again at the trolling canoe, it had raised its crane and was paddling for home.

Quickly he secured his catch and set sail, following the *tira*. Once he cleared the reef passage into the lagoon, he saw high, claw-shaped sails of other fishing craft, all converging on the same beach. What could be drawing them except word of the trader's arrival? This atoll man would do a good business today!

Rimapoa ran his outrigger onto the beach, tethering it to the bole of a coconut palm. Following the sound of the crowd, he hurried to the assembly ground, where everyone had gathered. Glancing down through the forest of tattooed legs, he glimpsed a large mat laid out with objects that flashed and shimmered in the sun.

The men in front crouched to inspect and handle the goods, letting Rimapoa see over their shoulders. He glimpsed fishhooks, and fine ones, too, made from sea-turtle shell or mother-of-pearl, shaped to spiral inward. Fish could not shake themselves free of them, yet a fisherman, with a deft twist, could pull off his catch and be ready to bait the hook again.

The *motu* man, wearing a necklace of dolphin teeth over his tattoo-bordered chest, squatted on his heels, his arms draped around his knees. He answered questions by grunting, and making gestures with his fingers, as if his customers did not really interest him. Rimapoa hung back, careful not to attract the trader's attention.

Tepua was right, he saw. The man would make a formidable opponent. He was well muscled, fierce looking, with strong features and an arrogant bearing. Often he slapped aside the hands of those who were too inquisitive, or growled in his version of Maohi speech. He made it clear that he would take *tapa* in trade for his goods, but not any foodstuffs.

A number of men ran home, returning with rolls of bark-cloth. Rimapoa recognized some of Tangled-net's relatives among them. Tangled-net, of course, was absent.

As soon as he had learned that Tepua was under the headman's protection, he had gone into hiding. The man was a pig, Rimapoa thought, fit only for sacrifice to the meanest gods.

Rimapoa tried to put his anger aside. He hung about the edge of the crowd, listening to the talk. If the *motu* man truly had an interest in Tepua, he might say something in passing. But the visitor said nothing to reveal himself. Soon many men had either made their bargains or given up in disgust. Rimapoa felt conspicuous in the small remaining crowd. He did not like the cold glances that Tangled-net's relatives were casting at him.

He turned toward his boat, thinking he should leave before trouble started. But he had nothing to tell Tepua and the trader was still talking. . . .

"This *tapa* is your family's work?" the *motu* man asked one of Tangled-net's uncles as he looked over the cloth that had been offered.

The uncle had a jovial face and a big belly, but his arms were thick with muscle and his eyes shrewd. "The women of our household make the finest *tapa* in the district," he replied proudly. "Not even the headman's servants can pound cloth so evenly and bleach it so white. I want these six fishhooks for my bundle." He pointed to a group he had set aside.

A glint awakened in the atoll man's eyes. He softened his voice so that Rimapoa had to strain to hear. "Yesterday I saw the headman's servants beating cloth. And I saw with them a skinny woman, not Maohi by her looks. Maybe she is distracting the others from their work. Maybe that is why their cloth is not so good." He added the last part jokingly.

"I have heard about that woman," said the uncle. "She is nobody. Just some *vahine* from one of your atolls."

Rimapoa clenched his fist to keep from groaning aloud at the man's loose talk.

"She interests me," said the trader. "For your *tapa* I will give the fishhooks you chose, and two others, if you tell me all you know about her. Even more, if you have her name and something of her ancestry."

Rimapoa hissed through his teeth. The savage was offering a far better deal than he had given the other men. This knowledge was worth something to him!

But then Rimapoa realized that he had edged dangerously close to the trader. He crouched behind a knot of men, peering out between them as Tangled-net's uncle answered quietly, "I cannot talk here. Come to the large canoe shed just after dark." He pointed to a place along the shore. When the trader nodded, the uncle handed over his cloth and picked up his fishhooks. After he had taken the first six, the trader brushed his hand away.

"The rest—later," said the *motu* man with a cold smile.

As he hurried from the assembly ground Rimapoa felt his fingers curl with rage. This uncle was playing a dangerous game for the sake of his nephew. Who could say what the savage intended? He might hope to reap a large reward by bringing Tepua home. But what would happen if he learned how Tangled-net had treated her?

Rimapoa scowled as he went to untie his canoe. The uncle must be scheming to get rid of Tepua so that his nephew could return from hiding. But how he meant to arrange this, Rimapoa could not guess. Tonight he would have to risk listening at the canoe shed. . . .

Just before sunset, Rimapoa squatted behind the bole of a coconut palm, peering at the outline of the shed against the sky. A long row of center posts supported an arched roof of thatch that nearly reached the ground. Beneath stood racks where boats were stored when not in use. Now, during the fishing season, the shed was nearly empty. Only one canoe remained.

Rimapoa knew that boat, a large heavy dugout. It was too ancient and cracked for open-ocean use and too clumsy for paddling about the lagoon. The old man who owned the ancient craft refused to give it up, saying that one day he would paddle it—when the gods called him to paradise.

Rimapoa turned for a moment toward the last glimmer of light along the shore. Then he heard quiet footsteps as five men approached the shed. He recognized the big-bellied uncle from his silhouette. Several of the uncle's companions were carrying war clubs.

The men all ducked under the thatched roof. Rimapoa, feeling alarmed, leaned against the rough bark of the palm. The voices were low, furtive. As twilight faded he scuttled closer, to hide behind another tree at the edge of the shed.

He heard the fishermen send one of their number to watch outside for the trader's approach. Hairs prickled on the back of Rimapoa's neck. This did not look like preparations for a friendly meeting.

The shed remained dark. No torches were lit. Rimapoa strained to hear the voices, and realized that the men were arguing.

"Let the *motu* man take away this troublesome *vahine,*" the uncle was saying. "That will be best for us. We should even offer to help him catch her."

"Catching her will be easy," another voice said with a laugh. "We just wait until she visits the fish stealer."

Rimapoa knotted his fists as a third voice joined in. This younger man had a reputation for being reckless and cruel. And coldly clever. "Uncle," the young fisherman said, "you still have not listened to me. I agree that we must get rid of the *motu* woman, but your way is too risky. Sending her back to her island would not be wise."

"And why not? When she is gone, Tangled-net can come home."

"But, Uncle, I am certain that this woman is of high birth—among her own people. For what other reason would the trader take such interest in her?"

"Tangled-net said she told great lies about herself."

"Forgive my presumption, honored uncle, but Tangled-net is not the most truthful of my brothers. Suppose this Tepua has the ancestry she claimed, and was maiden of the temple as well. If the savage takes her home, her kin will say that someone here defiled her."

Mutters broke out among them. Then the uncle said, "She will be killed for her carelessness. Good."

"Uncle, is your brain made of fermented breadfruit

mash? Her family will not rest at that. They will want revenge.''

''They may refuse to trade with us, that is all. We can find other sources of pearl-shell fishhooks.''

''Fishhooks?'' The younger man laughed. ''They will paddle into our lagoon at night and creep into our houses. You will wake up with a fish spear sticking through your great belly.''

The uncle grumbled and fumed, but the younger man's voice rose above his. ''Listen,'' he hissed fiercely. ''The one thing these atoll people understand is revenge. If the trader takes the woman away, they will come back after us, and our family will be destroyed.''

Rimapoa's mood darkened further. He sensed where the argument was heading.

''Then what would you do, my arrogant sage?'' Tangled-net's uncle asked resentfully.

''Club the *motu* man and feed his body to the sharks. And the same for the woman, of course. Before she can cause more trouble.''

A chill ran down Rimapoa's back. Tepua was safe now, so long as she stayed in the headman's compound. But as soon as she went outside . . . He shook off the grim thought and tried to hear what else the plotters would say.

''Getting rid of the trader will not be easy,'' Tangled-net's uncle grumbled. ''He has the bearing of a warrior and eyes that miss little. Do you think he will not be on his guard, if he comes at all?''

''We are five,'' said someone else, ''and he is one.''

''But his cries will be heard. This trader has the head-man's protection during his visit. If we are found out—''

''Listen,'' said the young man again. ''I will tell you what to do. See that old dugout on the rack? What would happen if it slipped off and fell on a man?''

''It will not fall,'' snorted Tangled-net's uncle, but Rimapoa heard murmurs of agreement and admiration for the young man's cleverness.

''The rack has been here for many seasons,'' said the young man. ''Perhaps the poles are cracked or the lashings loose. If someone were sitting just to the side there, the dugout might crush him before he could even cry out. And we have the bait to lure the man!''

Rimapoa began to shiver. Had these men no idea of what they were planning? To kill a man here would soil the canoe shed and anger the gods, ruining the fishing for everyone. There had to be a safer way to deal with the trader.

Tangled-net's uncle at once raised a similar objection, but the young instigator brushed his warning aside. ''The gods care nothing for the death of a *motu* savage,'' he said scornfully. ''And we can always have a priest purify the canoe shed afterward, just in case.''

More muttering followed, and then a general agreement. As the plotters began their preparations Rimapoa beat his fist soundlessly against the tree. Perhaps he should try to warn off the trader or alert the headman.

The trader meant nothing to him. He wanted only to do what was best for Tepua. But if these men murdered once and got away with it, they would not hesitate to try again. He did not see how anyone could protect her.

He trembled, sweating. His hand crept to the shell-bladed knife stuck through the knotting of his loincloth. No. He would have no chance against five such ruthless men. They already hated him. Given the slightest excuse, they would kill him as eagerly as they would their other chosen victims. But if he helped the trader, then Tepua might be taken away. . . .

He shook his head, unable to decide. Tepua's life would be in danger whether or not the trader was killed. Still struggling with this dilemma, he heard footsteps approaching, and realized that he had deliberated too long.

Now he saw two men, one carrying a torch of bundled coconut-leaf ribs, approaching the rear of the shed where he crouched. The trader, he realized, had turned cautious, bringing an escort. Rimapoa stood up, aware that he had no choice now but to greet the stranger. He signaled for caution. ''I must warn you,'' he whispered.

The *motu* man charged forward and grabbed Rimapoa tightly by the arm. Then the fisherman felt a spear point pressing through the thin cape over his back and knew that the bodyguard had slipped behind him. "I am not your enemy—" The sharp point pressed harder before he could explain.

"I will hold on to you, in case of trouble," said the trader. "Say nothing."

At that moment Tangled-net's uncle and the rest of the plotters emerged from the canoe house. "Who is this man?" the trader demanded as the others arrived.

A hand grabbed his chin, jerked his face toward the torchlight. "Rimapoa the fish stealer. A thief and a breaker of *tapu*. He is also the man who sleeps with that woman you are so curious about."

"Him!" The *motu* man gasped with astonishment. "Then she is not the one I seek. A chief's daughter was lost at sea, but such a maiden would not take up with one of your fishermen." The last words were spoken with the deepest contempt.

"Lies!" Rimapoa answered, no longer caring if the savage met his doom here. The man knew nothing about Tepua. Perhaps someday she would happily become a fisherman's *vahine*—Rimapoa's woman. "Tangled-net is the one who took her," he shouted. "Against her will! Do not blame me for his evil work."

"What is this?" asked the trader, glancing angrily from one man to the next. "She was forced?"

"Come inside the shed," said the uncle. "We need not discuss this in the open. I have learned the woman's name and I have also recovered part of the canoe that brought her. When you have these, you will know the truth."

"You go first," said the atoll man. He waited until the five had entered the shed. Then his bodyguard, who appeared to be a Tahitian from another district, seized Rimapoa and dragged him after them. The trader came in last, holding his torch.

"Come look at this wreck," said the uncle. Rimapoa had thought the uncle's promise a ruse, though he recalled some talk of "bait." Now he was astonished to see part of a broken outrigger canoe on the ground beside the rack that held the old dugout. Perhaps it was the piece that Front-tooth had found.

At this sight, the trader seemed to lose all caution. He rushed forward with the torch and fell on his knees beside the weathered poles and lashings.

Seeing the trap almost sprung made sweat run down Rimapoa's brow. Despite his anger at the trader, he knew the gods would not ignore this desecration. Rimapoa strained against the bodyguard's grip, wanting now only to get away.

"I know this work," the *motu* man said breathlessly. "It comes from our islands. Look—" Then a terrible splintering sound erupted, followed by a brief cry as the trader glanced up. But he could not react quickly enough. The torch flew aside in an arc as the rack collapsed and the heavy dugout rumbled down on top of him. The trader cried out once more. Then Rimapoa felt the alarmed bodyguard release his arm. The fisherman immediately rushed from the shed while the bodyguard fled in a different direction.

"Get Rimapoa," someone shouted, "before he can tell anyone."

But he was already outside, racing down the path that would take him to Tepua.

"Put out the fire," someone else called.

Rimapoa heard a crackle of flame behind him and risked one glance back. The fallen torch had started a blaze at the bottom of the roof. Now a ribbon of flame was leaping up the dry thatch, widening as it went, sending up heavy smoke. He saw the men scattering, one heading in his direction.

The blaze was spreading too quickly. He knew at once that the shed would be destroyed—swift punishment for the wrong that had been done there. But the wrath of the gods might not stop with this single act. With a shudder of fear, he ran faster.

Beneath the shelter of the women's sleeping house, Tepua lay curled on her mat, dreaming of home. She dreamed of a time, during the rains, when she had crouched under pandanus branches to stay dry. The rain had seeped through the leaves and dripped on her shoulders, running down her back, making her shiver. The tapping of the raindrops grew louder. . . .

She wriggled in her sleep and tried to squirm away, but finally the persistent sound woke her. That was not rain outside, she realized. The sounds she heard were of pebbles tossed against the cane walls of the house.

In the darkness she lay clutching the wrap that covered her and wishing that the noise would stop. Why would someone be tossing stones? Then she remembered Rimapoa's promise. Perhaps he had come with news about the trader.

Still groggy, she wound her wrap around her body against the night's chill. Feeling her way in the dark, careful to avoid waking anyone, she slipped outside. A half-moon gave enough light for her to find the bamboo fence. She moved away from the houses and called to Rimapoa softly, impatiently.

Then she saw the fisherman, his clothing in disarray, his chest heaving, glistening with sweat. His hair was wild and his eyes frightened. She felt him shaking when he reached past the fence and grabbed her arm. "You must come with me. Now."

She had never seen him like this. "For what?" She tried to pull away from his harsh grip, but he would not let go.

"Tangled-net's kin have killed the trader. You will be next."

"Next? How can they harm me here? They would not dare invade the headman's compound!"

"They are desperate men. They will wait until you are out digging yams or bathing in the stream. Then . . ." He made a sharp motion with his free hand, imitating a war club coming down.

"I must tell the headman," she said, her voice rising in anguish. "He will stop them."

The fisherman shook his head in dismay. She could see the urgency in his eyes. "Stop shadows? I do not know who all these men are. I recognized only two, and Tangled-net has many kin who pay the headman tribute. Will Pigs-run-out banish every one of them on the word of his daughter's dancing teacher?''

Tepua's breath came faster and thoughts about the headman whirled through her mind. She did not want to ask favors of the man who had intended to share her mat tonight. She had avoided his attentions only by bringing him an intoxicating drink of *ava,* which had put him into a stupor. Such a ruse could not succeed twice.

''Where can we go? How can we find refuge?'' she asked as all the indignities she had suffered here came back to her.

''The high chief will protect you. That is his obligation.''

''The high . . .'' Her voice trailed off. She had asked long ago to seek the high chief's aid, but Hoihoi had warned her that he lived far away. She knew something else about the high chief now. He was brother to that arrogant Matopahu!

''We must go,'' the fisherman pleaded. ''At once. Before they start looking for you. I am in danger as well.''

Tepua turned to look back at the women's house, its thatch roof glimmering faintly in moonlight. The thought of leaving her friend Hard-mallet made her want to weep. She had also grown fond of her pupil, Small-foot. If she agreed with Rimapoa's plan, she dared not go back, or tell anyone why she was leaving.

Suddenly a chorus of cries from beyond the compound made her head spin around. Heavy footsteps pounded up the path from the shore. ''Fire!'' came the voices. ''A big canoe shed is burning! Call the headman!''

''That is also the work of those pigs,'' Rimapoa hissed. ''Now will you listen?''

In a moment the uproar spread through the entire compound. Warriors hurried out through the gate. Servants spilled from the houses, pointed to the red-tinged sky, and began to moan and pray. Children awoke screaming.

The shouts hurt her ears. Her pulse pounded at her throat. In the midst of this pandemonium, Tepua could think only of getting away. Rimapoa released her arm and she followed the crowd, rushing out through the open gate.

''To my canoe,'' he said, when he met her on the other

side. "If we leave now, we can reach the high chief by
dawn."

She ran beside him toward the beach, so quickly that she
felt dizzy from exhaustion when she finally reached the
sand. When she had caught her breath, she helped drag his
boat into the surf. They nearly swamped the craft in their
urgency to launch it. As Tepua scrambled in, Rimapoa set
the mast and raised sail, stopping briefly to send anxious
looks up and down the shore. The fire was still burning,
glowing in the distance and filling the air with acrid smoke.
Frantically she paddled, helping the sail's pull until the
canoe was well away from shore.

At last a good stretch of open water separated the boat
from the fire. Rimapoa set his course, following the coastline, and lashed the sail in place. Then he picked up a
coconut from the bottom of the boat, but his hands trembled
so badly that he dropped it.

Tepua was also shaking, but she managed to retrieve the
coconut from the bilges of the canoe. She broke the nut open
with a flat stone she found there and handed it to the
fisherman. She certainly did not fault him for lack of
courage. What had he been through this night?

First he spoke a prayer, then poured the milk into the sea.
"I doubt such a small offering will undo what Tangled-net's
kin have done," he muttered, "but I must try." Then he
described what had happened since she last saw him.

When he was done, she understood. He was not shaking
as a coward might, but like a brave man whose reserves
were almost drained.

"You see why I must leave here," he said. "The gods are
angry. I fear they will punish us by keeping the albacore
from everyone's hooks. So if Tangled-net's kin do not kill
me, my life will be worthless anyway."

"You were right to go, Rimapoa," she said softly. "But
I am sorry for Hoihoi."

"She knows nothing of our woes. She will miss me,
perhaps. But soon her cousins will be visiting and she will
not be alone."

"Even so, I am sad for you."

"Perhaps it has worked out for the best, *tiare*," he answered. "I have too many enemies here. Even before you came, I was in danger. And living in some other place, perhaps you and I will not be kept so far apart."

"Yes. Perhaps. I had not thought of that." She sank down into the boat, too exhausted to say more. The cries from shore had faded, and Rimapoa fell silent as well. All she could hear now was the gentle lapping of lagoon water against the hull and the crashing of distant breakers.

Wishing she did not feel so weary, she splashed a bit of water on her face. Soon she would have to explain why she had fled. What could she say that would not make her troubles worse? As she tried to compose her words, imagining herself standing before the high chief, she kept seeing Matopahu's face.

10

A night's journey up the coast from where Tepua had set out, in the sacred courtyard of the high chief's *marae,* a long ceremony was nearing its end. Since dusk, Matopahu had been sitting on the chilly stone pavement. His joints felt stiff and his body cold from his nightlong vigil, for the priests had allowed him to wear only a loincloth.

Behind him, far off, he heard a cock crow, though he saw no hint of daylight overhead. That bird's reward would come quickly, Matopahu thought with a faint smile. One of the high chief's servants would go after the impatient fowl and seize it tightly by the neck. Knotted-cord did not like waking early.

Matopahu sighed, imagining his brother asleep on his warm mat. There was no comfort here for Matopahu, though he sat at his place of honor in the tribal *marae*. The low walls that surrounded the open-air shrine did little to block the wind.

Throughout the night the priests had been chanting. Now they began again. In the torchlight Matopahu watched the high priest, Ihetoa, kneeling before the huge *ahu,* the layered platform of rounded stones that towered over the far end of the courtyard. The priest, too, wore thin garments, a loincloth and a light fringed cape, exposing himself to the chill in order to gain the gods' favor.

Matopahu turned to glance at his friend, the underpriest Eye-to-heaven, who knelt at his own meditations. In the gloom he could see nothing of the expression on his *taio*'s face. It was at Matopahu's insistence that he and Eye-to-heaven had come to witness the high priest's ceremony, in hope that it might resolve the dispute over Matopahu's prophecy. This would be Ihetoa's third attempt at asking the gods for an answer. He had promised to call on the most powerful, the god of war, peace, and fertility, the great Oro.

The chanting continued, until at last the sky brightened. Now Matopahu could glimpse the lagoon through the surrounding trees. To his side, on high poles near the center of the courtyard, stood the bamboo altar platform. Varied fruits, as well as a choice pig, had been laid out as offerings. On and around the stepped-stone *ahu* stood numerous carved boards, painted with red ocher, hung with strips of *tapa* and tufts of red feathers to please the gods. *Soon,* thought Matopahu, feeling light-headed from lack of sleep. *Soon we will see if Ihetoa can keep up his sham.*

The high priest had never been pleased by the prophetic words that Matopahu spoke during his fits. Years earlier, Ihetoa had led the prominent men who opposed Matopahu's assumption of the chiefhood. Matopahu's father had given way to the influence of his advisers, altering the usual succession in favor of the younger son, Knotted-cord.

Priests, Matopahu had come to realize, did not like having their roles as oracles overshadowed. On some islands, such as Urietea, a man might be both high chief *and* oracle. Here in Tahiti, the nobles and priests were too jealous of their privileges to permit such power to reside in one man. So they had kept Matopahu from the high office, though they could do nothing to take away his god's voice. And Ihetoa was trying to disparage even that, by refusing to accept the prophesy.

Now, finally, the high priest stood up and turned to the rear of the courtyard. He took a step forward, holding out his arms as a signal to his attendants. A lesser priest hurried up to place the tall forward-curving headpiece on his brow while another removed his simple cape and replaced it with one decorated by a rich fringe of feathers.

From the tall *rata* trees that flanked the *marae* came a breathy moaning that made Matopahu's nape hairs stand on end. It was only the wind in the branches, he told himself, but he knew that many spirits haunted this sacred place.

Feathered cape billowing, the high priest stood watching Matopahu coldly. Ihetoa was an imposing man, broad across his shoulders and chest and solid through the belly. He had a face to match—wide, flat, with high cheekbones and full lips. An almost imperceptible nod of his head sent his assistants scurrying.

Then Matopahu heard the conch trumpet blown, a resonant blast that made him look over his shoulder at the cluster of ceremonial buildings outside the courtyard. He saw two priests approaching, bringing with them the sacred god's house from its keeping place. The ark was of polished wood, a closed chest covered by an arched roof of thatch. The men carried the ark suspended between two poles, and made their way carefully through the gap in the low wall surrounding the courtyard.

The high priest took a step closer while the ark was placed on posts set up to receive it. Beside Ihetoa came a wizened old man dressed in a white waist sash and loincloth, his hands entirely blackened by tattoos. He was the god-handler, the one who actually opened the ark, unwrapped the sacred image from its scented bed of *tapa* and drew it forth. His hands carried so much *mana,* so much sacred power, that he could not feed himself, lest he make his food too dangerous for his stomach.

A hush settled over the attendants as the old man came forward and reached under the thatch of the ark. There was but one opening, a round hole sealed with a sacred, white cloth. The god-handler slipped an age-withered forearm inside to draw out the image. To Matopahu, what emerged in the old man's hands looked almost alive. He drew in his breath as he looked at the oblong shape covered with bright feathers, glowing in crimson like the heart of fire or the spilled blood of war.

The high priest lifted his arms and chanted, "Oro, greatest and most terrible of gods, take on the mantle of these sacred feathers. Oro, fly to us from your place in the misty heights. Enter now into your image, your body, that we may hear you speak."

Matopahu's throat grew dry. The ruddy light of dawn shimmered on the feathered covering and a breeze stirred it gently. Suddenly Matopahu saw the god breathe and move. So bright was Oro that his eyes ached to look on him.

The acolytes and underpriests prostrated themselves before the image held aloft in the old man's hands. Matopahu cast himself down along with them.

He heard the high priest intone, "Oro, god of war and plenty, son of Ta'aroa and Hina-tu-atua, hear my plea. I beseech you to put away your wrath and offer us your wisdom." The high priest chanted more words of praise to the god, then asked in a rising tone, "What can we expect in the coming season, O mighty one? Will the breadfruit bear in plenty? Or will the crop fail—as Matopahu warns us—leaving us with empty bellies?"

The chief's brother felt his lips trembling. He had not expected his own name to be mentioned. Now any blame for disturbing the god would clearly fall on himself. Nervously he watched the priest continue. Ihetoa leaned close to the image, as if to hear its answer, but did not dare touch it. A renewed moaning in the trees made Matopahu's shivering grow worse.

The high priest muttered and the moaning sound came again. Then Ihetoa was speaking, uttering words of gratitude and praise to Oro. The god-handler lowered the image and replaced it inside the ark. But what was the answer? Matopahu turned to his *taio* and saw only a puzzled frown.

Ihetoa's face betrayed nothing. He stood in silence, waiting until the god's house was taken away. Then he raised his arms and turned toward the *ahu* of the temple. "Here is what great Oro has said to me," he intoned, his voice harsh in the cool, morning air. "These words are addressed directly to Matopahu. 'Have patience,' the god says. 'Do not try to be the first cock announcing the dawn. Remember what happens to the ones who crow too early.'" He lowered his arms, turned to the high chief's brother, his face displaying a faint smile of satisfaction.

"But that is no answer," Matopahu protested as he rose stiffly to his feet. "Telling me to have patience. That settles nothing."

"Then you have not understood it," Ihetoa replied

coldly. "Talk to your priestly friend and let him explain."
He turned, walking solemnly out of the courtyard. His
assistants lifted the god's house and followed behind him.

Matopahu understood the meaning well enough. It meant
that Ihetoa could continue to stall, refusing to announce that
the people should take action. And Matopahu already knew,
merely by observing the trees, that little remained of the
current breadfruit crop. Unless an effort was made to
preserve much of this, and the root crops as well, many
people would go hungry in the coming season.

Matopahu wondered if Oro had really spoken. If he had,
then perhaps the high priest had lost his ability to interpret
the mysterious sounds that the gods made. In fury, he turned
toward his *taio*.

"I cannot prove him wrong," whispered Eye-to-heaven.
"At least he has not flatly denied your claim. He would not
dare do that."

"But how long must we keep this to ourselves?"

"Our friends—your supporters—are quietly taking pre-
cautions, though it will not be enough if a real famine
strikes. For now we must be satisfied with that."

"I will be satisfied," answered Matopahu bitterly, "when
Ihetoa is no longer my brother's high priest."

A short time later Matopahu was walking along the
wooded shore. His earlier weariness had vanished, driven
off by his anger at the high priest, and he felt a need for
exercise.

In the *marae,* which lay on the nearby spit of land that
jutted into the lagoon, he had left the ceremonial garment
that the attendants had provided. Now he wore a waistcloth
and shoulder cape plaited from strips of hibiscus bark.
Unwilling, at this early hour, to don the elaborate head-
dresses affected by nobles at his brother's court, he had
wrapped his head with a turban, his only concession to
vanity being a long plume fastened above his forehead. He
walked barefoot, enjoying the feel of the sandy ground.

To walk here was a privilege that his brother no longer
could enjoy, Matopahu thought with a wry smile. Since

assuming his title, Knotted-cord was carried everywhere he went so that contact with the sacred personage might not accidentally sanctify a place used by commoners. Not long ago, the chief's bearer had stumbled, letting Knotted-cord's leg brush the outside of a noblewoman's dwelling. She had been forced to abandon the house, since it had been made sacred by the chief's touch. Matopahu shook his head at the thought of the owner's discomfiture, and dug his toes deeper into the sand.

Then, with a sigh, he turned, looking toward the fence of bamboo that surrounded the high chief's compound. Matopahu could see his brother's residence, with its high thatched roof and walls of canes set closely together. He assumed that Knotted-cord was still sleeping soundly within. Or perhaps not so soundly . . .

The dispute over the famine prophecy was only the latest in a series of conflicts that had threatened the peace of the district. Though he did not encourage them, some men whispered of deposing Knotted-cord and making Matopahu their chief. Matopahu did not take these mutterings seriously. His brother's hold on the high office was too strong now. Soon, Matopahu expected, the men who had pushed him aside would act to remove him from the court as well. In all likelihood, he would be forced into exile. Perhaps that would be for the good of all . . . except himself.

Matopahu's worried thoughts were interrupted by the soft *plunk* made by a canoe paddle. Turning, he was surprised to see an outrigger gliding across the still waters of the lagoon. He glanced at the weathered hull and low bow, with its flat bow board, recognizing the canoe as a fisherman's craft. The mast and sail had been taken down and stowed in the bottom.

A wiry bronzed man sat in the stern, handling the steering oar. Amidships a woman knelt, dipping a paddle. As she drew closer he studied her high forehead, large glistening eyes, and the note of determination in her face. She had a strange, exotic beauty, he thought. Then he laughed aloud as he recognized her. The dancer from the household of Pigs-run-out!

The canoe approached a stone jetty used by important visitors to dock. As soon as the two men who stood guard for the chief saw the battered outrigger canoe, they ran out, shouting and gesturing to warn it away. The man who steered the craft ignored them. The woman leaned forward and called, "We come seeking refuge. Does the high chief turn us back without a hearing?"

"I see no pigs or *tapa* in your canoe," one guard said. "What can you offer for my help?"

"Among my people," the woman retorted sharply, "a chief's hospitality is open to the poorest family of his island. I thought the same would hold here."

"We, too, must eat," the guard said, picking up a long spear and pointing it at the canoe.

"Then we must seek aid from better men!"

Matopahu scowled in shame for his brother's household. The guards had no right to ask for gifts. Quickly he walked toward them, emerging from the greenery so that he could be seen.

"Wait!" he cried just as the fisherman was about to paddle away. Matopahu saw the woman's eyes widen at his approach. Her lips parted, as if to speak his name, and her face reddened beneath the gold of her skin, but she kept silent. No, she had not forgotten him.

Matopahu strode out onto the jetty. "Your greediness dishonors this household," he scolded the men. "Stand aside, and hope that my brother does not put you to work grating coconuts." He turned, beckoning to the couple in the outrigger. "*Manava!* You are weary. Please come ashore."

Suddenly he remembered the woman's name—Tepua-mua. She rose halfway in her seat, apparently ready to accept his offer, but the man hesitated.

"I am the high chief's brother," Matopahu explained to him. "I can promise you a welcome here. If you wish an audience with Knotted-cord, I will arrange everything. Tell me what drives you from the headman's protection."

He glanced from the fisherman to Tepua. The man seemed about to reply, but she touched his arm and whispered something, then turned to Matopahu. "I cannot explain my situation simply," she answered in a controlled voice. "It will be better if I speak directly to the high chief."

Matopahu nodded, narrowing his eyes. He realized that she still simmered over his pretense of scorning her. What did that matter to him, when so many eager women were always at hand? Yet he felt an unexpected pleasure at seeing her again. "As you wish," he answered. He signaled for the guards to help her climb ashore. Then he turned, leading his visitors up the path toward the compound.

Once inside, Matopahu left the new arrivals with one of his retainers. They would be lodged in a guest house until Knotted-cord was ready to see them. Matopahu hoped this matter, whatever it was, could be settled quickly and without ill-will. He counted Pigs-run-out as his friend.

As for the woman, he did not know what to make of her. At the underchief's house she had confided in him, but he doubted that she had revealed the full truth about herself. He had taken her for a noblewoman, a displaced princess from a distant atoll. But what was she doing with this fisherman, who seemed more companion than servant?

Matopahu strode past the various outbuildings, the cook-houses for men and for women, the storehouses for the chief's riches, and stopped at the high chief's own dwelling. He realized he had come at the proper moment when he heard a cry from within the house. "The high chief is coming out," warned the herald's deep voice. "Stand back, stand back."

Matopahu recalled, for a moment, how his brother had been as a youth. Not tall, but well formed, with limbs that were strong, yet smooth. Now, as Matopahu glanced up at the chief being carried out, he saw one who had attained the majesty of girth that was the mark of important men.

"Why is my food not ready?" Knotted-cord complained as he emerged, blinking, into sunlight. The pouting face, the whiny voice, the childish impatience; they were not characteristic of the brother Matopahu had once known. They had come upon the chief with indulgence and indolence.

Knotted-cord rode the back of a new bearer, a huge young man who was already beginning to perspire under the load. Matopahu felt a twinge of sympathy for the fellow, but his thoughts remained with the unexpected visitors. "Noble brother, may I beg a favor of you?" he asked.

"If you are quick. I see that the imbeciles are still fetching my bowls of *poi*."

"A woman and a man have come to ask your help. Evidently it is something that Pigs-run-out could not handle. A matter requiring the high chief's wisdom—"

"There is my food! Next time have it ready when I come out!" The chief swatted his bearer as a signal to advance.

"Noble brother!" said Matopahu in a tone of annoyance.

"I will hold my usual audience this afternoon," grumbled Knotted-cord, turning his fat neck only briefly to give his answer. "Expect no favors."

After bathing, and rubbing himself with perfumed coconut oil, Matopahu put on a waist cloth of fresh white *tapa*, painted elegantly with crimson dye. About his neck, a servant tied a regal gorget made of feathers and cowrie shells. Shaped like a half circle hanging down, its shimmering border stuck out beyond his broad shoulders.

The servant took the headpiece outside before settling it on Matopahu's hair, for such a wide fan of feathers and plumes could not otherwise get through the doorway. The gorget was so large and stiff that Matopahu could not fold his arms, but had to clasp his hands behind him as he walked. He would have preferred his turban and a simple shell necklace, but he was the chief's brother and appearances had to be kept.

In full ceremonial dress, Matopahu walked swiftly to the open area where other courtiers, priests, and nobles stood about the audience rock. A crowd of common people had also gathered, a few to plead their cases before the high chief, the rest to gape at the spectacle and finery of the court. The one man he wished not to see, Ihetoa, stood in his usual place and did not acknowledge Matopahu's presence.

The boom of drums and the whistle of nose flutes announced the chief's impending arrival. Criers shouted above the noise and the words were taken up by other voices.

"The high chief flies to his people," called the royal herald. "Like the bird of paradise, like the sea eagle, he flies. Look up and behold him as he comes!"

Every gaze lifted, for the exalted man rode above the sea of heads, over nobles and commoners alike. He did not need as fine a costume as others in his court, his brother knew, for what was mere adornment compared with such elevation? Knotted-cord passed like a god among men, carried on the shoulders of his sturdy human mount.

It did not matter that his paunch pressed heavily on his bearer's neck, or that his skin had a pallid yellow-brown hue. To the gathered crowd, he was above all mortal failings and they worshiped him.

I could have been the one carried on those shoulders, adored by those eyes, Matopahu thought, letting the envy seep through. *But I would not have let myself become as pleasure-ridden and lazy.*

He remembered, with chagrin, that his brother had said almost the same thing long ago. Matopahu shook his head as he recalled the strong young man whose ideals and good intentions had been lost. Knotted-cord's corpulence had grown much faster than the wisdom and greatness that it was supposed to represent.

Yet Matopahu did not flatter himself with the notion that he could do better in resisting the temptations of the office. Perhaps everyone who accepted the chieftainship must pay such a great price. Matopahu looked warily at the faces about him, knowing that even thoughts carried danger. Here stood the high chief's orator, his sorcerer, his counselors, all ready to act should they sense any threat to Knotted-cord's power. And Ihetoa, the high priest, was the most dangerous of all.

Matopahu watched as attendants lowered his brother carefully, placing him on the audience rock and arranging his garments. Other attendants came up behind him, using feather-tipped sticks to chase off any flies that might dare to land on the chief. Knotted-cord held the long carved staff of his office, tapping it against the rock while he gazed, with a bored expression, at the crowd.

There were several petitioners to be heard that day. Matopahu took his place among the dignitaries and listened while his brother pondered cases that had been judged by underchiefs, but not to the plaintiff's satisfaction. Knotted-cord was in his usual hurry, eager to send the people away as quickly as possible.

At last Tepua and the fisherman came forward. Matopahu glanced once at his brother, though Knotted-cord had warned him to expect no help. Matopahu feared now that he had even harmed Tepua's prospects by mentioning her.

"The woman first," said the chief, leaning forward to squint at Tepua. "Who are you and what do you want of me? I am told you were under the protection of Pigs-run-out."

Matopahu watched Tepua hesitate before she spoke. He hoped she had been properly instructed by his retainer on how to behave before the chief. He regretted that he had not gone personally to prepare her for the audience.

Her bronze skin glowed in the afternoon light that slanted down across the lagoon. Her dark hair, cascading in waves over her shoulders, gleamed as she bent to place the token offering his servant had supplied—a trussed white fowl—at the high chief's feet. She was like a vision evoked by the chants of the storytellers. . . . No, Matopahu caught himself. She was just a *motu* woman, and one who might prove irksome.

"Glorious chief," she began. Matopahu saw that she kept her gaze averted slightly from the sacred person, as custom required. "I cast no aspersions on Pigs-run-out," she said. "He took me into his household and granted me his protection."

"Then why do you come to me?"

"Your underchief also offered his aid to a trader from the atolls, a man who entered his district recently. I learned that this trader meant to harm me. To avoid giving Pigs-run-out the difficult task of choosing between us, I left.''

Matopahu, studying her face as she spoke, noted signs of duplicity that he had seen in her once before. This woman always seemed to be hiding something. He glanced at the chief, whose bored expression had not changed. ''It might be interesting to learn, noble brother,'' said Matopahu openly, ''why this trader would want to harm the woman.''

The chief grunted. ''Answer,'' he ordered.

''I have enemies in the atolls,'' she replied in a strained voice. ''The trader wanted to take me back to them. He planned to use force, and he found men who were willing to help him.''

''Yet you said you belonged to the underchief's household,'' the chief said. ''Your interests would come before the trader's.''

''Pigs-run-out took me in as dancing teacher to his daughter,'' said Tepua. ''But the girl made little progress and her father thought I was to blame. Perhaps he welcomed the chance to be rid of me.''

''Hmm.'' The chief propped his chin on his plump hand and scowled into the distance. There was an awkward silence and Matopahu thought his brother might simply dismiss her. Before he could plan his words carefully, he cleared his throat and moved up beside the high chief's seat.

''Noble brother,'' Matopahu said quietly, ''I have visited the underchief's household, and I think there is more to the story. This is a spirited noblewoman before you, not a servant girl. When Pigs-run-out tried to offer her favors to his guests, she sometimes refused.''

The chief's bored expression suddenly brightened. ''Refused? That must have caused a commotion!''

Matopahu knew his brother liked nothing better than to see his underchiefs made fools of. ''Yes. It happened once when I was there. I had to intervene—somewhat delicately—to save her from his wrath.''

The chief nodded. ''I would have enjoyed seeing him swell up like a puffer fish. That is what Pigs-run-out looks like, you know. Especially when he gets angry.'' The chief turned to Tepua. "I find your plight amusing," he said in a kindlier tone. "What is it that you ask of me? To take refuge here? Or something more?"

Tepua's mouth fell open, as if she had not expected so generous a response. She turned for a moment, glancing at the fisherman behind her. When she faced the chief again, Knotted-cord smiled faintly, and Matopahu thought that his brother, too, must be struck by the odd beauty of this woman. "I am listening," the high chief said.

Tepua seemed to gather her resolve. "On my journey here I saw a performance house, nearby along the shore. I thought it might be where the Arioi dance."

"Do you wish to watch them?" the chief asked. "They will perform again in a few days. But that will not help your problem with the underchief."

"I wish to do more than watch, honored one. I have prayed that the god Oro will inspire me. I wish to enter the ranks of the Arioi."

Behind her, Matopahu saw the fisherman's jaw drop. Evidently he had expected some other request. A ripple of surprise went through the assembled courtiers as well.

"Ho-ho!" the chief laughed, turning to Matopahu. "You are right, noble brother. This one is no meek servant."

Tepua pressed her advantage. "I ask that you grant me permission to stay here until the performance. Then I will learn if the god has chosen me."

"And if he has not?"

Tepua lowered her gaze toward the ground and did not answer.

"You must have hard bones and be able to dance all night," the chief said. "My Arioi are the best in the island. They are often called to other districts as traveling players."

"It will be as the gods decide," Tepua said firmly.

"That is so," said the chief, dismissing her with a shake of his staff.

Now Matopahu watched the fisherman standing alone before the chief, another white fowl fluttering in his grip. The man looked so taken aback by Tepua's words that

Matopahu could only shake his head in puzzlement. What, he asked himself, was the relationship between these two?

"The man next," the chief said, growing impatient. "And last."

Matopahu's servant had to prod Rimapoa; the fisherman stumbled forward to drop the offering at the high chief's feet, then stepped back and bowed his head.

"Are you asleep, fisherman?" the chief boomed. "State what you want or I shall decide it for you."

"I brought—Tepua here—to keep her safe from the trader and his companions," he managed in a quavering voice. "By doing that, I made enemies in my district. Now I cannot return home."

"You also wish to remain here?"

He nodded without speaking.

"There are already too many fishermen in my district. Since you have gone to the effort of bringing this woman, I grant you permission to stay until the next new moon. Do not linger beyond the time I grant you." The chief lifted his heavy staff. "The audience is done. Bring my bearer."

Matopahu watched briefly as the court began to disperse. He itched to speak to Tepua again, but his concern for appearances held him back. In Tahitian eyes, after all, she had no standing. She was merely an atoll woman.

It would not do for him to show an interest in her. If he were merely after pleasure, and handled it discreetly, then no one would take notice. But he felt drawn to her in a way that he could not take lightly. He caught himself wondering what might happen if she did gain entrance to the Arioi. Through that means, and few others, a woman of no importance might rise to prominence.

He smiled and shook his head, trying to push aside these thoughts. Yet he continued to watch her through the dispersing crowd. *If you can dance all night, atoll woman,* he wondered, *what else can you do to please a man?*

When the audience ended, Tepua walked away in a daze. She wished she had planned this better, and had shared her hopes with Rimapoa. She had intended merely to ask for refuge, yet the chief's expression had softened briefly, and somehow—even with Matopahu staring at her—she had made her bold request.

She was sorry that Rimapoa had been startled and hurt by it, but she had made him no promises. She sighed, turning to see the fisherman standing under a breadfruit tree with his back toward her, his gaze on the ground. "Rimapoa, I did not know what would happen," she said as she came up behind him. "We came to him together. How could I foresee that the chief would send you away?"

Rimapoa would not look at her. "You are leaving me. That is all I care about," he said harshly. "This is my reward for saving you from Tangled-net's kin!"

She gasped, feeling as if he had struck her, yet she could not blame him.

"I did not plan it this way! If you will only listen—"

"No matter what you planned, I have lost you." He slapped his hand against his forehead. "Where is my shark's-tooth flail?"

She felt her eyes begin to sting. After all he had done for her, must they separate with such bitter feelings? One part of her wanted to embrace him, to say that she would cast aside her dreams and do whatever he wished. "Rimapoa, listen. The Arioi have influence with the high chief. If they take me in, perhaps they can also help you stay here."

"Now you listen to *my* plan," he said, turning to her, his face twisted with anguish. "It is far simpler, and does not need any help from this overstuffed chief. You can become my wife. We can take refuge somewhere else, in a distant part of the island. If you did not think so much of your high birth—"

She stamped her foot on the hard ground. Despite her anger, she felt the strong bond that had grown between them, forged by affection as well as necessity. "Do not blame everything on my birth! I have to refuse for another reason, and that is simple survival. My troubles will not end because one atoll trader was killed. Other men will come looking for me."

"If anyone tries to take you, he will die. I will be the great blue shark that protects the royal child."

"Oh, Rimapoa! Even a great shark will be worn down by many barracudas that circle him. I do not want you to spend your life fighting and fleeing."

"And how will your life with the Arioi be any safer?"

"The Arioi are warriors as well as performers. You know that. They protect their members, and there are hundreds of them."

"How can you be so certain about these people you have seen only once?"

"I talked to Hard-mallet and her friends. If I am accepted, I will live among the Arioi, inside one of their large compounds and away from the gaze of passersby. When I perform, I will always be masked or painted, and part of a large group. Even someone who knows my face will not recognize me."

"There is still a risk."

"Yes. But remember, Oro-the-peacekeeper watches over the Arioi. They have special immunities. Even when two chiefs are at war, one side dares not harm the Arioi of the other."

"So now you put your faith in *tapu*. I remember how little that did for you when Tangled-net took you to the shelter. What you need is a strong man—"

Impatiently she interrupted. "Rimapoa, you are brave and clever. But that is not enough against a determined band of warriors. You can be all those things and proud besides, but it will do you no good when I am lying on the sand with my skull smashed by a club!" She paused to calm herself. "I am sorry, but the trader's arrival convinced me of that. It is the truth of things and we both must accept it."

He locked his gaze with hers. Slowly the severe lines etched on his face by grief and anger softened. "What if the Arioi turn you away?"

"Then—then—" She faltered. She had been so sure of herself that she had not considered the possibility. If she failed in her quest, she doubted that the high chief would take her in. And now that she had seen Matopahu strutting in his finery, whispering about her to his brother, she could not stand the thought of remaining at court.

The answer came out before she could stop herself. "Then I will do as you asked," she said in a rush. "I will take you as my *tane*. I will be your wife."

"Ah, that is all I can hope for." He took her in his arms and held her affectionately, seemingly oblivious to who might be watching.

For a moment the memories came back of the day when they had walked to the waterfall. One part of her wanted to give up the struggle, to go with the fisherman wherever he asked. "Rimapoa," she said softly. "Let us accept that the gods will resolve this. They will decide whether the Arioi find me worthy."

"Yes," he said joyfully. "Yes, I understand. And I know what I must do now. I will bring an offering to the fisherman's *marae* that will make the priest's eyes bulge! The gods will hear my plea."

And I must also pray, she thought. *To Oro. To Oro-of-the-laid-down-spear. To show me that I know why I have come to Tahiti.*

11

BESIDE the shore, in a clearing bordered by tall, thick-rooted *rata* trees, Tepua found a shrine where women prayed to their guardian spirits. She must make her offering here, she knew, for ordinary women were forbidden to approach the places that men held sacred.

The shrine was simple, a small heap of water-smoothed stones surrounded by a fence of short sticks. The modest offering table of lashed bamboo stood at shoulder height. This shrine was dwarfed by the *marae* complex behind it. From where she stood, Tepua could see only a few gray walls and thatched roofs, but earlier she had glimpsed the huge *ahu* of stone that was the main *marae*'s heart. She sighed as she lifted her gifts, a few pieces of ripe fruit, and put them on the altar, beside other offerings of food and flowers.

She dared not presume to call on a great god directly; only a priest could do that. But she remembered how her protective spirit, Tapahi-roro-ariki, had comforted her in a dream. She wanted to call on her ancestress for help, but in this foreign place she did not feel the proper reverence.

Kneeling and closing her eyes, Tepua pictured the *marae* at home, its walls of weathered coral, its secret burial places beneath the paving stones. She shivered as she recalled the chants over the offerings, chants to draw the attention of the spirits: *Niu kura, niu taupe, niu toro . . .*

"Great ancestress," she begged at last, "speak to Oro for me. Remind him whose daughter I am. Ask him to grant me his favor." A sudden chill touched her and she knew the fear of the gods.

Tepua opened her eyes, rose, and walked humbly from the shrine. She realized how glad she was to be away from that place of spirits when she paused to cross a stream where it emptied into the lagoon. Here children were tossing *nono* fruits at each other, splashing and giggling. She wanted to throw her wrap aside and join them.

But something distracted her. When the children quieted for a moment, she heard drumming. The Arioi might be rehearsing, she realized. Pausing only to wash off the dust, she ran along the shoreline, following the sounds.

Soon she neared the huge open-walled building that she had seen from the canoe. Its thatched roof was loftier than that of the headman's grand dwelling. Its posts were the smoothed trunks of palm trees. Inside lay a raised platform for honored guests. In a corner, the drummers were practicing, and a few young dancers with them.

She saw other preparations under way. Workers carried a newly hewn plank to men who were repairing the wooden platform. She smelled the tang of sap and sawdust, mixed with the scent of dry grass scattered on the floor.

She did not enter, but went to a grove of breadfruit trees a short distance from the performance house. Here she thought she might dance to the drummers' beat without being seen. But her thoughts turned to Rimapoa, and she could not get started.

Where would he go when his time here ran out? He had spoken of seeking refuge with other chiefs, but had not mentioned any influential friends who might aid him. *I will help, somehow,* she vowed and then found herself able to focus on the drumming.

She began a slow dance, one that used graceful hand movements to tell stories. She started with the motion for *ori*—walking. With her upper arms held close to her body and elbows bent with palms facing up, she moved her hands up and down in the rhythm of someone striding along a trail.

I was walking . . .

She lifted her arms high, with palms facing each other, forming the profile of a valley with her hands. Then she put her hands to her eyes, keeping her elbows up and extended to each side.

Up a valley. I saw . . .

She dropped her fingertips onto her shoulders, so that her arms formed the outline of outspread wings.

A bird . . .

"That is very good," said a soft voice behind her.

Tepua, startled, turned toward the intruder. She saw a square face framed by flowing black hair, a yellow hibiscus blossom above one ear.

"I am Curling-leaf," the young woman said pleasantly. She was short, stocky, and plain, but her laughing eyes gave life to her face. "I am a novice with the Arioi. And you have taken my favorite spot."

"I did not know—"

"Please stay. The grove is large enough for two dancers and I would not mind having a companion." Something about Curling-leaf reminded Tepua of Hard-mallet. The young Arioi novice was not as pretty, but her disposition seemed more cheerful.

Tepua introduced herself, but said nothing of where she had come from. "So you are a *po'o,* a chest-slapper," she said. "Then you are the first Arioi I have met." Tepua knew that Curling-leaf held a provisional grade, one that must be passed before reaching the lowest regular rank of the order.

"I have been a *po'o* for some time."

"Even so, you are far ahead of me," said Tepua, trying not to show her envy.

Curling-leaf sighed. "Outsiders always think that my life must be wonderful. Let me tell you what it is really like."

Tepua did not want to be discouraged before she had even begun, but politeness and curiosity made her listen to the other woman's experiences. For three years, Curling-leaf had been a servant in the house of the Arioi lodge chiefess. All this time she had been preparing herself for promotion to the rank of Pointed-thorn, the order's lowest grade.

"I did not know it could take that long," said Tepua in a discouraged voice.

"There are so many chants to memorize, dances to practice, skills to develop," Curling-leaf explained. "But even though I am finally ready, I have another problem that holds me back."

"Yes?" Tepua sensed her new friend's reluctance to continue.

"This may not trouble you at all," said Curling-leaf. "Do you know that a member must provide a feast each time she advances a grade in the Arioi?"

Tepua frowned, puzzled.

"I am sorry to confess," the novice continued, her gaze now on the ground, "that my family cannot help me. My father and uncles are good men, but they have no land of their own. Providing my feast would be a great hardship for them."

Embarrassed by this admission, Tepua almost wished she had not pressed for an answer. At the same time she wondered angrily why no one had bothered to explain this to her. "My kin cannot help me either," Tepua whispered, touching Curling-leaf's hand in a gesture of sympathy.

"But do not worry, my new friend," the novice answered. "You are pretty enough to find an admirer. Some important man often comes forward when one of our female members is ready to advance. And, of course, she returns the gift in other ways."

So that is what they all expect of me! That is what everyone has assumed! Tepua felt her face burning as she considered the implications. But why should she concern herself over it now? She would be happy enough just to become a novice, even if she never went beyond that.

She turned her thoughts to Curling-leaf's situation, wondering if this young woman had spurned the attentions of her admirers. Perhaps that was not the reason. Curling-leaf had a pleasant disposition, but her plain features might not appeal to many men. "Despite all you tell me," said Tepua, "I am determined to try."

"Then I will pray for your success," said Curling-leaf. "And if you do find a place among us, I will be your friend. But I don't think that practicing your dancing will help you. I have watched many candidates who danced well, only to be found unworthy because they did not give themselves completely to Oro."

Tepua shut her eyes and leaned her head back against a

tree. She remembered how she had lost herself in dance, feeling the fire of divine strength run through her. She believed that Oro had seized her then, though she had certainly not spent any time practicing her art. If she had faith in the god, perhaps he would come to her again.

"Then I will do as you say, Curling-leaf," she answered softly, though the decision made her uneasy. "I will work no more at this. I will accept what skills I have and pray for Oro to inspire me." *And if the god fails me, then Rimapoa will win after all.*

As the evening of the Arioi performance approached, Tepua's apprehension grew. By then she had talked to other novices, finding some who disagreed with Curling-leaf's advice. "It would not hurt," said one girl, "to dress yourself properly so the god will know how eager you are to please him."

Following the novices' instructions, Tepua made a scarlet paint for her face from the juice of *mati* berries crushed with *tou* leaves. She combed out her hair until it glistened in the late-afternoon sunlight, then put on a headdress woven from bright yellow *ti* leaves. Over her wrap, she tied a girdle made from the same leaves as her headdress. Then she anointed herself with a dab of pomade, coconut oil scented with sandalwood dust.

Reds and violets of sunset streaked the sky as she finally made her way toward the performance house. People had started to gather, most taking seats outside the open walls of the building. Beneath the thatched roof of the great theater two bonfires crackled, lighting the mats hung from the expanse of the single rear wall and reflecting off the huge, polished pillars that supported the roofbeams.

The leaping bonfires and glow of candlenut tapers made the night outside seem darker. Tepua stood apart from the crowd massing around the building. The light dazzled and dismayed her. The theater was huge and she had never danced before such a large crowd. If Oro called her, she wondered how she could even make her way through the throng of people.

A sharp prickle started at the back of her neck as the

drumming began. The milling crowd moved aside, forming
a lane for a troupe of musicians and players who strode
toward the performance house. One man pounded a drum so
tall that it had to be carried before him on the backs of two
assistants. Tepua felt its bass beat through her toes as he
passed. Other men tapped double-ended drums slung over
their shoulders by straps, or hollowed-out logs with slits cut
at the top. These log drums gave out a *tok, tok* like the sound
of *tapa* mallets, but much sharper and louder.

The onlookers arranged themselves, sitting on the ground
outside the theater and looking in past its open walls to the
area where the performers would dance. The more privileged classes had seating inside, on the scented grass laid
out on the floor. The stools on the viewing platform
remained empty.

Tepua heard a court herald shout in his strong bass voice
above the clamor of the crowd: ''The high chief is coming.
He flies to the house of the players. Clear the sky, clear the
earth so that there may be no hesitation in his flight. Give
way, the high chief comes!''

The sound of running footsteps blended into the sound of
the drums. Knotted-cord, dressed magnificently in streaming robes of *tapa,* seemed to swoop down upon the crowd.
His headdress was shaped like a frigate bird with lifted
wings. The chief was carried so rapidly on the shoulders of
his bearer that Tepua thought the bird might rise from his
head and fly off.

With gasps and sighs, the people parted for their ruler.
Behind Knotted-cord came his chief wife, lesser wives,
relatives and favorites, all riding the shoulders of husky
men. The party was arrayed in cowries, feathers, mother-
of-pearl, and long lengths of the finest dyed and painted
tapa cloth. Matopahu was among them, wearing a feather-
fan headdress, but Tepua chose not to look at him.

She wished that he had stayed away. But why did it
matter? she asked herself. His opinions meant nothing
tonight. The Arioi would be the ones who judged her.

She watched Knotted-cord's bearer lift the chief to the

highest stool on the platform. In quick succession, the other notables were announced and took their lesser seats.

"Make way for the chiefs of our lodge! Make way for the blacklegs." At this cry, a man and a woman appeared at opposite sides of the performance house. Both wore the honored red loin girdle and elaborate flower crowns. Tepua knew that these were not the Arioi leaders she had watched with Hoihoi, but chiefs of a larger and far more famous lodge.

The two blacklegs launched into a high-kneed prance. They advanced toward each other with a strutting motion that made everyone in the crowd laugh and cheer. The man threw his head back and roared at the audience. "Ha-ha! It is I, Head-lifted, chief comedian of this lodge. I am here to entertain you with my troupe. My mountain is the highest, my cape seaward the most beautiful, my river the freshest. It is I, chief Arioi of the district where coconuts fall like rain."

The woman, who declared her name to be Aitofa, made a similar speech. Then the two blacklegs pranced toward the platform and took their seats on the remaining stools.

As the formalities continued Tepua's impatience grew. She feared half the night would pass before anyone began to dance. She felt foolish standing at the edge of the crowd, her face painted and her body decked out in yellow. People kept glancing at her as if expecting something marvelous to happen. Did they want her to disrupt the ceremonies? she wondered. Perhaps they were hoping that Oro might seize her now.

She stepped farther back as the players began to perform. The crowd roared with laughter at their antics, but Tepua did not. She felt a chill, and wished she had brought something warm to wrap around herself. Even the sight of a friendly face might help. She looked for Curling-leaf among the chest-slappers at the side of the hall, but could not find her.

And then, when she was not expecting it, the drumbeat quickened. The chest-slappers arranged themselves about the perimeter of the stage area. At a signal from the first in line, each began flapping the left arm, while slapping the upper chest with the right hand.

The painted and masked performers took their places and started to dance. Tepua watched the swirl of bright costumes, and was amazed at the skill of the best Arioi, the grace and speed of their movements.

She knew she was being dazzled by the thudding of the drum and the glare of the lights. But she had not come to gape, like the other spectators. Forcing herself to turn from the spectacle, she looked out into the moonlit landscape.

She could still hear the drumbeat, but her legs and arms felt heavy, refusing to start the dance. Who was she to challenge the Arioi on their own ground?

Facing away from the performers, into the darkness, she willed herself to move, her hips to start following the rhythm. The motions did not feel right. Her body was stiff and slow. Anyone looking at her would know she was not inspired.

Do not think, she told herself. *Dance. Just dance.*

As she continued, her muscles slowly warmed and her movements became lighter, faster. She flung back her head, rolling her hips easily. The undulation came up her legs, through her belly, her chest, and out along her arms. It felt good. She did it again, faster, freeing her muscles from the lock put on them by fear.

She tilted her head back. Now the motions grew smoother. A warmth rose from her center, growing like a young tree and sending its line of strength up through her body. She shivered with the delicious sensation and gave herself to the dance.

At last she turned again toward the performance house. Her attention focused, not on the high chief and his retinue, but on the Arioi blacklegs, the man and the woman. Still dancing, she neared the building but saw no way to break through the crowd. Everyone was watching the performers within.

She needed to get through! Out of desperation, she thrust her head back and gave a loud wavering howl. Heads turned among the spectators. People scuttled aside for her, whispering and pulling their children with them.

Questions rippled through the crowd as people watched her advance. "Who is this dancer? What household does she come from?"

Gathering her breath, she let forth a series of short yells, each one rising higher than the next. "I am of the household of the shark—mothered by sharks—fathered by sharks," she cried, her hips moving ever faster.

Her fever grew as she flung her head back and forth, her black hair lashing her shoulders. She heard her words as if another voice were speaking. "I am of the household of the canoe, mothered by canoes, fathered by canoes. I am of the household of the reef, mothered by coral, fathered by coral."

As she stamped her way to the front a new word came from the mouths of the crowd. *"Nevaneva,"* they breathed. "Oro's touch is on this woman."

But Tepua knew that the fever came from the intensity of her dancing, not from the god. The rapture still had not taken her. Even as she heard the cries she felt the fire of her performance die down. In the faces of those watching, she saw doubt and disappointment appearing.

For a moment her attention shifted to the end of the platform. There she saw Matopahu turn with a smile to speak with the man beside him. Was he laughing at her poor efforts? she wondered. If so, she refused to accept his scorn.

Tepua shouted again, braying in defiance across the heads of the audience. Now she did not care if the god supported her or not. She sprang forward until she was dancing beneath the roof of the performance house, her gaze sweeping the faces of the chest-slappers as she spun past them. They had paused in their arm striking as well as their chanting, but took it up again, increasing the pace as if challenging her. Then Curling-leaf stood in front of her, urging her on with her own slaps and cries.

The dance itself possessed Tepua, sending her in with the other performers. As she whirled among them they turned with looks of astonishment. The others backed away from her, leaving a clear space in their midst. It no longer mattered where she was or who watched. She no longer saw anything clearly, only a dazzle of colors and shadows, the shimmer of lights and the dizzying sway of bodies.

Her arms and hips moved with a will beyond hers, harder and faster than she had ever danced. Her breath came in gasps, her strength drained into the demands of the dance until she thought she could give no more. Her legs quivered, threatened to collapse. A voice within her cried out for more, but her body, exhausted, could not give it.

Then something flared inside her, and a brightness came. It was the blazing orange red of fire, of sun, of war. As she danced on, her legs stopped trembling. They burned with a new strength, the power of a young god—Oro, who presided over war but loved peace, Oro-of-the-laid-down-spear, whose power let enemy sit down beside enemy. Then he was beside her, within her, surrounding her, his passion devouring all else. . . .

Silence brought Tepua out of her trance. Hearing no drums, she staggered to a halt. Why had they stopped?

Feeling like a sleeper awakened, Tepua rubbed her eyes and stared at the circle of Arioi around her. The people in the audience were roaring with delight over her performance, pounding their thighs. She could read nothing on the players' faces, painted and masked as they were.

Two chest-slappers, Curling-leaf and a young man, approached her. They hesitated, wonder and fear shining in their eyes. "My frenzy is gone," Tepua said weakly, and leaned gratefully against them as they took her arms. Her head was spinning and her muscles ached. Cooling perspiration chilled her back.

They led her to the side of the hall where the female blackleg, Aitofa, stood watching her. The chiefess had come down from her perch! One tap on the shoulder, Tepua knew, would give her the chance she wanted. After a few ceremonial words, the ritual questions and answers, she would be accepted as a novice. Aitofa raised her hand. . . .

Suddenly another hand caught Aitofa's forearm. The

chiefess turned with annoyance to the stocky man who had come up beside her. He was the other blackleg, the leader of the Arioi men. "Why do you stop me, Head-lifted?" asked the woman.

"Do not be too hasty in judging this dancer," he answered.

"Have you any doubt that she was possessed by the god?"

"I see only that under her red paint and yellow leaves she is a foreigner. Who can say what savage spirit entered her tonight?"

"Perhaps you have doubts, but I have none. Seldom have any of us witnessed such a performance. The women's troupe needs another strong player."

"Then choose a Maohi woman," the red-girdled chief replied. "Someone who will not embarrass us."

"Show me a Maohi woman with the same promise!"

Suddenly a young player rushed up to the arguing pair. "Noble leaders, excuse my interruption," he said. "The high chief is growing impatient. He wishes the show to continue."

"Then we will finish the discussion later," Aitofa said coldly to Head-lifted. She made a quick motion to the two novices who were still holding Tepua. "Put her over there."

And then Aitofa was gone, leaving Tepua to stumble between the two chest-slappers to a seat in the dry grass beside the platform. Curling-leaf gave her a few words of encouragement. Then the novices ran back to their places at the edge of the hall.

Tepua closed her eyes briefly, still catching her breath, then slowly looked around. Close by, on one of the high stools, sat Matopahu, watching her. He gave her a wink. He spoke, but the drummers, starting again, drowned out his words.

The Arioi had given her no answer! And now she could not put Matopahu from her mind. She stole another quick glance at him, the well-formed limbs, the handsome, arrogant face beneath the black-and-white fan-feathered headdress.

Perhaps she had misjudged him, she thought. Perhaps he did wish her well tonight. But she could not go to him and hear what he had to say. No. She must sit here, where Aitofa had put her, and endure the rest of the entertainment.

It was going to be a long night.

12

When Tepua woke, she stared for a moment at the cane walls of an unfamiliar house. She remembered only hazily how she had come here after the performance. *The dance.* She blinked as she pushed herself up, feeling soreness now in every joint and muscle.

"Tepua . . ." called a soft voice from behind her. She turned and saw Curling-leaf standing at the doorway. Tepua could read nothing from her expression. The novice probably did not know what decision the lodge chiefs had finally made.

Tepua touched her face, felt the dried paint, and realized that she had forgotten to wash it off.

"Come with me to bathe," said Curling-leaf. "When you are done, Aitofa will see you."

They left the compound, coming soon to a stream that ran through a pleasant breadfruit grove. No one else was bathing. "The others were here long ago," Curling-leaf explained. "You slept late. Aitofa told us to let you rest."

"I am already showing bad habits," Tepua muttered as she hastily washed, then went to meet Aitofa in the spacious house that stood in the middle of the compound.

Aitofa sat, like other chiefs, on a four-legged bow-bottomed stool. Tepua had paid little attention to the blackleg's appearance during the nighttime revels. Now she saw a tall, handsome woman, someone undoubtedly of a noble family. Aitofa's features were strong, too severe to be beautiful. Squint-lines showed at the corners of her eyes.

Her short hair was decked by a simple wreath of flowers. About her shoulders, and drawn across her small breasts, she wore a finely plaited shoulder cape. Aitofa crossed her arms and studied Tepua with an expression that made the latter feel like a promising but annoying child.

"How many Arioi performances had you seen before deciding to dance among us?"

Tepua hesitated. "One, noble chiefess. Two, if you count the beginning of last night's show."

Aitofa threw back her head and laughed. "One! By Oro's navel, you are more reckless than I had thought. What are your reasons for seeking to join the Arioi?"

"The god possessed me last night. Is that not enough?"

"The god has his will, but we of flesh have ours. Sometimes the two conflict, and a person who enters the society regrets it later."

Tepua had thought she might be asked such a question. She had resolved to be frank about her hopes, but tell no more than Matopahu knew about her past. "I came from a good family on my island," she said. "But my ancestry means nothing to people here. With the Arioi, perhaps I can regain something of what I have lost. . . . And protection from my enemies, should they ever seek to find me."

Aitofa nodded. "I give you credit for thinking about your decision. But perhaps you have not considered everything."

"I thought I knew—" Tepua began.

"By the scared navel, they all think they know," said Aitofa in another burst of laughter. "You intrigue me, though, *motu* daughter. It is fortunate that you do, or else I would have given in to Head-lifted and thrown you out on your pretty little bottom." She held up one warning finger as Tepua opened her mouth to protest. "Now listen, and answer the questions that I put to you."

Tepua stiffened her spine, eyeing Aitofa warily. Amid the mixture of spice and generosity in the lodge leader, she sensed a tinge of ruthlessness that had probably served to propel her to this high position.

"There is one rule," said Aitofa, "that we enforce without exception. Though every initiate knows it, some women refuse to believe it until the truth falls upon them. Do you know which one I mean?"

"About—children?"

"We Arioi women have none."

"Yes."

"And not because we give up men. No. That would be too harsh a price for membership. But tell me this. What happens if a noblewoman of your island conceives the child of a commoner?"

Tepua answered without hesitation. "The child is done away with. Before it can draw breath. The family will not let it live."

"Then I need not explain to you how we Arioi remain childless."

Tepua swallowed. "You need not. Even so, I feel sorry for a woman who grows a child and then must destroy it. How much better if the child did not start at all. I thought the Arioi had ways—"

"One can make prayers to spirits, of course. And the sorcerers offer a few remedies, but none are certain. There are also ways of pleasure that do not require a man to spill his seed within you."

"Will I be taught these things?"

"You will."

"Then I will not conceive a child."

Aitofa looked away, her eyes becoming distant. "How clear this one is, shimmering like the mother-of-pearl of her island." Tepua heard her whisper.

"Is that all you wish to tell me?"

"That is only the first part," said Aitofa. "If you join us, you will start as a chest-slapper. Discard any notions of performing before a crowd as you did last night."

"I thought I had the talent—"

"Perhaps you do, but you first need the discipline and the knowledge to use it. Remember that we perform as a group. Each dancer is but one leaf on the tree. Is that clear?"

"Yes."

"Finally, let me remind you that a novice must serve in the household of a high-ranking Arioi. And we do not believe in assigning only light tasks. The character of a young woman is improved, we think, by husking coconuts, digging in the garden, carrying firewood."

"I was a servant in the household of Pigs-run-out,"
Tepua answered firmly.

"Good. If you join us, you may look back fondly on that
time. I ask you to think carefully about this. Head-lifted has
convinced me to go slowly in your case. I urge you to speak
to the novices you see around my house. Then come back
and tell me your decision."

"And if it is yes, will you accept me?"

"I have prayed for guidance. Let us hope the gods lead us
both in the same direction." Aitofa dismissed her with a
curt gesture.

Tepua, her head swimming, went out into the courtyard.
Part of her rebelled against Aitofa's imperious manner, the
chilly voice, the tattooed fingers crooked at her as if she
were a child. Yet how could she give up this chance? Oro
had called her! She already knew how she would choose.

She found Rimapoa near his canoe, on the shore beside
the fisherman's communal house. Behind him, water lapped
quietly at the black sand beach. "I watched you dance," he
said moodily as he repaired his lines. "I offered a fine pair
of albacore at the fisherman's *marae,* hoping that the god
would turn you away. Instead—"

"My acceptance is not certain yet," Tepua said softly,
wishing she could find some way to ease his pain.

"It will be." He turned from his work to study her face.
"I hear a new note in your voice, and I see how your eyes
shine."

Tepua sighed. "Yes. I believe the Arioi will take me in.
It is *your* problem that worries me now. When your month
here is over—"

"Ah, but the spirits did hear my plea. Though they would
not keep you from the Arioi, they granted me another
favor." He gazed at her with a satisfied expression.

"Must I guess?" she asked cautiously. How volatile he
could be, swinging from sullen anger to joy with the
swiftness of a child.

"No. Listen. Recently a local fisherman fell from a big
fishing canoe and drowned. This morning the other men

asked me to take his place in the boat until his son returns to claim it. I will be able to stay beyond the time that the high chief gave me.''

"Then I am glad," she said, taking his hand, seeking the familiar warmth. "You will be safe here. And I know you would like to fish from a *tira* again."

"And you may change your mind about the Arioi," he said. "After you stay with them a time, and learn how they treat you." He offered her his other hand and gave a gentle squeeze. "So you see, I have not given up my hopes."

"I do see," she answered with a laugh. *And I will prove you wrong.* But now, watching his roguish grin, she could not be angry at his persistence.

Two days later, under the high roof of the Arioi performance house, the women of the lodge assembled in rows. Tepua, standing alone before them, could see by their tattoos that these Arioi ranked from novice all the way up to grades just below blackleg. Aitofa, the only blackleg in the lodge, stood at the front of the group.

Tepua scanned their faces, some beautiful, some plain, some young, some approaching middle age. She had asked these women about their lives, as Aitofa suggested, but she knew her questions had been far too few. Now Aitofa stared intently at her. Her eyes spoke to Tepua, saying that if she wished to change her mind, she might still do it now. No. Tepua met the blackleg's gaze. She would not retreat.

"Here is our candidate," Aitofa said, turning to the women beside her. "And here is what she must pledge." She glanced again at Tepua before starting the ritual questions.

The candidate drew in her breath. Just a few words now, and all would be changed for her. Her skin prickled as she realized that she was entering a world she knew far too little about. She had been a chief's daughter and a servant, and now she would be less than a servant. Yet through talent and hard work she might become so much more. . . .

"Our new novice must obey her leaders without question

or hesitation,'' boomed Aitofa's voice. ''That is the first pledge. Does she agree?''

Tepua struggled to answer. ''I do,'' she said in a breathy whisper. When Aitofa scowled and cupped her hand behind her ear, Tepua repeated herself in a firmer voice. ''I will obey.''

''And she must dedicate herself to studying the history, chants, songs, and dances of our order.''

''I will.''

''She must uphold the ideals of the society by embracing youthfulness in all its aspects. She must strive for physical perfection and grace of movement.''

''I will.''

''She must never show cowardice, or refuse to fight. We Arioi women learn the skills of war and serve alongside the men if war should come to our district.''

''Yes,'' Tepua said, remembering her skills with bow and spear. She had exercised for sport at home, but she knew she could learn to fight.

''And last, she must swear to remain childless, so long as she is one of us.''

Tepua straightened her shoulders. This was the most difficult answer, and yet she was prepared to make it. ''I agree.''

Then Aitofa raised her hand, and gave the ritual words that Tepua knew must come. ''*Manau, manau, haere mai!* You are one of us, come here.''

Tepua stepped forward, her chin lifted, her pulse quickening. A sharp tap, almost a blow, fell upon her shoulder.

''Then welcome, blessed of Oro,'' chanted Aitofa. ''I invest you with the *maro pipi,* the girdle of the pea vine.'' Another woman, heavily tattooed with scroll designs from shoulders to hands, brought the novice's girdle to the blackleg. The ritual sash had been woven from fresh vines, dark pods showing amid the bright green leaves.

Tepua lifted her arms as Aitofa bound the sash around her waist. The other women broke into a chorus of songs and clapping, welcoming the new novice among them.

''It is done. Oro is pleased,'' Aitofa concluded. ''And

now we feast in honor of our new novice.'' The women filed out to the clearing beside the performance house, where places had been set—broad plantain leaves spaced neatly on the ground.

Tepua had not expected this. She glanced at the nearby sheltered cooking pit and saw servants already parceling out steamed plantains and yams, baked fowl and taro greens. She stepped closer and saw a huge fish, an albacore, that had just been unwrapped from its covering of fragrant leaves.

The new novice gazed at the bounty with astonishment. This morning, Curling-leaf had led her on a long walk through the hills, to gather flowers for the ceremony. All the preparations must have been done while they were away. But at whose expense?

Evidently noticing Tepua's confusion, Aitofa came to her. ''Usually the relatives of a candidate provide all her feasts,'' she explained. ''Since the first is a small one, and you have no kin here, I made the arrangements this one time.''

''Your kindness . . . honors me,'' Tepua answered, feeling awkward. Here was a gift she could not possibly repay.

''You will have ample opportunity to show your appreciation,'' said Aitofa sweetly. ''I have decided that your service will be in *my* household.''

Tepua tried to cover her surprise. ''I will be pleased to serve you,'' she said, hoping her words sounded humble. After all the chiefess had done for her, Tepua knew she should be glad of this chance to give something in return. Why then did she find the prospect so dismaying? ''This is a fine feast,'' Tepua added. ''I cannot imagine one better. Look at the albacore!''

''That part I did not provide,'' said the chiefess. ''A fisherman left it with one of the servants. He ran off without giving his name.''

Rimapoa!

Later, as she sat at her place, Tepua nodded with pleasure when a servant brought her portion of the repast. According to custom, women did not eat albacore. Yet Arioi women were different. At their feast, nothing was denied them.

But what did this offering from Rimapoa mean? He had not admitted defeat, but was still courting her. The gift of albacore proved that. He had not accepted her decision at all. . . .

Tepua took up her new life and found it as exacting as Aitofa had warned. The season for Arioi performances had ended, but this did not lighten the burden on the novices. Part of each day she spent training, practicing dance or mime or spear exercises as she was ordered. The chiefess had told her that she must stay close to the house and have nothing to do with men until she mastered the main body of chants. Exhausted after every day's work, Tepua found this restriction no burden.

Her mornings were always devoted to labor, usually grating coconut for use in making *monoi,* scented oil. Tepua sat on what the novices called a "grating pig," a short log that had a long piece of coral sticking out at one end. Pressing the white meat of a halved coconut against the coral, she gave a rotary motion to the shell, letting the shavings fall to a plantain leaf below.

The coconuts were well aged, the nut meat tough. The work went slowly, tiring her wrists, arms, and fingers until they felt numb. One day Curling-leaf sat beside her, waving flies away, occasionally dumping the shavings into a trough when the pile grew high.

"You are slowing down, and we have scarcely begun," said Curling-leaf as she handed Tepua another open nut to replace the one she had finished. The odor of rancid coconut milk made Tepua's stomach queasy. The buzzing of flies grew louder.

"Let's start on the creation chant again," said Curling-leaf. "Remember what Aitofa told you."

That I am a prisoner here until I learn all the basic chants. The long names of characters and places seemed to slip from her mind as if they were covered with grease.

"Oro dwelt with many gods in the sky's vault," Tepua

began. "Over them he ruled as high chief. He had his wife, Ax-with-eyes—"

"The wife's name was Stand-to-unfold-the-sky," interrupted Curling-leaf. "Ax-with-eyes was a daughter's name."

All right, go on, Tepua told herself. "He had his daughters, Ax-with-eyes, Eater-of-the-summit, and a son, Sworn-friend. Ooops, forgot the other daughter, Fog-of-many-owners." Tepua stopped to wipe sweat from her brow, then pushed the coconut down onto the grater again.

"One day, in a fit of anger, Oro pushed his wife out of the sky. Probably because he couldn't remember her name," Tepua added, and Curling-leaf giggled. "Oro missed his wife and grew lonely. His sisters, Darkness and Grossness, went to earth to find him another. Clad in *ti* leaves, they came to Tahiti.

"The people brought their finest women, but the god found none to suit him. So the sisters went on, until they reached Porapora. They found a great beauty named Water-of-man-of-war-birds, who lived in a place called Water-of-red-fig." She stopped to flick away a bug that was climbing the heap of shavings. "Or was that the other way around?" The two women began to laugh.

"Why must your legends be so long-winded?" Tepua asked. "I have had enough chanting for now."

"I know," said Curling-leaf. "We all feel discouraged at the start. But listen to me finish. It won't hurt to hear it through."

Then Curling-leaf continued the long story of Oro and his women and his gifts, finally telling of the great chief Tamatoa who had founded the Arioi society.

"You did that well," said Tepua, when she was done. *Your dancing is also good, and you are the best of us when it comes to handling a spear.* But Tepua did not say the rest aloud. She knew that her friend had long been ready to advance to Pointed-thorn. Only her inability to provide a feast stood in Curling-leaf's way.

A month passed while Tepua remained busy at Aitofa's compound. During this time Rimapoa often came to watch her as she labored in the yard, and to talk with her from afar. He was surprisingly cheerful, and seemingly unruffled by Aitofa's rules. Now he had gone away with the large canoe to fish near other islands, and would not be back for many days. She was surprised at how much she missed his visits.

Her head felt filled to bursting with the words of the legends. At night the chants continued in her dreams, droning on and on, allowing her no sleep. If only she could have an occasional day of freedom, she thought, the rest might be bearable.

Unexpectedly, one morning, her routine was interrupted. Aitofa summoned Tepua to meet her, not in her large house, but in a modest guest house in a secluded corner of the compound. When Tepua entered the room and saw who was seated on a four-legged stool beside the chiefess, she was so stunned that she almost ran back outside. *Matopahu!* She glared at him while a knot formed at her throat.

"The high chief's brother has asked for a word with you," Aitofa said coolly. "He has an interest in your career with us. I am sure you know the value of such an ally."

Tepua's cheeks grew warm as she remembered what Curling-leaf had said about the importance of having an admirer. But why, of all men, must it be Matopahu? As she recalled how Pigs-run-out had offered her to him, she felt a muscle jump in her jaw. Tepua needed no patron now. Advancement to Pointed-thorn was far off, might never come.

"I will leave you two to discuss this in private," said the chiefess.

Tepua took a breath, her thoughts so tangled that she could not speak. Her hands clenched and unclenched as she studied Matopahu, who sat with his elbows on his knees and his hands dangling between his thighs. He wore a simple cape thrown back over his shoulders. The broad, bare expanse of his chest gleamed with scented oil. *Such beauty . . . But I will not be another fancy feather for your turban.*

His face was almost as she remembered it—half-mocking eyes above wide flat cheekbones, crisp black curls about his forehead. But her vision was now adjusting to the light that diffused between the loose weave of the guest house wall. She saw unfamiliar lines about his mouth and at the corners of his eyes. His proud spirit seemed to have taken a beating, for he looked weary and downcast.

Yes, something had changed, but she could not say what.

He broke the silence. "You stand so still and stiff, as if your spine were made of ironwood."

"I want nothing from you," she whispered fiercely. "I need no patron. I wish you had not come."

"Do not judge me before I have spoken." His voice carried a rawness that told of hidden pain. "After you danced, I wanted to wish you success with the Arioi, but Aitofa asked me not to disturb her newest novice. Now that I am going away she permitted this meeting. I am being forced to leave the court for a time."

"Then I will not have to watch you laughing at me when I perform." The words came out with a spite that she instantly regretted. Matopahu stood up and caught her by the shoulders. Tepua thought he would shake or strike her, but he only held her, waiting until she looked into his eyes. The warmth of his hands kept her from pulling away.

"Tepua, I did not laugh," he said solemnly. "I cheered you on, I was glad to see that the god favored you."

She searched the rich brown of his eyes, finding an earnestness she wished to believe in. He was not mocking her. He truly rejoiced in her good fortune. She grew acutely aware of the closeness of his body. His sweet musky scent made her head start to spin.

I am not ready to lose myself. Not with this man. Though she trembled, she took his wrists and gently removed his hands from her shoulders. "Tell me the second reason you came."

"Because it may be my last chance to make amends for what happened at the underchief's house."

"Then you admit—"

"I admit only that I was stupid and smug and full of myself. Does that satisfy you?"

Grudgingly she accepted his partial apology. He was

right. His only transgression had been his arrogance, and she was hardly one to condemn that.

"Now you look less formidable," he said. "Perhaps you would even help me solve an irksome problem. People have given me too many gifts. I have no more room to hang rolls of *tapa* from the eaves of my house. And now that I must go away, what will become of my wealth? I fear it will vanish into the houses of my enemies."

"Give the *tapa* to your friends. They may have some use for it."

"That is exactly what I am doing. I would like to count you as such a friend. Aitofa has agreed to hold the cloth for you, and to trade it for the foodstuffs you will need when you advance to Pointed-thorn."

So he has already made the arrangements. Without even asking me. Her anger returned. Smiling scornfully, she said, "You are generous."

His expression brightened. "I am glad that you accept."

"I accept for my friend Curling-leaf," she said triumphantly, "who needs your help sooner than I do. The cloth will pay for *her* feast, and I will tell her of your kindness." Savoring his look of astonishment, she turned toward the doorway.

"Wait—" He started to come after her.

"Tell me, noble brother of the chief, why you have become so humble."

He leaned against the house pole and did not answer at once. "I have found that even an oracle can fall from favor," he said darkly. "Knotted-cord will not listen to my warning of the coming famine. The high priest refuses to accept my prophecy and even assures my brother that we will have plenty to eat. I wish I could believe he is right."

"And that is why you must leave the district?"

"That is one reason. In time, you may understand the rest."

Hearing this, Tepua could not help feeling a degree of sympathy for him. Now she understood why he seemed so troubled today. Without his feathers and his fancy capes, he no longer resembled the arrogant nobleman she had seen strutting with his peers. "I do not know much about oracles," she said. "I was told that a god speaks through your lips. But the high priest also has ways to commune with the gods."

"They deceive him or he deceives us, I cannot say which. I have warned Aitofa and my other friends. Those who trust me will prepare themselves for a harsh season. The breadfruit is almost gone, but we still have taro and yams. We must save what we can and hope that wild foods from the mountains will provide the rest."

"Then I will help gather and store food for Aitofa's household," she answered in a gentler tone. "Your warning is all I can accept from you. Let there be no gifts between us, no unspoken obligations."

He smiled sadly. "You have not lost any of your spirit. I leave it to you, then, to make your way among the Arioi however you can."

"So I will, noble brother of the chief." She was about to turn and leave, but instead found herself standing before him, not knowing why. She let him put his arms about her and draw her close. The warmth that she had sensed before enveloped her now, surrounding her with gentleness and strength.

When he pressed his nose to her cheek and inhaled softly, she felt a shiver that made her catch her breath. She could not stop herself from returning the embrace. Her fingertips glided up, over the smooth skin of his back. She leaned into him, wanting to feel her thighs and her belly against his. The tips of her breasts tingled as they brushed his chest.

This was the man as she had imagined him, in the moments before Pigs-run-out had exposed the truth. She had allowed herself to be deluded once. Now, here she stood, dusty and sweaty and covered with sticky bits of coconut . . . while Matopahu still pretended that she attracted him! In her embarrassment, she tried to back away from him.

"You have not told me the full truth about yourself," he said, holding her gently but refusing to let her free. "I think you are more than a *motu* noblewoman. Can it be that you are really a chief's daughter and a child of the gods?"

She closed her eyes, feeling the momentary excitement drain away. She had always been ready to believe that he desired her simply for herself. With a surge of anger, she squirmed free of him, racing out, her face hot and her tears brimming.

She tried to imagine how delighted Curling-leaf would be with her news of the gifts, but that only made the tears flow faster. *I am no longer a chief's daughter. If that is why he takes an interest in me, then he is worse than a fool.*

Rimapoa had almost lost track of how long he had been with the *tira*. Three new moons had passed, he thought, or perhaps four. Now, on a blustery afternoon, he sat with his companions on an unfamiliar beach as they waited for their food to cook.

His thoughts turned, as they often did, to Tepua. Secretly he had often watched her, muddied and perspiring, working Aitofa's garden plots. Despite the heavy labor, her determination to stay with the Arioi had shown no signs of wavering.

Rimapoa's own lot had not been easy either. The crew of the *tira* had long ago given up on albacore for the season, and had been reduced to makeshift methods of fishing. The men had rigged a sail, and traveled far from Tahiti in search of food. Today they had been fortunate, using small live fish to lure larger prey. Working together, they had subdued a large barracuda and dragged it into the boat.

Finally they had put in to this *motu* and shared their catch with the islanders. In return, the local people had brought heaps of clams, and pudding made from the fleshy inner part of the pandanus fruit. The islanders had also supplied coconut shells and husks for fueling the cookfire.

Now, as Rimapoa waited with the other men by the steaming pit oven, several young *motu* women provided entertainment. A crewman blew a piercing melody on his nose flute while the girls gaily swung their hips and fluttered their fingers. They lacked the skills of Arioi, Rimapoa saw, but their eagerness more than made up for that. The one in the center always seemed to be glancing at him. He could not help returning her smile.

Soon the music ended, and the dancers raced off, vanishing into a stand of narrow-leaved pandanus trees. But Rimapoa was certain the girls would be back later, after the men had eaten. These islanders had traditions of hospitality to their infrequent visitors that included keeping them warm during the night. Rimapoa began to feel aroused by this prospect, though he knew that no woman could make him forget Tepua. . . .

A call from the cook distracted him from his daydreams. Rimapoa turned to the pit oven, watching eagerly as the cook's assistants shoveled away its covering of leaves. The wind shifted, bringing aromas that made his mouth water. He and the others had eaten almost nothing for the last two days. Now, as soon as the food was passed out, they began to gorge.

"We are eating better than anyone back home," said Two-oars, the master of the *tira,* as he licked his stubby fingers.

"It is true," said another. "Last time we were there I saw people digging up *'ape* roots at the riverbanks."

Rimapoa scowled. He knew that *'ape,* whose broad leaves resembled those of taro, was eaten only in desperation. The starchy corms had to be baked for an entire day before they became edible.

He recalled his last visit to Tepua, and wondered if she, too, was beginning to feel the pinch. The Arioi must be better off than most people, he thought, yet in time they would also find their stores running low.

He worried less about Hoihoi. She had her own taro patch, as well as a huge storage pit for *mahi.* And she carried an ample reserve of flesh about her.

Every year had its season of scarcity; this one was just more severe than usual and was affecting almost every type of food. Surely the gods had turned away from the people, but no one could say why.

"I heard," said a crewman, "that the high priest at home is starting to worry. He is going to have another ceremony. Some say he plans to call for a 'two-legged fish.'"

The other men laughed nervously, and Rimapoa felt a

cold sweat on his back at the mention of a human offering. He was an outsider and his remaining time in Knotted-cord's district was almost gone. He had no family, no influential people to help him.

"A man can protect himself from that fate," said Two-oars, after devouring another piece of fish. "All he needs is a passionate woman—one with long fingernails."

"What sort of woman can let her nails grow?" growled the crewman beside him. "Only a highborn daughter, who sits in her house all day while servants do her work."

"Has anyone taken a good look at these island girls?" asked Two-oars.

"Not at their fingernails!" his companion answered.

"Well, a man can sometimes be lucky. Even if priests treat him as less than a man ever afterward." Two-oars turned and barked an order to his cook. "Bring me the rest of those clams!"

Rimapoa sat in the darkness, finishing his food, wishing he could stop thinking about women. It was no longer just *hanihani* that he longed for. A woman's touch could make a sacred thing profane. A woman could make a man no longer fit for the gods!

Another month passed. The trolling canoe returned to Tahiti several times and then went out again. On an overcast morning, as the boat's crew sailed home, Rimapoa learned that his time with the *tira* had finally ended. Two-oars informed him that the place he had occupied was about to be reclaimed.

The boat had been out only one night this time. Now it was bringing in several baskets filled with reef fish that the men had speared by torchlight. As the crew brought the *tira* to shore and used logs to roll it into a shed, raindrops began falling lightly. Two-oars parceled out the catch, leaving some behind for the afternoon meal, sending the rest home to the families of his crew.

Under the usual arrangement, the patrons of these fish-ermen supplied them with vegetable food at all seasons in return for fish whenever it was available. Now the patrons were finding they could not provide all that the crewmen needed.

Rimapoa, however, accepted a *tiputa,* a rain-cape woven of pandanus leaves, in place of part of his share. Despite the downpour, he went out looking for Tepua. The *tiputa* hung down in front and back, keeping his body dry as he headed inland.

He did not let the news from Two-oars discourage him. He had known it would come and had prepared himself. Now he had a new offer to make to Tepua. This one he thought she might accept.

As he walked he heard infants wailing inside the houses. He remembered life as a child during the scarce season, how he had hungered for breadfruit when there was nothing but grated taro root. Soon, he feared, the children would be glad to have even the poorest of substitutes.

He noticed a mud-smeared group of men coming down from the hills carrying bunches of wild green plantains, *fe'i,* hanging from poles laid across their shoulders. To gather *fe'i* was strenuous and dangerous work, he knew. The shortage was getting worse.

As he came to the side of the female blackleg's compound, the rain shower stopped. The air was heavy, rich with smells of damp vegetation. He looked over at Tepua's usual place in the yard, but did not see her. The dark pile of emptied shells made him wonder how many hundreds of coconuts she had grated since joining the Arioi. What an occupation for a woman of her birth! But now, he suspected, that task was finished for a time. He saw no husked coconuts waiting.

From under a nearby thatched roof he heard the droning of several voices in a chant.

"So it was arranged for the beautiful maiden to become Oro's wife. The god descended to earth as a rainbow in order to see her for himself. He was greatly pleased and agreed to the marriage. But when the day arrived, Oro had no earthly possessions, no gifts to bring to the feast. . . ."

Rimapoa listened awhile, pleased that he could pick out Tepua's voice from the others. At last, the instructor uttered a few words of praise for the novices and sent them to their other tasks.

When he saw Tepua emerge from the house, he had to tighten his fist to keep from crying out in joy. But what had happened to her proud spirit? Her shoulders were slumping and she kept her eyes on the damp ground.

Instead of going to her "grating pig," she turned, with her two companions, toward the compound gate. "Tepua," he whispered, but she was too far away to hear him.

Rimapoa hurried along the fence. Perhaps she was going out to work in the vegetable gardens. He hid near the path, behind the stout trunk of an ironwood tree, and picked up a stick from the ground.

Tepua walked last in the procession of young women. Rimapoa hissed and tossed his stick, dropping it neatly in her path. When she turned and saw him, her downcast expression brightened instantly.

She rushed up to greet him, pressing herself warmly into his arms. Her touch so filled him with delight that he could not speak at once. Deeply he inhaled the fragrance of her hair. She could make him forget everything, he realized, even his greatest fear. If she became his wife, he would never again worry about priests and their dark stone temples.

"I have learned the chants—all but one," she whispered happily. "And that one is short! Even Aitofa is impressed."

"Then will she let you out of your cage?" He had noticed how quiet the compound seemed today.

Tepua turned, glancing behind her, but no one was there to overhear. "Aitofa let some novices go back to their families," she answered in a rush. "Until next season begins there is little to do here, and she is having trouble feeding us all. If I could get away, where would I go?"

"I know a place," he answered with a smile. "I've been told of an atoll you would like very much. Its lagoon is full of fish, and nobody lives there!"

"Atoll!" She drew in her breath, her eyes opening wide.

"I would be happy to take you there." He stood beaming, waiting for her to answer.

"But what about your work in the *tira*?"

"That has ended," he answered, his feeling of excitement fading. "The drowned fisherman's son has come to take his father's place."

"But—the high chief will send you away—"

"Do not worry, *tiare*. I have a plan. That is why I must go to this coral island. I intend to gather a gift for Knotted-cord that will keep him from sending me away. And if you help, you will solve a problem of your own. But I cannot explain now. Tell me first if you will go."

"I must ask Aitofa," she answered uncertainly.

"Then ask her soon, *tiare*, but keep our destination secret. Do not tell anyone what we are planning."

13

On a bright morning three days later, Tepua hastened out of Aitofa's compound and onto the path toward the fishermen's house. She could scarcely believe that Aitofa had finally let her go, but Tepua had recited her last chant perfectly, and had demonstrated her growing skills in mime as well.

Tepua had said she was going to visit distant kin, and Aitofa had not questioned her, smiling knowingly as she gave her assent. *Would she have agreed so readily if she knew I was meeting a fisherman?* Tepua wondered. Aitofa always insisted that her novices choose their men from the upper classes. It would be best if she never learned about Rimapoa.

As Tepua hurried along the path, the fresh breeze cooling her face, she recalled what he had told her about his atoll. "The rarest birds are plentiful there. We can collect feathers as easily as a child collects shells. Do you know that a tail feather from the man-of-war bird, just one feather, can be traded for a whole pig?"

Tepua knew how feathers were valued for ornaments. The scarce red-and-yellow ones had a special importance because they were used when calling on the gods. Rimapoa thought he could gain favor with the high chief through a gift of rare feathers. He had suggested that she help him collect them, and use her share to provide for her feast when she advanced to Pointed-thorn.

His idea, at first, had attracted her. With resources of her own, she could avoid accepting a patron. But surely, she told herself, Rimapoa was not the only one who knew about that atoll. If brightly colored birds were so plentiful there, why did no one else gather the feathers?

She had mulled over his plan, finally deciding that it was a ruse. He was using his mysterious destination as a lure. All he really wanted was a way to be alone with her. Yet she had agreed to sail with him!

She knew what was going to happen. They would be together for days, traveling from one island to the next. At night, when they lay near each other on a quiet beach, he would draw her close to him. . . .

This prospect no longer daunted her. When she first joined Aitofa's household, she always turned her back when other women spoke of their lovers. Gradually, after so many months of sleeping alone, she had come to envy them.

It did not matter to her that the others took noblemen. Her chance to have a chief for a *tane* was gone. Rimapoa was the one man who deserved her affections, the only man she was willing to trust. Soon he was going away. He had waited for her so long, always kind and patient, and now she felt ready for him.

As she neared the beach the sight of the shimmering lagoon made her laugh aloud with pleasure. During her months of study she had not once been permitted to take this short walk from the compound. She had almost forgotten the beauty of the water here, its clear, azure color and distant whitecaps.

She found Rimapoa preparing the canoe, his supplies of food, water, and fishing gear already aboard. On the islands along the way, he had promised, they could find whatever else they needed. Looking as joyful as if he had just landed the choicest albacore in the sea, he launched the boat, then carried her through the surf and gently lowered her in.

The names of the islands, as he recited them, made a chant she liked better than any she had learned from the Arioi: Eimeo, Huahine, Porapora, Maupiti. She turned toward Eimeo, the only one close enough to be seen, its green slopes and rugged spires a startling sight on the horizon. That was their first destination, where they would spend the night.

Little whitecaps, topped with glistening foam, lapped against the outrigger's sides. Rimapoa's mat sail filled and the canoe's bow swung seaward, heading toward the pass through the reef. Soon they cleared the breakers.

The wind freshened, blowing gently from the southeast, and Rimapoa let the canoe run before it. The outrigger rose and fell in the rolling waves. Tepua sat in the stern, watching Rimapoa.

He looked bronzed and spare, wearing only a sunshade woven of coconut fronds, and the usual fishermen's *maro* about his loins. As he countered the pull of the wind in the sail with the steering oar, she watched the muscles bunch in his arms and chest. Droplets of water sparkled on his skin and the sun revealed flecks of gold in eyes that had always seemed so dark.

He looked happy in a way that she had never seen before, the worry lines gone from his face, his manner no longer guarded. She realized that she had never been with him on the open sea.

He was like the gulls that dipped about the mast's feather pennant, she thought, or the rainbow-colored *mahimahi* playing in the outrigger's wake. He was a creature of the sea. When one took the shimmering *mahimahi* out of the ocean, it lost its colors and became just another fish. Could such a thing be true of a man? Perhaps it was true of Rimapoa—that the colors of his spirit faded on land and renewed themselves at sea.

As the boat moved farther from Tahiti and out of the island's wind shadow, Tepua felt the breeze stiffen. Rimapoa pulled in the sail, and the canoe heeled as it gathered speed. The lean became more severe, driving the outrigger float beneath the surface, and he climbed out on the balance board to counterweight the wind's force against the sail.

Tepua noticed with alarm that water was racing past less than a handspan below the splashboard. "What are you doing?" she called with dismay.

He laughed, looking like a brown sea spider with his knees and elbows sticking out as he crouched at the end of the balance board. "I get my best speed this way," he called back.

"But we are in no hurry!" Ahead, Eimeo's green peaks already seemed near.

As if in defiance, he hauled the sail closer and the canoe tilted even further, its splashboard kissing the waves as Tepua tried to scramble up the slanting bottom.

"We will go nowhere if we capsize!" she shouted above the roar of water past the hull.

Rimapoa threw back his head and laughed, his teeth flashing in the sun. "I thought you had sailed before," he answered good-naturedly.

"I have!" Tepua grabbed for a handhold and tried to haul herself up. She slipped, skidded down into the bilges. "Rimapoa, if you do not stop this, we will go over!"

"Everything is lashed in, *tiare*," he sang back. "Nothing will be lost. I am not such a fool to think that we cannot be swamped. Why not come out here with me? You will be more comfortable, and the canoe won't heel so badly."

In response, she climbed up on the high side and perched there, peering uncertainly at the water rushing by below. "Come up, *tiare*," he coaxed. "It is not as terrifying as it looks."

If she refused, she thought he might swamp the boat just to spite her. With a sigh, she began to climb out on the narrow balance board, clutching the bamboo poles that ran along each side as tightly as she could, and trying not to look at the boiling wake below. The board seemed to sway, and she froze, breathing hard.

"Now turn yourself around," he said, "and sit with your back to me."

She peered up at him while spray dashed against her arms and face. "I think you are enjoying this," she answered.

"I am," he agreed, eyes sparkling. "Better turn around before you get washed away."

The worst part was switching hands, since both wanted to retain their panicked grip on the bamboo poles. But despite the canoe's porpoising and the sheets of spray that drenched her, she managed to plant her rump on the board.

Rimapoa grasped her arm, pulling her backward so that

she sat between his legs. "Lean against me. That way. Now we will see how fast our bird can fly!"

With their combined weight on the balance board, the canoe lessened its heel and the submerged outrigger float surfaced. Freed from the drag, the canoe bounded ahead. The water below became blurred streaks of white and blue. Rimapoa put his arm around her. He was wet and sticky with salt, but his skin was warm and the muscles beneath felt strong.

Gradually, Tepua's fear gave way to excitement, then exhilaration. Over the stern she saw the great emerald mass of Tahiti, its shores fringed by a curving line of breakers. Over the bow lay the oncoming new island, a wondrous panorama of mountain and shadow. From its heights fell silver ribbons of waterfalls that flashed in the sunlight.

A surge of joy made her tip her head back and laugh as Rimapoa had done. This was not frightening! This was wonderful! Never had she skimmed across the sea in a craft as light and swift as Rimapoa's. At any instant, she thought the canoe might leave the ocean and take flight into the sky.

And Rimapoa was master of this boat. Suddenly she felt a new respect for him. Out here, a man's ancestry counted for nothing. What mattered was knowledge, skill, and strength.

The wind blew harder and spray soaked her wrap. But the chill did not bother her, pressed as she was against his warm body, with his thighs straddling her hips. Beneath the rough cloth of his *maro,* she felt something swelling.

"Now there are three of us." He laughed as his erection grew harder.

"Keep your attention on the boat!" she answered.

Late that night, she woke and felt the warmth of Rimapoa close beside her. Under moonlight she saw that his smile of contentment still lingered. "Pearl woman, you are wonderful," she remembered him exclaiming. "Now you are indeed a woman. *My* woman."

She had felt too lazy and comfortable then to dispute his claim. Even now, when her glow of pleasure had faded, she was willing to admit he might be right. He had found her on the beach—a wreck tossed up by the sea. He had taken her in and cared for her. Why shouldn't she be his?

Only one reason. The Arioi.

She frowned, recalling all that he had told her. When they came back to Tahiti, the fisherman would have to find a new home. After this journey, she and Rimapoa would be forced to part. She looked up at the palm trees that leaned out over the beach and tried to count how many days and nights they would have together. Not many. She must savor every one. For a long time she did not sleep.

Huahine, Porapora. The days and islands passed quickly. One morning, before dawn, the two left Maupiti behind them, heading due west toward their final destination.

"There is a small *motu* along the way," he told her. "Not a comfortable place, but we can stop there."

Tepua sensed that he wanted more of a challenge than easy hopping from one island to another. "I have paddled by night," she reminded him, though she did not wish to remember her ordeal.

"You would not complain of the wet and cold?"

"No!"

"Good. Then we run straight for Fenua Ura."

The sky had not yet brightened. Over the bow, she saw a few stars setting. She stared at them, trying to fix the cluster in her mind. If the journey continued all day and into the next night, she might have to steer while he slept.

Later that morning, as they sped across open water, she joined Rimapoa on the balance board. They made good speed, gliding over the swells, racing the dolphins. Sometimes they glimpsed flying fish leaping across the waves.

Sitting on the balance board, with her back against Rimapoa's warm chest, she recalled the excitement of their crossing to Eimeo. That first night away, and every night since then, she had embraced him willingly, even eagerly. She had begun to feel that no other life could please her as much as this.

Her resolve had not weakened. She would not give up the

Arioi, and he knew that. But part of her would always be here, sailing between the islands with Rimapoa.

Late in the afternoon, Tepua curled up for a nap in the bottom of the outrigger canoe. She woke in darkness and glanced up at the star-jeweled sky. Rimapoa sat at the steering oar, seemingly content with his course. The star patterns did not look right to her. She shook the muzziness of sleep from her mind. No. She should not question his navigation. After all, he had taken them this far without mishap.

She gave him an affectionate embrace, then relieved him at the steering oar so that he could eat and drink. Suddenly she remembered something he had mentioned before they set out.

"We should be past the little *motu* by now," she said. "The one you told me about. Did you see it?"

"No. I thought my course would bring us close." He shrugged. "It is hard to see a low island." He was trying to sound as though it didn't matter, but a certain tension in his voice betrayed his uncertainty.

Her sense that the canoe was off course grew stronger. She scanned the sky, remembering the patterns she had studied as they left Maupiti. The trio of stars that had been setting then had not yet come full circle, and she found them higher up the sky. Rimapoa's course was off. If they continued in this direction, they would miss Fenua Ura, the red-feather island, and be carried beyond into the unknown western sea.

She opened her mouth to speak, then hesitated. After seeing Rimapoa manage the craft so well, she was reluctant to doubt his steering. But she knew that he normally stayed within sight of a high island's peaks. She had even heard Hoihoi disparage his knowledge of way-finding by the stars.

She tightened her hand on the steering oar. If she questioned Rimapoa's course, he might be annoyed, but better that than being lost.

"I know where we are, *tiare*," he said indulgently when she told him her concern. "You are right, we have gone a little south, but soon I will make my correction."

The wind hissed against the sail, and phosphorescent waves rushed by the hull. Rimapoa kept casting anxious looks at the bowl of sky overhead. Did he really know where he was going? she asked herself. He had never before sailed these waters.

The night wore on as the canoe climbed the swells and slid down into the troughs. Tepua became stiff and cold, both with weariness and fear.

He has chosen the wrong star and I know the right one, she thought furiously. *Why do I not insist?* "Perhaps we should stop," she suggested.

He laughed, but it sounded forced. "Once you are on the ocean, there is no stopping, *tiare*. Even if I cast out a sea anchor, we will drift, and then we will have no idea where we are. It is better to sail on."

"By the wrong guide star?" She took a breath. "Rimapoa, we are lost and you will not admit it."

He argued, first gently, then more heatedly. As patient a man as he was on land, at sea he obviously resented having his judgment questioned by a woman.

"You may have sailed between atolls on your father's canoes," he said angrily, "but that does not make you a master of the sea. I have spent my entire life on the ocean."

"But not in these waters," she retorted. "Throw away your seafarer's pride—or it will get us drowned."

He fell silent, and for a time she heard only the wind and the slap of waves against the canoe. Tepua felt the steering oar in her hand. One push would swing the bow over to her star. As if he could read her thoughts, he came to the stern and took the oar from her. She resisted briefly, then stopped when her struggling threatened to capsize the canoe.

Rimapoa's voice was low and fierce in her ear. "You try that, woman, and I will tie you up with sennit and stow you with the coconuts!"

"I would rather jump out and swim to Fenua Ura. At least then I might get there."

"Tell me why you are so certain." His voice showed no softening, but his grip on her wrist eased.

She pointed to the cluster that was now heading down

toward its pit beneath the horizon, and explained how she had sighted the same stars at dawn.

"I do not recognize that cluster of yours," he said. After a few moments of study, he added, "And now I see why. There is a wanderer in with the other two."

"Yet those stars move down like any others. And I know that wanderers follow the sun's track."

He hung his head and gave a deep sigh. "Ay," he said in a low voice. "They do." Then he moved the oar, her hand under his, so that it seemed as if he had made the choice.

By dawn they had spotted no sign of land. Dolefully Rimapoa stared out at the empty horizon. Tepua bit her lip. Perhaps her direction change had come too late. Perhaps she had even made things worse.

Rimapoa sighed. "It is never easy to find a low island that is far from others. That is one reason few people ever reach Fenua Ura."

Tepua stared into the bilges of the canoe. She knew the terrors of being lost on the ocean. She gripped the outrigger's splashboard tightly, painfully, as the memories returned. "Then we have to turn back, and sail toward the dawn," she said mournfully.

She felt Rimapoa's hand on her shoulder and looked up into his troubled face. "No, *tiare,*" he said. "If we are lost now, we have little hope of finding Maupiti on the way back. We may even miss Porapora."

"It is better to try—"

"Yes. We must try something, but I am not giving up yet. If I fail now, there is nothing for me back in Tahiti. We must find our bird island, using every skill we have." His voice took a humbler tone. "Your people are always sailing between atolls. If there is anything you learned from your canoe masters, I will listen."

Tepua tried to remember. Once she had met a young navigator who was studying his father's art. She had chatted with him a long time, always under Bone-needle's watchful gaze. "I have heard that clouds over an atoll sometimes reflect the color of the lagoon," Tepua said. "You may also see palm leaves and bits of bark adrift on the waves."

Rimapoa, in turn, told her to watch the flight of any birds that might pass; some might be heading for land. The height and direction of waves offered other clues, he said, but those were more difficult to follow.

Tepua searched the sky until her eyes ached from glare. She saw nothing of interest, except perhaps a patch of low cloud that seemed faintly tinged with aquamarine. When Rimapoa thought he also saw a patch of color, he brought the outrigger about. To rest her eyes, Tepua gazed down at the dark water.

Soon she noticed Rimapoa also staring down, leaning out of the canoe, studying ripples in the calm morning sea. She watched his eyes widen, his brows rise. He muttered something.

"What is it?" she asked.

"I think we may be downwind of land," he said. "Look how the water is so calm here. An island we cannot see must be breaking the force of the waves." He leaned so far over the canoe's side that Tepua grabbed the back of his loincloth for fear he would tumble in. "Two sets of wave crests are crossing each other. I have only noticed that in the lee of an island."

"So perhaps my steering saved us after all," Tepua lifted her chin.

"We will know soon," Rimapoa answered, his voice rising with hope. He took the steering oar again and asked her to handle the sail. Soon they were beating upwind into a light breeze. Tepua spotted a raft of debris in the water. It was a soggy tangle of rotting leaves and wood, but its presence meant that land might be near.

Then she caught sight of a distant line of breakers, plumes of white water shooting up as the sea crashed against a hidden reef. A flock of birds wheeled overhead. And finally she caught a glimpse of palm trees, crowns just visible on the horizon. A coral island!

She watched intently as another small *motu* came into view, land jutting darkly just above the sea. The brilliant blue of a lagoon shimmered through the opening between the two islands. She almost felt that she was coming home.

"Fenua Ura!" the fisherman shouted. "It has to be. It fits every description I've heard." He put his arm around her. "Together, we found it." She hugged him, her doubts almost forgotten. As they drew closer to shore she saw beneath the trees flashes of wings, many brightly colored.

Rimapoa would get plenty of feathers here, she thought. He could take as many as he wanted. Whether they would help him end his troubles with the high chief, she did not know.

14

As the canoe rocked gently beneath him Rimapoa caught whiffs of heated air, heavy with smells of atoll vegetation. The low shore remained at a distance while he studied the obstacle ahead—the outer reef flat that sometimes broke the water's surface, then slipped below when swells lifted the boat.

An old man Rimapoa had met while traveling with the *tira* had told him about Fenua Ura in trade for a fine fishhook. Now Rimapoa wondered who had gotten the best of that bargain. Unbroken reef surrounded most of the atoll, which contained four islets spaced around the lagoon. To reach the calm waters within he would have to negotiate a hazardous channel.

He watched huge breakers churning in the distance and imagined the sea boiling through a narrow opening in the reef, carrying the boat before it like a piece of chaff. Then he turned to Tepua and pointed past the end of the nearest islet. "The pass is over there, but too dangerous. Another reason people do not come here."

"Then what will we do?"

"The water is calmer on this side," he said. "In a small boat like mine, we may be able to cross the coral. That is our best hope."

He had already trimmed the sail. Now he began to paddle, keeping a careful watch on what lay ahead. The reef fell off sharply along an irregular front. At one moment he could be floating safely in deep water, at another, smashed on the rock. Nearly close enough to touch he saw dangerous coral heads, pink and gray and mottled green. If a wave came before he was ready . . .

"Look!" he shouted. Ahead he saw what appeared to be

a shallow channel, barely awash. He paddled fiercely, positioning the boat, holding it ready until a swell could lift it. Then, in a rush, he was over, struggling to find his way across the treacherous shallows. Behind him Tepua probed the bottom with a pole, but he was moving too fast to get much help that way. Whenever the swells dropped, he braced himself for the sound of wood grating against stone. "My hull is thick and solid," he cried out, trying to reassure her. Only once did the bottom scrape, and then, with his paddling and her poling, they worked the boat free.

Ahead lay the exposed edge of dark, weathered coral that formed the shore. He saw no place to land there. Painstakingly he made his way toward the more sheltered end of the islet, coming at last to a beach of smoothed coral stones. A thicket of flowering bushes, glistening in white and green, grew almost to the water's edge.

Birds screeched as he stepped out into the knee-deep current, the submerged rocks slippery under his feet. Tepua scrambled up onto the narrow beach, and Rimapoa began handing her their supplies. These included bamboo poles, hardwood-tipped arrows, and an archery bow that Tepua had made on an earlier island. In small baskets they also carried leaf-wrapped packets of food and a dark lump of breadfruit sap.

Something else lay in one food basket, a dried piece of root that Tepua knew nothing about. For a moment, as he carried it ashore, that root seemed to cry out for attention, rattling itself against the stiff leaves of its container. Rimapoa splashed loudly to cover the sound, then laughed at himself for his foolishness.

When all had been unloaded, Tepua helped him drag the canoe through an opening in the bushes, up onto higher ground. Then they decided to take a quick look around.

"So much like my home!" she called excitedly. Continuing along the seaward shore, they reached the end of the islet and turned inward toward the lagoon. The calm water was turquoise, its color richer than the sky's. Tepua's face shone with excitement as she pointed to a crescent of dazzling white beach.

She is lovelier than anything here, Rimapoa thought, wanting to hold her against him and feel the warmth of her skin. But there was no time for *hanihani* now. He turned inland to the stands of atoll trees—hibiscus, green-berried *tafanu,* and fuzzy-leaved beach heliotrope. Here he glimpsed splashes of brilliant color among the broad leaves and low-hanging branches. Birds of a dozen varieties called to each other or flitted past on iridescent wings.

A whistling sound made him glance up as a pair of purple parakeets with creamy white breasts swooped from tree to tree. A larger parakeet, with variegated plumage in all colors of the rainbow, preened its feathers on a low bough, then stopped and stared at him with hard shiny eyes.

"That is Tu-tave," said Rimapoa softly, extending his arm toward the parakeet.

"I know that bird from legends," Tepua answered.

Then you know also that birds are the shadows of the gods, carrying their sacredness to earth. Rimapoa said nothing aloud, but admitted to himself that this bird could keep its feathers. It was the shadow of Tu, a god revered by *motu* people. For Tepua's sake, he would not harm a Tu-tave.

They went several more steps, then halted as a chorus of squawks and screeches came from overhead. Other birds appeared in such a brilliant array of colors that it almost hurt the eyes to look at them.

"I know that one, too," said Tepua, indicating another parakeet whose feathers shone in scarlet and emerald green. "The Arioi legends mention him. He is A'a-taevaco, the shadow of Oro-of-the-red-girdle."

"We have truly found it," said Rimapoa, his growing sense of awe making him surprisingly uncomfortable. "The island of feathers!" Despite his words, his feeling of jubilation had almost vanished. There was more *mana* in this place than he had thought possible.

"I never expected the island to be so splendid. It has a sacred feel about it, Rimapoa. I know these birds of the high gods must not be disturbed. How can we—"

"Do not worry, *tiare,*" he said, giving the answers he

thought about for so long. "We will find plenty of feathers
on the ground. If we must pluck some from the birds, we
will choose only those that are shadows of lesser gods."

Then, as his gaze followed a black-tailed man-of-war bird
swooping down to the edge of the water, he noticed the
thing that he had expected—and did not wish to see. His
brow began to sweat, far more heavily than when he had
been steering the canoe across the reef.

Close to shore, on a prominent rise, stood a carved
wooden post, held upright by blocks of coral. The faces cut
into the weathered wood seemed to be glaring at him,
warning him away. He blinked, wishing the unwanted thing
would somehow vanish. Tepua spotted it at the same
moment, her fingers trembling as she pointed.

"Yes, *tiare,* I see it," he replied, trying to contain his
frustration. "Some chief has placed a *tapu* on this shore. No
one may gather feathers here."

"Then what—"

"I knew we would find such a post, but it only applies to
this one stretch of coastline. If we are out of sight of a *tapu*
marker, then we may do as we please."

She came up to him, her eyes narrowed, her brow
furrowed with doubt. "If we are forbidden to be here, then
let us go to another place," she said. "It is not worth the
risk."

"I have told you that we will break no *tapu,*" he
answered, trying to keep the nervous edge from his voice.
After all, the old man had warned him of the difficulty, and
had hinted at a way around it. "You must trust me, *tiare.*"
They turned from shore and began to walk toward the
lagoon.

Soon Tepua saw a type of palm tree that she had known
all her life, but had seldom seen in Tahiti. "*Fara!*" she
cried, and ran to the pandanus, reaching up to embrace the
thin trunk while her feet straddled its cluster of aerial roots.

While Rimapoa went ahead she twisted a lumpy fruit
cluster from the tree. She used a piece of shell to pry off one
of its cone-shaped sections, then began to suck on the juice

at its base. She closed her eyes. With the familiar flavor filling her mouth and the sound of wind hissing through the leaves, she could almost imagine that she stood beside her father's house.

The spell was broken when Rimapoa returned for her. "You don't have to eat that," he said. "We still have provisions and we can fish in the lagoon."

"But I like this!" she protested.

"You get so little out of it. In Tahiti we eat *fara* only when there is nothing else."

She shook her head and sighed. How could she explain to a high islander what *fara* meant to her people, giving both shelter and food? For a moment she recalled how, at home, men thatched roofs with the tough leaves, and women sat together, scraping starch from the cooked fruit to make a pudding called *kapenu*. If she built a fire here, she could make her own *kapenu*.

"I have found fresh water," said Rimapoa. "That is more important. You will see other *fara* trees." He led Tepua inland, over ground covered by long creeping vines, to a pit that had weathered out of the coral. Or perhaps someone had carved the hole. The thought that other people came here gave her goose bumps. She gazed down at the cistern, like so many she had seen on coral islands. Though the water would allow them to stay longer, she was not overjoyed. Despite Rimapoa's assurances, the *tupu* post worried her. This was a lovely *motu,* as fine as any in her own atoll, but she did not want to remain here long.

Nonetheless, she could not refuse when Rimapoa urged her to explore with him. Turning toward the inner shore, they reached the blinding white sand at the edge of the lagoon. Here she could see to the bottom of the clear water, where anemones waved lazily and brilliant fish flitted among the coral heads. The heat rising from the sand made her dizzy.

"We will spear fish here at night, by torchlight," said Rimapoa. "That is the easiest way to catch them." She gazed across the water, seeing only a few stretches of high ground about the lagoon. Most of the surrounding reef was submerged and barely visible. The *motu* they were standing on appeared to be the largest in the atoll.

This islet's riches, she learned quickly, had already been claimed by others. Wherever she went with Rimapoa, they came across *tapu* signs warning them away. "Let us make a shelter," the fisherman said in a tense voice. "Tomorrow we can explore the rest."

When she woke the next morning, she found herself alone. Now she remembered how quiet and distant Rimapoa had seemed when they curled up for sleep the past night. For the first time since starting their journey, he had not wanted to make love. They had pressed against each other for warmth, but that was all.

Rimapoa was afraid of the island, though he would not admit it. How could she convince him to leave it after coming so far? She shook her head, crawled out from under the lean-to of branches, and began searching for a *fara* tree. Maybe, after she refreshed herself, she would think of something. . . . But then she heard footsteps. "Come, *tiare*," he called excitedly from behind her. "I have found a place where we can hunt feathers."

They carried some of their supplies as he led the way back to the lagoon, then continued along its sandy shore. "There is no *tapu* mark here," he said, sweeping his hand across a stretch of beach. Tepua did not like the nervous way he spoke, but agreed that she could not see one.

They moved into the shade, pressed the sticky gum they had brought onto the ends of several bamboo poles, then stood the poles upright in the ground. Any bird taking a perch would be trapped by the gum. Then Tepua strung the bow she had made days earlier. She checked to be sure that the wood was still springy and limber, and that no damage had been done by sun or sea. But she had no desire to shoot at birds. In Tahiti, as on her home island, archery was a sport, and arrows were never aimed at living things.

"Let us see what feathers we can find on the ground," Rimapoa suggested when he saw her reluctance to use the bow. They began to search beneath the trees. "There is one,'' he said, bending to pick up a long yellow tail feather in fine condition. ''If we poke around under the chaff we may find others.''

Gradually, Tepua warmed to the hunt. So long as she was not harming the birds, she thought she was doing no wrong. After a time, their hands grew full. They stopped near the beach and heaped their treasure on a pile of dry leaves.

''I will make a basket for the feathers,'' Tepua said, breaking off a young palm frond, slitting it down the midrib with her fingernail. While Rimapoa continued his search she sat in the shade of a *fara* tree and began work, interweaving the leaflets in a twilled pattern. When she finally closed off the bottom, the finished basket was narrow, long, and deep.

It was not until she stood up from her work and stretched her legs and back that she noticed the *tapu* sign just a few steps behind where she had been sitting. Rimapoa was just coming back along the shore. ''The chief who raised that post has forgotten it by now,'' he said in a bitter tone as he scooped the collected feathers into her basket.

If that was so, she wondered, then why did he look so frightened?

Rimapoa could not get rid of his fear. It was foolish, he kept telling himself. He was safe here on this island, far from priests, far from the *marae* where men were offered to the gods.

Yet he broke out into a cold sweat as a parakeet winged overhead, its plumage of crimson and blue shining.

Shadows. Shadows of divine ones who hunger for the flesh of men.

Tepua thought that everything he collected came from the ground. He had not shown her how accurately he could fling a stone, surprising a bird on its perch. He had no need for her bow and arrows, playthings of a noblewoman.

He wanted to be gone from this place, where the gods seemed to watch him from every side. Yet the feathers—the brilliant feathers. He could not turn away from them.

In Tahiti, he no longer had a home. His skills were of little use in waters that teemed with fishermen, but with these feathers he could get almost anything he wanted. He imagined presenting them to the high chief. In return he might receive far more than permission to live in the district. Perhaps he would get what no man of his class could hope to have—a parcel of coastal land, well planted and supplied with pigs. What would Tepua think of him then? How could she refuse to be his wife?

With this prospect in mind, he turned, stone in hand, toward the bushes. He threw silently and his aim proved true. His prey, a tropic bird, fluttered once, then lay still on the ground. He stripped scarlet feathers from the tail, held them against the sky, and saw how they danced like fire in his hands.

If these are the gods' shadows, he asked himself, *then what must the gods themselves be like? They must shine so fiercely that no man can look at them. Their vengeance must be terrible.* When he began to tremble again, he clenched his fists until the shaking went away.

Rimapoa could not keep the fears from his mind. Each day they grew more intense, but he persisted in his hunting, and spoke nothing of this to Tepua. She might help him, in the end. He was not willing to tell her how.

There was a way to protect himself that Two-oars had spoken of. He could make himself so distasteful to the gods that they would turn away in repugnance.

It was to this end that Rimapoa had dug up a certain rare root that a shark fisherman had once told him about. He recalled now how he had found it, in a damp forest deep within a valley. After searching all morning, he had come on a shoot of pallid waxy green peeking out from the lusher undergrowth.

Probing eagerly with his digging stick, he had loosened the soil, lifted the entire plant, and cupped it in his hand. Once the dirt was brushed away, he saw that it was white and full, suggesting in its voluptuous curves the shape of a woman's body. . . .

Now, each day, when the sun rose and he felt strong, he put his plan away with disgust, for he could not bear doing such a thing to his beloved. Once or twice he nearly cast the pale root into the sea. But as each day wore on, and the calls of the birds echoed in his ears, the dark thoughts returned.

Oh, to be free of this terror, he thought. *I know no other way. And it will not hurt her. . . .*

Tepua did not see where Rimapoa went on his own, but he continued to bring feathers long after she had given up searching under the trees. Every morning she assured him that they had gathered more than enough and asked him to leave the island. So far she had not been able to sway him.

What a different man he had become on Fenua Ura. She wished to have the sea-loving Rimapoa back again. As soon as they left Tahiti, she had started to view him in a new light. Her dream of serving Oro had not changed. Yet she had begun to think that one day, when her past was long forgotten, she might give up the Arioi—for Rimapoa, if he still wanted her.

Why was he acting so strangely now? she kept asking herself. Simply being off the sea could not explain it. This once-lusty fisherman had stopped caressing her, or even speaking words of affection. And why had he asked her to take care of her fingernails, letting them grow long?

Her feeling that she did not belong on Fenua Ura constantly troubled her. She sensed the need to tread lightly, to be careful not to disturb anything that lived here. The moist shade beneath the trees and the scents of the overhanging flowers brought her no joy. Even the bright lagoon had lost its attraction.

Finally, one afternoon, Rimapoa emerged from the brush and announced that their task was done. He dropped the closed basket at her feet, but cautioned her not to open it. "The sight of so many sacred feathers will burn your eyes," he warned. "Let us eat well today and leave at dawn."

Alone here, she and Rimapoa had grown lax in following the food *tapus*. They cooked in the same oven, though Tepua always used one side and he the other. Now she glanced over at their shallow pit and saw that the fire, lit earlier, had burned down. The hot stones were ready.

Under a pile of coconut leaves lay two parrotfish he had

speared last night. As she was wrapping them to be baked she noticed Rimapoa grinding something on a flat stone. He scooped a yellow-white paste onto a strand of *fara* leaf and came with it to the oven.

"Ginger," he said. "We've no more coconut sauce."

Tepua nodded, remembering the assortment of roots he had brought along with his other supplies. She had grown fond of the tangy Tahitian ginger. This time the color looked a bit odd, she thought, but she spread some over her fish while he took care of his own.

When it was time to eat, he carried his portion aside, as he always did. But today he seemed to put an unusually large space between them, turning his back to her.

She glanced at him where he crouched, melding into the shadows of late afternoon, and frowned. She could think only of leaving, of the relief she would feel when they were back on the sea.

Hungry now, Tepua unwrapped her fish and tasted it. She had used all the ginger that Rimapoa had given her, and now she enjoyed its sweet tanginess. But she noticed a tart aftertaste and wondered if the root had gotten too old.

She had almost finished eating when she felt a prickling sensation on her lips. She rubbed her mouth with the back of her hand. A wave of heat rolled through her, making her pulse jump and her head swim. She tried to get up, found herself unsteady on her feet, and sank back to her knees.

Fish poisoning!

"Rimapoa!" she tried to call, though the words came out in a hoarse gasp. "Do not eat yours." But she knew her warning was too late. Her hands and arms were stinging and prickling as if she had been lying on them. The feeling spread rapidly over her body, making every area of skin intensely sensitive.

What she had to do now was break open a coconut and drink its milk. That was the way she had been taught to counter such a poison, but she could not summon the will to stand up. Instead, she rubbed at her twitching thighs, letting her fingers travel higher. The sensation between her legs, when she accidentally touched herself, was so delicious that she forgot everything else.

Suddenly she caught herself. This was not fish poisoning. She had been stricken once as a child and remembered the experience. Now she felt no nausea, just an odd fluttery feeling in the pit of her stomach.

"Rimapoa!" she called again. Why didn't he come? Why did he stay crouched in the shadows, like something waiting for its prey? She fell forward on her hands and knees, gasping as a surge of ovenlike heat passed through her. This time it did not ebb as before, but withdrew to glowing knots in her breasts and an intense throbbing between her legs.

He came forward at last. She lifted her head to look at him. He seemed to shimmer, glowing with a red halo. She fell back on her rump, feeling suddenly light-headed. Everything she glanced at now had red halos.

But Rimapoa's mood remained serious. Why had the spice not affected him? Perhaps, while he sat apart, he had not eaten his fish at all! A part of her shrieked an alarm, but the sound was forgotten in the rush of her arousal.

She looked at Rimapoa's sweat-shined chest, taut belly, and narrow waist. She felt a hunger that added to the heaviness in her breasts and the wet heat between her thighs. She desired him. It did not matter what he had fed her. She needed him inside her, pumping. . . .

She could wait no longer. Rising, first on her knees, then in a crouch, she lurched forward, knocking him over. She climbed atop him, dragging her breasts hard against his chest. "I want you," she said harshly. She ground her hips against his. His eyes were slitted. Specks of red seemed to dance in his pupils.

Suddenly he embraced her, held her tightly to him, so tightly that she almost wished to be free. "I did not know what it would do to you," he whispered. "I did not think it would be so strong."

"It does not matter. Later I will be angry, not now. Now all I care about is this." She clawed at his loincloth, tore it away, and wiggled onto the hardness that emerged from beneath. She arched her spine, straining her head back, quivering.

"Quickly," she said, and moaned when the tip of his manhood slipped between engorged petals. "I want to feel every part of you."

He slid in, growing stiffer as she clutched him to her. She felt explosions of pleasure that merged into pain. And then, when he was as far in as he could go, she wrenched him over so that he was on top and she below. Drawing up her legs, she grabbed his buttocks and writhed against him. Her nails moved up his spine, over the bumps of his ribs.

Everything was crimson. His skin, the sand beneath, even the canopy of leaves had a fiery haze. The red was in her, making her wild and demanding. The red was in her fingertips as they traveled up his back, clenched, and drew down again, her nails cutting him.

She thrust against him harder, only faintly hearing his cries as he drove into her. In her frenzy, she clutched and clawed him until her hands grew wet and slippery with his blood. And then her release came, sending her body into uncontrollable shudders and jerks and her mind down into darkness.

Sprawled on sticks and leaves that pressed against her back, Tepua woke and saw the light of early morning. She rolled over, groaning at the stiffness in her limbs and the buzzing in her head. The memory of what had happened came to her as if from a dream. Then she glanced at her fingers and saw dried blood beneath torn and jagged nails.

With a rush of revulsion, she staggered to her feet and headed for the lagoon. She felt tainted and befouled, as if she had been taken again by Tangled-net. All she wanted was the clean embrace of the water.

Then a wave of nausea and dizziness swept over her and she fell. She vomited, lay panting, trying to gather strength to rise again. She could only hold herself up on her hands, her hair tumbling down over her face.

Rimapoa.

And then he was beside her, pulling her against him,

brushing aside her hair, giving her a sip of cool water to take away the taste of bile. . . .

She wrenched from his grip, spilling the water.

"Tiare," he said, extending his hands to her, his face stricken with grief and guilt. "Forgive me. I did not know it would have such an effect on you. I only thought it would make you—passionate—"

"Passionate?" She shrieked the word in his face. "How frenzied must a woman be to please you?"

Eyes shimmering with a strange triumph, he stood up, turned around, and showed her his back. It looked as if he had been lashed with the barb of a stingray. Blood-encrusted gashes ran from the tops of his shoulders to his waist.

Tepua had seen men who were scratched by their lovers, but this lay beyond her experience. The marks were not of love but of madness. *And he had insisted that she let her nails grow!*

"Why?" she asked again, her voice breaking. "I needed no—sorcerer's potion. I was glad to—wanted—to give you pleasure."

"It was not pleasure I needed last night," said the fisherman in a strange cold voice. He turned to her, his eyes feverish. "I have escaped the priests. They cannot take me now. The gods will hate the taste of me. I am safe. The fear is gone. I am finally free of it. Do you understand? I am free!"

Tepua could only stare at him, blank with incomprehension.

"Ah, *tiare.* On your island, they do not offer up the 'two-legged fish.' That's why you are so puzzled. Our priests will not take a man who bears scars inflicted by a woman. They say he is not fit for the gods." The fisherman swallowed. "So now, *tiare,* my only fear is that I have hurt you."

"More than hurt!" she said in a voice of fury. "You were not sure what would happen to me! Yet you risked it, and gave me no warning. That is far worse than any pain." Shakily, she tried again to stand. This time, strengthened by her anger, she was able to walk to the lagoon. She waded in and fell to her knees in the transparent water. The lagoon was pure. Its gentle touch would cleanse her.

For a long while she lay stretched out in the shallow water. Bright fish flitted about her legs. Under her, the soft sand made a comfortable bed. Best of all, when she let the water lap over her ears, it cut off the sounds that had begun to torment her—the endless cries of the birds. She scrubbed her fingertips again and again until they were free of Rimapoa's blood.

At last she stood up, staring with sudden detachment at the man who sat on the beach, his head down on his crossed forearms. Now she knew the real reason he had brought her on this journey. Not to gather feathers, as he had claimed. Not for *hanihani* either. Not even for a last attempt at wooing her from Aitofa. "Why did you need me at all?" she asked him. "Why not simply scrape your back with coral?"

He lifted his head, but stared in another direction. "The priests can detect trickery," he answered in a tone of despair. "They have secret ways."

"If you had explained—" She cut herself off. What man would admit to his fears? What man would beg his *vahine* to pretend a frenzy that he could not arouse in her? Knowing this, she still could not excuse him.

She gathered her wrap about her and began to walk away. "Wait," he called hoarsely. "I have something more to say. Yes, I admit that I mistreated you! It was not an easy thing to do. But do not forget how you rewarded me for taking you away from your enemies—abandoning me to go off with your Arioi. Do not look down on me, *motu* princess. We two are fish that feed on the same shoal."

She turned her back on him and stumbled toward the shelter.

"Listen!" he cried, coming up behind her. "Yesterday I felt the gods all around me, so close that I could scarcely breathe. I heard their hearts beating, their stomachs churning with hunger. For me. For my soul. Please understand, *tiare*."

She stopped, turned to stare at him. He seemed a pitiful

figure, covered with salt and dust, unable to meet her gaze. Yes, she did understand his terrors. He could not help but be affected by this place, with its aura of sacredness and its god shadows in every tree. She had tried to convince him to leave long ago, but perhaps she had not tried hard enough.

He came closer, reaching out to touch her hand. She flinched, like an animal withdrawing from something it knows not to trust. She saw the pain in his eyes as his fingers fell away.

"So you are afraid of me now," he said with a groan.

"I bear part of the blame for this," she admitted softly. "I am sorry. We must leave here. Now. Before anything else happens to us."

"The canoe is ready to be launched. I am taking only some water and coconuts . . . and the basket."

The basket. A shiver came over her at the thought. She realized that she no longer wanted anything to do with the treasure that she and Rimapoa had gathered. *Let him have it. Let him have it all.* She blinked back her tears as she followed him to the coral-strewn shore.

15

WEARY from days of sailing, Rimapoa neared the familiar coastline of Knotted-cord's district. Ahead, jutting out into the water, lay the forested spit of land where the great *marae* stood. His journey was almost at its end.

He sadly turned his gaze to Tepua, who sat in the bow facing away from him. She was leaving him now. He did not know when he might see her again.

She had forgiven him, she said. Yet they had slept apart every night since leaving Fenua Ura. And she wanted nothing to do with the treasure they had gathered.

Slowly, reluctantly, he brought the canoe in to a thickly wooded shore. *"Tiare,"* he said, trying to explain himself once more, as she got out and waded through shallows to the rocky beach. "Remember this. It was for your sake that I took so many feathers. So I could provide for you if you ever chose to leave the Arioi. And if you need me, I will still be here to help."

Waves lapping gently at her feet, she glanced at him briefly. She opened her mouth as if to speak, and her eyes glistened, but then she shook her head and turned away. He wanted to jump out of the boat and run after her, but he knew that she would only resist his embrace. She must have time, he thought, time to heal her hurt. Then, perhaps, she would truly forgive him.

As soon as she vanished between the trees, he paddled away. The parting meant nothing, he kept telling himself. She would come back to him, just as she had done before. Yet he could not get free of the desire to gash himself and groan aloud.

He tightened his fist and refused to give in to his misery.

He was about to approach the high chief. He must go as a man of courage, not one who whimpers over women.

Soon he reached the mouth of a stream that emptied into the lagoon. He stopped to bathe in the fresh water, then asked for a few dabs of *monoi* from some young people sitting on the bank. After rubbing his arms and chest with the fragrant coconut oil, he felt presentable, ready to face Knotted-cord.

When Rimapoa brought the canoe up to the high chief's jetty, however, he was dismayed to see a familiar and hostile figure—the guard who had tried to keep him from landing when he first arrived with Tepua. "So you are back," the chief's man said with a snarl. "I know you, fisherman. You are not welcome."

"Let the high chief decide that," said Rimapoa.

"He decided long ago. I was there at your audience, but you were too busy stumbling in the dust to notice me."

"And now I will have another hearing. I bring a gift that will make the high chief eager to see me."

"Gift?" the guard snorted. "Are you keeping it under your fishing lines? He peered into the boat, poking at the gear with his spear point. At last he reached the basket with the feathers.

"That is my gift," Rimapoa said. "Only Knotted-cord may open it."

"It is my duty to inspect it first," said the guard coldly. "Men have been known to offer the chief baskets filled with poisonous centipedes."

"Then look if you dare. The sight is not for a commoner." He had examined the feathers as he gathered them, but had carefully kept the basket closed as he added each new prize. Such a concentration of sacredness was too much for the eyes to bear. Now, his hands trembling, he picked up the basket and held it open.

For a moment sunlight gleamed on the brilliance of red and yellow plumage within. Rimapoa felt a stabbing pain in his eyes and immediately looked away. The guard gasped and stepped back, throwing his hand over his face. "I am blinded by the power of the gods!" he shouted.

"That is your just punishment. Now help me up." The fisherman closed the basket, then leaned out to place it atop the jetty. When the guard only moaned and wailed, Rimapoa tied up the boat without assistance and climbed ashore.

The guard remained on his knees, rubbing at his eyes. "You should have warned me," he said miserably.

"Get up, you lazy sow, and take me to the high chief." The fisherman shook the guard's shoulder. Gradually the man seemed to recover. He stood up, shakily, and finally retrieved the weapon he had dropped.

"What kind of fisherman are you?" the guard muttered. "Do birds come to your hooks?"

Rimapoa did not answer, but followed the man's broad back up the path. The basket in his hands suddenly felt unwieldy. What if he dropped it, or lost his footing? Rimapoa shook his head, wishing he could get rid of his doubts.

Entering the compound, he tried to ignore the bustle of courtiers and servants, the chickens fluttering underfoot, the shouting children. He fixed his gaze on the high chief's house, its doorway covered by a painted mat and flanked by guards. He paused, carefully holding his basket.

The man from the jetty went forward to confer with the other guards. One beckoned him closer. "The noble chief is sleeping," the guard whispered. "Leave your gift. When he wakes, we will send it in."

"I will wait," said Rimapoa firmly.

"What is the trouble?" asked a voice from inside.

"A fisherman brings an offering to our exalted one," said the guard from the jetty. "I have inspected it, and I assure you that it is worthy of the chief's attention."

"Then hand it in. The noble one is awake and looking for amusement."

Rimapoa watched with both satisfaction and uneasiness as a plump hand pushed the hanging mat aside and took the basket. Never before in his life had he found a chance to rise above his humble station. When the high chief saw this magnificent gift, he would grant Rimapoa anything he wanted.

He tried to imagine having his own house and land, with so many trees that he could make frequent gifts of coconut and breadfruit to his less fortunate friends. And what if he should father a son? What a feast he would give! He imagined the details, growing hungry as he pictured the yams and bananas and pork. . . .

"You. Fisherman." A guard's deep voice startled Rimapoa from his daydreams. A hand grabbed him harshly by the arm. "You will wait until the high chief is ready to deal with you." The guard pulled him roughly away from Knotted-cord's house, taking him toward a small hut at the edge of the compound. Rimapoa saw another spearman behind him and did not dare protest.

"Stay in here. And be quiet," the guard ordered, pushing him in through the low doorway. A stale and unpleasant odor filled the small space within. Rimapoa saw that the dry grass on the floor had not been changed in a long time. The cane walls were cracked and rotting.

Why were they treating him so? This stinking hut was no place to put a man who brought royal gifts. He felt perspiration on his face and chest, and a need to relieve himself. Crickets chirped in the roof thatch, giving him no cheer.

He approached the nearest wall, wrapped his thin fingers around the weathered canes, and tested their strength. The cords that bound them were frayed; he could break through before anyone noticed, race out into the compound. . . .

But for what? The guards would catch him in the end and bring him back. No. He must stand fast and carry himself with assurance. If anyone accused him of misdeeds, he would firmly deny them.

The fisherman sighed and loosened his grip. He pressed his face to a gap and found that he could glimpse the front part of Knotted-cord's house. All was quiet there now. He closed his eyes as he pressed his forehead painfully against the bamboo.

When he heard voices, he looked out and saw the high priest, Ihetoa, his white cape flying behind him as he strode up to Knotted-cord's door. The high priest was a tall man, broad of shoulder, and quick for a man of his bulk. Ihetoa did not enter the chief's house, but waited until the mat was pulled aside before he peered in. The priest seemed to be speaking to someone, perhaps to Knotted-cord himself. Then Ihetoa turned and walked across the courtyard.

Rimapoa's pulse quickened when he saw the priest heading in his direction. He stood away from his peephole and straightened his shoulders, determined to answer well whatever questions might be put to him. The priest should be pleased, after all. The sacred power of the new feathers would add much to the ceremonies and artifacts of the temple.

Ihetoa's expression bore no sign of gratitude as he burst into the room. "So you are the fisherman who comes with so many glorious feathers."

Seeing that broad, livid face, Rimapoa lost his resolve. He stammered nervously. "They—they are gifts—to the high chief and his court. So they may earn—the gods' favors."

"Ah, so you wish to please the gods."

Rimapoa felt a sudden burning at the base of his skull, at the place where sacrificial victims were struck. He sucked in his breath but could not answer.

"Very well. Then you will come to my *marae*. That is the place for a man such as yourself."

And the place where the sacrifice is offered! "I—I first beg a moment's patience while I visit the fishermen's shrine."

"For what purpose? To call on some menial spirit? Let us go where the gods of true power can listen. You will explain to *them* how you came by these feathers, and they will say what is to be done." The priest turned sharply and walked toward the compound's gate. Guards flanked Rimapoa, holding him tightly by each arm, forcing him to follow.

Leaving the gate, Ihetoa turned to the path that led out along the point. Ahead, rising amid a grove of ancient trees, stood the awesome *ahu* of stone. Suddenly the old fears gripped Rimapoa. The scars from Tepua's hands, won at such a terrible cost, no longer made him feel safe. He looked with dread at the high chief's *marae*.

Until now, the modest shrine belonging to Pigs-run-out was the largest temple he had approached. Even at a distance, the *mana* of this place made him tremble. How many men had been offered here? he wondered. The place was haunted by their spirits. He heard their voices as the wind rustled through the boughs overhead.

Rimapoa could scarcely force one foot to follow another. Carved spirit figures, guardians of the *marae*, glowered at him from the shadows of *rata* trees. Beside him, the warriors paused to remove their capes in a gesture of respect for the gods. Rimapoa, who wore a simple loincloth, could only bow his head.

"Here. Come this way, fisherman. This is as far as we need go." Ihetoa stopped well outside the quadrangle that was surrounded by a low wall of rounded stones.

Several temple attendants, known as *opu-nui* or "noble stomachs," were sweeping fallen leaves from the paved floor of the courtyard. When they saw the high priest, they scurried away. Rimapoa glanced at the painted, carved boards that adorned the *ahu*, and at the low stone uprights that marked special places of worship. He could not avoid looking at the largest altar, a high wooden platform set on legs that rose above his head.

Atop it lay an offering of fruit, and the rotting corpse of a man. When the wind shifted, the odor made him gag. "The gods have demanded another sacrifice," the priest proclaimed. "Once that is done, I feel certain that our season of scarcity will end. You have chosen a good moment, fisherman. Your arrival comes just when we need you."

"But my—"

"Silence, until I ask you my questions. Tell me how you got those feathers."

"I—" He struggled to find breath. "I—gathered—them on an island."

"Name it."

Rimapoa swallowed hard. The gods were listening now. He no longer could convince himself that he was safe from them. And even if the priest spared him, he must still deal with the ghosts that haunted this place. What revenge might they take if he lied? "Fen—Fenua Ura."

The high priest smiled coldly, displaying yellowed teeth. "You speak the truth. No other island in these parts has such riches." Ihetoa glanced up at the towering stones, then fixed Rimapoa with a penetrating stare. "Did you not know that Fenua Ura is restricted by the chiefs? Did you not see the *tapu* signs posted all around the island?"

The fisherman retreated under the priest's stare, but behind him he felt the bulk of four armed men. He had planned his story, should this question arise. He had practiced it often when he was away from Tepua.

May the ghosts torment me for this lie, he thought. *But I will not give it up.* "In one place," he whispered. "In one place, along the shore, no sign was posted. I thought that I was free to hunt there. Maybe there were warnings once, but the wind blew them down."

"*Wind?*" Ihetoa laughed, making a dry cackle that chilled Rimapoa in his bowels. Then he spoke in a low and vicious tone. "You did not need to see the signs! The place is *tapu*. You felt it every time you took a step."

"Then," Rimapoa managed, the words barely audible. "Then I was careless. I beg you—forgive my mistake."

"Ah. What is to be done with such a man?" the priest said, addressing the stones of the temple. "He steals feathers that are reserved for the high chiefs and he calls it a mere mistake!" Again he turned to Rimapoa. "Only your life can atone for this sacrilege, fisherman. I am sure you know this. But you can be glad that your sacrifice serves another purpose as well. You are to be our two-legged fish." He made a signal to one of the guards.

My scars!

The words caught in Rimapoa's throat. He saw, behind him, the man with the war club raising his arm. Rimapoa screamed, wrenching free of the hands that gripped him, throwing himself at the high priest's feet.

"What is this?" Ihetoa asked in a tone of fury. "What are these marks on your back? Why did no one mention them?

Guards, where are your eyes?'' When no one answered, he spoke again. ''Fisherman, explain quickly.''

''A—a woman,'' he gasped. ''A woman—made them.''

The guards began to laugh and jest among themselves.

''It is true!'' Rimapoa wailed.

''Such scars can be made by other means,'' said the priest.

''There is—no trick.'' He felt their stares burning his flesh. ''I can—show you—the woman. Then you will know.''

''There is no woman,'' said the priest. ''Not for this liar, this *tapu*-breaker.''

Rimapoa squirmed. ''If you are wrong—''

''Silence!'' Ihetoa roared. Then he turned to the guards and shouted an order. ''Take him and check his story. Be quick. The gods are impatient.''

As Tepua made her way along a shaded path she tried not to think of Rimapoa or of the long journey that had ended so bitterly. She felt exhausted from lack of sleep and weak from hunger. Worst of all, she knew she must soon face Aitofa and resume her exhausting duties as a novice.

She walked listlessly, following a track between the houses, the smell of wood smoke teasing her as she went. People were readying their ovens for the principal meal of the day, but what were they preparing? She glimpsed a basket of purple stems from some wild vine. In another yard, the women sat around a heap of fern roots, wrapping them in leaves for baking. *Famine foods*. When Tepua glanced up into the breadfruit trees, she saw no sign of the tiny buds and catkins that must precede the next crop.

Despite her slow pace, Tepua arrived all too soon at Aitofa's household. She was sent at once to join the remaining young women in the yam garden outside the compound. The food that came from this field was precious now, she understood. ''Dig carefully when you harvest,'' Curling-leaf told her. ''The roots must come out unbroken.''

Flies buzzed around Tepua's head as she squatted to probe the ground with a pointed stick. Her eyes kept

shutting. Whenever they did, she saw flashes of bright
plumage and birds fluttering just out of reach. If only she
could forget them . . .

Again she probed the soil, and this time she found so
large a tuber that she could not dig it up. It seemed to run
underground across the entire field. She worked feverishly
with the stick, thinking how many people her discovery
would feed, when she felt a hand squeezing her arm.

"You fell asleep," said Pecking-bird, a young novice
who seemed to delight in Tepua's misfortunes. "But now
you have visitors." Pecking-bird raised her voice so that all
the others could hear. "The high priest's men have come to
talk to you."

The digging sticks halted as everyone turned to Tepua.
"What have you done?" whispered Curling-leaf. But Tepua
could not answer. Nor could she keep her own stick in her
trembling fingers.

Perspiration chilled the back of Tepua's neck as she rose
from the yam patch and brushed soil from her knees. Then
a group of warriors burst from between the surrounding
trees, thrusting their prisoner before them. Tepua's throat
tightened when she saw Rimapoa, his arms bound behind
him, his face smeared with dust, his eyes wide with fear and
despair.

"Is she the one?" the leader of the warriors asked
Rimapoa. Mutely he raised his eyebrows, signifying yes.

"Come closer," the leader said, beckoning to Tepua. The
other novices had all backed away. Only Curling-leaf still
stood close by her. "This fisherman has fresh scars on his
body," the warrior continued. "He says you clawed him
while you two were rutting. Is this true?"

Tepua heard an outbreak of gasps from the novices
behind her. "With *that* man?" said Pecking-bird. The other
women laughed nervously. "Not even our *motu* princess
would want him!"

"Answer, woman! The high priest has chosen this man
for sacrifice. Tell us the fisherman is lying so we can get on
with it."

Lie? Tepua stared at Rimapoa, unable to reply. She could

still hear Pecking-bird's words of disdain and the scornful laughter of the other novices.

And then a terrifying thought came. Admitting that she had been with him might be tantamount to making a far more serious confession. The high chief should have rewarded him. Instead . . .

Tepua narrowed her eyes. There was only one explanation. Yes, Rimapoa had lied. To *her*—about the *tapu* markers on the island. And that made her guilty as well!

"What is keeping you, woman?"

She opened her mouth to deny Rimapoa's claim, but her voice would not come. It was true that he had lured her to Fenua Ura, then drugged her to the point of madness. But seeing him now, staring at her, lost in his own fears, she no longer felt anger, only sorrow.

"Take him back to the *marae*," said the leader to the other warriors. "His falsehoods have struck this woman dumb, but we know the answer."

"Wait!" she cried. "I made those scars. We were together and—I forgot myself." She looked away as Rimapoa gave a long sigh and sagged between his two guards.

"Turn him around," ordered the leader. "You." He indicated one of his men. "Take her hand and place it on his back. See if her fingers line up with the scars."

Before she could protest, the man grabbed Tepua's wrist and spread her fingers over the marks. Then, with contempt, he flung her away. Her eyes burned. It was not enough for them to hear her confession; they had to prove it in front of this audience. Behind her, the novices whispered furiously, and she heard Pecking-bird's voice rise. "They say that all savages rip up their men—"

Another novice sneered. "That one's no man. He's a slimy eel. She fornicates with eels."

"What is this commotion?" demanded another voice. Aitofa appeared on the path from the compound. "Who disturbs my novices at their work?"

"We beg your forgiveness for this intrusion, noble chiefess," said the warrior leader. "The high priest needed to ask a question of this woman.'' He pointed to Tepua. ''But now we are done with her.''

''If Ihetoa wishes anything from the Arioi women, he must first ask me,'' Aitofa answered, her eyes flashing. ''You had no right to intrude and harass my novices. Go!''

Tepua gaped at the woman's audacity. She understood that Arioi chiefs were protected by strict sanctions. But to dismiss the high priest's warriors with an imperious wave of her hand . . .

The guard nodded. ''We are leaving. I hope we need not disturb you again.'' He sent his men on ahead of him. Rimapoa, still bound, stumbled between them, barely keeping up. He gave Tepua one final look of anguish and was gone.

She did not want to think what might happen to him now. If they did not kill him outright, they would probably exile him to some hostile shore.

''Now,'' Aitofa said, her gaze traveling over the novices and settling on Tepua. ''Explain what they wanted.''

A dozen voices started up.

''Stop gabbling like a cageful of fowls. Remember that you are Arioi!'' Aitofa snapped. ''Go back to your work. Tepua-mua, come with me.''

Tepua tried to obey, but was so numb from shock that she stumbled, falling to her knees. Curling-leaf caught her arm, steadying her.

''She is weak from her journey,'' Curling-leaf said. ''Will the noble chiefess permit me to help her?''

''She will come with me. Alone,'' said Aitofa.

Tepua leaned briefly on her friend. A squeeze from Curling-leaf's hand helped calm her. Then, lifting her chin, she followed the chiefess into the house.

Aitofa's lips formed a thin, tight line as she listened to Tepua repeat her confession. ''A novice of the Arioi would not consort with such a person as this Rimapoa,'' said the chiefess haughtily, ''much less be moved to the passion you admitted. If I had been in the garden, I would have refused to let those men speak to you. I would have forced the high priest to make his own determination.''

Tepua closed her eyes.

"You have embarrassed us enough that I am tempted to dismiss you from the lodge. Have you anything to say?"

Tepua hesitated. She dared not let more of the story emerge. If Rimapoa kept silent about the rest, then perhaps her part in the transgression would remain secret.

"Noble chiefess . . ." she managed. "I wish only—to say this. If I had not confessed . . ."

"Yes?"

"Then the high priest—would have greatly angered the gods with his offering."

Aitofa tossed her head. "Angered them? That is what the men would have us believe."

"Do you—do you doubt?" Tepua stared at the chiefess in astonishment.

"The priests tell us that the touch of a woman makes a thing profane—unsuitable to be offered. You have left the sign of your touch on that fisherman, and that is why he cannot be sacrificed. But remember this. The men say that no woman may handle their holy things, yet if a woman becomes high chief, she stands in their *marae* and wears the sacred girdle of feathers."

"Then—" Her mouth fell open. She had never heard anyone voice such a challenge. Aitofa's anger appeared to be directed at the priests rather than Tepua.

"We are heading into dangerous waters," said Aitofa quickly. "Let us get back to deciding whether you deserve to remain with the Arioi. Come outside, and I will show you the one way to sway me." In the courtyard, the blackleg clapped her hands sharply to summon her novices.

"Stand up on that flat rock," Aitofa told Tepua, "and prove yourself."

Prove? Tepua glanced at the sunlit rock where novices often stood to make their recitations. Once, but only once, she had managed to get through all the chants. She had not thought about them for many days.

"You may start with the founding of the order," said Aitofa. "Climb onto the rock and begin. And be certain you make no error."

Tepua could not even bring to mind the first phrase. She advanced slowly toward the rock, aware that every novice was staring at her. She saw Curling-leaf beckoning her forward. Of all the faces, only Curling-leaf's showed any sympathy for her plight. The other novices seemed to be enjoying the spectacle, welcoming the respite from their tasks.

"Now!" ordered Aitofa. "And anyone else who speaks gets a turn to recite as well."

Tepua stepped up onto the small platform. The sun beat on her head, making her dizzy. Her lips felt dry, and she wondered when she had last had a drink. Then she remembered her illustrious forbear, Tapahi-roro-ariki, who had proved long ago that a woman could stand in the *marae,* and rule over the land as well as any man. Tepua offered a silent prayer. *Ancestor spirit, I call on you now once again.*

The founding of the order. She could not remember a word of that chant, yet her mouth opened and she began to speak. . . .

16

FOR the next few days, Tepua did everything she could to keep out of Aitofa's sight. She had expressed her appreciation, both to her guardian spirit and to the chiefess, for being allowed to remain with the Arioi. Now Tepua wished only to forget the incident.

She dared not ask anyone about Rimapoa's fate. So far, there had been no questions about her own part in his misadventure. When the chiefess finally summoned her, she knew what the interview would be about. With her mouth dry and her fingers trembling, she went to the small guest house at the side of the compound. She had met Matopahu here, long ago, she remembered with a twinge. This time only Aitofa sat waiting.

"I thought the incident finished," said Aitofa coldly, "but now I see it is not. The high priest has learned that you were away while your fisherman was raiding that island. He believes that you went with the man and helped steal the feathers."

Tepua looked at the grass-strewn floor, unable to reply. For two nights she had lain awake, worrying about the accusation that must come.

"I would like to let the high priest have you for questioning," said Aitofa. "If you are guilty, then you deserve whatever punishment he decrees. You must tell the truth now, all of it. It will be better for you if _I_ decide your fate."

Tepua remembered the high priest, Ihetoa. She had seen him, wearing his elegant cape, standing near Knotted-cord on the day of her audience. His expression of disapproval had chilled her when she dared a glance in his direction. Perhaps he despised her merely for being a foreigner, a person ignorant of Maohi ways. Now she imagined Ihetoa standing over her, his face livid, as he questioned her about her journey with the fisherman.

All thoughts of denial fled. "I should have stopped Rimapoa," she answered with a moan. "He deceived me about the *tapu* signs, but I should have seen through his lies."

"So you admit that you helped him?"

Tepua let out a long sigh. "I did not harm the birds, but I did pick feathers from the ground."

"Then you must be punished, but not by Ihetoa's command. I do not intend to weaken the power of the Arioi by giving in to a priest. I will refuse him. That does not mean you are safe."

"Then—" Tepua fell silent under Aitofa's stern gaze.

"I will not have another incident, with warriors forcing their way into the compound. I want you away from here for a time so you can do no more harm."

"Where can I go?"

"To the mountains. With provisions running short, there are always groups going up to gather wild food. I will send you with the next party of Arioi."

"That—that is good of you."

"Wait until you have heard the rest. I have spent some time planning this." Aitofa cast a wary glance at the latticework walls. "Come closer," she whispered. "There are spies everywhere."

Wishing for something to hold on to, Tepua took a shaky step nearer.

"The man you met in this house fled to the highlands and remains there in exile. When the food gathering is done, you must not return here with the others. If you find this man, he will give you refuge. It is important to me that you find him."

Tepua felt dizzy with confusion. "Mato—"

"Speak no names!" Aitofa cut her off, then lowered her voice again. "There is great agitation in the court. Now that the famine is real, people are muttering against Ihetoa. Knotted-cord still defends him, and the unrest grows. It is

important that our friend be kept informed. I want you to
take him a message.''

Tepua frowned. ''But why not—''

''Why not send someone else? Because the hills are full
of spies, priests who walk by day and by night. They know
who stands with our friend, but they do not know *your*
loyalties. There are risks, yes, but would you prefer to stay
here and face the high priest? At least, this way, your
absence will serve another purpose.''

Tepua could only give one answer. ''I will go,'' she said
softly.

''Good. Until then, you will not leave the compound, not
even to wash.''

A few days later a party of young Arioi men and women
set out for the interior of the island. Tepua had garbed
herself like the others, with a sunshade of plaited coconut
leaves about her head. She still felt conspicuous, out of
place in the party.

The others were too cheerful, singing and laughing as
they went. To them this was little more than an excuse to
leave their usual routine. If the scarcity of food troubled
them, they did not show it. Tepua knew that the stocks of
mahi were low and the vegetable gardens almost exhausted.

As they climbed a gently rising path she could not bring
herself to imitate the high spirits of the others. How could
she feign a joy she did not feel? The prospect of a meeting
with Matopahu—if she could find him—gave her no cheer.

Curling-leaf, who walked beside her, whispered, ''There
is another one,'' and nudged her with an elbow.

Tepua did not have to be reminded that priests, seemingly
absorbed in recitations, stood at the vantage points all along
the path. She tried not to look at the white-garbed man as
she went by him.

Why had Aitofa sent her with this message? she asked
herself. Another Arioi might have been a better choice.
Then, as Tepua crossed a glimmering brook, the answer
came to her. She gasped, lost her footing, and fell to her
knees in the running water.

"What is wrong?" asked Curling-leaf, helping her up.

"It is nothing," Tepua answered, though her cheeks burned in fury. *Matopahu had planned this long ago!* Before he left, he had certainly arranged for spies to keep him informed of matters at court. He must have also asked Aitofa to find an excuse to send up his "dancer." And the message Tepua had just memorized to tell him—meaningless, of course.

As she went on, Tepua tried to console herself. She had been spared a confrontation with the high priest, at least for a while. Aitofa had gotten her away safely, even if only out of friendship for Matopahu. And the chief's brother, who thought he could call her to him like a tail-wagging pup—she would deal with him later.

The group climbed ever higher, until they came to a place where *fe'i,* wild bananas, grew on upright stalks. The grove was small and quickly exhausted. A few young men left for home, carrying bunches of ripe, orange-skinned bananas tied onto long poles. The rest of the group moved on, to steeper terrain, but found no more fruit that day.

In the morning, after sleeping under a shelter of branches, they reached a cascade that plunged from sheer heights into a rocky pool. A cool spray, smelling of mossy stones, drifted from the falls. Ropes dangled over the stones along the side of the waterfall, offering a way to ascend. The land above, from the little that showed, appeared lush.

"Up there," said one of the men. "That is where to find the best fruit." He grabbed one end of the closest rope and began to ascend the slippery face.

Tepua gaped at his daring. The thought of dangling so high made her dizzy. And Aitofa had told her, just before she left, that Matopahu was up there! She watched how the climber put his feet onto tiny ledges barely large enough to support his toes. Only a lizard could ascend that path.

Dismay came over her, drawing sweat to her palms. She remembered the outing to the hills with Rimapoa. Even that modest height had disoriented her, making her lose her balance. That climb had been a mere stroll compared to this!

She caught herself. It was a disgrace to show cowardice

among the Arioi. Young Pecking-bird was already seizing a hibiscus-bark rope and mounting the base of the cliff.

This is too much to expect, she wanted to shout. *You Maohi have climbed heights all your life, while I have never scaled anything higher than a coconut tree.*

Yes, and she had been afraid to climb those at first, she recalled. The trees had looked as high to her then as this cliff did now. She gritted her teeth and waited for the lowest rope to be free again. Then she grabbed the end, set her toes in the narrow footholds, and began to climb before fear could stop her.

"That's good!" called Curling-leaf, encouraging her from below.

Tepua turned her head to call back to her friend, then caught a glimpse of the foaming pool below. She shut her eyes, but the dizziness was upon her, freezing her where she clung.

The whole cliff seemed to sway beneath Tepua as she gripped the rope. She forced herself to look up, to feel with her toes for the next foothold. In her first rush up the face she had ignored the little springs that trickled down the rockface, making it wet and slippery. Now, as she frantically sought purchase for her feet, she felt the clammy algae scum covering the rocks. When she tried to shift her weight, her foot skidded out from beneath her, leaving her dangling by her arms.

At last, after slipping several more times, she reached the next ledge. Here the rope ended. She saw that she would be forced to sidestep along a narrow shelf to grab the next one.

She laid her head against the damp stone and closed her eyes. It was bad enough climbing when she had a rope to hold on to. Now she would have to leave even that small security and move out on the face with her belly to the rock and her heels hanging out over a sheer drop.

She held the rope as long as she could, but the terrible moment came when she had to release it. She inched sideways, her cheek against the stone, her eyes on the next section of rope, afraid that if she stopped for a moment, she would never continue.

She whispered a plea to her guardian spirit. "Make the handholds dry. Keep the ledge from crumbling." Then she looked at the next rope, just ahead, swinging a little from the movements of the climber above. Each of her sideways steps seemed to bring it no closer. She imagined what might happen if her fingers loosened or the ledge gave way. She would topple backward, falling in a graceful arc into the pool below. At least it would be a pretty death, for those watching.

Her groping palm struck something thick and fibrous. Her fingers recognized the rope and clamped onto it before her fear-numbed mind could realize that she had reached safety.

From here, the face tilted inward, so that she could walk up it by bracing her heels against the stone and leaning back against the rope. On this final stretch, the rocks were drier and the going easier. And then, just as the breeze was starting to dry the sweat on her face and she was wondering if, someday, she might even learn to enjoy this, her head came up over the cliff edge and someone thrust out a hand to pull her to safety. A friend?

Pecking-bird!

"I did not expect you to make it, lover-of-eels," said the girl, pulling her up roughly. "You savages are not easy to kill."

Tepua, still catching her breath, gave no reply. She glared as Pecking-bird ran, laughing, toward the others, joining them beside a stand of purple-stalked *fe'i*. Then she straightened up and hastened away from the steep drop behind her. Ahead lay relatively level ground, where fanlike *anuhe* ferns stood almost as tall as the low trees.

Earlier, Tepua had hinted to Curling-leaf that she would not stay with the foraging party. Now, after glancing around to see that no one was watching, she began to follow the stream away from its cascade. Up here the water flowed quietly over smooth black rocks.

After a time Tepua paused to wade into the water and splash herself. She glanced up at the dark peak that towered over the plateau. Aitofa had told her to search for a cave near its base, but she still had far to go. She paused to listen for voices but no longer heard the noisy group of Arioi she had abandoned.

She could not tell what lay immediately ahead. Around the stream's banks the low forest closed in. The watercourse turned, and boulders blocked her view of what lay upstream. Alone in this isolated place, she felt a sudden prickle of fear.

A deep snorting in the underbrush made her spin around. She saw low branches stirring, as if moved by something beneath them. *A wild hog?* She had heard tales of fierce boars in the mountains, but not until now had she believed them.

Another snort. She had no weapon. In the water at her feet lay rounded stones the size of her fist.

The bushes shook so violently that she thought a whole family of pigs was coming at her. The snorting began again, but as she tensed herself for the attack she heard the sound dissolve into peals of human laughter.

Two men wearing loincloths emerged from the underbrush. It took her a moment to recognize Matopahu. She did not know the other man.

Enraged by the prank, Tepua tossed a few rocks, but the men dodged them nimbly and splashed toward her through the stream. "Is that how you greet us?" Matopahu asked with a grin.

"I do not greet you at all." She picked up another stone, ready to use it if he tried to come closer.

"You made a pretty sight climbing with those ropes," he added.

"You watched?" Her cheeks burned at the thought.

"My lookouts warned me a large party was coming. I did not expect to find you among them."

"Did not expect me? Aitofa sent me to you! And for someone in exile, you look surprisingly cheerful." The man she saw now, clad in rough cloth and a simple turban, seemed to have changed once again. Evidently the life here suited him. His broad, beaming face showed no trace of his woes.

"You, on the other hand, look in need of a bath," he chided, laughing.

She pitched the rock at him and picked up another. "And you hope that I will bathe while you watch. Well, that is not my plan. Aitofa ordered me to give you a message, so I came. After that I am going back to the Arioi."

"I am listening," he said, his expression suddenly sober.

She glanced at the other man, who was older than Matopahu but apparently equally fit. "No one else must hear it."

Matopahu nodded toward the other. "This is Eye-to-heaven, my *taio*."

Tepua frowned. The other man was his sworn friend, and this was all silly play. Even so, she would not disobey Aitofa.

"All right," said Matopahu, when she remained silent. "I will come closer so you can whisper in my ear."

Tepua lifted the rock again. "Put your hands behind your back," she insisted. "I know how fast they can move."

"There is a *tapu* against hitting the chief's brother with a rock," said Matopahu with a wink. "Is that not right, *taio*?" He glanced at his friend. "Eye-to-heaven is a priest. He will tell you."

Priest? Tepua took a step back and narrowed her eyes.

"Do not think that all priests are against me," said Matopahu hurriedly, his mood serious again. "We are both in exile. Eye-to-heaven confirmed my prophecy, but Ihetoa overruled him."

She stared once more at the other man. He was shorter and stockier than Matopahu, with a round pleasant face. He was broad of shoulder and well muscled, his belly protruding gently above his loincloth. She thought he seemed too amiable to be a priest.

"I am waiting," said Matopahu softly, and now she realized that he had come up just in front of her, his ear cocked toward her lips.

"When—" She cleared her throat and began again. What a child's game this had become. But Aitofa had told her to say these words: "When the ghosts stop walking."

"That is all?"

She had repeated the phrase in front of Aitofa until she knew it better than any Arioi chant. "When the ghosts stop walking, the eye must start."

"Ah, that is the news we have been waiting for," Matopahu exclaimed. Then his arms went around her and he was pressing his nose gently against hers.

"Eye!" she said, making a halfhearted effort to wriggle free. "That is your friend's name. Now the message makes some sense."

"I will explain it all to you. Later." He bent down, clasped her by the legs, heaved her over his shoulder. She felt wildly dizzy as he carried her toward deeper water. "I thought you had something to take care of upstream," he called jovially to the priest while Tepua thrashed in his arms.

"Yes," answered Eye-to-heaven. "I will get nothing done if I sit here enjoying these games." Tepua caught a glimpse of him vanishing into the shrubbery.

"My cloth is getting soaked!" she complained. Matopahu's answer was to unwrap her, throwing the garment onto the bank. She took that opportunity to slip from his wet grasp. Diving under him, she grabbed his feet and toppled him into the stream. "Now we will both have our baths," she said, spitting cool water as she came up.

Matopahu stripped off his own waist cloth and tossed it aside. He came after her, but she was too quick for him, splashing through the shallows and then into a deeper pool. She realized that she was laughing like a child.

Suddenly she caught herself. This game could only lead to one thing, and she was not sure she wanted it. After Rimapoa's betrayal . . .

Matopahu plunged in after her, and she held him off with a barrage of splashing. He stood, grinning, with his arms open, as the water cascaded down his broad, glistening chest. Then he reached up onto the bank and broke off a long banana shoot. "Do you know what this means, daughter of coral?" he asked as he waved the leaf. "It is our sign for peace and friendship."

"I am not feeling friendly," she answered, trying to keep her tone serious.

"I cannot afford to have more enemies." He reached up and plucked another shoot. "Here. You hold one, too. Then we will discuss the terms of truce."

His eyes shone with reflected sunlight. Droplets danced on his cheeks. His mood was so cheerful that she could not hold herself back. Her hand reached out and took the stalk he offered.

With his free hand, he drew her closer. This Matopahu was nothing like the man she had scorned so many days before. She wanted to trust him. She wanted far more than that.

When he gave her the nose kiss, she did not try to pull away. He rubbed his cheek against hers, then against her shoulder, then her breasts. Gently he lifted her, carrying her to the bank, setting her down with her feet trailing in the water.

She lay on cool springy moss while she felt his gentle touch moving over her, his fingers across her belly, his lips along her thighs and in the hollows behind her knees.

He picked a creamy petal from a flower on the bank, then touched its softness to her belly. She realized that all thoughts of resisting him had fled. She felt so comfortable now that she parted her legs when his fingers moved lower. He began to stroke her inner thighs with the petal, pausing once in a while to add a caress with his nose or his lips.

The stroking sent little tickles of pleasure up between her legs. Matopahu brought the petal to his nose and closed his eyes with blissful enjoyment.

"How wonderful are the perfumes of love—the aroma of flowers and the scent of a desiring woman."

He put the petal in the stream and let the rivulets carry it away while he stroked her inner thigh again, this time with the tips of his fingers.

"Your skin here is so soft and smooth," he whispered. "Softer than the petal. I have a place like that." He moved up, laying his stiffening member against her. The silky tip rose and he moved his hips so that it traveled down the sensitive area where he had been stroking, across the little nest, up the inside of the other thigh, then down again.

She could feel herself growing engorged with desire as the tingles became intense waves of pleasure, rippling up from her inner thighs into her loins. She breathed out a low moan and began slowly rocking her hips.

"No, not yet," he whispered, laying his cheek along hers. With his nose and chin, he laid a trail of caresses from her throat down between her breasts to her belly. Aglow now with desire, she clasped his head against her belly, winding her fingers in his curly hair and pushing her loins against his chest.

His hands massaged her, spreading their warmth over her flanks and belly, then briefly reaching to her breasts and stroking her nipples. She was astonished at the joy surging through her at that touch.

She thrust with her hips, searching for that hard member that had teased her. "You are merciless!" she cried, until at last she felt the silky spear pressing at her entrance, gliding inside with a smooth, long thrust.

She thought then that he would start moving and that she would find joyful release, but he stopped, holding himself as deep as he could. She felt him trembling, saw how his head strained back as he leaned on his hands.

Inside, she could feel him expanding into her deepest recesses, growing until she became deliciously tight about him. She lay, eyes closed beneath him, wanting this to last forever, wanting him to keep getting larger until he completely filled her.

She thought she was already climbing the peak to ecstasy when he started to move in easy gliding strokes. The pearl of her womanhood became an intense center of blue-white fire that radiated into every part of her body. . . .

Then it exploded. She knew dimly that she was wiggling, kicking and shouting in abandonment, caught in an eruption of fire that consumed all else.

When she regained her senses, she still felt gentler waves of pleasure sweeping over her. Now Matopahu was nearing his own release, thrusting deep into her moist slickness, tossing his head wildly, clenching his hands into fists. His eyes wide and bright with need, he withdrew from her then plunged in again, giving a great groan as shudders racked his body.

He collapsed atop her, then rolled to the side, still giving little shivers of pleasure. She stroked his neck, starting in the damp hair behind his ears, drawing her fingers down across the bronzed cords of muscle in his neck.

They dozed awhile, and when they woke they strolled upstream to where the flow narrowed and the water ran faster. They joined again, this time atop a smooth, flat rock, with the stream rushing past them. The chill of the spray on Tepua's skin only heightened her excitement and she reached climax with rainbows dancing about her head.

He swung her up and carried her out of the stream into the shade. She felt languid, golden. She could not imagine a satisfaction deeper than this.

But another part of her still felt distant, even resentful. He had teased her, pushing her to the extremes of desire. He had held her entranced, withholding himself for as long as he wished.

He could do exactly what he wanted with her, she thought, and he knew that. She looked at him as he lay on his side, his head propped up on one elbow, his spent member lolling along one thigh. Reaching out, he ran the back of his hand along her jawline and raised his eyebrows.

She looked down, away.

"My loving is not good enough, pearl woman?" He paused. "Or is it too good?"

Her face warmed. How was it that he somehow knew her thoughts even before she spoke them?

Did he have some unspoken command over her, some ability to draw her to him? She rebelled at the thought. After joining the Arioi and setting her own course for her life, she had hoped that no man would ever rule her, either by force or by charm.

She brushed back her hair and tossed it over her shoulder, watching him narrowly.

"Woman, what is it? You cannot say that I gave you no pleasure. Your cries were loud enough."

She gave him a level look, letting a slight, scornful smile touch her lips. "I think you have lost your turban, brother-of-the-chief."

The sun had passed noon by the time Tepua finished washing herself in the stream. She slowly put on her wrap, aware that Matopahu had been staring at her the entire time. "I think my business here is finished," she said, forcing the unkind words. "I have done everything that Aitofa sent me for."

Matopahu, sitting on the bank, groaned and slapped his forehead. "You still believe that I conspired with Aitofa to lure you here!"

"Why else would she have chosen me, except at your request?"

"If she thought to please me, it was her own idea. Perhaps there was some other reason she sent you."

Tepua answered in a quiet voice. "I had to go away awhile, and she thought I could stay here. But you are not the only one living in the highlands. I heard today that a group of Arioi has a temporary settlement near the base of the falls. I can stay with them."

"What is this? You are also in exile?"

"For a foolish mistake. I will make amends to the gods somehow. It is not for myself that I grieve—" Tepua felt a catch in her throat. She had not intended to tell anyone about Fenua Ura. Now, suddenly, she could not hold back. It did not matter if he despised her for taking up with a fisherman, or laughed at her folly. She sank down beside him and spoke until her tears ceased to flow.

"That rascal!" said Matopahu when she was done. "At least you are rid of him now."

"But the priests cannot kill him!"

Matopahu rested his chin in his hand. "Maybe not, but he will be put on some small, distant island, where nobody will ever see him again."

Her voice fell. "Then he will die anyway."

"Perhaps. In that case it will be the gods' doing and not the hands of men."

Tepua felt slightly relieved. Wherever Ihetoa sent him, so long as the sea was nearby, Rimapoa could probably catch something to eat.

"Come now. After all that, you surely do not care what happens to him."

"I should not care," Tepua said angrily, but tears threatened again.

Matopahu gently put his arm around her. "I would like to have you stay with me. When my *taio* leaves, it will be very lonely up here. It is your message that will take him from me."

She sighed. "You still have not explained that message."

"It is simple. We—my friends and I—are trying to get rid of Ihetoa and put Eye-to-heaven in his place."

Tepua scowled, remembering her conversation with the chiefess. "Aitofa hinted at that. She said that your brother still supports the high priest."

"That is so, from all I have heard. Now you told me, 'When the ghosts stop walking, the Eye must start.' Five nights after the moon is full, the spirits stop troubling us. That is when my *taio* must go home. By then, my friends think that Knotted-cord will be ready to back down. They want Eye-to-heaven to be there to assert his candidacy."

"Your friend will replace the high priest?"

"That is our plan."

"Then I will have to deal with him in the end," she said moodily.

"About the feathers? Yes. That is likely." For a moment the thought seemed to weigh on him.

"Then tell me," she said, "since I have confessed so much to you. Is Ihetoa the only man you wish to see replaced? Is it possible also that you envy your brother's office."

"You misjudge me, Tepua. Do you think I would like to be carried everywhere I go, and have food brought to my mouth by servants? That is the life of an infant. No. My only aim is to give my brother the guidance he sorely needs—by making Eye-to-heaven his high priest.''

"If that succeeds, will you be able to go home?"

"Yes. Would you be glad to see me back?"

When she did not answer, he stood up and held out his hand. "We need not talk of that now. For you, I am still a mountain man, and I do live well up here. Come along, and I will show you."

As the afternoon passed Tepua realized that she had almost forgotten about rejoining her Arioi party. The thought of dangling from the ropes again made her knees watery. She could not imagine going back right away.

The ropes were not the only reason, she admitted. The Matopahu of the heights was far more appealing than the Matopahu of the high chief's court. If he returned to his old life, she believed she would come to despise him once again. For now she found herself enjoying every aspect of his wild existence.

First he showed her the pinnacles that he and his friends used as lookout points, though she declined to climb them. Then he led her toward the shaded pools where he fished. She saw Eye-to-heaven returning with evidence that he had not just disappeared out of politeness. He carried three fine brook fish, strung through the gills on a hooked twig.

Tepua glanced at the priest, wondering what sort of man he was. The priests she had known did not soil their hands with common tasks. They always had servants and attendants about them. But here was Eye-to-heaven, humming to himself, a smile on his lips as he ambled along the trail with his catch.

"We build fires far from where we live," explained Matopahu as his friend continued in the opposite direction. "That way, if someone finds the ashes, they will not know where to look for us."

But he did not show her today's cooking place at once. Instead, they followed the stream, up one bank and down the other, until the afternoon was half-gone. Finally they reached a clearing where the priest sat beside a fire.

"Now you will learn an easy way to cook," said the priest with a smile. "Without a pit oven. Just watch me, and then you can do it."

Beside him lay several sections of stout, green bamboo. He cleaned a fish, cut it into small pieces, and slipped these into a bamboo hollow. After he had stopped up the open end with leaves, he placed the bamboo on the coals.

Tepua prepared her own fish in the same manner, then added chunks of *fe'i*. The moist bamboo fibers sizzled in the heat and finally began to blacken, at which point everything was taken out of the fire.

"Now I know why you two look so fit," Tepua said when she tasted the meal. "Down below, we are lucky to have yams."

The priest shook his head glumly. "Only a few people can live up here. What they need below is breadfruit. The time for flowering has come, and still, I am told, the trees show no buds. Ihetoa's offerings have not pleased the gods."

Tepua nodded. She had seen the barren trees, and she knew the importance of breadfruit. All the other sources of food combined could not replace it.

"We must find an answer soon," said the priest, "or many will die."

"*You* are the answer, my *taio*," said Matopahu, clapping his friend on the shoulder. "When you stand in the *marae* and offer your prayers, the gods will listen."

After the three had eaten, Matopahu led Tepua to a rough face of rock. "Here is our cave," he said. "You must climb a few steps."

Tepua looked up, but saw no opening.

"That is the marvel of the place," he said. "It cannot be seen from the ground." He pointed out the handholds and toeholds, and helped her take the first large step up. Then her head was above the stone lip and she could see into the cave's small mouth.

The place was only a few paces deep. She pulled herself over the lip and crawled inside. The floor had been covered with a layer of fragrant ferns. A few pieces of wood served as crude seats.

The men came in, bringing with them leaf-wrapped packets of food left over from the meal. The priest hung these by cords from the ceiling. "In case of rats," he explained.

Soon Eye-to-heaven retired to the rear of the cave. Tepua and Matopahu stayed at the mouth, and she curled up against him. Soft whistling snores soon told her that the priest had gone to sleep.

"Eye-to-heaven is a good man," said Matopahu. "Do you like him?"

She answered sleepily. "Yes, I do."

"Yet you seem shy around him," Matopahu said, drawing her head into his lap and stroking her hair.

"I am still wary of priests. What I did on that island—"

Matopahu touched a finger to her lips. "We will not tell him about that yet. He has other, more pressing problems. For now I think you should follow Aitofa's advice and turn your efforts to your work with the Arioi."

"But your *taio* will learn soon enough. When he returns to the district, he will certainly hear about it. And if he becomes high priest—"

"If so, he will be far more sympathetic than Ihetoa would have been. For now we say nothing. I am enjoying your visit too much to have it spoiled by more gloomy talk." He continued to caress her. Her drowsiness gave way gradually to a warm feeling of arousal. The earlier urgency was gone, replaced by a gentler desire.

"You will find the nights chilly here," he whispered as he led her back into the cave, to his bed of sweet-smelling ferns. "But I have only this one cape to spread over us. We must lie close together."

"I am not cold yet," she answered, feeling a sly grin cross her face. Then she felt the warmth of his chest against her back, like the sun's heat baking her. She reached behind to stroke his thigh, discovering quickly that he had already shed his loincloth. . . .

* * *

In the early light of morning, Tepua woke to the sound of a low moan. She reached for Matopahu and realized that he was not beside her. She sat up, full of fears she could not explain.

At the side of the cave, she saw Eye-to-heaven crouched by Matopahu's sweat-slicked trembling body. "You must go out now," said the priest firmly when he saw her crawling closer.

Tepua hesitated, baffled. Matopahu had shown no sign of oncoming illness. Now, suddenly, this. She stared with alarm at his contorted face and the jerky motions of his limbs.

Then she noticed that Matopahu's left hand was wrapped in bark-cloth. He held it stiffly upright as if injured. Once again a strange windy moan came from his throat.

"What has happened to his hand?" she demanded.

"I am sorry, but you must leave," Eye-to-heaven insisted. He reached out to block her, but she got past him and seized Matopahu's wrapped hand. Beneath the bindings it felt twisted, deformed. Shivers crawled along her spine.

Biting her lip in terror, she tried to unwrap the binding. Eye-to-heaven seized her wrists and pulled her away. She was almost glad to let Matopahu's hand be torn from her grip, suddenly afraid of what she might expose beneath the cloth.

Now she understood. She had seen other men in god-induced fits. But this time it was Matopahu who lay on the ground, foaming and flailing, waving a bound arm that no longer seemed his own.

She felt an urgency to obey Eye-to-heaven's command and scramble from the cave, leaving the priest to deal with this nightmare. Then she saw Matopahu's unbound right hand moving to the floor, fingers opening and closing, as if desperately reaching for someone. Sending a defiant look at the priest, she grabbed Matopahu's palm tightly. The skin was damp and hot, the touch filled with urgency.

"He wants you here," said the priest in a tone of defeat. "You can stay, but keep quiet. We must listen carefully."

Matopahu continued to moan in a harsh, breathy voice, but Tepua could hear no words. She prayed silently that the god would depart and cease tormenting him. Instead, he began to babble in a language she did not understand.

"Even I cannot interpret that," Eye-to-heaven whispered.

Matopahu stiffened, his hand clenching Tepua's convulsively. She fought against his strength, trying to keep him from thrashing and hurting himself. Then suddenly a new, and deeper, voice boomed through the cave. Its resonance held the awesome glory of the *marae,* of dark stone crypts, of images wrapped in feathers. Tepua felt her gooseflesh rising.

The voice grated in Matopahu's throat. "The spear of bamboo is cast at the branches made bare. The tree is of the lance, the club, it stands. The tree is bare, the man pierced to the heart . . . pierced to the heart. . . ."

The words meant nothing, yet filled her with dread. Her body trembled and she scarcely dared to breathe until the voice was finally done. Then she heard a long sigh, felt Matopahu's grip weaken, saw his body fall still.

Eye-to-heaven continued to crouch over him, the priest's face intent with concentration. He began to mutter, more to himself than to her. "What is it? What can it mean?"

"Has the god departed?" she asked fretfully. "Is Matopahu all right?"

"Yes. He will sleep now. While I am left to struggle with his words."

Frowning with doubt, Tepua lay down beside Matopahu and wrapped his cape around them. His skin felt cooler, no longer radiating the fierce heat of the god-touched. She pressed against him, trying to warm him with her own body.

"The branches are bare," murmured the priest. "That refers to the breadfruit, of course. Pierced to the heart means that some great wrong is behind this. Spear-of-bamboo, *ihe-ohe.* That sounds like the name of the high priest, but now I am only guessing." He sighed, looking down at Matopahu with a mixture of affection and frustration. "Yes, *ihe-ohe* does sound like the high priest's name, if we say 'Ihe-toa.' ''

Tepua wished the priest would cease his muttering, at least until Matopahu recovered. Now she could find no rest for herself. Her thoughts kept spinning. Against her will, she found herself trying to interpret the message.

She knew that the gods' words were often cryptic, and that men sometimes spent days trying to explain them. ''Why must the gods torture Matopahu so,'' she complained, ''only to confuse us?''

''He did not suffer,'' the priest said. ''When he wakes, he will remember nothing. But what am I to make of this? *Ihe-toa,* spear-of-ironwood.''

The more Tepua thought about it, the more the mystery annoyed her. *So what if the priest was called spear-of-bamboo instead of ironwood? He still had a sharp point!* ''Tell me, Eye-to-heaven,'' she asked. ''How do your friends plan to force Ihetoa from his office?''

''They will accuse him of having lost the favor of the gods. They will say that the high ones misled him, making him reject the warning about famine.''

She was familiar with such accusations. Her father had once had troubles with a priest. ''Sometimes an evil spirit influences a man,'' she said. ''Ihetoa may say that a demon misguided him, and that now he has driven it away.''

''He has a clever tongue. That is why my friends needed to wait so long. Even now they may not succeed.''

''Then perhaps these words we are puzzling over were meant to help you.''

''You are quick-witted. Now I begin to understand why Matopahu spoke of you so often.''

She felt her cheeks prickle at that piece of news. She was glad the dimness shadowed her face as she replied, ''Up here, away from women, a man cannot help thinking about them.''

''That is true,'' Eye-to-heaven said with a sigh and fell silent.

She cradled Matopahu awhile longer, trying to sort out her feelings. She felt an odd new tenderness toward him, as if he were an extraordinary yet fragile child. When he woke, he would be himself again, the free-living man of the mountains. But she would not forget that she had seen him shuddering on the cave floor, in the grip of something more powerful than any man.

It was said that the gods only spoke through those they favored. Yet Tepua wondered how anyone could call this an honor—subject to the whims of some unknown spirit, forced to speak words that might be nonsense, unaware of what happened during the seizure.

Sacred or not, she would not wish for such a thing. Her own small gifts were frightening enough. She closed her eyes, waiting for him to wake, and drifted back into sleep.

Matopahu woke slowly, rising from slumber as if he were coming up from deep water. He felt a dryness in his mouth and a stiffness in his muscles that could only mean one thing. . . .

He lay on his side, staring at his left hand, feeling and seeing the wrapping of bark-cloth about his fingers and palm. Yes, he dimly remembered winding it around his hand when he felt the aura coming on.

And—the woman. Had she been here?

He turned to glance at Tepua, sleeping, curled up against him. Feeling his dismay grow, he pulled away from her. What had he said? What had he looked like, thrashing on the floor like a speared lizard?

Quietly he crawled to the priest and shook him awake. He put a finger to his mouth, telling Eye-to-heaven to move silently, without waking Tepua. When he slipped down out of the cave, Matopahu saw that they had all slept late. He stood blinking in the bright sunlight, then walked a short distance to the stream.

"I had hoped the god might leave me alone awhile," Matopahu said wearily to the priest. "Tell me what the voice said this time."

Eye-to-heaven repeated the enigmatic words.

"You are probably right about *ihe-ohe* and Ihe-toa," said Matopahu, "but there is still a puzzle." He rubbed behind his neck, realizing that he must have strained it when he thrust his head back. Eye-to-heaven said he often did that when the god entered him. "I hope you got Tepua away before I—"

"I am sorry, *taio*. She insisted on staying. And when you reached out to her, there was nothing I could do."

Matopahu stopped at the stream's bank and stared at the priest. "I—reached out to her?"

"Or the god did."

Angrily Matopahu tossed aside his wrap and plunged into the cool water. He stayed down as long as he could, and when he brought his dripping head up, he did not speak at once. "Why do the sacred ones make me forget what I have done?" he complained. "One day I will wake up to learn that I have bitten a shark—or coupled with a wild boar."

"If that happens, the shark or boar will have my sympathy," answered the priest cheerfully.

"I can always depend on you for a wise answer, my *taio*," Matopahu said. He paused, then approached again the question that troubled him. "So Tepua saw me. She must have been frightened. What woman would not be at such a sight?"

Eye-to-heaven put his hand on Matopahu's shoulder. "She insisted on remaining at your side. She was afraid, perhaps, but she wanted to help you."

Matopahu let his breath hiss through his teeth. He had never before cared that a woman saw him babbling nonsense and squirming like an infant. Instead of feeling honored by the god's visit, he now felt shame. Tepua was an outsider. For all he knew, she might view what had happened to him as a sign of weakness.

He turned to his friend, who was staring at him with a puzzled expression. No, the priest would not understand. Matopahu could not even explain these feelings to himself. "Do not discuss this in front of her," Matopahu said quickly. *If she does not see it happen again, she may forget.*

When Tepua woke, she found the men gone. Matopahu must have recovered, she thought with relief. She imagined that he was out scaling cliffs while she still rubbed sleep from her eyes.

Hungry, she nibbled on some baked banana wrapped in a leaf. While she ate she stared at a long piece of cord that had suspended the packet of food from the ceiling. Now it hung free.

When she finished eating, she decided to go out to wash. She was about to try the tricky descent from the cave when her gaze fell again on the hanging cord. A long time had passed since she last felt a need to make string figures. Now she had a good reason.

She pulled the cord loose, wrapped it around her arm. Then she crawled from the cave, feetfirst, easing herself over the lip as she tried to find a purchase for her toes. Birds screeched overhead, laughing at her clumsiness, she thought. Bits of broken rock clattered below. At last she steadied herself and dared to look down.

It was not so far to the ground, she realized. Gripping an edge of stone near her waist, she lowered one foot, then the other. She arrived at the bottom, panting, but unhurt.

Now she would have some time to herself before the men came back. The sound of running water beyond a stand of fern trees called to her.

Tepua did not linger at her bath. After she had dried off in the sun, she moved to the cool shade. Then she took the cord from her arm and made it into a loop.

The string figures! How she missed them. They helped her to relax, let her mind wander onto new paths. Now she hoped they might lead her to understand Matopahu's mysterious pronouncement. The gods had guided her before, in this way . . . She started with a prayer to her guardian spirit, Tapahi-roro-ariki.

When she was ready, Tepua began with simple figures, loosening her hands. *Priests and spears*. The shapes did not match her thoughts. This one resembled an ironwood tree just a little. Bamboo? Perhaps this one. She tried the more difficult forms of *fai*.

After a time she groaned with frustration and put down the cord. The insight was not coming. She was trying to force the figures in one direction or another. She needed to let them flow of their own accord. Once more she called on her ancestress for aid.

Again she began, this time barely watching what her fingers wove. The cord moved so quickly that sometimes it seemed to blur. She glimpsed tantalizing visions that were gone before she could interpret them. Then she paused for a moment to rest her tired fingers.

Glancing down, she saw a new shape in the string—an upraised hand. And then she was looking at an image far away—at a hand of flesh, at a man in a tall feather head-dress, at a high altar in a *marae*. The image grew startlingly clear.

The man was smiling, his expression mocking the solemn proceedings. He was praying before the altar, yet his face wore a sly grin. And the offering, she saw with a shudder, was a man.

Tepua fell back under the force of the vision and lay on the ground. Her eyes were shut now, and the image had vanished. But the face—she could not forget it. She had seen that face before.

At last she got up and began to walk aimlessly along the stream's banks. Shiny lizards, sunning themselves on the rocks, darted into crevices as she approached. She paused now and then to stare into the glistening water. Then she remembered her audience, months before, with the high chief. The man from her vision, garbed in priestly white, had been standing close to Knotted-cord that day. It was his face—Ihetoa's mocking countenance—that she had just seen.

"Walk quietly, or you will scare the fish," came a whisper that startled her out of her reverie. She glanced up to see Eye-to-heaven, holding a two-pronged spear, bending over a pool at the side of the stream.

"Where is Matopahu?" she asked.

"Walking alone and thinking. Shh." He shifted the spear, his eyes intent on the quarry.

Tepua stamped impatiently. "Eye-to-heaven, I have something to ask you about that is more important than your dinner.''

His arm came down in a sudden thrust. He gave a cry of triumph as he pulled back the spear, bringing with it a struggling perch. ''I am listening now,'' he said as he dropped his catch into a basket.

''I do not know all your words. What do you call it when a priest fails to show the proper reverence?''

Eye-to-heaven put down his spear and turned his attention fully on her. He frowned as he answered. ''That is called *hara,* a grave sin.''

''If a priest is irreverent, then how do the gods view his offering? Surely they turn away in anger.''

''Certainly. But I do not see—''

''Because,'' she said excitedly. ''We are puzzling over the meaning of 'spear-of-bamboo.' You say the offense of irreverence is called *hara,* and I have heard of a kind of bamboo called *hara-tavai.*''

Eye-to-heaven stared at her for a moment. His eyes widened and his mouth opened and then he sank to his knees. ''So that is the word game the gods have played on us,'' he said with awe. ''Two names for bamboo. Two meanings for *hara.* By these rules, *ihe-ohe* becomes the 'spear-that-sinned.' ''

''Then—''

''It is all clear to me now, Tepua,'' he said, pounding his fist against the ground. ''And you have unraveled it. 'Spear-that-sinned is cast at the bare branches.' Ihetoa must be guilty of *hara,* and that is why our breadfruit still does not flower.'' He glanced down into the pool, his eyes narrowed. ''All this time he blamed the famine on the people's shortcomings. No one dared suggest that Ihetoa himself was at fault.''

''Then what can be done? Is it possible to accuse him of his crime?'' Tepua's exhilaration was already fading. She had solved one problem only to raise another.

Eye-to-heaven sat and put his chin in his hand. ''That is what I must decide. The high priest can always cast doubt on Matopahu's words. He has had plenty of practice at doing it. If only someone had seen his transgression—"

Tepua almost spoke, but what point would there be in saying that she had seen the high priest's crime in a vision? No one would take her word for it.

"I will not wait here while my friends plot among themselves," said Eye-to-heaven. "I must return at once and see how I can use this knowledge."

"But the message from Aitofa said to wait—"

"The ones who sent it did not know about Ihetoa's misdeeds. Come. We must find Matopahu."

17

As evening approached, Tepua sat with the two men, looking out through the cave's mouth at the lengthening shadows below.

"If we leave early tomorrow," said Eye-to-heaven, "we can catch Ihetoa at his afternoon nap. I would like to confront him when the priests and attendants are all drowsy."

Matopahu grinned. "That will be the best time. Before he can clear his thoughts and invent new lies." He turned to Tepua. "I do not want to leave you up here alone. You mentioned a camp of Arioi—"

"No," she interrupted. "I want to return with you."

"It will be dangerous," said the priest.

"Not if I keep out of sight."

"And if we fail?"

"Then I will run back to the hills." She lifted her chin and stared at Eye-to-heaven. Did the priest want to deny her a part in the plan? She hoped she would not have to remind him how she had untied the mystery of the oracle's words.

"Until we are close to the high priest's *marae,* we must all stay hidden," said Matopahu, breaking the impasse. Again, he turned to Tepua. "If we fail there, we will need you to carry a message to our friends. You cannot follow us where we are going—onto sacred ground. There is a boundary that no woman may cross."

"I know about that boundary," she answered coldly, recalling Aitofa's rebellious words. "I can take refuge at the women's shrine nearby."

"Then let us get some sleep," said the priest. "My belly is full and I am already nodding." He turned and went deeper into the cave.

Tepua remained. She had not told why she was so eager
to follow the men to the *marae,* and she was glad that they
had not asked. Eye-to-heaven's questions at the stream had
helped her remember another detail from her vision. She had
seen a second man, a temple attendant, a witness to the high
priest's transgression. If she could somehow find him . . .

Matopahu drew closer and put his arm about her. "The
night will be cold again," he said in a whisper.

And it may well be our last together. She tried not to let
that dampen her spirits. Tomorrow he might be killed for his
arrogance in accusing the high priest. Or he might succeed
in pushing Ihetoa from his office. In that case, Matopahu
could probably take up his old life—a life in which she did
not fit.

It was possible, of course, that he would merely be forced
back into exile. If he lost to Ihetoa tomorrow, she felt certain
that the famine would continue. She was not so selfish as to
want that.

"Listen," said Matopahu with a wink as the last gleam of
sunlight vanished. He nodded back into the cave. "Our
friend is already snoring. And I am not even sleepy."

She shook off her worries. "I know a way to tire you
out," she answered, teasing. "At least one part of you."
She let her hand travel slowly down his hard belly, coming
to rest on the even harder erection in his lap.

"I am not sure I can tire out *you,*" he replied. "But I am
willing to try."

The men woke Tepua when there was barely light enough
to find their way out of the cave. They emerged into the
early-morning coolness, hurried along the streambed, past
the *fe'i* trees to the edge of the cliff.

"It is easier going down," Matopahu said when he saw
her hesitate. "I will do it first, to show you."

He chose a place where two hibiscus-fiber ropes hung
side by side. He drew up one line and knotted it about his
waist, then took a firm grasp of the other and backed over
the cliff. Tepua tried to watch him as he went, but the sight
of the ground far below made her head swim.

Then she heard him call that he had finished the first leg of the descent. She pulled up one line, fastened it around her waist, and wound her fingers about the other. Her hands were already shaking. She suspected she would always feel this way when facing heights—she would have to go ahead anyway.

Hand over hand, she let herself down, bracing her heels against the damp rock. She focused on her feet, refusing to look anywhere else.

And then she was out of rope, forced to balance on a ledge while she untied herself. For the next part of the descent, she had only a single rope for her hands. She inched down the slope while she tried to imagine that she was only a few steps above the ground.

The illusion sustained her awhile. She fell into a daze, no longer searching for handholds or footholds, but letting her body find them. Abruptly she was startled by Matopahu's voice from below.

"Slide the rest of the way," he shouted. "It is quicker."

She dared a look down. *Not much worse than the drop from the cave's mouth.* She tried wrapping her legs and arms about the line, letting herself slide until she hit the ground. Her hands stung from the cord, but she was safe.

While Tepua caught her breath Eye-to-heaven arrived, looking as if he had enjoyed the dizzying descent as much as a good meal. She felt briefly envious of the men as they moved on, following the trails she had taken with the Arioi.

Wistfully, she recalled the leisurely pace of her friends on the way up. Her current companions seemed never to need rest. Sometimes they even led her into strenuous "short-cuts," plunging through a thicket or down a streambed, to emerge again onto another section of trail. The sun was only a little past its peak when they neared the coastal plain.

From here on, the three had to avoid the main trails completely. Matopahu led the way along a winding course, through stands of hibiscus that hid them in shadow, then down a dry gully flanked by withering ferns. They detoured around the chief's compound and finally approached the great *marae*.

"You must stay there," whispered Eye-to-heaven, point-ing in the direction of the women's shrine that Tepua had visited several times before. She agreed, and waited for the men to go ahead. When they were almost out of sight, she followed them, hiding in the shadows beneath the high, leafy *rata* trees.

Not far ahead, she glimpsed the carved figures that marked the borders of sacred ground. Except in the rarest of circumstances, no woman could step beyond them and expect to live. But Tepua had an urgent reason for going on. She wanted a look at the attendants, the *opu-nui*, who served the priests.

Her pulse quickened as Matopahu and Eye-to-heaven approached the boundary—and crossed it. Thinking she might lose them, she tightened her fist in despair. Keeping just outside the forbidden ground, she followed, watching the two men pass the low stone walls of the sacred courtyard.

Near the *marae* wall almost hidden in the shadows of the overhanging trees, stood a group of small houses. In front of the doorways, several temple attendants lay asleep. While her companions approached from one side Tepua circled around to approach from another.

She could not be certain if the houses themselves stood on sacred ground. Yet she crept up to the largest, keeping to the side that faced away from the *marae,* while the men went to the doorway and entered without announcing themselves.

She peered through a gap in the wall and saw the high priest jump up with surprise from his sleeping mat. "Where are my attendants?" he shouted. "Get up, you lazy pigs! Look who dares come here—the false prophet, and the upstart who would like to take my place."

"We come for no personal gain," answered Eye-to-heaven. "The famine forces us to seek you out."

His calm manner seemed to infuriate Ihetoa. "There is no famine!" the high priest retorted. He poked Eye-to-heaven in the stomach with a forefinger. "Look at your fine belly if you think otherwise." Ihetoa turned to regard Matopahu.

"Why should I care if the chief's brother insists on seeing bad fortune all around him? The buds are a little late, but the breadfruit will come. I have declared it so."

"Declare it louder, for the trees have not listened," Matopahu said. "In the night sky, the Seven Little Warriors are also announcing the season of plenty. Yet I see only leaves on the breadfruit trees. You delude yourself and your people, high priest."

"That is the last I will endure from you." Ihetoa turned, shouted an order to his attendants who stood at the door. Tepua saw a dozen brown-girdled *opu-nui* rush in carrying heavy sticks.

She shivered as she watched Matopahu hold up his hand—the same hand that he had wrapped in bark-cloth. "If you touch me, you will bring the anger of Knotted-cord down on you," he said to the men. "I may be in exile, but I am of the high chief's blood. An insult to me is an affront to him as well."

The temple attendants glanced at each other uneasily.

"Your slick tongue can be silenced," Ihetoa said, narrowing his eyes as he studied Matopahu. "I have the power to arrange it."

Tepua saw Eye-to-heaven step forward. "Now your own words betray you, Ihetoa. You admit, before us all, that you play with the lives of men."

The high priest's eyes went cold and glittery. All motion in the room froze. "Do not cross me, small priest," Ihetoa said, "unless you wish to suffer the same fate."

"Your threats mean nothing," said Matopahu. "You have abused your office, Ihetoa, and now you must answer for what has happened. Look all around you. There may be no famine for us of the higher ranks, but what of those less fortunate?" He turned to one temple attendant. "Have you begun to worry about starvation? Speak the truth!"

The man glanced nervously at Ihetoa and did not reply.

"I know you are afraid to answer," said Matopahu. "You are fed well here, after all. But what of your family and your neighbors?"

The man looked away and took a step backward, but Tepua heard muttered agreement from his companions.

"I will go outside and ask the others," Matopahu challenged. The attendants made way for him. Tepua remained hidden as he came out, peering at the scene from behind a bush. In front of the houses, evidently drawn by the commotion, a larger group of *opu-nui* and priests were gathering.

"Listen to me," said Matopahu to the growing crowd. "Ihetoa denies there is a famine because he is to blame for not ending it. He made offerings to the gods, and they ignored his pleas. *For good reasons!* It was his irreverence that angered the gods and made them punish us. I accuse the high priest of *hara.*"

Hostile whispers passed through the crowd. Several attendants shifted their sticks nervously from one hand to the other.

Ihetoa emerged from the house and strode into the crowd. "Anyone who disobeys me now will be meat for the altar," he declared in a steady voice. "You men let yourselves be swayed too easily. I tell you, the gods will take care of us. When I make the final offerings, you can be certain that my prayers will be heard."

"Answer the charge of *hara!*" an underpriest bellowed.

Ihetoa drew himself up. "How can I answer such a falsehood? I have been high priest here since Knotted-cord was a child. Not once has anyone found fault with my reverence." He turned slowly, surveying the faces. "You have all served with me. You have all been in the *marae* and felt the sacred touch of the gods as they descended. Every season I carried out the holy rituals, and they were always successful."

"It is true," several men replied.

"There is more," said Ihetoa. "When a fever gripped Knotted-cord and no one could drive it off, do you remember what happened? *I* went to the *marae* and asked the gods to take me in his stead. Matopahu did not stand beside me, nor did this other fellow who calls himself a priest. No. It was *my* humble plea that convinced the divine ones to save our high chief.''

"He does have the gods' favor," muttered several more *opu-nui.*

"He once had it," Matopahu countered. "But no longer."

"Enough!" said Ihetoa to his men. "Take these trouble-makers to Knotted-cord. He will know how to keep them from spreading their lies."

Once more Matopahu held up his hand, but this time the attendants surged toward him. Tepua anxiously scanned their faces, hoping she might still find the man she sought, an *opu-nui* from her vision who had been standing close to the high priest. But now it was too late. Matopahu and Eye-to-heaven, despite their vigorous protests, were being dragged away from Ihetoa's house.

In desperation, she sprang from behind the bush and shouted over the noise of the crowd. "One of you saw it. One of you witnessed the high priest's sin." She pointed at the center of the throng.

The crowd of men spun to face her. "She profanes the *marae!*" shouted the high priest, his voice at a frightening pitch. He turned savagely on Matopahu. "This is the kind of man who accuses me of *hara.* One who brings a woman to soil the temple grounds!"

"I am not on sacred ground," Tepua shouted back, though she could not be certain.

A party had started toward her with upraised sticks when Eye-to-heaven pointed to the boundary markers, stones set in the dirt beside the houses. The *opu-nui* grumbled among themselves, but agreed sullenly that Tepua had not violated the sanctuary. Even so, they glared at her and held their sticks ready.

She gestured again at the crowd, crying out that the witness should be questioned. Which one was he? The face from her vision was nowhere in sight, but another man seemed to shrink from her accusations. She watched this *opu-nui* retreating to the rear of the assembly.

"Enough!" Ihetoa roared. "Before you stands the true cause of our trouble. I know about this woman. She is the worst of these sinners, and the men have schemed to keep her from being punished. Take all three to the high chief.''

The temple attendants looked confused. They held back for a moment, as if reluctant to touch a woman.

Ihetoa shouted, ''She is the one who broke *tapu* on Fenua Ura and stole feathers from the shadows of the gods. It is dangerous to touch her. Drive her before you with your weapons.''

Tepua glanced behind her, searching for a path of escape, but for a moment longer she stood her ground. ''Ihetoa wants you to forget the charges against him,'' she answered. ''That is why he accuses me now. Let him question instead the man who witnessed his own sin. Look! The rascal is trying to run away.''

In the confusion, every man glanced at his neighbor, and small arguments broke out among the *opu-nui*. Then, from the rear of the crowd, came shouts and the sound of blows. Two men dragged another forward.

Tepua stared at the small fat face, the pursed lips, the tangle of beard on the chin. She could not be sure that this was the man from her vision, but his expression of fear betrayed him.

''Let the *opu-nui* speak,'' said Matopahu.

''I have nothing to say,'' the temple attendant squeaked, fear making his sparse beard shake with the quivering of his chin. Ihetoa tried to interrupt the proceedings, but the sudden raising of sticks silenced him.

Matopahu turned to the quaking *opu-nui*. ''If you will not speak the truth, we can learn it another way. Eye-to-heaven will perform a divination.''

At this, the man went even paler, and sweat shone on his face. He cast a pleading look at the high priest, but now Ihetoa had no help to offer.

Then the accused man turned to Tepua, his expression changing to one of awe. ''How could you have known this?'' he asked her in a quavering voice. ''It is said that the gods sometimes speak to a woman when no man will listen. They must have chosen you to help me purge myself of this hateful knowledge.'' Visibly overwhelmed, he flung himself at Matopahu's feet.

"Have mercy, noble one!'' he cried. "I did see the high priest's irreverence, but I kept silent. When he offered a 'two-legged fish' on the altar, I saw him grin with triumph. I knew he was not thinking of the gods, but of his own victory, for he had long sought to do away with that man.''

Matopahu and Eye-to-heaven picked the attendant up, setting him on his feet. Tepua watched Matopahu shade his eyes and scan the group. "Are there others who can add to this testimony?'' Matopahu asked.

After a brief silence, an old dignified priest from the lesser ranks came forward. He said that he, too, had witnessed Ihetoa's failings. He had grieved over them, but had kept silent out of fear. "I am also guilty,'' said the old man, "for not telling what I knew. This has long troubled me. Now I must make amends for my lack of courage.''

"At last we have something worth bringing to Knottedcord's attention,'' Eye-to-heaven replied. "Let us go to him and repeat what has been said here. Let the high chief decide the outcome.''

"Wait,'' said Ihetoa. "Two men may see the same fish, but each tells a different story about its length. In my own eyes, I have done no wrong. If I appeared pleased during the offerings, it was only because I knew that I was making the gods happy.''

"There is more to it than that,'' answered the old priest.

"I have not finished explaining,'' said Ihetoa.

"You must step down,'' said the old priest. "That is the only way to settle this. Let another take your place, until you are freed from your sin. Give this new high priest a chance to make prayers. If the breadfruit trees bud, then we will know I am right.''

"And if they do not?''

"Then take back your office, confident that your innocence has been proved. If that comes to pass, put *me* up on your altar and see if my flesh will appease the divine ones.''

When the old man stopped speaking, the crowd of *opu-nui,* swelled now by all the priests from the *marae,* began to shout and wave whatever weapons they carried. They advanced on Ihetoa, and his protests could not hold them back. The flood of men surged from the *marae* and toward the high chief's compound.

Tepua fled, taking another route, until she found refuge in a quiet grove near the shore. Then she fell down and hugged the warm sand until her trembling ceased.

She did not hear anyone approach. The sound of a voice made her start, and she jumped up to flee again.

"I have been searching everywhere," said Matopahu softly, sitting beside her, taking her in his arms. She could not believe how reassuring his touch felt at that moment.

Her heart was still pounding. "I did not know—what they would do to me."

"You are safe now," he answered. "My brother has been forced to give Eye-to-heaven the high priest's office."

"And Ihetoa?"

"He will be sent away—to serve at a lesser temple until he can cleanse himself of the sin."

She let her breath out slowly. "Then you have all you wanted."

"I have a victory. Are you not pleased?"

"For you, yes. And for the people harmed by Ihetoa. But I fear that your *taio* will learn about my offense now. He heard the priest's accusation. He will ask questions."

"Do not fret, my coral flower. Eye-to-heaven cannot treat you as an ordinary woman. Not after the way you found that *opu-nui*. You must—as the poor fellow said—possess some gift from the gods."

"I—"

He pressed his nose warmly against hers. "There is something you have not told me," he said gently. "How did you solve the riddle of my oracle?"

She stiffened, remembering Bone-needle's many warnings, but saw no way to keep her secret now. Of all men, surely Matopahu would be the most willing to understand. "I had a vision," she confessed quietly, and explained how she used string figures to bring it on. "Ihetoa appeared, and

I witnessed his offense in the *marae*. I saw the other man also, but not so clearly."

Matopahu's eyebrows arched in surprise. He told her that he had never heard of such an ability. "Then you *are* blessed by the gods," he said, drawing back from her, leaving a sudden space of chilly air between them.

"Does that make me different in your eyes?"

His brows knitted. "It does not change my feelings."

"Even so, you will return to court now," she said, a bitter tone entering her voice. "And I, to the Arioi. There will be no more sporting in caves or splashing in mountain brooks." As she spoke she realized that her own words had ended the short idyll. Had she kept silent about the insight from her vision, even for a day, she and Matopahu would have had that much more time together. It had been so brief. . . .

"Tepua," he answered sadly, "I cannot say what will happen yet. I do not even know how my brother will like having me back here. And what if that old priest is proved wrong? What if the breadfruit still does not flower?"

"Then the gods have forsaken us all." She wiped away a tear.

"No, I do not think so. The gods have been angry many times, but they have always helped us when our need was great." He rose on one knee, as if ready to depart. "You must return to Aitofa now," he said. "Eye-to-heaven has gone to explain why you disobeyed her orders and returned from the mountains with us. Now that Ihetoa has no power to harm you, it is best that you remain here."

"And near you . . ." She stared at him expectantly. He still had said nothing of what was to happen between them.

His gaze turned from her. "You must understand this, Tepua. People will be watching me, reporting everything I do. It will be difficult—"

"To consort with a *motu* woman!"

"Do not be angry. It will not hurt us to stay apart for a while. Later, when this uproar over the change of priests has subsided—"

"Then you will send for me," she answered harshly, "as you would for your favorite dog." She pushed herself up and stood away from him. "Perhaps I will surprise you. Perhaps I will not come." Before he could soothe her with his whispers and warm touch, she raced from the clearing.

Late that afternoon, in one corner of the high chief's compound, servants were readying Matopahu's house to be occupied again. Matopahu stood outside, watching the men carry in sleeping mats, when he saw Eye-to-heaven approaching. The priest's mood seemed unusually somber.

"What is it, my *taio*?" asked the chief's brother.

"I must speak with you. About Tepua."

Matopahu regarded his friend with narrowed eyes. *Has the new high priest no more pressing problem?* he wondered as he motioned for his *taio* to join him in the shade.

"It concerns her trip to Fenua Ura," said the priest.

"I heard about it," Matopahu growled. "And if I ever find that eel of a fisherman who led her there, I know what I'll do to him."

"So she has admitted it to you. I was not sure what to make of Ihetoa's blustering."

Matopahu clenched his fist, wishing his fingers were around the fisherman's neck. "She was tricked. I understand what happened. The wretch concealed some *tapu* markers to ease her fears. Otherwise, she would not have stayed on the island."

"Even so, the gods must be angry at her. She escaped Ihetoa's wrath only through Aitofa's protection. Yet something must be done. The gods can choose to strike her at an unexpected moment. Knowing this may drive her to despair."

"Can you help?"

"Yes, but it will not be easy. The Arioi can protect her from any penalty I decree. She must come to me and agree to follow my instructions. Many prayers and offerings will be needed, and this will take time."

"She is shy of priests, but I believe she trusts you, Eye-to-heaven," said Matopahu. "Perhaps a suggestion on my part . . ."

"Or better, from Aitofa. I must tell you this as well, my

taio. It is prudent that you stay away from this woman until she is freed of her sin.''

Matopahu felt his face flush. He was not willing to admit, even to his *taio,* the true depths of his feelings for Tepua. ''She will return to her place among the Arioi,'' he said. ''But I had thought, after a brief time—''

''As a friend, I cannot forbid you such pleasures, yet as a priest I urge you not to see her until she has come into harmony again with the gods.''

Matopahu gazed at his *taio* and felt his dismay turning to doubt. He and the priest had been close for so many seasons that he seldom questioned the man's motivations. Now he wondered whether jealousy might be influencing Eye-to-heaven's words.

Tepua's presence had already disrupted the partnership. She had explained the riddle that Matopahu's god spewed forth, succeeding where the priest had only met frustration. Perhaps Eye-to-heaven sought to restore things as they had been. Matopahu glanced at the priest and felt pangs of remorse. *He has always acted with my best interests at heart, yet now I find myself doubting him.* ''For how long would you make her atone?'' Matopahu asked.

''Several months, at least. I will know better after I have spoken to her.'' Eye-to-heaven paused. ''My *taio,* I see doubt on your face. My only wish is to restore Tepua to you, renewed and purified.''

Matopahu dropped his gaze. ''Yes, of course.''

''Then tomorrow I will consult with the Arioi chiefess,'' said Eye-to-heaven. ''Now I must prepare myself for another task, a most important one—a night of prayer in the *marae.*''

''I wish you well,'' Matopahu replied coolly. At that moment he could not think about the problems that weighed on everyone. The priest departed, leaving the high chief's brother to stare into the dust. Servants approached, asking how to arrange the sleeping mats. *What does that matter,* Matopahu thought, *if I must sleep on them alone?*

He turned and stalked off, reaching the shore and plunging into the choppy waters. A storm was coming, but he paid no heed to it. He swam out into the lagoon, trying to exhaust himself so that he could think no more about her.

Why had he not been born a flying fish or a sleek-sided porpoise? The sea's creatures chose their own mates. They asked no permission from chiefs or priests.

18

THE afternoon was almost gone when Tepua reached Aitofa's compound. She hoped fervently that the chiefess would be preoccupied, too busy to call her. Tepua wanted only to throw herself down on her mat and weep.

When she came through the gate, she heard no sounds of laughter in the courtyard. No one was pounding cloth or husking coconuts. A lone servant stared at her.

"Where is everyone?" Tepua asked.

"The noble chiefess has just gone out. The novices are still in the hills collecting food."

"Ah." *Aitofa gone!* With relief, Tepua went to the novices' quarters and unrolled her mat. She was too tired to cry; instantly, she fell asleep.

Later she woke in darkness, and thought she felt Matopahu's warmth beside her. No, it was only the cover that she had wrapped herself in. Suddenly she realized that she was alone, in a large and empty house. And this was a night when the long-toothed ghosts roamed. . . .

She shivered, wishing for another wrap. It did not help that Ihetoa had announced her guilt within earshot of the *marae*. Not only the priests and *opu-nui,* but every spirit that lingered there had heard it. Against living men she might have a chance, but she was helpless against ghosts.

Tepua moaned softly, and prayed to Tapahi-roro-ariki. "I will dedicate myself anew to the Arioi," she promised her ancestress. "I will work harder than the other novices so that I can quickly advance to Pointed-thorn. And tomorrow, at first light, I will bring you a fine offering."

She tried to sleep, but whenever the thatch rustled overhead, her pulse quickened. In the near silence she heard insects clicking, rats rustling and squeaking. These sounds might be messages from the spirits, but she lacked the skill to interpret them. The thought made her shiver anew, yet finally she dozed off.

When Tepua woke, with a start, she saw the morning's welcome light filtering through the walls. She stood up, glanced at her body, ran fingers over her face. No harm had been done to her! At once she hurried out to find the gift she had promised her protector.

She had forgotten how difficult it would be to find a suitable offering at this season. In Aitofa's dusty storehouse she discovered only yams and taro. "These will not do!" she cried. One did not bring such lowly roots to an altar of the gods.

She headed toward the shore, hoping to find an overlooked coconut under the palms. Along her way she passed beneath the breadfruit trees, barely glancing up at the canopy of branches. Once these boughs had bent under the weight of heavy fruit. Now only shiny scalloped leaves hung there.

But amid the greenery something new caught her attention. She stepped up on a fallen branch and peered closely at the boughs. Was it possible? She rubbed her eyes, thinking she must still be half-asleep. When she looked again, she knew she could not be mistaken.

Just out of reach a bud was emerging, a speckled yellow-and-green catkin. When she glanced higher, she saw others. The tree was preparing to bear fruit again!

She was so excited that she almost lost her balance on the branch. She hurried back to the compound, shouting to the few remaining servants. "The gods have forgiven us! Come see! Everyone come!" She said nothing of her own part in this. But she felt certain that it was Ihetoa's dismissal that had brought this sign of hope.

The servants scrambled after her, and when they saw the buds for themselves, they began to dance about the grove, singing and clapping. Then they raced along the shore to spread the news.

Staring after them, Tepua remembered her unfulfilled pledge. Perhaps in the nearby hills she would find something. A *nono,* or some other small fruit would do for the altar, so long as it was unblemished.

She chose a steep path, ascending while the sun rose, but found nothing of interest along the way. Hot and thirsty, she sat to rest awhile as the sun approached noon. Then she heard shouts from the trail above. She looked up and saw a crowd of Arioi descending, the same foraging party that had taken her to the mountains.

They filed past, their faces damp and dusty, their clusters of ripening *fe'i* hanging heavily from poles laid across their shoulders. When they heard Tepua's news, they began to shout and sing.

At last Tepua spotted Curling-leaf, who was carrying a basket of small mountain apples. They walked together to Aitofa's courtyard, where the Arioi threw down their burdens. The others rushed to the breadfruit groves, but Tepua, with three of Curling-leaf's best apples, made her way to the women's shrine.

The altar stood almost bare. Tepua's gift seemed a trifle in the midst of that emptiness, yet she knelt in prayer. "Here is my gift, Tapahi-roro-ariki," she said. "I beg you to intercede for me with the high gods and ask them to forgive my transgressions against them." She kept silent about Matopahu, and the harsh words she had said to him. He would forget them in time, she thought. He would not forget their afternoon together in the highlands.

But how long must she wait before he called her into his arms again? And how would she put by her pride when he did? She stared at the heap of black stones, the *ahu* of the shrine, but found no answer.

As she headed back she heard a sound that had been missing far too long—drumming. Following the deep-toned rhythm, she reached the performance house, where a group of Arioi were starting an impromptu celebration. Fires were already burning in the pit ovens, though she could see from the preparations that the mountain food would be used sparingly. After all, many days must pass before the new breadfruit was ready to be eaten.

When Tepua saw the others celebrating, she rushed to

join them. *Dance. Dance for Oro. Chant praises to the god.*
That was all she wanted to do now. But before she could
even start, a servant came after her. "Aitofa calls you," the
girl said. Tepua's words of joy died in her throat. With a
heavy step she followed the servant.

"I did not expect to see you here so soon," the chiefess
said coldly as Tepua stepped into the guest house. "But I
am willing to accept what Eye-to-heaven told me. Let us say
nothing more of your . . . adventures in the mountains. Or
of what took place among the *opu-nui* yesterday." She
paused and took a long breath. "I have other things to say
to you."

Tepua, squirming inwardly, forced herself to stand erect.
"Eye-to-heaven has spoken to me of your troubles," the
chiefess continued. "He has offered to perform whatever
ceremonies are needed to help you. But you must take time
to atone. Until then, you remain under a cloud."

"That is—a kind offer—by the new high priest."

"It is. And he asked that you speak with him about it."

"Yes, I will do that," Tepua said softly. But the thought
of approaching Matopahu's *taio* filled her with dismay. She
was certain that he, too, would be a far different man here
from the one she had known in the highlands. She wished
she could find some other way to redeem herself.

"There is something else," said Aitofa sharply. "Con-
cerning our important friend, whose name I need not
speak. I must tell you that he will not be calling you to his
mat. Eye-to-heaven insists. Your guilt might taint our
friend. Your touch might even cause his god to fall silent!"

Tepua reeled under the impact of Aitofa's words. *It is too
late. In the stream, he touched every part of me, yet his god
still came to him.* She dared not say this aloud.

Her fury at Matopahu flared again. He had warned her
that they must part. He had said that people would be
watching him, but not that the gods would be watching as
well!

Or was this a convenient lie, making it easy for Matopahu
to cast her aside? Her throat tightened. "The man does not

matter,'' she whispered. ''I must rise to Pointed-thorn. That is my only wish now.''

''I would also like to see you advance,'' said Aitofa. ''Eye-to-heaven believes that the gods will now grant us our season of plenty. And you may be ready before it ends. Yet you still have the burden of providing a feast for the entire company. Other novices made their arrangements long ago, but you were too proud.''

''I will do anything,'' said Tepua. ''I do not need M— I do not need—''

Aitofa frowned. ''With your reputation, what man of rank would be interested? Everyone knows how you clawed that fisherman.''

She bristled at the reminder. Was it her fault that Rimapoa's foul trick had sent her into a frenzy? But she did not wish to argue with Aitofa. ''Then what am I to do?'' Tepua asked in desperation.

''Your only hope is to find a patron who cares nothing about what others think of him, who does not even listen to priests. . . .'' Her voice trailed off into awkward silence. A gust of wind blew, making the rafters creak. ''I know one such man, only one,'' Aitofa said at last. ''Even then, I hesitate.''

''Tell me.''

''He is not young and you will not like his appearance. He drinks too much *ava*. Do you know what that does to the skin? I have sent other novices to him, but none stayed.''

''I will. Let it be part of my punishment.''

Aitofa sighed. ''That is appropriate.''

''Then you will talk to the man?''

Again Aitofa paused. ''I see no other way to help you. And Head-lifted often reminds me that I should not have taken you in. If you advance to Pointed-thorn faster than anyone else has, then I will have a way to answer him.''

In the next few days, the Arioi who had gone away during the idle season returned to the lodge house. Every morning and afternoon the drums sounded as the dancers practiced again. When her turn came, Tepua joined them, standing in

formation with the other novices and following the lead of
the dancing master.

She had found that blending her performance with the
troupe's was more difficult than the dancing itself. At home
she had grown used to being the featured dancer, dazzling
the audience with her speed and agility while the other girls
formed a backdrop for her performance. Now Tepua had to
match her movements with the others. Yet sometimes she
lost control, and every so often she found herself so caught
up in the music that she forgot everyone around her. Then
she would see the leader's angry face and have to bear his
tirade.

Tepua still was obliged to labor for Aitofa every day. She
spent her mornings sitting cross-legged, making finely
plaited mats to be given as gifts. When she had time, she
also practiced weapon handling or mime. One warm afternoon, while Tepua exercised with an ironwood spear,
Curling-leaf interrupted her. "Aitofa sends word," she
whispered, "of an admirer who wishes to see you. You
must go to him now."

Tepua felt gooseflesh as she turned to stare at her friend.
She had accepted Aitofa's offer in the heat of her anger at
Matopahu. Now she felt far less certain about it. "First I
must wash," she answered. "I am covered with dust." With
one final lunge, she drove her weapon into the target of tied
straw.

They walked to the stream, and when Tepua felt the cool
water around her, she wanted to prolong the bath as long as
possible. Curling-leaf was already dry, and arranging her
wrap. With her head down, Tepua came out on the bank,
then listlessly rubbed herself with scented oil from a
coconut shell. The other women in the stream were laughing
excitedly as they discussed the men they were preparing to
meet. Tepua had no one to care about now. Perhaps she was
better off that way.

Curling-leaf vanished for a few moments, returning with
a garland of coconut leaves and hibiscus flowers for
Tepua's hair. "Now I will lead you to his house," Curling-

leaf said. "To the house of the man called Feet-out-of-water."

They took a wooded path that paralleled the shore. Here, stately ironwoods dangled needlelike leaves over a thicket of smaller trees. "Why were you chosen to lead me?" asked Tepua. When Curling-leaf did not answer, a discomfiting thought reached Tepua. "Is it because you know the way?"

"Yes," her friend answered unhappily.

"You went to this man, and yet you remained a novice."

"I could not please him," Curling-leaf replied, turning so that Tepua could not see her face. "He sent me away."

"Then I cannot hope to do better."

"You are prettier," the other woman insisted. "And I have seen how you dance. Feet-out-of-water will not send you back."

Tepua frowned. For a moment she thought she might not be able to go through with Aitofa's plan. She stared at her downcast friend, trying to imagine what had happened between Curling-leaf and the nobleman.

Then anger strengthened Tepua's will. She had come this far with the Arioi. She had learned their chants until she could say them awake or asleep. Now she would not give up her hopes.

Breathing deeply, trying to keep her thoughts from what was to come, she followed Curling-leaf. They passed a stand of glossy-leaved *hotu*, crossed a stream, and approached the shore. Here breadfruit trees stood in neat rows, surrounding a compound that was almost as large as the headman's.

"Remember that this is a nobleman you are visiting," said Curling-leaf as they drew closer to the low fence. "His father was a well-known chief, long ago. This man has influence as well as wealth. He can help you."

"Are those your words or Aitofa's?"

The other woman hesitated. "Those were the words Aitofa used when she sent me to him. I hope you heed them better than I did." Curling-leaf embraced her quickly. Tepua saw the glimmer of a tear on her friend's face as Curling-leaf turned back to the path.

Standing alone now before the compound fence, Tepua recalled the words of challenge she had shouted so many days ago. The people at the performance had asked who she was, and Tepua had answered: *I am the sister of the shark. I am the daughter of the reef.* She straightened her wrap, swept her black hair over her shoulders. Proudly she strode toward the guard who stood watching her.

A servant came to take her in. Children glanced up from their games, then looked away. Brown dogs eyed her and returned to scratching their fleas. *Good,* she thought, *I draw no attention.*

But suddenly it seemed that every woman of the household was watching her. She saw mats pulled aside at the doorways and faces pressed to cane walls. Her cheeks burned as several finely dressed women came out into the courtyard to gaze at her openly. Tepua forced herself to meet the challenging stares.

The servant led her, not to the main house, but to a smaller one with latticework walls that lay at the edge of the compound.

"Welcome to my little guest house," said a deep voice from within. "I am pleased that you accepted my invitation."

The servant stepped aside, allowing Tepua to enter alone. Her eyes took a moment to accustom themselves to the dimmer light within. Then she saw a heavy, pale-skinned man sitting on a broad stool. He was of middle years, a good deal older than either Matopahu or Rimapoa, and was dressed in a simple printed wrap that did not disguise the bulge of his belly. Beside him lay polished coconut shells and a wooden bowl filled with muddy-colored liquid. Tepua sniffed the peppery scent of *ava* root.

She stepped boldly into the room.

"The last time I saw you," he said, "was the night your face was smeared with red paint. I could not get a good look at you then. Now I see that you are as beautiful as Aitofa promised."

"You are kind," she answered quietly. Her stomach fluttered.

He smiled. "I could not stop watching you that night. I would like to see you dance again."

Tepua lowered her gaze. "Oro came to me. I cannot call up such a frenzy at will."

"Frenzy? No. This is not a sacred occasion!" He picked up one of his cups and dipped it into the bowl of murky *ava*, then shouted an order through the wall.

From just outside, the sound of a drum began softly. Tepua remained before Feet-out-of-water, trying not to stare at the white, scaly patches that covered his skin—the result of overindulgence in *ava*. The thought of touching him repulsed her.

"Is the beat to your taste?" he asked. "Tell the drummer what you want."

"It will do." She remembered how she had managed to begin on the night she danced for the Arioi. Perhaps if she did not have to endure his stare . . . She turned, facing the source of the drumbeat. Through the wall's openings, she caught a glimpse of the drummer's smooth, well-muscled back. If she were dancing for him instead of this wreck of a man, she might manage a bit more enthusiasm.

She began the movements. She could will herself to follow the beat, but that was all. Her arms moved heavily; her fingers felt clumsy. Slowly she turned to face Feet-out-of-water.

"Yes," he said, smiling as he put down the cup he had just emptied. "Aitofa did not mislead me."

Or you are too besotted with drink to care. She continued to roll her hips, turning her body until she had made a full circle.

"That is good, but enough for now," he said, sending the drummer away with a curt order. "I do not want to exhaust you. Sit down and join me." He dipped a cup into the bowl and held it out for her.

Tepua sucked in her breath. It had been her honor to serve this drink, when it was available, to her father's most important guests. She had not been permitted to sample it herself.

"Have some," he said. "It will make you happy. I see too much sadness in your face."

She did not know if Aitofa would approve, but the chiefess had sent her here. With a defiant laugh, Tepua sat down and took the cup.

"In one draught. That is how we drink it."

Tepua eyed the contents warily. Then she raised the cup to her mouth and swallowed. Only when she finished did she notice the sharp, peppery taste of the roots that had gone into it. Her tongue felt slightly numb.

"Good?" Feet-out-of-water was beaming broadly and Tepua felt her own glum mood lifting. "I will tell you a secret," he said in a mock whisper. "I have the best *ava* on Tahiti. There is a special place in the woods where I grow it. Maybe someday I will take you there."

"The only roots I know are taro and yam," Tepua answered. *And I am learning about the one between a man's legs.* But she kept herself from saying the last part.

"Yes," he answered. "I have heard how Aitofa puts you novices to work in her gardens. That is why I try to help when I can." He leaned forward, reaching out to pat her hand, when suddenly he toppled from his stool and fell heavily onto the mat-covered floor at her feet.

Tepua cried out with concern when she saw him make no attempt to rise. "It is nothing," he said. "When I take too much, the drink makes my legs heavy. Come, lie next to me."

She had never seen anyone drink enough to be made helpless. Now she was moved by pity as well as disgust. She also felt light-headed from her own drink, though she had only downed one cup.

"Come here," he said. "And I will tell you a story about a man and a woman."

"I have heard plenty of those." With a sigh of resignation she lay down beside him, leaving a small space between them. He whispered to her. Reluctantly, she wriggled closer.

"That is better," he said. "You must bring your face to me. I cannot move."

At last, with an effort of will, she rolled up to him,

pressing her nose against his broad and fleshy cheek. It was a strange sensation, not as unpleasant as she had expected.

"Now, here is my story," said Feet-out-of-water. "There was a woman so beautiful that all the men envied the one who took her to his hut. But her would-be lover drank too much *ava*. He drank so much that his spear would not rise. Even so, the couple laughed together and enjoyed each other's company. Even without *hanihani*."

"That is a good story. I will remember it."

"Behind me, you will find a bowl of scented oil. I would like you to roll me onto my back and rub my chest. When I am able, I promise to do the same for you."

Tepua agreed to do as he asked. It seemed a more agreeable task than the one she had expected to perform. His eyes closed while she worked, her palms gliding over his slick, soft flesh. She felt his breathing slow into the rhythm of sleep. Her own eyelids began to feel heavy. She remembered how long she had spent plaiting mats this morning. . . .

When Tepua woke, the interior of the hut was almost dark. Feet-out-of-water was gone. She hurried to the doorway and saw a young womanservant waiting for her. "You must go home now," said the girl. "A boat is ready."

"Boat?" Tepua followed her out through the gate and down to the black sand beach. Four husky men were standing beside a large outrigger canoe. When they saw her, they launched the boat, then held it steady just offshore. One man came forward, picked her up, and carried her through the surf to put her in.

This is the way a noblewoman rides. Tepua felt a glow of pleasure as she watched the men dipping their oars, speeding her along the shoreline. She felt, for a moment, as if she were going to her real home. If she closed her eyes, she could imagine that these were her father's oarsmen. . . .

She was still feeling proud when she strode into Aitofa's compound just as the brilliant sunset faded. Curling-leaf ran up to her. "It was not bad—this time," Tepua confided.

"Then I am happy for you. We may both make Pointed-thorn together."

* * *

Tepua expected Feet-out-of-water to send for her again,
but he did not do so at once. Meanwhile, she heard talk from
the other novices that made her face hot. Matopahu had
become wildly popular since his triumphant return from the
mountains. He was now traveling through the district,
enjoying the hospitality of one underchief after another.
Some women were being made happy, she thought. Tepua
could not help imagining Hard-mallet's expression when he
arrived at the compound of Pigs-run-out. . . .

There were whisperings that more people wanted to put
Matopahu in his brother's place. "But he does not wish to
be chief," Tepua blurted out before she could stop herself.
The others stared at her, as if wondering how she could
know such a thing. She bit her lip. "That is what I have
heard," she added hastily.

The thought chilled her. *Matopahu as high chief?* In her
imagination she saw him mounted on the shoulders of his
bearer, his newly bulging stomach pushing out his noble
garments. She saw the disdain in his eyes when he looked at
her, and wanted to weep. That was not the way her
mountain man should end up.

She resolved to say no more about him, and to try not to
listen when others mentioned his name. When she heard that
Feet-out-of-water had sent for her again, she welcomed the
distraction with a gaiety that surprised her.

"A boat is coming for you soon," the messenger said.
This time she prepared herself for the meeting with more
enthusiasm. She walked down to the beach, and her mouth
fell open when she saw what awaited her—a large double
canoe, outfitted with a small thatched house in the middle of
its deck. Colored pennants fluttered from the bow posts.
Sunlight gleamed on the arms and backs of the paddlers.
What a sight for someone who had spent the morning
pounding cloth!

When she slipped inside the hut, she found Feet-out-of-
water smiling at her. "Today I am taking you to my secret
place," he announced as he pressed his nose against hers.

"Where the *ava* roots grow?"

"No. A better place than that."

The men rowed them swiftly past the wooded shore. Children raced along the narrow beach, calling and waving. She glanced out the doorway at the fine young paddlers and tried not to wish that one of them were beside her, instead of the aging nobleman.

"You are still sad, I see," said Feet-out-of-water, patting her arm. "I must ask Aitofa to take better care of you."

"It is not Aitofa. . . ." She fell silent, listening to the creak of timber and cord and the steady rhythm of the paddlers. She wondered if she might mention the question that troubled her. "I am worried—about these rumors of replacing the high chief."

"Ah," said Feet-out-of-water. "It is no surprise that people are grumbling. Knotted-cord supported Ihetoa far too long."

"I do not know how chiefs are judged here," she said. "Is one mistake enough to turn people against him?"

"It should not be. Knotted-cord is far from the worst chief we have had. And with Eye-to-heaven's advice to guide him now, he will do far better."

"Then why do people talk of pushing him aside?"

"Ha. It is foolish, I agree," said Feet-out-of-water. "Matopahu is not suited for the chiefhood." He gave her a curious look. "Surely you are bored with this talk of politics."

"No. Please go on."

"I have no quarrel with the chief's brother. He is superior in wit and character to poor Knotted-cord. It is this business of being an oracle that worries me. There is danger in having one man serve as both high chief and oracle."

"I have heard that on some islands it is even worse. The same man is high priest as well."

"Quite so. I am impressed with your knowledge, little novice. Such a man may come to think of himself as a god, but he can only be a man, and must make the mistakes of men. This could happen here—in our district of Tahiti."

"Would the nobles and underchiefs tolerate it?"

"For a time. Then they would cast him out as well, probably kill him."

Kill him! Tepua's breath quickened and she found that she could not speak. So this was what Matopahu risked. A humbler man might change his course, but Matopahu was far from humble.

She became aware that Feet-out-of-water was looking at her, raising his eyebrows at her sudden silence.

"It is nothing," she said hastily, then donned a pleasant expression as she would a costume. "I was just . . . surprised."

Feet-out-of-water sighed and stretched himself. "Politics can be very tiresome. Let us turn our thoughts to more pleasant things, eh? I think you will enjoy the place where we are going."

Through the doorway she saw that the canoe had turned away from shore. Ahead, graceful arches of coconut palms rose above the surf. Then the rest of a small coral island came into view.

Fortunately, this place in no way resembled Fenua Ura. It was a tiny *motu,* with only ironwoods and a few coconut palms sprouting from its sandy soil. The ground had been carefully swept of fallen leaves and debris.

One man carried her ashore, but two were needed to lift her host and bring him over. When he stood up on his own, he used a walking stick to steady himself. "This is where I come when my household grows too noisy," he said. He pointed to a thatched shelter beneath the trees.

His men carried in mats and supplies from the canoe. He waved the boatmen away and led Tepua inside.

"I have given up my *ava* for a while," he said jovially, "so that we may better enjoy each other's company." He lowered himself heavily onto the mat beside her and pressed his nose to hers. At once his fingers moved to her wrap and began to fumble with the knot. Tepua could not help stiffening as he loosened the tie.

"Are you afraid, pretty one? Or repulsed? The unappealing tone of my skin cannot harm you. In fact, it is looking much better after these few days without my drink."

Tepua swallowed, not knowing what to say. She allowed him to unwind her wrap. Then, at his order, she turned her buttocks to him.

She willed herself not to flinch at his touch. Drawing in her breath, she held herself rigid as he began to caress her with a gentle motion. "Sweet globes," he crooned. "Mangoes ripening on the tree."

To her surprise, she found the warmth of his hands not unpleasant. From a coconut bottle he poured scented oil and began to rub it gently into her skin, working upward over the small of her back and onto her shoulders. She began to tingle.

She felt herself loosening. Perhaps it was not the man at all, but the lovely island and pleasant little hut that were affecting her so. Now that she could not see him, she might as well imagine that the broad-shouldered paddler lay behind her, rubbing her with his supple hands.

"How I like you Arioi girls," he said. "All the dancing and exercise makes you nicely firm. Other women are so soft and flabby." He pressed his body against her. She felt his length hardening, and she did not pull away. It was pointless to think that she might turn back now.

He caressed her for a few more moments, bringing his slick hands around to stroke her breasts. The tingling grew stronger, preparing her for what was to come. Then she felt him push inside her and give a few frenzied thrusts. After a shudder, he collapsed with a deep sigh of contentment.

For a moment she bore the weight of his paunch pressing against her back. Then she gently tipped him sideways so that he rolled away, already snoring, onto the mat. She drew her wrap over herself for a cover and lay down beside him, feeling a mixture of relief and regret.

The act had been less repulsive than she had feared. If this was the worst she must endure, then she knew she could bear it. So long as Oro was pleased, what did her own feelings matter?

As the nobleman lay sleeping beside her, her thoughts returned to their conversation on the boat. What he lacked as a lover, Feet-out-of-water made up for in other ways. He had talked with her as few men had ever done, listening carefully to her opinions. He understood well why Matopahu should not be chief.

Matopahu's supporters had won a victory when Ihetoa was forced out of office. Perhaps they could keep the former high priest from ever returning. But to cause more changes would be folly. Why could they not see that?

Folly. The word drifted through her mind as she closed her eyes sleepily. The Arioi were masters at exposing foolishness. Matopahu himself had once told her how important this was. If the Arioi felt a need to do so, they could ridicule even the doings of the high chief's brother. . . .

19

IN a torchlit courtyard, drummers started a rapid beat, sending six young women dancers into frenzied motion. Matopahu, watching from his seat of honor, whispered a few compliments to his host. The entertainment had been lavish and had gone on so long that now Matopahu wished to stand and stretch his legs. The dancers' hips moved in a blur. The girls were pretty, yet he could not work up an interest in any of them.

Matopahu's gaze turned to the other guests, men of the district, who still watched with rapt attention. Then he glanced at his host, a young nobleman called River-dry, one of Knotted-cord's underchiefs. The young man's narrow face was aglow as he watched the entertainment. He seemed guileless at this moment, but Matopahu knew otherwise.

Earlier, while speaking in private, River-dry had hinted strongly that he would support Matopahu if he wished to displace his brother. Matopahu had merely smiled at these suggestions. It was far too soon to tell anyone what he might be planning.

Now, as the guest looked away from his host's intent face, he found his thoughts drifting elsewhere. These dancers meant nothing to him. There was only one dancer he wanted.

When Matopahu had first heard about Tepua and Feet-out-of-water, he had laughed scornfully. Everyone knew that the old fool was useless to a woman. But gradually Matopahu's feeling of helpless anger had grown. Now, as he thought about it, he imagined his would-be rival drowning in a huge vat of *ava*. Here was a fitting end for him!

Feet-out-of-water has nothing to lose, Matopahu reminded himself bitterly. The aging nobleman held chiefly titles but no power. He lived as he pleased on his large estate and paid no attention to what others said. If he wanted a *motu* woman as his consort, not even the high priest's disapproval would stop him. . . .

Abruptly Matopahu realized that the drumming had stopped and entertainment ended. Everyone was staring at him, waiting for him to rise first. He smiled, stood up, aware that he had become the center of attention. The crowd opened to let him pass.

"My good friend," said River-dry as they walked back toward the underchief's house. "There is a favor I would ask of you, a delicate matter. I have heard much about your remarkable god-voice. Of course, if you are weary . . ."

The high chief's brother was far from surprised at this request. It had become almost a ritual, repeated in one household after another. "I can promise nothing," he said, giving his usual reply. "But the god has proved agreeable lately, as you may have heard." He signaled to his *taio,* who had been traveling with him, helping to assure the people that the gods' favors had been fully restored.

Eye-to-heaven continued to serve as interpreter of Matopahu's pronouncements. Recently his task had proved easy, since the words had been surprisingly clear. Both men knew that something had changed. The spirit who seized Matopahu now was far different from the one of earlier days—the one who had warned of famine and of Ihetoa's guilt.

It was not uncommon for one god to leave a man and be replaced by another. Yet Eye-to-heaven had begun to express his concern about this one. "The new voice worries me, *taio,*" he had said on several occasions. "I believe it speaks truthfully, but I sense a malicious streak. Be wary of letting it seize you too easily." Matopahu saw that warning again in the priest's expression as Eye-to-heaven joined him at the underchief's doorway.

Only a small party of important men came with them into the house. The others remained outside, keeping a respectful distance. "I want only a single light," Matopahu insisted.

The smoky torches were taken away. The select audience took its place on the grass-strewn floor.

Matopahu sat on a thick pile of mats in the middle of the floor. Eye-to-heaven brought a candlenut taper and sat cross-legged beside him. "You may all chant softly, along with me," said the priest, when everyone had settled.

The chant was simple, two lines repeated endlessly. Matopahu stared at the small sputtering light and tried to make himself comfortable. In earlier days he had never tried seeking the god-voice; it had always come to him when it chose. He had been happy when it left him alone.

Now his reputation as a prophet had spread throughout Tahiti. People from outlying settlements flocked to wherever he was in hope of hearing some new message. He had found a way to keep from disappointing them.

As he watched the blue-tinged flame he slowly began to relax. He put aside all his troubling thoughts and let the light draw him in. His breathing deepened and slowed.

Then a prickly sensation began at his nape and spread gradually down his back, taking a long time to reach the soles of his feet. His body began to feel so light that he thought it could be lifted by a puff of wind. Soon he could not feel the mats that lay under him. He seemed to float in the darkness, with only the small, bright center for company.

The chant droned in his ears. He no longer heard the words, only the repeating rhythms. In his mind, he spoke a chant of his own.

> Come to me, spirit, I am waiting.
> Come to me, in the darkness.
> I long to hear your voice.

For a time he knew nothing, thought nothing. There was only the chill of emptiness about him. Then he felt a sudden disturbance. His left arm shuddered and a groan sounded. He sensed only dimly that something was being wrapped about his hand.

A sound emerged from a mouth, but the mouth was not

his own. "Ahhh," the voice said, in a strange and frightening tone. "Ahhh, I am here . . . in the world of flesh." Matopahu felt his shoulders twitch and his legs tremble. The light vanished, leaving him nothing to hold onto. Yet there were sounds. . . .

He heard a frenzied whispering, then a firm and familiar voice speaking aloud. "O spirit who favors us by your presence," said Eye-to-heaven. "I beg you answer one question."

"Who—who asks it?" The god-voice rasped and squeaked.

"A worthy man. The noble chief who calls himself River-dry."

"River-dry? I—do not know him."

"He is here with us, spirit. He is eager to please you."

"To please me—he must be generous. I—crave the things of the living. Let this River-dry bring offerings. Have—Matopahu—take them in my name."

"You will have gifts, wise spirit," said River-dry. "I have rolls of scented cloth already waiting for you."

"And a woman. Yes. This is what I crave tonight."

"Any woman you please," the underchief answered quickly.

Matopahu scarcely heeded what was said. He had no part in this now. All he could do was listen. "Then ask. Ask your question," said the god-voice.

The underchief seemed to have trouble getting out his words. "I—I would like to know, gracious spirit. About my first child. Will it be a son or a daughter?"

"Ahhh," the god-voice squeaked. "Here we have a wise question. Here we have no simple answer. Why is that? Why is the outcome so confused?" The voice began to click and squawk and gabble. Matopahu knew his limbs were thrashing, but he felt nothing, suspended as he was in another place. Then clear words came again. "Twins! That is what you have coming. A boy and a girl. I cannot say which will be first from the womb."

"That—that is a fine prophecy," River-dry answered.

"And all I can tell you," the god-voice squeaked. "I

have worked up a hunger. Bring me the woman now. Wait. Bring me two. I will choose. I want—both your sisters.''

Matopahu heard a hiss of indrawn breath. It was customary, he knew in his dreamy haze, for the guest to be entertained by the wife or consort of the host. The host's sisters, on the other hand, must be treated as chastely as if they were the guest's own kin. But now it was a god speaking, not a man, and no one could refuse the demands. The women would feel honored to be called.

''Uh . . . as you wish, noble spirit,'' replied River-dry.

Later, toward dawn, Matopahu woke and felt the warmth of the women, one on each side of him. What a pity, he thought, that he could not remember the pleasure they had given his body. That had been for the god and the god alone.

He stretched, feeling the stiffness and aches that always followed these visitations. He quietly rose and went out, glad to feel a fresh breeze on his face. ''You are up early, my *taio*,'' came the voice of Eye-to-heaven, who was already outside.

''Come. Let us walk,'' said Matopahu. The shore lay just ahead and the tide was low. In the growing light he watched small waves lap the exposed beach. ''All went well last night, I trust. I cannot remember much.''

''River-dry and his family will have something to talk about for a while.''

''But you are not pleased, my *taio*. I hear it in your voice.'' Matopahu waded a short distance out, letting the cool water swirl around his feet.

''I am thinking that I would like to go back to the simple life of a priest. I have had enough of being an honored guest night after night, traveling from one nobleman's house to another.''

''Yes, it is tiring,'' said Matopahu. ''But we have our obligations. It is important to restore the people's confidence in their gods—and in their high priests.'' He did not add that he still keenly enjoyed being the focus of attention. At home, he was constantly overshadowed by his brother.

''You know I cannot desert you,'' said the priest. ''It is

not only a matter of our friendship. What would people think? To leave you would mean breaking up all the good work we have done.''

"Then let us continue this tour for a time, my friend. Maybe you will come to think differently.''

"No, I will not change, my *taio*," the priest answered with a sigh. "You are the changed one. You let men's whispers fill you with ambition. You do not discourage the rumors.''

Matopahu smiled. "I say nothing.''

"But men try to guess your thoughts. As do I. What will happen if someone dares ask your god the question that all wish asked?''

"If I will be chief?" Matopahu laughed coldly. "To that question, I can only hope that the god will answer in riddles. It is your job to be sure no one asks. That is one reason I need you with me.''

"Then I will stay, my *taio*, but I urge you to reconsider what you are doing.''

In a clearing near the Arioi house, Tepua sat with a group of other novices watching Pecking-bird and her friends improvise a skit. Preparing these little comedies was part of their training. There was to be a competition, judged by high-ranking Arioi, to select the best performance.

Pecking-bird, holding an imaginary chief's staff, sat stiffly on a rock. "Fishermen, what is taking you so long?" she asked, looking down haughtily, her voice pitched low to imitate a man's.

In front of her, three young women pretended to struggle with a net. So far, no one in the small audience was laughing at her playlet.

"Fishermen, I am hungry," said Pecking-bird. "And you are slow!''

"This will fill your belly, noble chief," said one of the mock fishermen. The others mimed lifting a huge fish from the net. Still, nobody laughed.

In exasperation, Pecking-bird turned her back on the

players and sat down in the shade beside the onlookers. "Let me see who can do better," she challenged.

Tepua felt her muscles tensing. While she watched Pecking-bird's group, ideas for her own playlet had continued to grow. Ever since her discussion with Feet-out-of-water, she had wondered how to bring her thoughts into the open. She did not know what the other novices would say, but now she wanted to find out. "Let me try," she answered.

"I am already laughing," said Pecking-bird.

Tepua ignored her. She picked up a wooden bowl, a prop that someone had left on the ground. "Curling-leaf, will you join me?" She held out the bowl.

"What—what am I supposed to do with it?" Curling-leaf took the bowl but remained seated.

"Imagine that it is filled with *poi*," said Tepua. "And pretend to eat."

"And what about you?"

Tepua assumed her own regal pose and forced her voice into the lower registers. "I am the high chief."

Peking-bird gave a shrill cry of scorn.

"But I am no ordinary high chief," Tepua continued. "You have all heard of me, I am Rooster-crows-too-early-gets-head-lopped-off." She saw a few smiles, but now she hesitated. What she wanted to do next would raise eyebrows, might even be viewed as sacrilegious. Yet the Arioi, by turning things around, seemed to get away with the most outrageous buffoonery.

"What makes me special is this." She picked up a piece of bark-cloth and wrapped it around her hand. She heard indrawn breaths as the audience recognized the sign of the god-possessed. She hoped that they would also notice that she wasn't exactly imitating the behavior of a god-seized prophet, for she had made a point of wrapping the cloth about her right hand instead of the left.

Abruptly she adopted a different voice, one that quavered and squeaked. "I am not only the chief. I am an oracle, too." Several novices gaped at this pronouncement. "And what I say is for all of you to hear. This is what the divine ones demand of you. You must give up your old habits. From now on, when you eat *poi,* you must do it with one eye closed.''

''That is silly.'' Curling-leaf squinted at Tepua, trying to keep one eye shut as she dipped into her imaginary *poi.*

''It is supposed to be,'' Tepua whispered. A few in the audience were giggling while others looked on with puzzlement.

Tepua raised her wrapped hand again. ''There is more, my obedient ones,'' she said in her squeaky voice. ''When you eat your *poi,* not only must you close one eye, but you may use only your crooked little finger. At the same time, you must stand on one foot.''

Curling-leaf made a show of trying to follow orders, dipping into the bowl with her little finger while balancing awkwardly on one leg.

''Now you are supposed to look doubtful and question the interpretation of my words,'' whispered Tepua.

Curling-leaf giggled. ''Can this truly be what the gods expect of us?'' she asked. ''I must consult the high priest.''

''I am the chief *and* the oracle,'' Tepua intoned. ''I am so filled with *mana* that I do not have to listen to any priest. Do as you were ordered.''

''I think I know what this is about,'' said Curling-leaf, with a sly look.

Tepua felt her face redden. She puffed herself up to look indignant. ''How dare you speak out of turn? And where are the gifts you promised? Bring me pigs and *tapa,* you son of a sea snail!''

''Enough!'' cried Pecking-bird. ''I will watch no more. We are novices. We cannot poke fun at great men.''

Or at great fools? ''Pecking-bird, I always thought that the Arioi were *supposed* to do just that,'' Tepua retorted. ''If you do not like my skit, work on your own, and we will see whose is better.'' She stalked off, and was glad to see Curling-leaf coming with her.

For their rehearsals, the two found another clearing, farther from the Arioi house. After a day, other girls came.

With more players, Tepua began to embellish the little production. Yet she kept worrying about how Aitofa would react to it.

At times she considered asking the chiefess if hers was an acceptable mode of satire. But what if Aitofa told her to stop? If Tepua did not ask permission first, then later she could not be accused of disobedience.

Days passed as the senior Arioi prepared for a major performance for the coming Ripening-of-the-year celebration. The novices continued to work at their own comedies, often giving up their afternoon sleep to practice. The time for the competition finally arrived.

Early one morning a nervous troupe of novices, men and women, assembled inside the Arioi house. Both blacklegs, Aitofa and Head-lifted, sat with other high-ranking Arioi on the viewing platform. Tepua watched the judges, seeing several yawning or with sleepy expressions. They would rather still be dozing on their mats, she realized. Perhaps they did not care how much time the novices had spent preparing for this.

Head-lifted clapped his hands and called for the first group to start. A small troupe of men began a pantomime on canoe building that brought peals of laughter from every side. The first man swung an imaginary stone adze at an imaginary log, grimacing with astonishment as the tool rebounded from the hard wood. When he tried swinging again, the invisible head flew from his adze and struck another player, whose silent reaction of pain as he clutched his belly made the audience roar. Though they used no props, the skill and timing of the mimes let the audience almost see the misbehaving tools that kept dogging their efforts to build the canoe. Tepua could not help but admit to herself that this skit was far better than her own.

When Curling-leaf glanced at her, Tepua merely smiled. But each group that came on seemed almost as good as the first. At last it was Tepua's turn.

With straw stuffed under her wrap to pad her belly, the "high chief" took her place on a stool in the center of the stage. She studied the dour faces of the judges. The comedies so far had been amusing, but none had touched on politics. Perhaps she was about to break some rule that everyone else understood. . . .

Tepua swallowed once, and began. "I am the high chief. I am Rooster-crows-too-early-gets-head-lopped off." Not a single smile. She tried to ignore her audience and focus on the performance.

As the chief's pronouncements became more bizarre, and the action with *poi* bowls more frenzied, the onlookers began to warm to it. In the final scene, the players started a mad scramble to depose the demanding high chief. Tepua saw Aitofa's lips twitch, and even noticed several judges giving vent to subdued laughter. But Tepua had seen their responses to the other comedies. Hers ranked near the bottom. She tried not to show her dismay as she led her players off.

Tepua was not surprised when Aitofa called her late that afternoon. She still felt stung by her defeat, although she did not begrudge the "canoe builders" their victory. They were expert mimes, almost as good as seasoned players. But Pecking-bird's silly piece on fishing had also been declared a winner.

Aitofa sat on her stool, staring at Tepua with an expression that she could not interpret.

"I hope that our performance gave no offense," Tepua said hastily. "I did not mean to be irreverent."

Aitofa raised an eyebrow. "I give you credit for daring, if nothing else. I cannot remember when a novice last took on such a dangerous subject."

"Then—you are not angry?"

"I did not say that. I will tell you, however, that Head-lifted and I have spent some time discussing your skit."

"We should all forget it," said Tepua sadly. "Compared with the others—"

"It showed poorly. That is correct. You have much more to learn before you can amuse an audience. Yet your performance was not entirely without merit. The piece had a satirical bite that I found refreshing."

Tepua's eyes widened.

"With work, it might be made into a worthy comedy."

"To be shown?"

"Yes. To the people."

Tepua felt a sudden panic. She had started this, after all, with a hope that the senior Arioi might follow her lead. Now that it seemed possible, why did she wish to stop it? "But—if it is presented—"

"There will be effects, both good and bad, I agree. Everyone will know whom we are mocking."

Tepua struggled to explain her feelings, which pulled her in two directions. "It is not the man himself, I would mock, but what other people wish to make of him. They are pushing him into something he does not really want."

Aitofa smiled grimly. "Do not think that you alone have had these thoughts. As it happens, Head-lifted and I talked some time ago about this. We spoke of presenting a comedy to poke fun at our noble friend. After all, that is what we Arioi are expected to do. But the Ripening Celebration attracts visitors from other districts and even from other islands. We did not want to air our problems before strangers."

Tepua felt vaguely relieved. "Then later, perhaps."

"No," said Aitofa. "We cannot keep your playlet a secret now. Too many people have seen it, and they will talk. If we do not put on a finished play at the first opportunity, then everyone will believe that we Arioi have lost our keen edge, that we are afraid of important people. Now you have forced our hand."

Tepua looked down. The thought of how Matopahu might take this made her deeply uneasy. She knew that she had been moved by spite more than by any interest in politics. Yet she truly believed that Matopahu's life would be destroyed if he gained the high chief's office.

"What do you say, my rash novice? Do you wish now that you had chosen a more innocent subject?"

She lifted her head and answered hoarsely, "That is not the Arioi way."

"Good. Then do not be surprised when you see our players tossing bowls of *poi*."

The breadfruit grew fat on the trees as preparations for the performances went forward. The experienced players took the skit and transformed it into a masterpiece of comedy. Even Tepua burst out in gales of laughter when she saw the rehearsals.

Whenever she met Feet-out-of-water, Tepua tried to amuse him by imitating portions of the Arioi play. The nobleman did not call her often, for he had begun to suffer from an illness that even abstention from *ava* did not cure. Sometimes when she arrived, she found him in good spirits. At other times, when he seemed gloomy, she did her best to cheer him.

Meanwhile she kept hearing of Matopahu's exploits, not only in the high chief's district but in other parts of the island. Matopahu's pronouncements continued to win him renown. Men from outlying areas were seen almost daily carrying gifts to leave at his house.

People spoke of these exploits in admiring voices. When Tepua heard such talk, she focused her thoughts on the festivities to come. After the comedy was presented, some of these admirers might have second thoughts!

The time of celebration was almost at hand. Visitors began arriving from all over Tahiti, and from other islands as well. Every day Tepua saw new canoes drawn up on the beach. It had occurred to her that the guests might include *motu* people.

Atoll traders visited Knotted-cord on occasion, but so far she had avoided them by staying close to Aitofa's compound. This time she could not hide; on the night of the performance, she would have to stand with the other novices.

The risk of being seen began to worry her even more than how Matopahu would react to the play. She had known, when she joined the players, that some time she must face this. Now she wondered if she had put too much trust in the ability of the Arioi to protect her.

Every day she nervously searched the beach. Among polished hulls bearing upright bow- and stern-posts, she feared she might find the simpler but more seaworthy double-ended craft from her own islands. She found none.

Preparations grew feverish as the night of the performance approached. *Tapa* mallets clattered all day. Drums and nose flutes sounded as the Arioi practiced dance and pantomime. Tepua stood in the line of chest-slappers, swaying and chanting, never missing a beat.

At last the moment came when she found herself in costume, sitting with the other novices beneath the roof of the great performance house. She blinked, gazing up at the firelight reflecting from the timbers of the theater, listening to the roar of the bonfire. Then she turned to watch the festivities begin.

"The high chief!" came the cry, booming across the heads of the audience as Knotted-cord swooped into the performance house on the shoulders of his bearer. His face glowed with satisfaction as he was carried to his seat. Tepua wondered if he had been informed about the comedy to come. Perhaps he was eagerly awaiting the ridicule that would be heaped on his brother.

Next the royal family and favorites arrived. Missing from this privileged group, of course, was Ihetoa. The dismissed high priest would not wish to be seen now, in the depths of his disgrace.

Another man's popularity had taken an upsurge. Tepua could not help watching the arrival of Matopahu, resplendent in a tall black-and-red headdress and feather cape. He rode his human mount with evident enjoyment, waving to the crowd while the applause swelled around him. Yet his expression seemed forced, and she sensed a darker mood behind the gaiety. Perhaps he, too, knew what was to come.

With a burst of thigh-pounding applause, Matopahu was installed on a high seat near Knotted-cord. He sat regally, keeping up his confident appearance. But when the crowd's attention turned to something else, she saw a gloomy look appear. Then she noticed him send a searching glance around the theater, as if looking for someone he could not find.

Tepua turned away. She had painted herself thoroughly, and had draped herself with garlands and necklaces in a style she did not normally use. Matopahu—or anyone else—would have difficulty recognizing her tonight.

The time came for arrival of the Arioi. Aitofa and Head-lifted, howling and cock-strutting across the open floor, made the ritual greeting, casting the braided coconut leaf at the high chief's feet. Now, Tepua thought, the introductions would begin as each noble guest appeared and recited his or her lineage. She forgot her other worries when she realized that she had not gone today to look at the visitors' canoes.

The introductions began with Maohi high chiefs. As the genealogical recitations droned on, Tepua sighed softly to herself. So many noble families, not only from Tahiti, but from all the neighboring high islands!

She had fallen into a daze, staring at the firelight, when the crier's voice abruptly changed its tone. "Here is the welcome to noble guests, who come to us in their seaworthy canoes. Here is the greeting to far travelers. Here is the welcome we offer to the chiefess Hoatu and her consort, Ro'onui.''

Tepua instantly ducked behind Pecking-bird. She was trembling so that she barely registered the names that had been cried. But she had seen enough. Nobles from the coral islands had come, people who might recognize her. Tepua had heard of this visiting chiefess, who ruled an atoll not far from her own. She raised her head enough to see past Pecking-bird's shoulder.

The *motu* chiefess was arrayed in a regal headdress, a high wicker cylinder covered with iridescent green pigeon and parakeet feathers, decorated with shark's teeth and pearls. She wore finely woven garments of white hibiscus bark, fringed at the edges. The man beside her wore a simpler headdress. She stared at him, openmouthed, as she took in his familiar face. *Rongonui!*

She realized that the crier, unable to pronounce the nasal "ng" sound, had garbled her brother's name. As she watched the guests take their seats she continued to marvel. Rongonui had seemed so young when she left home, and did not look much different now. Yet her brother had become consort to chiefess Hoatu!

Tepua stared at the woman, who seemed notably older than Rongonui. Tepua could not fault her for her choice. Hoatu could have her pick of men, so why not take one in his prime?

As the pair came forward the firelight shone on their faces. The chiefess appeared calm, with the serene dignity of one who accepted homage as her right. Yet Tepua could see a hidden ferocity in her high-boned cheeks and the sculpted flair of her nostrils. She was a sturdy woman, with plenty of strength to put behind a spear thrust. If Hoatu's tribe went to war, Tepua could easily imagine this woman standing in the forefront of her warriors.

Beside her walked Rongonui. He was as tall as their father, his arms and torso thick with muscle. His eyes were the most striking part of his oval face. Black-lashed, they seemed to have been drawn in charcoal on his bronzed skin. His gaze was the same as Tepua remembered it—measuring, challenging, but she noted a new element, a sense of smoldering resentment. How different it must be for him to live always in the shadow of power.

She barely listened as first Hoatu and then Rongonui recited their lineages. How she wanted to run to her brother and ask what had happened at home. But she could not go to him. Not now . . . not even at the end of the night's festivities. He must never learn of her presence here.

Tepua was caught in such a fever of longing and despair that she wondered if she would be able to concentrate on her performance. Soon the novices were getting to their feet around her and forming the line of chest-slappers that made a living boundary to the Arioi stage. Hurriedly she found her place.

For a brief time she was able to lose herself in the rhythmic beat of chants and songs. The Arioi performed a dance symbolizing the graceful beauty of the breadfruit tree. Then came another dance and then it was time for her comedy.

Rongonui's arrival had nearly made Tepua forget about Matopahu. She cast a glance at Knotted-cord's brother and imagined that she saw him narrow his eyes. Hastily she looked away. She could not think about him now. Her mind was too full of thoughts about her family.

The play began with the chorus chanting "praises" for the new high chief. Each compliment carried its barb, and soon laughter from the audience almost drowned out the words.

Then the "high chief" bound his right hand with a gaily painted cloth and began to stride about, miming his procla- mations. For this scene, the Arioi used no props. But when the "subjects" dipped their little fingers into their imagi- nary bowls, Tepua could almost see the long, gooey strands. Soon pandemonium reigned, with bowls flying and imagi- nary *poi* getting smeared everywhere.

Knotted-cord roared so hard that Tepua thought his high stool might tip over. Matopahu wore a faintly embarrassed grin, but Tepua saw his hands fiercely gripping the under- side of his seat. She felt a moment of pity and wondered if she might have found a subtler way to handle the subject.

At last the play ended in a flourish as the subjects rebelled, dumped *poi* on their troublesome ruler, and pan- tomimed tossing him over a cliff. The audience broke into a rumble of thigh pounding as the players bowed. It took a long time for Knotted-cord to stop laughing, and Matopahu's rigid smile seemed carved on his face.

The festivities continued, but Tepua began to think that the high point had been her satire. From Knotted-cord's reaction, he would probably want the skit done at each Arioi performance for the rest of the season. She assumed that the Arioi would be glad to oblige. Poor Matopahu!

Her gaze turned back to her brother. She waited impa- tiently for the end of the evening's celebration, yet at the same time she dreaded that moment. If she went to Rongonui, would he recognize her? And what would happen when Rongonui sent word to their father that she still lived? He would insist that she come home, and then he would learn of her defilement. She gazed at the Arioi around her. She did not know if they would defend her from the wishes of her own family.

The celebration ended for the night. The chest-slappers began to file from the hall. Tepua saw her brother rise, his profile clear against the dying flames of the bonfire. Had he sorrowed over losing her? she wondered.

Rongonui turned, staring her way, as if he could see her, though she knew that she blended into the crowd. Perhaps he sensed something.

Curling-leaf tugged Tepua's hand impatiently. The novices were leaving. Tepua thought of going with them—to hide like a rat under a leaf.

Her decision to conceal herself from the trader had been easy, but now it was her brother who stood here. How could she know if she would ever see him again, or anyone else from her family? Suddenly she broke Curling-leaf's grip. She cut through the milling throng toward her brother, crying out to him in the atoll tongue.

The scuffling and muttering of the crowd ceased at the sound of her shouts. Rongonui turned, raising his brows in confusion, even fright. "Who speaks with the voice of my lost sister?" he challenged.

The costume and the face paint! Tepua spat on her wrist, scrubbed her forehead, then her cheek. As the paint wore away, Rongonui's expression turned to one of astonishment.

"Tepua-mua?" He came down from the platform.

"Yes, my brother. I survived the storm and drifted here, to Tahiti."

Rongonui opened his arms and Tepua flung herself into his embrace. "So many tears have been shed for you, so many prayers spoken," he said. "Why did you not send word that you were safe?"

"I had no way to reach you. I did not even know if any of my kin had survived."

"But our traders come here often," he answered, in a tone of rebuke. "And yes, we certainly did survive. We kept most of our canoes from capsizing, and lost no one but you. I thank the gods that the squall was brief.'' Rongonui grasped her shoulders and held her away from him, studying her keenly. She became aware that others were watching, especially those still seated on the platform. The high chief cleared his throat.

Her brother turned to Knotted-cord. "You have been a gracious host, noble high chief. This is a gift I did not expect. It gives me great happiness."

Knotted-cord leaned forward on his perch, glancing first at Tepua and then at Rongonui. "This woman is your sister?"

"Yes. We had thought her dead, but I see that you have kept her safe. For that, my father Kohekapu will be greatly pleased."

Hearing these words gave Tepua a chill. Soon she might have to confess that she had not been cared for as well as her brother assumed. If she could somehow avoid that . . .

Knotted-cord puffed himself up. "She wished to enter the Arioi. I recognized her worthiness and aided her."

"My family is honored to receive your help."

Knotted-cord flicked his elegantly carved fan. "It may be," he said cautiously, "that a few fools disregarded your sister's rank. You can be certain that they will be more careful after this."

With that, the high chief grunted an order to his bearer and waited to be lifted from his seat. Suddenly he turned to Matopahu, who was staring with evident astonishment at the scene. "I trust you enjoyed the entertainment, noble brother," Knotted-cord said with a parting laugh as the bearer lifted him.

Hoatu, the chiefess, took Tepua into her own embrace and spoke to her in the atoll tongue. "I am glad to find you alive, Tepua-mua, after hearing so much about your family's grief. When we take you back with us, I will order a great feast. All your kin will come—"

Tepua stiffened. "Let us talk of that later."

"Then join us in our guest house," said Hoatu. "I wish to get to know the sister of my husband."

Tepua glanced again at Matopahu, who had scorned his

bearers to remain on his stool. Clearly he had heard the
conversation between Rongonui and the high chief. Now
Matopahu looked bewildered. Did it please or dismay him
that his guess about her ancestry had proved true? And how
badly had the play stung him? She wanted to run to him, to
say *something* that might heal the breach between them. . . .
With a sigh, she turned away, to go with her brother.

"I will visit with you, but I must sleep in my own
quarters," Tepua said at last as she walked with Rongonui
outside the performance house. Servants carrying palm-rib
torches lit the way to the high chief's compound. "I am still
bound by the rules of my lodge."

"You should stay with us," said her brother, brushing
back a strand of wavy hair that fell over his face. "One of
our family should not debase herself by capering with
Tahitian players. You will be returning home now, so you
may as well tell your troupe leader that you are resigning."

Tepua spun around to face her brother. The black-lashed
eyes were cold. "That is not my plan," she answered.

He grasped her arm. "There is no question. You are
Kohekapu's daughter, and that is what he expects of you.
You must forget this Arioi nonsense and return to your
sacred duties until another marriage can be arranged."

"Rongonui," said Hoatu sharply. "We are in Tahiti now,
where we have no authority. Let us not offend our hosts by
quarreling."

"You would let her defy her father's wishes? I think I
know already why she refuses to return. She cannot have
stayed so long among these dissolute Tahitians without
taking a lover." Rongonui pulled Tepua to him, stared
down at her with a hard gaze. "Have you been corrupted by
these eaters of *poi*? Have you lost your purity?"

Tepua tried to tear herself free from him.

"So I am right." He gripped her so hard that she nearly
cried out from pain. She gasped, then stamped down,
grinding her heel on his bare toe. Rongonui let go and she
pulled away.

Hoatu interposed herself between the two. "My husband

and his sister will not fight,'' she said calmly. ''Rongonui, you disgrace yourself.''

''Will you stand by while she destroys the reputation of my family?'' Tepua's brother hissed. For the moment the chiefess gave no answer.

Just ahead stood the guest house, where servants were bringing in candlenut tapers. Others carried coconuts freshly opened for drinking, and bowls filled with fruit. Hoatu waved the servants out as soon as they had delivered the refreshments.

The chiefess seated herself on the highest stool. Tepua saw her brother's resentful expression as he took another seat. ''You leave me with a problem, Tepua,'' said Hoatu. ''It is true that your father will expect you to come back to him.''

''I have not joined the Arioi for frivolous reasons,'' Tepua answered in a firm voice. ''The god Oro seized me. Everyone saw that I was inspired. To tear me away from here—from the path I have chosen—would risk angering Oro.''

''How do I know that?'' asked her brother bitterly.

''Do not answer spitefully, my young husband,'' chided Hoatu. ''I understand something of Tahitian customs. The Arioi would not have taken her in if they had not seen her in a state of *nevaneva*.''

Tepua turned to Rongonui. ''You have said, noble brother, that I was the only one lost in that storm. Does that not tell you something? The gods wanted me to leave my home island and come here. If you try to take me away, how do you think they will answer?''

He beat his fist against the leg of the stool. ''You are my sister and Kohekapu's daughter. Yet you wish to serve as a lowly chest-slapper in the Arioi! This is the disgrace that everyone will know about. Even if we hide your defilement from our father, he will hear this.''

His hand shot out, grasping her wrist. She gave an angry cry as he brought the back of her hand closer to the light, showing the altered tattoo. ''And this is the final proof of your debasement,'' he shouted. ''You have defaced our emblem, the mark of our ancestors. How can I tolerate such an insult?''

"Is it true, sister?" asked Hoatu.

Tepua pulled her hand free. "It was the only way I knew to keep the wrong people from finding me. I would have been carried home in a trader's boat, like a fat sow, and bartered to my father."

"As you deserve—" Rongonui began.

Hoatu interrupted, "Enough, husband! I know it was no easy decision for Tepua to make. And now she can again wear the emblem of her family. I would like her to do that. But this question of being an Arioi chest-slapper . . ." She gave Tepua a penetrating look.

"I will not remain so for long. I will advance to Pointed-thorn, and then higher." She paused, thinking for a moment of Feet-out-of-water and the promises he had made to her. No, she need say nothing of that. "If you wish me to rise quickly, to the most honored ranks of the Arioi, here is what you can do. You can ask Kohekapu to send me gifts of pearl shells and fishhooks, so that I can arrange my advancement feasts. That is the way to end this quarrel with honor."

"Well-spoken, sister of my husband," said Hoatu. "I see no other way out. I am not willing to bring the gods' wrath down on us to satisfy Rongonui."

"I will make no such request of my father," said Rongonui petulantly.

"Then I will," said Hoatu. "Furthermore, I, too, will send gifts, Tepua. I would find it an honor to be kin to a high-ranking Arioi. I would prefer, of course, that you married one of our island chiefs, but I see now that it cannot be."

"You are kind and wise, noble chiefess," said Tepua. *Far more so than Rongonui can ever be.* Her eyes stung, threatening tears. She had no chance for a reconciliation with the rest of her family, she thought. Hoatu's sympathy and assistance were the most she could hope for.

And there was Matopahu. What would happen if he learned who was ultimately responsible for the play? She sighed, giving up the battle against her tears as one spilled over and slid down her cheek.

She turned her face, hiding her pain. She wanted to run out now, to race along the beach in the moonlight and forget how cruelly her brother had treated her.

But custom required her to stay with Hoatu and sullen Rongonui, talking lightly of the evening's entertainments, until the chiefess began to yawn. At last Tepua gave Hoatu a parting embrace, and endured one from her brother. Then she walked out into the quiet night.

As Tepua left the high chief's compound she paused before taking the path toward Aitofa's. Turning toward the point, she could just make out the high stones of the *marae* gleaming in moonlight. The sight made her shiver, yet she did not turn away.

For too long, she knew, she had been avoiding Eye-to-heaven. By declaring her unfit for Matopahu's company, he had so angered her that she had never gone to see him about her atonement ceremony. Instead she had put it off, plunging herself into the Arioi work, making amends for her sin through offerings at the women's shrine. But now so much had changed. . . .

Tepua recited her prayer against night-walking spirits as she took the dark path toward the *marae*. She knew the way to the high priest's dwelling. Carefully skirting the sacred boundaries, she came up behind the house and saw a glimmer of light filtering through the walls. She called softly to Eye-to-heaven.

The pattern of light shifted and she dared to peer through the wall. Eye-to-heaven, seated on a stool, was talking to another priest. Tepua waited until the other man left, then called again. This time, the high priest heard her and came to the wall.

"Tepua-mua!" he whispered. "I am so pleased to see you. But you must not come inside. Stay there and I will walk with you."

He came out, embraced her warmly, then led her to a place where they could sit and look out at the full moon reflected on the water. His white robes seemed to give off a pale light of their own. "Matopahu has changed very much since we were all together," he said sadly. "That is not what you came to see me about, is it?"

She wanted to confide in him, but she could not forget how he had kept Matopahu from her. She tried to keep any resentment out of her voice as she said, "Matopahu is part of the reason. I have heard much about his recent exploits, though I tried not to listen."

Eye-to-heaven shook his head sorrowfully. "When I traveled with him about the island, he became more arrogant every day. Wherever we went, the orators made speeches exaggerating his virtues, and I think he began to believe them."

"And what of his pronouncements? I heard such tales."

"Yes," the priest agreed. "I know now that an evil spirit has replaced his wise oracle. For a long time, I tried to make myself believe otherwise. The people also suspect but do not seem to mind. They act as if it is an honor to satisfy the desires of this demon."

Her eyes widened. "Surely you can drive the spirit away."

"Not without Matopahu's help. He must be willing to make an atonement. Sometimes it is not easy to bring oneself to the proper state of mind." He turned to stare at Tepua. His face was shadowed, but the moonlight let her see his raised eyebrows.

She felt her cheeks burning. "Yes. It is true. I also must make my atonement. I feel now that I am ready."

"Good. You have suffered long enough, and Aitofa tells me you have served the Arioi well. As soon as these festivities are over, I will arrange the ceremony that will cleanse you."

"And Matopahu?"

"His case is not so easy."

"Perhaps the comedy—"

"Yes," said the priest with a sigh. "I heard about that performance, but I cannot tell you how he took it. The satire may help him regain his old self."

"If I could talk with him—"

"Let me try first," said the priest. "You see, I feel some responsibility for his woes. When I told him to stay away from you, I did not realize how harsh a demand I made on him. I think this anguish weakened him. To forget you, he indulged his basest impulses, and that made it easy for the evil spirit to push aside his old god."

"And has he forgotten me?" She heard her pulse beating as she waited for an answer.

The priest touched her hand. "Tepua, you are always in his thoughts. I am certain of that."

Certain? The priest's words made her dizzy. "If I had known this sooner—" No. It did not matter what had caused Matopahu's foolishness. She still would have wanted to expose it.

"I will speak with him tomorrow," said Eye-to-heaven, "and see if he has come to his senses about his ambitions. Until I have settled this, I ask you not to see him." The priest paused. "There is another problem as well. I do not wish to worry you needlessly, but I feel you should know."

Tepua stirred uncomfortably. Too much had already happened tonight, but if this new development threatened Matopahu . . .

"I am concerned about Ihetoa," said Eye-to-heaven.

"I thought he was gone."

"He should be where we sent him, at a shrine far from here, making his own amends. But he had hopes of eventually regaining his old office. Now, I fear, he has grown anxious about his future. I think he realizes that the people will never accept him back as their high priest. At least, that is what Ihetoa himself muttered to one of his fellow underpriests some days ago. And now our troublesome friend has vanished."

"Where would he go?"

Moonlight touched the lines on Eye-to-heaven's round face, turning his pleasant expression solemn. "That is what I cannot learn. And why I must warn Matopahu."

20

RIMAPOA stirred on his hard, gritty bed, wishing he could stay asleep. With a groan of despair, he crawled out from under the small, leafy shrub that served as his shelter. He looked around at his coral-strewn shore and saw that nothing had changed.

Behind him he heard the relentless pounding of waves against the nearby reef. White sand glistened under the morning sun, but he found no joy in its beauty. He could think only of finding something to eat.

Not a single coconut tree stood on this tiny island of his exile. The high priest's men had left him in a place where only a few shrubs grew, so that he could not build even the flimsiest of water craft. He had long ago given up the idea of escape.

The search for food had become his sole preoccupation. On many days—he had lost track of how many—he had found nothing. Now, fighting the weakness of his body, he stood up to scan the shore.

To his delight, he saw a small, white crab dancing back and forth near the water's edge. Salivating for the tiny morsel, he picked up a piece of broken coral—his only source of tools or weapons here. Cautiously he stalked his prey, aware how fast the crab could scuttle out of sight. Not daring to step any closer, he threw. . . .

The missile landed just short of its mark, startling the crab back into its sandy hole. Rimapoa howled his anger, then stood still for a moment while he mustered his strength. Just offshore, in the shallows that surrounded his tiny *motu*, he saw a flash of red fin, but he did not go after it. Lacking hook, net, or spear, he had little chance of catching anything that could swim away from him.

He had found shellfish when he first arrived, but now those were all gone. Sometimes, under moonlight, he had managed to catch a sluggish fish in his hands. He had even put together an octopus lure, tying glossy cowrie shells about a twig and lowering it over the edge of the reef on a line of twisted bark. The lure had worked—once—providing him with an octopus that he greedily devoured raw. But then his fragile lashings had fallen apart. None of the shrubs here had bark that could be rolled into proper cord.

Right now his thirst troubled him more than his hunger. Seeing nothing else of interest on the shore, he turned inland to his water supply.

A few natural cisterns in the rock caught rainwater whenever there was a storm. He had been trying to deepen the holes, but the process of scraping coral against coral went slowly and took too much of his strength. He knew a time would come when the basins dried up.

With a sigh, he bent down to sip from the dank hole. The water level was as low as he had seen it. He turned to study the sky, but saw no clouds.

Rimapoa had never imagined that he would die of thirst. He had always expected the sea to claim him. Perhaps, when the moment neared, he would have enough strength left to heave himself into the water. Better to be devoured by sharks, he thought, than to be carved up slowly by crabs while he still lived.

He returned to his sheltering bush, where he had piled slender sticks in the hope that he might weave them into a trap for fish. Without cordage, he had been unable to hold the contrivance together. But yesterday he had found some tough strands of kelp washed up on the windward side of his island. Now he thought he might be able to tie the sticks together into a mesh.

His fingers felt clumsy as he leaned over the work. Things kept slipping away from him. If he could only fill his belly once in a while, he might have the strength. . . . And then, as he was about to abandon his attempt, he noticed a man-of-war bird standing but an arm's length from him, its attention on the surf.

He could not miss such an easy target. He picked up a stone. The long-tailed bird seemed not to notice. *Shadow of the gods.*

No! He could not do it. He pressed his face into his hands and sprawled on his hollow belly. . . .

Later, when he heard a voice shouting over the roar of the surf, he knew he was still dreaming. He rolled over, trying to find shade. He heard the voice again, and finally opened his eyes. Now he was certainly awake, and he still heard it!

He stood up, raced to the lee of the island, and saw a small three-man outrigger approaching shore. One of the paddlers waved at him. Rimapoa rubbed his eyes, then began to whisper praises and promises to his god. "A dozen albacore!" he muttered. "White-bellies or larger. Give me the freedom to catch them, and they are yours!"

"You are looking thin, fisherman," called the steersman of the canoe. His own proud belly hung heavily over his spray-soaked loincloth. The man looked familiar, but Rimapoa could not place him. Perhaps he had seen him at the fishermen's house. Then Rimapoa's mouth fell open in disbelief.

"Ihetoa!" Without his headdress and fancy cape, the high priest's grandeur was gone. Rimapoa sensed that Ihetoa had lost more than his fine clothing.

"Let us talk," said Ihetoa, wading across the submerged reef and onto the island. He turned his back on the two crewmen left behind in the canoe.

Rimapoa came closer, moving slowly to conserve his strength. He could not grasp what this was about.

"I am willing to take you back to Tahiti," said Ihetoa.

The fisherman gaped.

"But only if you agree to help me. My enemies there have pushed me out of my *marae*. They are trying to keep me from my proper place. I need you to help me destroy them."

Rimapoa licked his dry lips. He wanted to go to his pool for a drink, but now his gaze was fastened on the high priest's haggard face.

"That *motu* woman who clawed you is one," said Ihetoa.

"As soon as you were gone, she took up with the high chief's brother. The two of them accused me—"

"Tepua?" the fisherman rasped. "With a strutting nobleman?" He felt weak and light-headed. The ground seemed to tilt beneath his feet.

"Be careful, fisherman," said the priest, grabbing Rimapoa's arm to keep him from falling. "Now listen to what I tell you. All the *opu-nui* saw those two together. What is more, the *motu* woman expects to advance in the Arioi. I have heard that she is planning her feast—"

"Feast! Then—" Rimapoa could barely speak. She had told him she wanted red feathers to barter for that feast, but then she had refused to take them. Now she was going through with her advancement after all! He groaned and sank to his knees, for he could draw only one conclusion. She must have planned this betrayal from the start—with her highborn friends. She had let him gather the feathers just so she could have them taken from him. So that she could have them *all*.

"Then that is why I am here—parched—starving," wailed the fisherman. "While she is in Tahiti rutting with that pig of a nobleman." Picking up a sharp piece of coral, he began to gash his forehead.

Ihetoa put a reassuring hand on his shoulder. "Yes," he said glibly. "Matopahu and the woman are the source of all your woes. And now that you know this, you will help me take revenge on them both. I need you to lure her from the Arioi women's compound. It must be done in secret. I want her simply to vanish, along with Matopahu, leaving not even a bone or patch of blood behind. Then all will be as before, and all the harm undone."

Rimapoa looked up but could not answer. He was breathing quickly, as if he had just been running along a beach.

"Come with me to the canoe and refresh yourself," said Ihetoa gently. "I saved some coconuts for you. And *fe'i*, baked yesterday. Your last meal here will be a good one."

Inside the novices' house at Aitofa's compound, Tepua yawned and turned over.

"Our *motu* princess is finally getting up," came Pecking-bird's shrill voice.

Tepua yawned again and opened one eye. She saw the other young women coming back from their baths.

"Now," said Pecking-bird, "that we know how highborn she is, I imagine she will expect us to become her servants."

Tepua sat up and glared at Pecking-bird. She groped for a suitable retort, and remembered Pecking-bird's playlet.

Crossing her arms, she spoke in a deep voice. "Fishermen, what is taking you so long? I am hungry and you are slow." This imitation of Pecking-bird's own performance set the whole houseful of novices laughing. "Are you not afraid of your high chief?" Tepua continued, improvising some additional lines. "I am fierce. I am a *motu* man. If you do not obey me, I will cook you all for my dinner."

Pecking-bird's face reddened and she stormed from the house. The other novices, still laughing, clustered about Tepua. "It does not matter to me," said Curling-leaf, "if you are of high birth or low. You have always been my friend."

"I am the same person I was yesterday," said Tepua. "My ancestry means little. My family is far away, and has no influence here. We are all novices together, and we must help each other any way we can."

"In that case," said Curling-leaf with a sly grin, "I think we should help you take your bath. Look. You still have paint smears on your face."

For a moment the others held back. But when Curling-leaf took Tepua's arm, they joined in, half dragging, half carrying her to the stream, all the while laughing and joking. They threw her in the bathing pool, then began scrubbing at her face and arms.

Tepua came up spitting bubbles. She knew she deserved this treatment. Too often, without thinking, she had held herself aloof from the others. Now that her background had come out, and she had scorned the idea of accepting special treatment, perhaps she could finally feel that she was a true member of the group.

"Enough!" she cried. "I have lost all my paint, and some of my skin as well!"

At last the other women relented, allowing her to climb back onto the bank. While everyone was drying off in the sun, Tepua noticed something out of the corner of her eye. She turned, saw only a few leaves trembling. "I think we had an audience," she said with a laugh.

"If so, they are being quiet about it," said someone else.

"After last night," said another, "I think the men will be happy to stay away from us this morning."

Tepua understood. Following the Arioi performance, men and women had gone off together to share the excitement the evening's performance had inspired. After so much lovemaking, the men were probably sprawled, exhausted, under the trees. Yet someone had been watching from behind the bushes.

"We are going down to the beach to say farewell to the guests," said Curling-leaf.

Tepua stiffened. "I have already said my parting words to my brother."

"But it will be fun," coaxed Curling-leaf. "Seeing all those boats in the water."

"Maybe Aitofa needs me to grate coconuts." When Tepua saw the look of disappointment on her friend's face, she followed the group down to the shore. There, to her relief, she found no sign of the huge double canoe that an atoll chiefess traveled in. Evidently Hoatu and Rongonui had left early.

Now other craft of all sizes were setting forth, bright pennants fluttering, paddles glistening, prows arching gracefully over the waves. To accompany the visitors on the first part of their journey, the Arioi had launched several of their own festive canoes. Aboard them stood men and women decked out in fresh garlands and glistening leaves.

Tepua watched the spectacle awhile, but could not lose herself in the gaiety. She could only envy the people returning to their homes and their families. The Arioi and a few friends were all she had.

Matopahu. Even if she knew what to say to him, she

could not go looking for him now. Eye-to-heaven had insisted that she wait. And what about Feet-out-of-water, whose recurring bouts of illness had kept her from him for so long? She knew that his family had called a disenchanter, a priest who specialized in undoing the work of sorcerers. If sorcery had not caused his illness, then the disenchanter would fail. Tepua despaired now of seeing that kindly nobleman again. . . .

With a sigh, she glanced at the novices around her. They were so caught up in the spectacle that they would not notice if she slipped away. Quietly she turned toward the path that led back to Aitofa's compound. . . . *What was that?* Someone had just ducked out of sight.

Tepua felt a sharp apprehension. She took a few steps into the deeper shade beneath the coconut palms. She peered around but saw no one.

Her heartbeat quickened. What if her brother had decided to take her home by force? He might have pretended to depart while sending men to watch for her. She asked herself if Rongonui could do such a thing in defiance of Hoatu.

She did not leave the shore at once, but waited until she saw a noisy group coming down through the grove. Then she hurried by them, raced through Aitofa's gate and into the novices' house. The spears that were used in exercises stood against one wall. Tepua took one out to the side yard and practiced skewering a straw "victim."

She had been working at this for some time when a wavering voice interrupted her. She turned to see a solemn-faced young man. "My master, Feet-out-of-water, is ill again," he said. "This time he is worse than before. If you do not hurry, it may be too late."

Tepua scowled. *A trick?* She realized that she had seen this servant at the nobleman's compound. For days, she had been expecting news from Feet-out-of-water, hoping for his recovery. "Have you come by boat?" she asked anxiously.

"There were none to spare. All the outlying kin are being summoned."

She did not look forward to walking the long, wooded

path. Hefting the spear, she decided to take it with her. As they left the compound the youth eyed her with surprise when he saw her still carrying the weapon. "No one at my master's house will harm you," he said.

"I have other enemies," she answered, explaining nothing more.

They quickly reached the path through the trees. The messenger, clearly in a hurry, did not seem to care that she was falling behind. Tepua called to him, but he merely beckoned for her to follow.

As she went she stayed alert to every sound and movement. An uncanny silence reigned. The insects had fallen still. The birds did not call to each other. The leaves hung motionless in the moist, heavy air.

Instead of fearing for her own safety, she chided herself, she should be thinking about Feet-out-of-water. He had always been pleasant to her, asking so little in return. He had never laughed at her ignorance of Maohi ways. . . .

Nearby, a stick snapped, and she jumped in sudden fright. Before she could call again to the messenger, she heard a hiss followed by the soft sound of her name.

When she glimpsed the figure that came toward her from the underbrush, she forgot both Rongonui and Feet-out-of-water. For a moment she could not breathe. She tried to level her spear, but her arms felt like stone. *Ghosts do not walk in the daytime,* she kept telling herself.

"Rima—poa," she whispered. What little flesh he had once possessed had melted away. Now she saw a skeletal figure, the shapes of ribs and shoulder bones showing through sun-blackened skin. His face was drawn, his eyes fevered.

"I escaped, *tiare,*" he answered in a dry voice. "Ask no more."

"But you—"

"I cannot stay here," he said, hanging back in the shadows. "If I am caught, the high chief will feed me to the eels. Let us meet later, after dark, and I will tell you all that has happened."

"Later. Yes." Her mouth hung open. Seeing him in this

pitiful state, she felt willing to forgive him for whatever he had done to her. Clearly he had suffered enough. "You must leave Tahiti," she insisted. "Take refuge with some other chief."

"I will go away," he promised. "But first, I beg you to meet me tonight. Come at moonrise. Behind Aitofa's compound."

She could not linger now—not while Feet-out-of-water was dying. Hastily, she whispered her assent and hurried off, hoping she could catch up with the nobleman's messenger. *Rimapoa was alive!* But he looked so weak. If the high chief's guards saw him, he could not hope to outrun them.

She arrived, out of breath, at the compound of Feet-out-of-water. Never before had she dared to enter the main house, but now the messenger beckoned her inside. She shivered as she heard the chanting of a priest within and cries of the women.

She stepped inside. The nobleman's sister gave her a single, piercing glance before continuing her wails. All the women held shark's-tooth flails, and blood trickled down their foreheads.

Tepua approached Feet-out-of-water, who lay stretched out rigidly on his back, his face pale, his eyes shut. The thought that she had come too late made her own tears start. At once she took a flail that someone handed her and gashed her own forehead, but she barely noticed the pain. She hit herself again, this time feeling blood drip down to mix with her tears.

The priest continued to wave his hands and pray, trying to entice the soul back into the body. As she stared at Feet-out-of-water she thought the appearance of life remained.

On the nobleman's fingers were tied red feathers, to protect his departing soul from evil spirits. Had it left him? She thought she saw his chest rising and falling slightly. He was not gone yet! The priest must have also noticed this, for he intensified his frenzied efforts.

Feet-out-of-water opened his eyes. In an instant the wailing ceased and the mourners crowded about him. The priest warned them back.

The sick man raised his head slightly, searching the crowd around him. "Te—Tepua," he whispered. The others glanced at each other in dismay, but stood aside to let her through. "Tepua. I—I have missed you." He drew in a ragged breath, then tried to reach toward her with his hand.

"Do no touch him," said the priest in a low, harsh voice. "For your own sake."

She understood. *The contamination from the dead and dying.* The substance of whatever evil was destroying him could move from his body to hers. Yet how could she refuse him this last small embrace? In defiance, she clutched his hand, felt the cool skin that seemed to grow colder as she knelt there. Once more the priest began to chant. . . .

So the rites continued, through the afternoon and well into the night. The priest was relieved by another, more vigorous man, whose efforts brought Feet-out-of-water's soul once more back into his body. Again the spirit slipped away and again it was called back. Tepua had no idea how long she had sat there, her head spinning from the incessant chanting and wailing.

At last the priest gave up his attempts to revive the nobleman and turned his energy to easing the spirit on its journey. He also dispatched a diviner, whose job was to paddle out in a canoe and watch the house from the water, until a vision showed him the reason for the poor man's demise.

While the priest inside chanted, the mourners waited anxiously for the diviner to return. If the death had been caused by sorcery, the culprit would be found and the attack avenged. If the death had been sent by the gods as punishment for some offense, then offerings would be made to keep the relatives from also being harmed.

Tepua remembered Eye-to-heaven's warning that she might bring woe to Matopahu because of her own transgression. Her *hara* might affect anyone she touched. Of course, Feet-out-of-water had known of this risk, but he had scoffed at it. It could not be true, she told herself now. She refused to believe that the gods would punish a man for caressing her. But what did the women of the household believe?

She searched their weary, grief-stained faces and saw only contempt for her in their eyes. It did not matter to them that she was now acknowledged as a high chief's daughter. "A *motu* princess is still a savage," she imagined them muttering among themselves. If her *hara* had contaminated Feet-out-of-water, then what might it do to the rest of the household?

These thoughts plagued Tepua while she waited for the diviner to return. She knew the night was waning. The time for her meeting with Rimapoa had passed, and she did not know if she would find him.

Suddenly she could no longer stand the hostile glances of the women. She stood up and walked to the center of the room. "I gave him joy in his last days," she said loudly. "I helped him laugh. Do not hate me for that." The women stared at her with widened eyes and said nothing. The men merely looked away.

Not caring now what the diviner would report, she went out through the doorway into the gloomy yard. The night sky was just beginning to show hints of dawn, and she had a long walk ahead of her.

Where was her spear? She remembered leaving it propped up against the outside wall of the house, but it was gone, and she could not face going back inside to ask after it. Now she had no need of a weapon. Her fear that Rongonui was trying to capture her had proved false. Rimapoa was the one who had spied on her at the stream and by the beach.

Empty-handed, she hurried from the compound. In the dim light she could make out the path, but every shadow seemed to hide a frightening shape. This was the wrong night for ghosts to be walking, yet malevolent spirits always congregated around the house of a dead man. Some descended from the sky. Others emerged from hiding places beneath the trees.

She tried her chant again, hoping it could ward off even

these powerful influences. The air remained still as she followed the trail, the smell of decaying leaves rising all about her.

A bird cried in the distance. She chanted louder. A rat scurried across her path, startling her, making her stumble into a clump of saplings. As she clawed herself free of them she heard more scuttling in the underbrush, but the noise seemed too loud for vermin.

She began to run, trying all the while not to hear the strange sounds about her. A huge *rata* tree, surrounded by twisting buttresses, loomed ahead, its bark gleaming faintly.

She paused, clutching one of the buttresses as she called on her guardian spirit for aid. Then she raced on, hearing the rustling grow closer. Aitofa's compound was not far. Two more bends in the path and a long, straight run.

Suddenly she saw a demonic figure rear up ahead of her in the middle of the trail. It held a club in one outstretched hand. She dodged around the apparition, crashing through the brush and heading toward the beach. . . .

"*Tiare,* do not run from me," came the ghostly voice.

"Rimapoa!"

She dropped to her knees and tried to catch her breath.

He brandished the crude weapon and spoke in a voice that chilled her. "I waited for you. Then I remembered you had gone this way, and wondered if you had come back."

Something in the way he spoke gave her fresh alarm. She blamed his ordeal. "Tell me how you escaped."

He interrupted. "First, you must not worry, *tiare.* I never told the priests that you came with me to Fenua Ura." His voice carried an undercurrent of deceit. "For my exile, they sent me to a little *motu.* Even you would not have found that place agreeable. I prayed to my god, and one day he let a fallen palm tree wash up on my shore. I made a crude raft."

"And paddled back to Tahiti on it? I heard that story in a chant. And I did not believe it then either."

He sighed, moving closer. She looked up, tensing, not certain what to expect. "Ah, *tiare,* it does not matter how I escaped. Another month on that island and the birds would have feasted on my eyes. I saved my life, but the cost is very great. Let me see the light of dawn on your face.'' He reached down toward her, but she drew back.

''Still afraid of me?'' he asked. ''But why do I see bloodstains on your brow?''

''I am mourning for Feet-out-of-water,'' she answered bitterly. ''He was going to help me. Without him I will not make Pointed-thorn after all. First the feathers, now this.'' She felt so miserable at that moment that she almost did not care what the fisherman planned to do to her. She watched his hands tightening on the heavy stick. A voice within tried to make her flee, but her muscles did not respond.

''What are you saying?'' he asked angrily. ''Your feast is taken care of.''

''My patron is dead. My only hope now is Hoatu, my brother's wife.''

He pounded the end of the stick against the ground. ''No, I do not understand. You and that strutting Matopahu plotted against me. That is why the high chief stole my feathers and sent me to exile. Then he gave them back to you. With that treasure, you can go as high as you want in the Arioi.''

''You are mistaken, my fisherman,'' she answered softly. ''The feathers are gone. And Matopahu had nothing to do with them.''

He pounded with his stick again. ''Then tell me why Ihetoa saw you two together by the *marae* And why he is so eager to be rid of you both.''

''Ihetoa!'' The name jolted her from the trancelike state she had fallen into. She stood up and faced Rimapoa, putting her hand on his where he held the club. ''Did Ihetoa put you up to this?''

The fisherman pulled back and grimly held on to the weapon. His gaze bore into her, but he did not answer.

''The high chief took away Ihetoa's office,'' she shouted, ''because we exposed his lies!''

''That is not how Ihetoa tells the story.''

''Did he confess what his own priest saw? Your friend Ihetoa is guilty of *hara*! The gods spurned his offerings. His victims died for no purpose.''

Rimapoa tightened his fist. She saw the muscles twitch at the back of his jaw.

"Have you forgotten how you almost joined the sacrifices on the altar?"

"I remember how you saved me, *tiare*," he answered hoarsely, still clutching the weapon. "But you still have not explained why you and Matopahu were together."

"Because Aitofa sent me to him—in the mountains. With a message for his *taio*. Then the three of us came back together."

"That was all? Just a message? No *hanihani*?"

She was breathing quickly and her pulse was racing. The ground was covered by a tangle of slippery roots, making the footing treacherous. If she tried to flee, she would surely stumble.

"You do not answer, *tiare*."

"*Hanihani*, yes," she answered bitterly. "In the mountains, where none of his highborn friends could see us. But it is finished now. The new high priest told me I must not touch Matopahu. Ask Ihetoa if you do not believe that."

"Scorpion of a nobleman! Scorpion of a priest!" Rimapoa smashed the club against the side of a heavy tree. He swung it repeatedly until the wood splintered in his hand. Finally he slumped to the ground. "Ihetoa would have put me on the altar if I had not explained my scars. And now you tell me that he mocked the gods."

Tepua was still trembling. She came forward slowly, finally crouching beside him and putting her arm about his shoulder, soothing the weathered skin. "Look at what has happened here," she said. "With Ihetoa gone from the *marae*, the trees are heavy with fruit. That is the final proof of his wrongdoings."

"Yes, I have seen that." He reached over and gently took her hand. "*Tiare*, I do not think I could have done what that tainted priest asked of me. Even if all those lies I believed were true. But I will not ask forgiveness of you again. I will only give you this warning. Ihetoa wants to rid himself of his enemies, and you are one. Guard yourself. Never go anywhere without an escort. Never leave your compound at night.''

''And what will you do?''

''Tell him you failed to meet me, and pretend I will try again. But now I must go.'' He embraced her for a long moment, pressed his nose to hers once more. Then, with a sigh, he stood up and vanished into the shadows.

Out of breath and exhausted from running, Tepua entered Aitofa's compound. Glancing up, she noticed how bright the sky had become. Soon everyone would be awake. She knew she had to spread the warning. If Ihetoa meant to destroy his enemies, he would be looking for Eye-to-heaven as well as Matopahu. Perhaps he was already setting his traps.

She went back to the gate and glanced at the sleepy warrior standing guard. ''There may be trouble,'' she told him.

''We have had peace in this district for a long time,'' he answered with a yawn.

''Have you seen any strangers tonight?'' She wondered if Ihetoa's men had been careless.

''No.''

''Have you seen the old high priest—Ihctoa?''

The guard jerked his head up. ''Why would that sad fool be wandering about?''

''A fool can still kill a man,'' she retorted. ''I will take this. You can get another.'' Before he could stop her, she grabbed one of the spears resting against the wall beside him.

She hurried toward the high priest's *marae,* dreading the prospect of entering the deep shadow that surrounded it. A man could hide easily behind one of the ancient trees. As she neared the turnoff to the woman's shrine, she saw a pair of *opu-nui* coming out on the path from the main temple.

''Go back,'' they shouted, waving briskly. ''Do not enter, woman.''

''Then call Eye-to-heaven for me,'' she replied as she tried to catch her breath.

"He will not like being disturbed."

"I bring news of Ihetoa!"

At those words, both men turned and rushed back in the direction they had come. Tepua stood there, holding her weapon upright and leaning on it for support until the high priest came running out to meet her.

"What is this about Ihetoa?" Eye-to-heaven asked, his oval face perspiring despite the coolness of the morning air.

She described her encounter with the fisherman and watched the priest's expression darken. "If Ihetoa has come seeking revenge," he said, "then perhaps some evil god is helping him."

"Evil—why?"

"Because Feet-out-of-water has died. Ah, you are confused. Your friend was of high birth. Now he will be mourned with all the fervor his family can muster. It will be a dangerous time for everyone when those people start to run wild."

She frowned in confusion. She had watched funeral rites that became frenzied, but none that menaced bystanders.

"You have not seen our ghost-masquers," the priest continued. "The dead man's kin and friends will paint their faces and become madmen, rushing through the settlements, swinging clubs or slashing with shark-toothed swords at anyone who gets in their way. Do you understand why I am worried?"

"Then—Matopahu—"

"I will warn him. Do not worry. We Tahitians are used to this. We take refuge in the *marae,* where the mourners dare not come. You are safe from them because you are Arioi. Even a crazed mourner will not harm an Arioi. Go home now. You are *not* safe from Ihetoa. You must keep out of sight until this is over."

Tepua stared at him. In the distance, she heard the faint sound of chanting. "Go," the priest insisted, "before the ghost-masquers reach us."

Tepua clutched her spear. Perhaps he was right. Ihetoa might send someone else after her when he realized that

Rimapoa had failed him. And Matopahu could take care of himself.

"Listen—I hear them!" said the priest.

Ghost-masquers? She turned and fled toward Aitofa's compound.

21

INSIDE a decaying, deserted house that stood alone on a hillside, Rimapoa crouched, staring up at Ihetoa and his men. The fisherman had spent the morning in the nearby hills, trying to keep out of sight while he gathered supplies that the priest had ordered. By now the sun had passed noon, its heat beating down on the broken thatch overhead. Small patches of sunlight lit the bare dirt floor.

"More coals!" Ihetoa demanded.

Rimapoa looked at the string of charred candlenuts that lay cooling at his feet. He gingerly touched one and found it did not burn his fingers. "These are ready," he answered, handing a piece of charcoal to each man in Ihetoa's party.

The warriors, who bore unfamiliar tattoos and frightening scars, began to paint black stripes on each other's faces. Rimapoa could not guess where the priest had found these men, or how he had induced them to help him. They were not Maohi, for they spoke with grunts that the fisherman could not understand. He assumed they were savages, who cared nothing about offending the gods by taking a man's life.

A rat scuttled across the floor. One warrior casually tossed a club, catching the creature with a glancing blow. It scampered off, squealing in pain, while the other men laughed.

"That is what you will get, fisherman," said Ihetoa, "if you miss the atoll woman another time. And we will cut off a part of you that you are fond of."

Rimapoa bit his lip and busied himself with his next task—kneading sticky breadfruit sap into a heap of white clay. The resulting paste would also be used to decorate the men. He thought he understood their foul purpose.

The fisherman had considered running away at daybreak rather than returning to tell Ihetoa that he had failed to catch

Tepua. But then, how would he know what this fiend was planning? For Tepua's sake he had let himself be drawn into Ihetoa's new scheme.

Silently he watched the warriors dab red sap on the unblackened parts of their cheeks, then paint red and black stripes on their bodies. Wherever these men were from, they certainly knew Maohi decorations. When they finished, no one would be able to distinguish them from real mourners.

"You will remain undisguised, fisherman," said Ihetoa as the warriors grinned at each other, their teeth flashing against their shadowy faces. "I want the woman to have no trouble recognizing you."

Mutely Rimapoa nodded. Ihetoa's men would also have no trouble recognizing him, he thought glumly, if they decided he no longer was of service to their master. He watched them adding stripes and circles with the gummy white clay mixture. Then they donned traditional head-dresses made of ferns and bright red berries. Finally they took up clubs and *paehos,* fiendish weapons made of shark's teeth sewn onto heavy sticks.

The priest did not disguise himself like the others. Rimapoa offered him a candlenut, but Ihetoa contemptuously slapped it from Rimapoa's hand. "Your work is done here, fisherman," he said with a snarl. "Go and do what you came for." He handed Rimapoa a four-sided club the length of his arm.

The fisherman rushed out, glad to be away from Ihetoa and his men, but his relief lasted only a moment. The mourners were a greater danger to him now than were the painted warriors of the priest. From his high vantage point he could see down into paths between the houses. The compound of the dead man lay far to the side and by the shore, but he glimpsed a cluster of mourners much closer. Turning, he fled the sound of their wailing.

His route wound back and forth along the hillside, sometimes taking him closer to Aitofa's compound and sometimes farther away. He did not know these hills; during his visit here, he had rarely strayed far from the water. He whispered to his god, begging for guidance.

Then, much closer, he heard a noise that made his hair stand on end. It was the hollow sound of oyster-shell clappers announcing the presence of ghost-masquers. Another group! They would attack anyone they caught.

He darted off the trail, but the mourners were fanning out, sweeping through the bush for anyone who had not fled their noise. The foliage rattled near the fisherman and he leaped from his hiding place. A shaft of sunlight dazzled him, then fell on a horribly contorted face, gashed and bleeding, eyes wild with grief, torn hair flying. The apparition lashed out at Rimapoa with the shark's-tooth *paeho.* The fisherman dodged and heard the hiss of the blade.

As the mourner recklessly swung his weapon back Rimapoa saw an opening and kicked the berserk man in the belly, doubling him up. With a bound, Rimapoa was away and running down the hill, ignoring the trails, pushing through underbrush that slapped and scraped at his face and body. The mourners might be anywhere. He did not know how to stay clear of them.

Only two thoughts came to him. He must protect Tepua, get her to safety. And he must find charcoal and paint to disguise himself, or he would not survive the afternoon.

Despite the disruption caused by the funeral, Tepua and the other women tried to get on with their tasks. A dozen Arioi warriors stood guarding the compound, but they could not keep out the cries of the mourners. "I should go," said Tepua to Curling-leaf as they stood by the compound fence, looking out. "I should blacken my face and mourn the man who was my friend."

"If you do, then I will come," said Curling-leaf. "No one wishes to harm *me.*"

"You should not take the risk."

Curling-leaf put her hand on Tepua's shoulder. "Then why should you? You have already wept for Feet-out-of-water."

"It is not just the mourning," Tepua whispered. "Mato-pahu worries me. He was warned to take refuge in the *marae,* but I know how stubborn he is."

"If your friend is in danger, then he may need my help, too."

"I do not want—"

"I will follow you in any case," said Curling-leaf. "Have you forgotten the gifts Matopahu left for me? I owe him much."

They found charcoal and face paint among Aitofa's supplies. Arming themselves with spears, they hastened out past the guards. In the distance, Tepua heard shrill yells from half-crazed mourners. She thought once more about Feet-out-of-water, but did not turn to join his grieving kin.

With Curling-leaf just behind her, Tepua took the path to the high chief's compound. The gate stood unguarded. She found the grounds empty, and so eerily silent that the back of her neck prickled. Peering in through the doorway of Matopahu's cane-walled house, she saw the sleeping mats in disarray. A coconut cup lay overturned.

"I hear footsteps," warned Curling-leaf. Tepua turned quickly, tensing for a fight. Across the courtyard came not an enemy, but Eye-to-heaven, his white *tapa* cape fluttering behind him as he ran toward the two women.

"You almost fooled me," said the high priest, pointing at their sooty faces. "You should not be here."

"Nor should you," Tepua replied. "And where is Matopahu?"

"He did not listen," answered the priest in a worried voice. "The others fled to the temple. Even Knotted-cord is there, but I cannot find my *taio*."

"Then we must look for him," said Tepua, running for the compound gate.

Matopahu jumped at the crash of a *paeho* sword cutting through brush. He had his own sword now, its grip slicked with the sweat of his palms, the wood shaft and serrated blade wet with a darker stain. Some of the blood on those savage teeth was his; he had tasted the bite of that blade before wrenching it from the mourner's hand.

Another black-smeared madman was coming at him. He knew now that these were the impostors that Eye-to-heaven

had warned him to expect. The men were garbed as
mourners, but their actions betrayed their purpose. They
made no warning noise with their clappers, as true mourners
did, but had tried to ambush him. Instead of rampaging
through the settlements, looking for other victims, they
stalked only him.

Earlier, Matopahu had left the compound with the others
who sought refuge in the *marae*. He had deliberately
lingered on the path so that the mourners—false and
real—could catch sight of him. He had hoped that Ihetoa
himself might appear. Instead, he had met only these
wild-eyed troublemakers.

At first he had enjoyed the fight. With the club he carried
in his other hand, he had crept up from behind to whack one
fellow on the buttocks, or knock loose another's headdress.
Now he was tired of horseplay, and he realized that his
opponents were in no lighthearted frame of mind.

Aaah! A *paeho* sliced down through the underbrush
where he crouched, nearly grazing his arm. He erupted out
of the leaves with a howl, meeting the blows with flurries of
his own. Parrying with his club, he cracked shark's teeth
from his opponent's *paeho,* so that shards flew about the
fighters and stuck in the skin like small, vicious knives.

Swinging the club again, Matopahu bashed the other
man's sword into his face and watched him fall back,
clutching the bridge of his nose. His triumph was cut off by
a trickle of fear when he saw two more specters advancing
on him, each carrying another fearsome *paeho*.

There was a boundary between courage and foolishness,
he decided, and he had overstepped it. Keeping his head
low, holding his club and sword close to his body to avoid
snagging them in the brush, he headed at last toward the
refuge of the *marae*.

The false mourners got ahead of him, barring his path
before he could get within shouting distance. He retreated,
then circled back, but once more found himself cut off from
refuge. He felt leaves and forest litter sticking to his
sweat-smeared face. Branches tore at his loincloth and
scratched his body like the nails of long-toothed ghosts.

This could be my death, Matopahu realized as he paused a moment to rest. The thought made him turn cold in his bath of sweat. He heard in his mind the warnings from Eye-to-heaven. *Do not let the wrong god seize you.* Yet he had persisted, night after night inviting the greedy spirit to possess him. Now, perhaps, the moment had come for his punishment. . . .

Matopahu put his thoughts aside as he caught the sharp smell of another assailant. He peered through the branches and realized that now he had three men stalking him. Then he glanced down at the ragged edge of his sword. Many teeth were broken, but the weapon could still make a serious gash. He was alone against three.

He crouched, heart banging in his chest, waiting for the instant when the two in front would come within range. He tensed, ready to spring up in a twisting attack, sweeping the sword across both men at once. He imagined red blood spraying across their blackened skins.

He jumped, but too late. As he uncoiled himself a club smacked his elbow. A bolt of pain shot down his left arm, but he managed to follow through on the sword stroke with his other. He had been thrown off balance and only scored one assailant across the belly, but that one dropped, howling.

With his head, he rammed the second man in the gut, sending him retching into the bushes. Still clutching the sword firmly in his other hand, Matopahu leaned down and forced tingling fingers to scoop up his fallen club. His hurt arm hung heavily, weighted with pain and numbness, and he could not raise it. Turning just in time, he kicked sharply at the third attacker's flanks and made him stagger.

Before he could strike with his weapon, he felt another blow, against the back of his shoulder. The second man was up again, and Matopahu spun to face him, enraged by the fire roaring down toward his damaged elbow. He began slashing and sweeping in a one-armed frenzy. But beneath the madness of pain lay the freezing knowledge that he was no longer a match for one man, let alone two. His left arm only shrieked agony when he begged it to rise. . . .

He was slowing down. He could not help himself. Each

time he fended off a club or *paeho* strike, he thought it came just a little nearer to his skull. He tried to retreat, but the trees were too thick behind him. The bared teeth of his two opponents showed against their blackened faces as the men closed in.

A blow to the side of his head sent him sprawling. A foot pressed heavily on his chest, holding him down, while a four-faced club descended to finish him. As if his mind and eyes wished to postpone the moment of death, he saw the club move with increasing slowness, dragging against the sky. Even now, he thought, he still might cry out a last plea to his guardian spirit. . . .

And then the hand opened and the club, instead of swinging in its killing arc, spun off in another direction, tumbling harmlessly away. The man who had held it cried out and toppled, clutching at a spear that had just pierced his shoulder.

People were yelling, their cries reverberating in his head, making it throb as painfully as his wounded arm. Shrill voices. Women's voices. One he knew well.

"Tepua—" he started to say, but a great buzzing blackness descended upon him, wiping out the sky and everything beneath.

With alarm, Tepua watched Matopahu's face go slack, his eyes roll up, and his head fall to one side. She knelt beside him, but Eye-to-heaven was quicker, raising his *taio* in his arms and cradling his head. Tepua caught the flash of jealousy that went through her, the wish to push the high priest aside and take the fallen warrior into her own arms. Instead she mouthed a silent prayer for his life.

She saw at once that Matopahu still breathed. His eyelids started to flutter. When Eye-to-heaven put pressure on his friend's left arm, Matopahu gave a jump and a yelp. The priest made him sit up, held the arm gingerly, and traced with one finger the outlines of an enormous bruise spreading all over the back of Matopahu's shoulder.

Tepua let her breath out in a rush. "I thought they had broken his head," she whispered.

"Nothing will break this skull," the high priest answered, stroking Matopahu's matted hair. "It is harder than ironwood."

Tepua turned as she heard Curling-leaf's voice approaching. "Three men are down," said Curling-leaf. "None is Ihetoa. And I don't see any more of them." Yet behind Curling-leaf loomed a figure smeared in black. Tepua pointed, shouting her warning before she recognized the gaunt shape of this other mourner's body. *Rimapoa!*

"Tepua, I warned you of the danger," the fisherman called in a loud whisper. "Why did you not listen?"

"This man is my friend," she said hastily to the others as Rimapoa came forward, showing his paint-smeared face. "He told me about Ihetoa's plans."

Rimapoa stepped closer, glancing only once at the wounded nobleman on the ground. "It was not for *his* sake that I gave you the warning, *tiare,*" he chided. "And instead of listening, you did this. Think of the danger!"

"Until we catch up with Ihetoa," she snapped, "we will all be in danger. How safe are you, behind that layer of paint?"

She turned back to Matopahu and saw that Eye-to-heaven was massaging his friend's arm. "It was my *taio* who rescued me," said the chief's brother. "I do not ask fishermen or women to fight my battles."

"And I do not ask men to fight mine!" she retorted. "I will find Ihetoa myself and settle the score between us." She turned to Rimapoa. "Tell me how he is dressed," she demanded.

"That priest is too clever," Rimapoa said angrily. "He waited until I left before donning his mourner's garb—if he put on a costume at all."

Eye-to-heaven looked thoughtful. "He will certainly disguise himself. But we cannot go around knocking down all the mourners and ripping off their costumes to find him."

"You are high priest," Tepua said. "Can you not order the real mourners to stop? Then we could find the false ones."

"Can one order a hurricane not to blow?" Eye-to-heaven replied. "While their grief still rages they listen to no one.

Even Knotted-cord must cower in the *marae*. Eventually the wind will die down by itself.''

"*Tiare,* there may be another way,'' said Rimapoa. ''Ihetoa will want to learn if his men have succeeded. He will be eager to talk to me. Then I can lure him into a trap.''

"If you can find him,'' growled Matopahu, ''then we will simply go after him.''

"*You* are not going very far,'' answered Eye-to-heaven to his *taio*. ''Not today.''

"In any case,'' said the fisherman, ''the rest of you cannot hope to hunt him down. The house where I left him has too good a vantage point. He will see you coming and slip away.''

"Then how can we lure him?'' Tepua asked. ''With what bait?''

"The bait is lying there.'' The fisherman cast a scornful glance in Matopahu's direction. ''Of course, if your noble friend would rather hide in the *marae,* then—''

Eye-to-heaven struggled to keep Matopahu from jumping to his feet. ''When we are done with this, fisherman,'' said the chief's brother, ''I will remember what I owe you— some fresh scars to go with the ones Tepua gave you. Now let me hear your plan.''

"I will tell Ihetoa that you were badly hurt,'' said Rimapoa. ''And that you crawled into shelter to wait your death.'' He turned, then pointed to a small cane-walled house in a nearby clearing. ''There. That place will do, and it should be empty. Everyone sensible is in hiding.''

"What makes you certain he will come?'' Matopahu had managed to sit up, though his face appeared pale from the effort.

Rimapoa smiled grimly as he answered. ''I know that vengeful priest. He will not trust my word. He will have to see for himself that you are finished.''

"I say we should try this plan,'' said Eye-to-heaven. ''If it fails, then we have lost nothing. You go to the house while the rest of us keep out of sight.''

Matopahu sighed. ''All right. I will be your bait. But I

will also defend myself. Give me a weapon. If that priest comes after me, I will be ready for him.''

Silently she picked up the *paeho* of one of the fallen assailants and handed it to Matopahu. *Ihetoa will not get to you,* Tepua vowed to herself. *You arrogant, oracle-making son of an eel . . . I will see to it.*

''Go find Ihetoa,'' Matopahu said to the fisherman as he heaved himself finally to his feet. He staggered toward the house in the clearing, but refused even his *taio*'s assistance in walking. One arm hung limp, apparently useless.

''Do not be afraid,'' whispered Eye-to-heaven to Tepua. ''He will gather strength. When Ihetoa comes, he will be ready.''

Rimapoa was sweating heavily by the time he neared the isolated house. If the priest remained inside, Rimapoa thought, he must be watching through a gap in the wall. And Ihetoa had ordered him not to disguise himself!

Squatting by the bank of a brook, Rimapoa rubbed his face with a handful of gravel. Plumes of sooty water streamed away from him as he worked. With dismay, he looked down at his charcoal-smeared body. He had no time to finish the job. The sun was already low. Ihetoa must be lured now, or the chance would be lost.

Warily, he proceeded up the last steep stretch. Across the front of the house, ruddy sunlight fell brightly on decaying, latticework walls. Rimapoa listened and heard nothing, not even the whine of mosquitoes. Perhaps Ihetoa had gone away. ''I bring news, priest,'' the fisherman announced in a tremulous voice.

''Then approach,'' came the answer. ''Stand by the doorway, but do not enter.''

With heavy footsteps, Rimapoa walked around to the side of the house. The doorway lay deep in shadow and he could see nothing of the man within. ''Is she dead?'' asked Ihetoa, his voice slightly muffled by the wall.

''N—not yet. But I will have a good chance at her tonight.''

''That was not what I expected to hear from you!''

"She—she painted herself like a mourner. And stayed with a group. I could not get close."

"Then I should have left you on that island!" Ihetoa fell silent a moment. "Come closer," he said. "Tell me what happened to the others."

Rimapoa saw streaks of sunlight across the dark floor, but still could not make out the priest's figure. A shadow moved, a long and ominous shape, and he jumped back in fear. "There was a fight. The chief's brother defended himself."

"But he is dead."

"By now, yes."

"By now?" Another shadow moved. A sharp cracking sound, like that of a heavy club hitting a post, made Rimapoa start. "What do you mean?" demanded the priest.

"He—was bleeding badly. Crawled into some hiding place. He will not last long. I am sure of it."

"I am not sure of anything. Where are the rest of my men?"

"Matopahu fought well. The others are lying under the bushes."

The response came in a deep hiss. "Then where is Matopahu?"

"In a small house. I can show you."

"Where?" the priest insisted. "Describe it exactly."

"Halfway—halfway along the path from the high chief's compound to the fishermen's *marae*." Rimapoa paused to gather his thoughts. "The fence is falling down on one side. There is a pile of coconut husks near the door."

"Yes. I know the house you describe. But you are too slippery, my tainted fisherman. Swear to me on your god that Matopahu is there."

Rimapoa replied with his oath, but the priest still remained hidden.

"Then tell me, if you saw him crawl inside, why you did not follow and finish him off? Is he not the one who stole your woman as well as your feathers?"

Rimapoa drew in his breath. "There was no reason to soil my hands with him. What purpose in killing a man who is already dead?"

Ihetoa pounded his stick again, making Rimapoa jump. "You will do it now. For me. Just to make certain."

"Ye—yes. If that is your wish." Rimapoa looked down in dismay at the small club he carried. Perhaps he could use it against Ihetoa instead. But the man refused to show himself, and Rimapoa could not guess what weapons he had with him in the house.

"Good," said Ihetoa. "I am ready now. You lead the way and I will be right behind you."

The fisherman took a few steps forward, but heard nothing from Ihetoa. He glanced back at the open doorway. "I am coming, fisherman. I will let you get ahead."

With his face exposed, Rimapoa did not wish to travel in the open. He was too likely to be attacked by mourners. Hastily he ducked from the shade of the house into a stand of hibiscus trees. He paused, turned to look behind him.

He heard a rustling of brush, but still could not make out the priest. Then he did catch sight of something that made him shiver. It was only the priest's shadow, elongated by the slanting light, but Rimapoa recognized the bulky outline of a chief mourner's costume. Now he understood why Ihetoa had sneered at the suggestion that he blacken his face. In this garb, his head and upper body were fully concealed. No one could possibly recognize him.

"Go on," said Ihetoa irritably. "Why are you so slow? The sun is almost down!"

Rimapoa scrambled ahead. The priest was too clever, he saw now. When they reached the house, Ihetoa would remain far back, well out of sight, and the trap would fail. In the gathering darkness, he would vanish before anyone could catch up with him.

He saw no way to fight the priest—who carried a *paeho* in one hand and an enormous club in the other. He could only hope to beat him by playing the fool.

"It is still a long way," said Rimapoa, turning to call to his invisible pursuer. "Can you move faster?"

"I am keeping up," came the distant voice.

The fisherman began to lope between the trees. Ahead, in

the gloom, he saw what he needed. Perhaps he could fake a
mishap and not really hurt himself badly. . . .

He braced himself for pain as he ran full tilt toward a
fallen log, screamed as he leaped over it, and went down.
Then he tried in earnest to get up, but when he put his
weight on the leg, he groaned aloud in agony.

"Clumsy pig!" shouted the priest behind him. "Now
what good are you?"

"I will be all right," Rimapoa insisted. He leaned on his
club and limped awkwardly a few steps, then a few steps
more, panting heavily. He heard the footsteps coming
closer, but dared not turn around. He was hopping for his
life, leaning into the makeshift crutch, when a blinding bolt
of pain struck the back of his skull. . . .

Tepua, hiding a short distance from the house where
Matopahu lay, watched afternoon fade toward twilight. Her
legs had grown stiff from sitting. She kept watch in both
directions along the path, but all remained still.

At last, she could sit no more. She signaled Curling-leaf
to stay behind, then picked up a spear. "It is too quiet," she
whispered. "I want to scout the woods."

"Alone?" Curling-leaf frowned.

"I will go. You watch the doorway from here."

Using underbrush to stay hidden, Tepua worked her way
around the house to the far corner, but saw no sign of
intruders. She glanced at the sky, now starting to pale and
redden with evening's approach. Settling against a tree, she
decided to try watching from this new vantage point. If Ihetoa
was coming, he might not use the most obvious route.

Sunset was almost at hand. She wondered if Ihetoa was
waiting for nightfall. If he did not fear the creatures of night,
he might hold back awhile longer.

Crickets began their shrilling chorus, joined by the
overhead rattling of palm fronds in the breeze. The distant
cries of mourners began to fade. Tepua became alert when
she saw low branches at the other corner of the house start
to ripple. That was not wind! She tensed, clutching her
spear, watching clouds of pollen billow from late-blooming

flowers to swirl in the failing light. A bough dipped, and then a monstrous figure emerged into the clearing and turned in her direction.

She took in her breath with a gasp. Could Ihetoa summon shades from the other world and bend them to his will? The creature had limbs and a body, even a head, but it lacked a face. A silvered blankness hid the front of its head. Behind the featureless visage, spikes fanned out to form a sinister halo.

The breast and shoulders were covered by a huge upturned crescent that was set with shimmering disks. Beneath hung an undulating curtain that seemed alive with its myriad tiny, gleaming parts.

Blind the apparition looked, but blind it surely was not, for it turned one way and then the other as if surveying the scene. And it carried a blazing torch! Tepua felt invisible eyes watching her. Sweat beaded on her skin and began to trickle down her face.

If Ihetoa could call forth such a shade, what chance did she have against him? A cry of dismay gathered in her throat, but she held it back, afraid the creature might turn on her. She knew that Curling-leaf and Eye-to-heaven could not see the intruder, for the house shielded him from their view.

The specter raised its torch, casting an orange light on the leaf-strewn ground beside the house. About this, lesser shadows seemed to gather, as if the demon had brought minions to serve it. Tepua shivered. Oh, great must be the power of a man who could summon such aid!

When the apparition turned its blank face to the house and began to advance slowly toward it, she considered her choices. If the thing was from the world of shades, she had no hope, nor did Matopahu. But if it was mortal . . .

She wished, suddenly, that she had a length of sennit cord to wind about her fingers. If she could divine the nature of her enemy, she might understand how to face it. She stared at her hands, imagining the strings slipping from one shape to the next. *Tapahi-roro-ariki,* she mouthed silently. *Show me the answer.* The imaginary strings stopped, holding one form. And then, just for an instant, she saw the same vision that had come to her in the mountains. *Ihetoa!*

She came out of the trance when the specter was still several paces from the house. She picked up her spear. The huge head turned slightly, as if sensing her presence, and Tepua stanched a cry. The specter's face suddenly came ablaze with a brilliant red light. What mortal possessed a visage of fire? She felt despair weighting her arms.

No. She could not abandon Matopahu. If the intruder was a man, she would battle it as a man, and if it was a spirit, she would fight as best she could. She crept through the brush, her spear lifted, as the figure stalked toward the far wall of the house.

Then she saw that the silver fire of the apparition's face was the dying sunlight reflected from the surface of a pearl-shell mask, a mask so flat and featureless that it made the figure appear blind. When the mask turned from the sun, the glow died and she discerned the narrow slits that allowed the wearer to see.

Was this Ihetoa under the bulky costume? Tepua strained her eyes against the murkiness of twilight. The figure, as if it knew she watched, passed into an envelope of shadow.

Now she kept silent for a new reason—she did not want to frighten the intruder away. She knew that her friends would see him as soon as he went to the other side of the house. But first he stepped up to the closest wall and pressed his face to a gap. Suddenly he began moving beneath the edge of the roof, his purpose now evident as his torch swept the thatch. Berating herself for slowness, Tepua launched herself toward him. The dry roof caught, crackling and smoking while the intruder stooped to ignite the cane walls as well.

"Ihetoa!" Tepua shouted, and saw the apparition turn sharply at the sound of the name. Then the figure rushed away from her and around the periphery of the house, all the while setting fire as it went.

"Gods eat your soul!" she hissed. By the time she reached the front, the cloth flap over the doorway was a sheet of flame. She screamed Matopahu's name, her heartbeat drumming frantically. The crackle of burning thatch was loud, and the harsh smoke almost overwhelming. She hurried after Ihetoa.

From the corner of her eye she saw her companions breaking from the bush, running, weapons lifted, toward the house. They were too distant; they would come too late to help her.

A banging and cracking inside sounded faintly above the growing voice of the blaze. Matopahu was trapped! On the far side of the house, the sounds were loudest. There, the monstrous form had set the final wall afire. Howling her throat raw, Tepua charged Ihetoa.

He tossed the torch aside and lifted his tooth-edged sword. She feinted with her weapon, heard his blade hiss past, then danced out of range. She clenched the spear shaft, sighting on the one vulnerable place that wasn't guarded by the heavy cloth or shell of the costume. The sweat-gleamed patch of skin at Ihetoa's neck seemed to beckon the spear tip as he raised his sword again.

Baring her teeth, Tepua drew back and cast the weapon with such force that the handgrip stung her fingers. And then the false ghost-masquer was reeling, hands clutching a shaft that transfixed his throat and pinned him to a wall post of the fiercely burning house. He arched, the spasm making him rise to his toes while the hole in his throat tried vainly to quench the flames with a torrent of red. Then he sagged and hung limp, held up only by the spear shaft still embedded in the wood.

Tepua knew the heady swell of triumph that comes from seeing an enemy broken. She panted fiercely, drawing her lips back against her teeth. The red of his blood was the red of her hatred. She could think of nothing else as she leaned one hand against the body and yanked out the spear. She was about to plunge it into him again when the snarl of the fire reminded her that she had more to think of than revenge.

Whirling, she faced the house again, heard the thumps from inside, saw that the wall was sheeted with flame. She wailed in dismay and rising horror.

"No!" she screamed, and swung up her spear. In a frenzy she attacked the barrier that stood between her and Matopahu, ignoring the red feathers that seemed to flutter all around her. Each touch left a searing track on her skin. Dimly she felt people beside her, hands on her arms, drawing her back.

"It will come down! Get away or you will be killed, too!"

She did not know who shrilled the warning in her ear—she was too immersed in the flood of grief that made her struggle and scream like a maddened animal. She knew her friends were dragging her away slowly, for she fought them for every step of ground.

Before her, the wall bulged as if pressed from within by the exploding pressure of the fire. Nothing inside could survive such heat. Yet she saw something—the tip of a *paeho* blade, perhaps—poke through the one part of the wall that was not yet ablaze.

Then the hole widened and Matopahu tumbled out like a thrown club, garments alive with flame. Caught in the middle of a tearful wail, Tepua turned it into a full-throated screech. Fire seemed to lash after Matopahu, but he rolled and clawed his way to safety. In the ruddy light she saw the burn and soot marks that crisscrossed his back, almost obscuring the huge bruise on his shoulder.

His loincloth was bedecked with shimmering tongues of red and yellow. She threw herself beside him, rolling him, swatting at the fire, and ripping away the burning cloth.

And then, when at last he lay on his side, hands outstretched, Tepua fell on top of him, yelling and crying in joy as well as grief.

"Woman, you will make a new river in Tahiti with your tears," said a muffled voice beneath her. "I am dazed, not dead. What about Ihetoa?"

"Roasting in the fire with a hole through his neck."

"That was to be *my* job."

"You eel!" she shouted. "You crawler-in-the-bushes. You useless climber of cliffs. Is there nothing you will let a woman do for you?"

He managed to put one arm around her and pull her closer. "I will think of something," he said with a muffled laugh.

22

WHEN Rimapoa opened his eyes and saw Hoihoi's stout figure looming over him, he thought he had somehow never left home. It had all been a dream—Tepua, the feathers, Ihetoa. Now he would get up, ready his boat, go out fishing for albacore. . . .

But when he tried to move, the pain at the back of his head made him gasp.

"So, brother. You went off with that atoll *vahine,* and look what it cost you." His sister's stout fingers closed about his arm. "You are nothing but bones. Even a hungry *motu* savage would not bother with you now."

The fisherman sighed. "My head—"

"It will heal. Now sit up and drink."

Rimapoa gingerly tried to comply. He felt the polished coconut shell pressed to his lips and forced himself to take a swallow of the milk. Then he glanced around.

He did not recognize the hut where he lay, though he noticed that the mats were worn and thin. "Where?" He moved his arm weakly.

"Servants' quarters. We are in the high chief's compound, but I would not call you an honored guest."

"I was—exiled—but I came back."

"I have heard all about that," she snapped. "You are fortunate, my wandering brother. The new high priest is not going to be harsh on you. The gods spared your life, he says, by letting you survive on that tiny *motu*. Provided that you leave Tahiti quickly, there will be no further punishment."

"And where else can I go?" Rimapoa glanced up at Hoihoi's broad, fleshy face.

Her eyes gleamed in a way he had not seen in many seasons. "It may surprise you, brother, to learn that I have found a husband. My *tane* lives on Eimeo and he is taking us back with him. We will have a house close to the lagoon. He says there is good fishing nearby.''

"Eimeo!" He could not help recalling the wondrous night he had spent with Tepua on the beach there. In misery, he slumped back onto the mat. "That place would not be my choice.''

"You will see. There are plenty of women on Eimeo. Even a rascal like yourself might find one. But first you need some flesh on those bones!''

"Say nothing to me about women,'' he replied with disgust.

"Good. Then you have forgotten your *motu* princess.''

"I do not even know what happened to her. After Ihetoa clubbed me—''

"Ihetoa is dead. And you may as well know this, brother. There is going to be a ceremony at the great *marae*. Tepua and Matopahu—''

"A marriage!'' He sat up suddenly, though the pain made him groan anew.

"Not a marriage. And now that you are up, you can eat some of this *poi* I made for you.'' She shoved a bowl at him, but he pushed it aside.

"What are they going to do at the *marae*?'' he demanded.

"Ah, brother. I forgot that you were away so long on that island. Maybe you did not hear about Matopahu's grand tour of the districts.''

"I would rather he took a tour of the ocean's bed.''

She sighed. "When he came to visit Pigs run-out, we all clustered around the compound trying to catch a glimpse of him. There was such a crowd that the headman's fence was thrown down and he sent his guards to chase us away. But we all got to see Matopahu.''

"That useless nobleman went to visit Pigs-run-out many times,'' the fisherman answered bitterly. "Nobody cared about him then.''

"Ah, but that was *before* he became so renowned. This time we knew the stories about him. Every woman of the district prayed he would call her to his mat.''

Rimapoa wanted to grab the bowl of *poi* and dump it over his sister's head, but she seemed to sense his intent and pulled it out of range. "What does all this have to do with a ceremony?" he persisted.

"You will have to ask the new high priest to explain it. All I know is that Matopahu's god deserted him, and that an evil one began to speak through his lips. The ceremony is to free him from whatever sins allowed that to happen. And to free *her* from the guilt of her visit to Fenua Ura."

Rimapoa frowned. "So you know everything, sister," he answered hoarsely. "But I still do not see why they are going to do this thing together."

"One sin may be connected to the other. The high priest did not take me into his confidence."

Rimapoa tightened his fist. "No. It can only mean this. They are going to marry."

"I do not think so," said Hoihoi, still holding the *poi* close to her.

"Explain!"

"I have talked with your *motu* princess. She says that her exalted kin are sending her gifts so that she can rise in the Arioi. Matopahu will not marry a woman who is forbidden to give him children."

The fisherman glanced at Hoihoi's grin and felt an unexpected surge of good feeling toward his sister. "This is no lie?"

"I think I know that woman, brother. If she is determined to be an Arioi, then she will let no man's wishes get in her way."

"I would also send her gifts, if I had any. To make sure she stays with the Arioi."

"Your gift to her will be to get well—as quickly as you can—and leave for Eimeo. That is why she sent for me to take care of you."

He smiled. "*She* did that?" He reached cautiously to touch the back of his head, but winced as he pressed on the *tapa* dressing. "Then maybe I am not sorry that I led Ihetoa into her trap."

"Are you ready to eat your *poi*?"

Rimapoa reached for the bowl. "I will not dump it on your head today, my dear sister."

The morning of the ceremony dawned with mist hanging in the trees, but soon a brisk wind cleared the air. Tepua left the women's Arioi compound, accompanied by Aitofa and Curling-leaf. She wore only a simple *tapa* wrap and carried a sprig from the sacred *miro* tree. Curling-leaf carried a trussed white fowl beneath her arm, its beak tied so that it would not interrupt the proceedings by squawking.

The *miro* twig, plucked earlier that morning, was still fresh and dewy. Tepua touched its heart-shaped leaves and fingered the rose-colored wood. The flowers were striking—a vivid sun yellow whose black center held a reddish sheen. It was an offering worthy of the gods, and she hoped it would please them.

A priest walked before the three, escorting them toward the *marae* where Eye-to-Heaven waited. As Tepua's party neared the path to the temple, she saw another priest approaching, accompanied by Matopahu and a servant. She could not help noticing how well the chief's brother looked, walking with his usual confident manner, his head thrown back and his shoulders straight. From this distance, she could not even see the scars left from his fight with the ghost-masquers.

It had puzzled her, at first, when the high priest suggested performing both ceremonies at once. He had not chosen to do this merely to save himself effort. The offenses were entangled with each other, Eye-to-heaven had said as he explained the ceremony of *taraehara,* the untying of *hara.* Now she and Matopahu must be untangled—from their sins and from each other.

She sighed, wishing the last part could somehow prove untrue. But Matopahu had asked her to leave the Arioi for him, something she could not do. And now, impossible as it seemed, the time for a final parting had come. . . .

Overhead, dark branches rustled. At the border of sacred ground Tepua saw the fierce wooden figures glaring at her. She remembered all too well the furor raised when temple attendants thought that a woman had crossed that boundary. "We may enter," said Aitofa, beside her. "See? Mats are spread so that our feet will not touch the sacred stones."

Tepua thought she heard bitterness in Aitofa's words. Yes, it was true that the gods' wishes seemed to favor the men who proclaimed them. There were exceptions only for women of the highest rank. A chiefess might tread the bare stones, but Tepua was no chiefess.

She turned to Curling-leaf, whose humble birth prevented her from following into the temple enclosure. Tepua embraced her friend, then took the offering fowl she had carried. "I will stay here and listen," promised Curling-leaf, wiping a joyful tear from her eye. "And offer my own prayers for your future."

Tepua turned, reluctantly, finally treading the path of mats that led through a gap in the *marae*'s black stone wall. This temple was far more imposing than any she had seen on coral islands. Passing into the courtyard, she saw at close hand the sacred uprights and the wooden altars laden with offerings of fruit and flesh. She drew in her breath, walking with caution lest she accidentally touch some sacred object.

The high priest, Eye-to-heaven, was draped in *tapa* bleached so white that it hurt the eyes to look at him. Beneath his tall headdress he did not look at all like the friendly priest she knew. Behind him, closer than she had ever seen it, loomed the stepped platform of rounded stones, layer piled on layer, the *ahu* of the temple. She trembled as she realized that on this high perch the gods and spirits would assemble to hear her plea.

Her hands were shaking as she held her two offerings, advancing slowly until the priest signaled her to stop. Then she knelt and waited for Eye-to-heaven to call on the gods. Despite the mat, she could sense the chill of the stones beneath her and the frightening power that they held. The warmth seemed to drain from her body.

The priest began his long chant. As she listened to the mystical words, she dared not move or even glance sideways. After a time she sensed a change without directly seeing it, a darkening of the air, a movement that touched her cheek. She tensed as she heard a flutter of wings. Birds—the shadows of the gods—were coming to alight on the *ahu*.

Then the priest whispered to her. It was time to recite the words of ritual she had learned. Her lips trembled and all she could manage was a whisper. "Here am I. . . ." *Louder!* "Here am I, and here are my offerings." *Louder still!* "I bring the chicken and the *miro* sprig to atone for my sin. It was I who stole red feathers from Fenua Ura. Forgive me that transgression. . . ."

Then, for a time, no words were spoken. From the signs around him, the priest would decide now if the gods had accepted her plea. She listened to the pulsing of her blood and struggled to keep herself upright. All around her, the spirits were whispering. . . .

"These offerings are accepted for the *marae*," the priest intoned at last. At once, the strange chill began to leave her. A band of sunlight broke through the trees and bathed her shoulders and back.

Matopahu came forward next, holding out his gifts. Tepua glanced at him as he knelt and bowed his head, saying the words of repentance. He spoke boldly, with no evident fear.

". . . to atone for my sin of allowing pride and vanity to darken my spirit, so that a demon entered me and displaced the god of my prophecies . . ."

She gazed at the rich gold of his skin and the expression of confidence on his face. For a moment she allowed herself to imagine that she had renounced the Arioi and agreed to his demands. She could still hear the words he had said after she pulled him from the fire. "You will be my wife now. There will be no more quarrels between us. And if Eye-to-heaven stands in my way, I will hoist him by his holy loincloth and toss him into the sea."

She had refused him then. If he asked, she would refuse him again, despite her pain. But she was letting her thoughts drift, when she should be watching the ceremony. . . .

Eye-to-heaven lifted his arms and cried, "Come hither!

May you live! Come again to the god's light. But go first and be cleansed of your debasement.''

The high priest left the *marae* and strode toward the sea. After him came Tepua, Matopahu, and Aitofa. Leaving the shadowed stones behind brought Tepua only a mild relief. She would be free of her sins now, but she saw little joy coming in the days ahead.

Matopahu fell into step beside her and she did not have the heart to move away from him.

"Why do you look so downcast, atoll flower?" he whispered. "One would think from your expression that a burden is being placed on your shoulders, not lifted from them."

"We should not talk now," she answered.

The breeze blew in her face, carrying spray that tingled on her lips. She reached a black-sand cove that stood opposite a break in the reef. Eye-to-heaven waded out in the quietly rolling surf, letting his robe of white *tapa* trail in the sea. While Aitofa stayed on shore, Tepua and Matopahu followed the priest.

They knelt, side by side, on the soft sand while the sea caressed their necks and shoulders. Eye-to-heaven came first to Tepua, opening his arms above her and raising his voice over the sound of the breaking surf.

"Hearken, O gods, to thy worshipers! Cleanse the woman who has offended, that her sin of taking the sacred feathers be washed in the ocean, be lost in the murmuring sea. Restore her to harmony, that she may take up the noble life decreed for her, that she may dance and chant for the Arioi. Hearken to us, O gods."

Then he stood over Matopahu.

"Cleanse the man who has offended, that his sin of harboring a false god be washed away. Restore him to harmony, that he may stand beside the chief once more as his loyal brother, that the voice within him may speak truth.''

At the priest's signal, Tepua lay back into the sea, feeling the waves wash over her, around her, sweeping away the unhappiness, fear, and guilt.

"There is prayer in the moving ocean," Eye-to-heaven chanted. "The sea is the great *marae* of the world."

Tepua felt the truth of his words deep within herself. Men could build temples of stone, but one day those might fall. Only the sea would remain, fluid, unchanging, with a mystery to rival that of the gods.

"You are cleaned, purified, ready again to walk in the world," the priest intoned, casting seawater over both of them. The ceremony was finished. Eye-to-heaven, wearing a satisfied look, walked slowly ashore.

But Tepua remained in the ocean, drawing strength and comfort from the surging water around her. She threw her head back, allowing the waves to play with her hair. She flung out her arms, letting them drift. A hand crept into hers. Matopahu's.

"There is something we have yet to settle," he said in a quiet voice.

"I think not, my valiant nobleman. I made my plans clear to you and now I cannot change them. Eye-to-heaven has just promised my service to Oro!"

"Yes, I heard that," he answered. "But suppose I make no demands you cannot meet?"

She turned toward him as he drifted near her in the surf, his eyebrows raised expectantly. "I remember what you told me," she said. "That a man of your line must have children. That no woman in Tahiti would refuse the chance to bear them." She blinked, unwilling to let him see her tears.

"I would like to pretend I did not say that, Tepua. It is true that I want sons. But I have learned that sometimes a man must wait for the things he wants most." He pulled her closer. "Stay with the Arioi, if that is your wish," he said softly. "But do not let that keep us apart. We will have children, but later, when you have fulfilled your obligations to Oro."

She studied him, slowly taking in what he had said. "But you must have sons—"

He laughed. "If I get impatient, I can always foster a boy

from one of my relatives. That is a common practice among us.''

Staring at his intent features as he waited for her to speak, she felt a tingle of confusion, surprise, and delight. But before she could think how to answer him, she felt Matopahu's hand stiffen, then grab her wrist. ''Look!'' he said, pointing to a dark fin cutting through the waves. Then another shark appeared. ''Two of them!'' He pulled on her arm, wordlessly urging her to retreat. From shore came other shouts of warning.

She held her ground for a moment, squinting, trying to make out the shape of the fins. Not mako, or tiger or white. They looked eerily familiar. ''Great blues!'' Tepua cried aloud. ''They came to me once before. Do not be afraid.''

''But—such sharks come only to bless the highest chiefs!''

''Perhaps, in the eyes of the gods, we are as important as high chiefs. We must welcome them and show we are worthy.'' She lifted her head and took a step forward, though she felt her pulse beating ever faster as the sharks approached.

Matopahu hesitated. ''Woman, are you certain? I have never refused to face an enemy. But these—''

''They are no enemies. Now that we are freed from our sins, the gods will not let us be harmed.'' When she insisted on remaining, he sighed and put his arm about her. Together they waded farther out into the waves.

Together, side by side, the great blues approached. Sunlight struck a brilliant deep ocean blue from their backs. As they turned, the color flashed into silver with a shimmer of yellow green. The long upper fin of their tails made lazy sweeps through the water.

The motion of their tails slowed. One great fish glided forward to Matopahu, the other to Tepua. She felt his hand grow rigid in hers. ''This is how they greet us,'' she whispered.

She felt a pointed snout nudge her—gently. The shark tilted its head and grazed up at her with an eye of deep black. Carefully she lowered her hand until her fingertips rested for a moment on the shark's grainy snout.

Then the swirl of water caressed her skin as the great blue swam past. Beside her, Matopahu was staring down in awe at the back of the second blue. Slowly he dipped his hand in the water and touched the shark above the gills. With patient dignity, it accepted the touch.

"You are right, Tepua. This is a blessing," Matopahu breathed. "Only the greatest chiefs are so honored."

The great blues swam around the couple, brushing by them so gently that the rough sharkskin did not make the smallest scrape. Then the huge fish withdrew a short distance out into the lagoon.

"Perhaps this is an omen of what the gods have in store for us," Tepua said.

Gently Matopahu drew her against his chest, cradling her in his arms as the wash of surf rocked them. "I am content with what we have now," he murmured, smoothing her hair back from her face. She threw her arms about his neck and pressed her nose to his.

"Look at the sharks," he whispered.

The great blues were playing, swimming together and brushing against each other as they circled.

"They are courting. One is *tane,* the other, *vahine,*" said Tepua with a laugh.

"Then that is how we must be," said Matopahu.

Yes, that is how we must be.

Glossary

aahi: albacore tuna. Tahitians had specific names for albacore of different sizes, such as *aahi perepererau* for young ones, *aahi araroa* for the very largest, etc.

ahu: stone platform, sometimes built of layers in pyramidal fashion, typically placed at one end of a *marae.* This was not an altar, but a sacred resting place for spirits who attended the ceremonies.

'ape: wild plant with large, glossy leaves. The thick root required long baking, and was eaten only in times of famine. *Alocasia macrorrhiza.*

ari'i (ariki): a chief, or a person of the highest class.

Arioi society: a cult devoted to worship of Oro in his peaceful aspect as Oro-of-the-laid-down-spear. In this role he also served as a fertility god.

atoll: a ring of coral islands that surrounds or partially surrounds a lagoon.

ava: a relative of black pepper. The roots and stems were used to make an intoxicating, nonalcoholic drink. (Known as *kava,* and still popular today in the Fiji Islands and elsewhere.) *Piper methysticum.*

breadfruit: the staple food of ancient Tahiti. A single tree can produce hundreds of pounds of fruit. When eaten baked, it resembles the flavor and texture of yam or squash. *Artocarpus incisa.*

candlenut: oily nut of the candlenut tree, *Aleurites molucanna.* The shelled seeds were strung on a coconut leaf midrib and one was set afire, each nut burning in turn, to light the interior of a house.

Eimeo: the island known today as Moorea, about eleven miles northwest of Tahiti.

fai: the art of making string figures, popular throughout Polynesia; "cat's cradle."

fara: pandanus or screwpine trees. A principal source of food (seeds and fruit) for many atoll people. Also an excellent source of thatch for roofs.

fe'i: mountain plantain. Bears small bananalike fruits that turn reddish yellow when ripe. Eaten cooked. *Musa fehi.*

Fenua Ura: an atoll known today as Scilly Island or Manuae, lying at the western extremity of French Polynesia.

hanihani: to caress, fondle.

hara: transgression, guilt. Often thought of as a substance that could flow from one person to another.

heiva: a festivity that typically includes feasting, performances, and dancing.

hotu: a large tree of the Brazil-nut family. The seeds were used as a fish poison. *Barringtonia.*

ihe: a dart or spear.

mafera: to fish for *aahi* at night.

mahi: sour paste made of fermented breadfruit; certain types of *mahi* will keep for months.

mahimahi: the dolphin fish, not the marine mammal.

mana: sacred power, which was considered capable of transmission by touch. Humans as well as objects possessed *mana* to varying degrees.

manahune: the lowest class of landowning people.

manava: expression of welcome.

Maohi: the Tahitians' word for themselves; literally "native."

marae: an open-air place of worship, usually a rectangular courtyard bounded by low stone walls, with an *ahu* at one end.

maro: a narrow piece of cloth worn by men about the hips, made of bark-cloth or finely plaited matting.

mati: a tree whose berries were an ingredient of the Tahitians' crimson dye. *Ficus tinctoria.*

Matopahu: lit., "steep-sided rock."

miro: Tahitian rosewood, *Thespesia populnea.* Considered sacred, it was planted about the *marae* and its boughs were used in religious ceremonies.

monoi: aromatic coconut oil, scented with such ingredients as sandalwood, gardenia, and jasmine.

motu: a low island created by the exposed part of a coral reef.

nevaneva: an ecstatic frenzy said to be caused by a god possessing a dancer or actor.

nono: small green warty fruit. *Morinda citrifolia.*

opu-nui: marae attendants. The name may be translated as "big bellies" or "august stomachs," referring to their partaking of food that was imbued with *mana.*

Oro: Polynesian god of war. Son of Ta'aroa and Hina. Patron god of the Arioi. One of the major gods of Tahiti at the time of European contact. Worship of Oro spread to Tahiti from Raiatea.

paeho: a weapon made of a length of wood with shark's teeth bound along one edge.

pandanus: see *fara.*

Papara: a district of Tahiti's western coast.

Paparangi: an atoll word for the sweet-smelling paradise where people of high birth went after death.

pipi: beach pea, a Tahitian vine used for making sashes worn by initiates into the Arioi society.

poi (poipoi): a pudding. In Tahiti, cooked and/or fermented breadfruit was generally the main ingredient. Many versions of *poi* were eaten.

po'o: a chest-slapper, or novice in the Arioi society.

Porapora: island known today as Bora Bora.

rata (mape): the Tahitian chestnut tree, *Inocarpus fagiferus.*

Rimapoa: lit., "one who fearlessly handles the unpleasant."

sennit: a cord made from softened fibers of the coconut husk.

Ta'aroa (Tangaroa). generally viewed as the god who created all else. Considered too far removed from human affairs to be addressed directly in worship.

taio: a sworn friend, joined with another through a formal friendship pact.

tane: man, husband, lover.

Tane: a principal god of Tahiti, to whom many *marae* were dedicated.

tapa: bark-cloth, made by pounding the softened inner bark of the paper mulberry, breadfruit, or hibiscus tree. Cloth was often dyed or painted, the best colors being scarlet and yellow. Rolls of *tapa* were prized as gifts, not only for their utility and beauty but because of the amount of labor they represented.

Tapahi-roro-ariki: legendary female atoll chief (lit. "Brains-cleaving-chief").

tapu: sacred, forbidden. Something that is restricted.

taro: a widely cultivated plant of Tahiti. The root, when baked, is somewhat like a potato. The cooked leaves have the taste of mild spinach. *Colocosia esculenta* and *Colocasia antiquorum.*

tatatau: person who marks the skin; a tattoo artist.

te: definite article, "the."

Tepua-mua: lit., "foremost flower."

teuteu: landless people, servants or laborers.

ti: small tree with many colorful varieties. Used for decoration and in sacred rituals. *Cordyline terminalis.*

tiare-maohi: famous Tahitian flower known for brilliant white petals in stellate formation, and delicate fragrance. *Gardenia tahitensis.*

tira: a twin-hulled canoe used in surface trolling for albacore.

toa: ironwood (*casuarina*), a hardwood tree with many uses.

Urietea: the island known today as Raiatea, located about 130 miles northwest of Tahiti. The center of the Oro cult was located here. Ruins of the great *marae* at Opoa can still be seen today.

ura: red feathers, the most valuable commodity the Tahitians possessed, essential for religious rituals and decorating sacred objects.

vahine: woman, wife, lover.

Selected Reading

Adams, Henry Brooks, *Tahiti; Memoirs of Arii Taimai.* Gregg Press, Ridgewood, N.J., 1968.

Bovis, Edmond de, *Tahitian Society Before the Arrival of the Europeans,* translated by Robert D. Craig, second edition. The Institute for Polynesian Studies, Laie, Hawaii, 1980.

Danielsson, Bengt, *Love in the South Seas,* translated by F. H. Lyon. Reynal & Co., New York, N.Y., 1956.

Davies, John, *A Tahitian and English Dictionary, with Introductory Remarks on the Polynesian Language and a Short Grammar of the Tahitian Dialect.* London Missionary Society Press, London, 1851.

Dodd, Edward, *Polynesia's Sacred Isle.* Dodd, Mead & Company, New York, 1976.

Emory, Kenneth P., *Material Culture of the Tuamotu Archipelago—Pacific Anthropological Records No. 22.* Department of Anthropology, Bernice P. Bishop Museum, Honolulu, 1975.

————, *Stone Remains in the Society Islands.* Bernice P. Bishop Museum Bulletin No. 116, Honolulu, 1933.

Ferdon, Edwin N., *Early Tahiti As the Explorers Saw It 1767–1797.* University of Arizona Press, Tucson, Az., 1981.

Finney, Ben R., "Voyaging," chapter 14 in Jennings, Jesse D., *The Prehistory of Polynesia.* Harvard University Press, Cambridge, Mass., 1979.

Haddon, A. C., and Hornell, James, *Canoes of Oceania: Vol. 1, The Canoes of Polynesia, Fiji and Micronesia.* Bernice P. Bishop Museum, Special Publication No. 27, Honolulu, 1936.

Henry, Teuira, *Ancient Tahiti.* Bishop Museum Bulletin No. 48, Honolulu, 1928.

Morrison, James, *The Journal of James Morrison Boatswain's Mate of the Bounty Describing the Mutiny and Subsequent Misfortunes of the Mutineers Together with an Account of the Island of Tahiti.* Golden Cockerel Press, Great Britain, 1933.

Moulin, Jane Freeman, *The Dance of Tahiti.* C. Gleizel/Editions du Pacifique, Papeete, Tahiti, 1979.

Nordhoff, Charles, "Notes on the Off-Shore Fishing of the Society

Islands.'' *Journal of the Polynesian Society,* 39 (1930): 137–173, 221–262.

Oliver, Douglas L., *Ancient Tahitian Society,* three volumes. University of Hawaii Press, Honolulu, 1974.

Parkinson, Sydney, *Journal of a Voyage to the South Seas.* Caliban Books, Hampstead, London, 1984.

Saquet, Jean-Louis, *The Tahiti Handbook,* translated by Nancy and Dominique Bernard. Tahiti, 1989.

Varady, Ralph, *Many Lagoons.* William Morrow and Co., New York, N.Y., 1958.

SPECIAL PREVIEW

If you enjoyed *Daughter of the Reef*, you won't want to miss the continuing saga of Tepua and her people . . .

    SISTER OF THE SUN by Clare Coleman

. . . an epic story of life and love, as beautiful and timeless as the islands themselves.

Here is an exclusive excerpt from the next captivating novel—coming soon from Jove Books . . .

UNEXPECTEDLY cast into a deadly current, Tepua sputtered as she came up for air. On both sides of the channel, sharp walls of coral hemmed her in. Men shouted to her from the canoe, now far ahead, but the hurtling craft could not turn back for her.

Tepua's head went under. Stroking fiercely, she emerged in a mass of foam. Now the coral wall rose just in front of her, its harsh edges glistening with seawater. In a frenzy she turned away and fought the current as waves pulled her down into a deep trough, lifted her and dropped her again.

Then she was swimming underwater, heading for the center of the channel, only dimly sensing pain on the side of her leg. Ahead she saw hints of calmer water, but the current was treacherous here, swirling her away from her path.

Then, at last, she was free of the undertow, and she saw overhead the quiet surface of the lagoon. She came up, gasping, pushing dark strands of hair from her face. Canoes were coming toward her. She was wet and exhausted, but she was home!

"Get her out! Quick!" came cries from shore. Someone helped Tepua from the canoe and she splashed into the warm embrace of Ehi, her foster mother. For a long moment they held onto each other.

"This was not . . . the homecoming I expected," Tepua gasped. Everything had gone well until the last maneuver, entering the lagoon through its only pass.

"Everyone knows," said Ehi, "there is an evil spirit dwelling in that pass. But the gods kept you safe and brought you back to us, if only for a short while. And now, your father is waiting for you. Let me help you get ready."

* * *

In a short while, Tepua was following a broad, shaded path beneath the coconut palms. She breathed the familiar fragrance, a mixture of salt spray and faint perfumes from blossoming trees. Underfoot she felt the crushed coral that covered much of the island. *Home!* Every scent was delicious; every sensation brought back memories of an earlier time.

Just ahead lay her father's house, the most important dwelling on the atoll, oblong in shape and thatched with slender *fara* leaves. It had once seemed huge to Tepua, and she wondered if it had somehow grown smaller. She pulled aside the hanging that covered the low entranceway and ducked into the dim interior.

Kohekapu lay stretched on his thick pile of finely plaited mats, his head on the smoothed log that served as headrest for himself and his wife. Another mat, plaited of coarser leaves, covered him to his neck. Beside him crouched a *tahunga*, a priest of healing, who chanted and waved a small tuft of red feathers. Kohekapu grunted a command, sending the *tahunga* back a few steps.

Tepua knelt beside her father and pressed her nose to his cheek. The sparse whiskers of his beard seemed whiter than she remembered, the wrinkles of his forehead deeper.

"Come to me, first daughter," said Kohekapu in a cracked and tired voice. "Let me see for myself that the sea gods did not take you."

Swallowing hard, she said, "I am well, Father. My guardian spirit has protected me."

"Speak to me," he insisted. "Tell me of your life in Tahiti. I heard such tales after your brother's visit that I do not know what to believe."

Recalling the incident, Tepua frowned and clenched her fist in anger. Her married brother had come to Tahiti for the Ripening Festival. When he found Tepua there he demanded that she return with him to her father. She had refused, earning her brother's contempt. He knew only atoll ways. He could not understand that the gods had brought her to Tahiti and wished her to remain there.

"Father," she said softly. "I have joined the Arioi sect, as you must know. I have pledged myself to serve a high-island god, Oro-of-the-laid-down-spear."

Kohekapu cleared his throat. "I am familiar with this god. The people of Tahiti make much of him. But such a power does not bother with people like us, so distant from the lands that he watches over. We must look to our ancestors in times of trouble. The great Oro will not hear us."

Tepua did not know how to answer him. In her thoughts, she was now a high-islander. While living on Tahiti, the problems of her kin had seemed remote.

"But what will become of you, my sweet flower?" he asked, "with your wild dancing and your foreign god? I know that Arioi women must not bear children. What kind of life will that be, with no sons and daughters?"

"One day, Father, when I have finished my duty, I will leave the Arioi. Then I will have sons. My children will be of the *ariki*, of the high chiefs, not only here but in Tahiti."

"Then you have a man, and one of high birth. I am glad to hear that, but I regret he is so far away. It is important that you remain with your own people awhile. That is what the *ringoringo* seems to be telling us."

As she took in his words, Tepua's mouth fell open and a chill touched her shoulders. From time to time a child-ghost, or *ringoringo,* flew out from the Vast Darkness, crying faintly beyond the roar of the surf. The voice brought a warning—that some great change was coming.

"Every morning at dawn we have heard it," said her father. "For seven days. The priests tried divination, but learned nothing of what is to come."

Tepua felt her throat tighten. She clasped her father's weathered hand, whispering, "I will stay with you. Until you have an answer, and are well."

"Ah, daughter, do not fool yourself. Soon my spirit will leave here to join the ancestors. I will learn what is coming, and then I will send you a message."

She blinked away a tear. "Go now," Kohekapu continued, giving her hand a gentle squeeze. "I must rest. We will talk later."

With a sigh Tepua turned away. Long ago, after consultation with the gods, the ruling succession had been decided. Tepua's half-brother, Umia, was to be the next high chief. As was customary, Kohekapu retained power until the boy reached a proper age to take up his duties.

Tepua frowned as she headed for the doorway. Young as he was, Umia might be chief sooner than anyone expected. She hoped the priests and elders had prepared him well.

Outside again, Tepua blinked, dazzled by the sudden brightness. She looked up and saw that the earlier clouds had blown away, leaving a blue sky and a brilliant sun.

She remembered how homesick she had been during her first days in Tahiti. The sights and smells of the atoll had never been far from her mind. Now she wanted to stop for a moment just to look around.

Glancing across the lagoon, its color pale as sand in the shallows, rich azure farther out, Tepua studied distant islets. She and her cousin Maukiri had a favorite . . .

"Tepua!"

She turned, and her mood brightened at once. Here came Maukiri running along the sandy beach, sturdy brown legs flying. Tepua eagerly embraced her young cousin. "I was gathering clams," Maukiri explained, breathlessly. "I just heard you were back."

"Ah, it has been so long." Tepua stood back to look at her cousin, the broad face and full lips, the dark hair astir in the breeze.

"I prayed every day that the spirits would bring you back to me," said Maukiri, taking Tepua's arm and leading her along the narrow beach. "And now it will be just like before. We will go to our islet, where no one can find us. Stretch out in the shade and say whatever we please."

Tepua recalled the islet, the special *motu*, that she and Maukiri had claimed as their own. It was too small for a family to live on. Coral heads studded the surrounding waters, discouraging casual visitors from risking their canoes. But for one who knew how to get onto the tiny beach, it was a perfect refuge.

"The sun is getting hotter," said Maukiri. "We should go now, before someone finds work for us."

Tepua laughed. Maukiri was talking as if the two of them were still children. She glanced back toward Kohekapu's house.

"You have seen him?" Maukiri whispered, her expression suddenly solemn.

"Yes. He is resting. The *tahunga* hopes for some improvement. There is nothing more I can do now."

"Look," said Maukiri, pointing to a battered *vaka*, a single-hulled canoe with an outrigger float, that was drawn high up on the sand.

Tepua studied the old canoe for a moment before she recognized it as one they had often used for paddling about the lagoon. "Have you gotten your brothers to tighten the seams yet?" she asked. Her people built their hulls from small planks, fitted edge to edge, and sewn together with coconut fiber cord. After much use, the seams began to leak intolerably. She and Maukiri used to argue about who was to bail, waiting until the hull was half filled with water before finally getting started.

"Come with me and find out," Maukiri answered in a teasing voice.

Tepua could not resist. Together, she and Maukiri pushed the small outrigger canoe into the warm, shallow water. They waded a short way out over the soft bottom, then climbed into the boat.

A slight breeze ruffled the surface of the lagoon as the two young women began to paddle. Looking down into deep, clear water Tepua saw gardens of yellow coral, a swarm of striped fish, a baby eel. Dark sea cucumbers lay motionless on the bottom.

The hot sun felt good on her back after the chill of the morning's wind. The canoe rocked gently, stabilized by the long outrigger float that was attached by slender poles. Across the water, trees of other islets stood in clusters.

Suddenly she noticed that her feet were getting wet again.

"So your boat is leaky as ever!" she complained, as a thin layer of water began sloshing in the bottom of the canoe.

"Not as bad as before," Maukiri protested. "But since you are the honored visitor, I will bail today."

At last they reached the channel they had long ago discovered, threading their way between coral heads that broke the surface with each gentle motion of the waves. Half the small *motu* was well-shaded by palms and thorny-leaved *fara* trees. On the other half, a white sand beach glistened in the afternoon sunlight.

Tepua helped her cousin pull the canoe ashore, then ran over the hot sand into the cool beneath the palms. Thirsty after her paddling, she picked up a freshly fallen green coconut and shook it to listen for the water. It was a *viavia*, the best kind for drinking.

The sharp stake that she remembered still stood upright in the ground beneath one of the trees. With a well-practiced blow, Tepua rammed the coconut's husk onto the stalk and started tearing away the thick, fibrous covering.

"That is something new," said Maukiri, when she caught up with her.

Tepua looked down at what she was doing, and felt her face burn. In the past, she recalled, she had always prevailed on Maukiri to do the heavy work of opening coconuts. Tepua had insisted that a chief's daughter must save her strength for more delicate tasks. But in Tahiti, as servant to a chiefess of the Arioi, Tepua had husked enough coconuts—more than enough—to feed everyone on her atoll.

"And I see you are good at it!" Maukiri laughed and went searching for a drinking nut of her own. Tepua paused for a moment, then continued her work. There was no point pretending she did not know how. With a seashell knife that was kept conveniently beside the stake, Tepua cut through the "mouth" of the nut and began to drink.

She swallowed the cool, sweet liquid greedily. Even in Tahiti, the coconuts did not taste quite as rich as this one. Within the *viavia*, the soft, white meat had a special fragrance. Tepua held the drained nut in one hand, tapped it sharply about the middle with a rock, and quickly broke it open. With her fingers she scooped out the first tender morsel.

At last, thirst and hunger satisfied, the two young women stretched out on a shady part of the beach. "Now you will tell me everything," said Maukiri. "Everything about the men of Tahiti."

Tepua laughed. "They are like our men, of course, but a little fatter. You have seen Tahitian traders."

"I am not talking about what they look like! Surely you have a lover by now. Tell me what their *hanihani* is like."

Tepua pursed her lips. Maukiri had reminded her of an old sore point between them. While Tepua had lived here she had foregone the love games that Maukiri and other young people enjoyed. Because of her noble station, Tepua's virginity had been protected by a chaperon—old Bone-needle—as well as by *tapu*.

"I do have someone . . . at least I did," said Tepua at last, recalling uncomfortably how she had listened, long ago, to Maukiri chatter about her first boyfriends. "He is Matopahu. Brother of a high chief, and a great man of Tahiti."

"I hear some doubt in your voice."

"It is not so simple," said Tepua irritably. "He asked me to be his wife and I refused—until I can complete my service to the Arioi. He said he would wait, but now he grows impatient. Someone told me he has another *vahine*."

"Then you must find someone else," said Maukiri cheerfully.

"I can be happy without a man," Tepua retorted. "Remember how much practice I had."

"Maybe you can," said Maukiri. "But I remember how you used to talk about Paruru. When Bone-needle was not looking you would waggle your hips when he passed, and see if he looked at you."

Tepua smiled faintly as she thought of her father's chief warrior, who had brought her from Tahiti for this visit. "I just spent ten days sailing with Paruru! I will be happy to see no more of him for a while."

"I think, cousin, that you are not telling me the truth. And I know for certain that now he *does* look at you."

Tepua rolled away in mock disgust. On the journey, her father's warrior had behaved toward her with formal aloofness, though she sensed his interest. And it was true that as a girl she had often thought about his dark eyes and his capable fingers.

"Maukiri, I have heard enough about men. I want to ask you a serious question. Why have I seen so many worried faces? Almost no one seems happy to see me home."

Her cousin did not answer at once. Tepua turned and saw her lying on her belly, tracing patterns in the sand with her fingers. "It is because of the priest, Faka-ora, and all this talk of ghost voices," Maukiri said. "Faka-ora has been telling people that a time of trial is at hand, and that Umia is not ready to lead our people through it."

"If my father recovers, then Umia will not have to."

"And what if we lose Kohekapu? Faka-ora says that the gods may have a new plan for us."

Tepua frowned, unwilling to admit to herself that the old man's spirit might depart. "I still do not see—"

"Ah, Tepua. There is certain to be a dispute now. I have heard what some priests and elders are saying. You are the oldest living child of Kohekapu. It is you who should be our next chief."